FIGHTING WITH SHADOWS

Dermot Healy

FIGHTING WITH SHADOWS

OR *SCIAMACHY*

A NOVEL

Edited, with an Introduction,
by Neil Murphy & Keith Hopper

DALKEY ARCHIVE PRESS

LIBRARY OF CONGRESS CATALOGING-IN-PUBLICATION DATA

Healy, Dermot, 1947-2014.
  Fighting with shadows or, Sciamachy / by Dermot Healy ; edited, with an introduction, by Neil Murphy and Keith Hopper. -- First Dalkey Archive edition
     pages cm
  "Originally co-published in 1984 by Allison & Busby and Brandon Books; a second
edition was published in 1986 by Allison & Busby" -- Verso title page.
  Includes bibliographical references.
  Summary: "Fighting with Shadows tells of violently sundered geographical borders,
of maddening religious differences, of the anguished gaps between people as they
struggle to find each other, and of how the dead reside among its inhabitants long
after they've passed. The imagination's encounter with reality registers Dermot Healey's
relentless fascination with the way things are seen and with the things themselves, or
the "erotica of little things." A realist account and nightmarish fable, Fighting with
Shadows is critical to the history of modern Irish fiction" -- Provided by publisher.
  ISBN 978-1-56478-585-5 (pbk. : alk. paper)
  1. Ireland--Fiction. I. Murphy, Neil, editor, writer of introduction. II. Hopper,
Keith, editor writer of introduction. III. Title. IV. Title: Fighting with shadows. V.
Title: Sciamachy.

PR6058.E19F5 2015
823'.914--dc23
                                   2015017096

Partially funded by a grant by the Illinois Arts Council, a state agency

Dalkey Archive Press publications are, in part, made possible through the support of
the University of Houston-Victoria and its program in creative writing, publishing,
and translation. www.uhv.edu/asa/

Dalkey Archive Press
Victoria, TX / Dublin / London
www.dalkeyarchive.com

Printed on permanent / durable acid-free paper

CONTENTS

Editors' Introduction: "Anything strange?"

Dermot Healy's *Fighting with Shadows* opens with an unanswered question: "Anything strange?" The same question is asked again almost a hundred pages later, but on this occasion it is answered in the negative; Frank Allen shakes his head and denies that anything is strange. But Frank is not being honest; a few moments earlier he had experienced a disorientating out-of-body experience that has challenged his sense of self: "Who was I a minute ago? Had he cried at all?" (131). Things are, in fact, very strange, as the switch in pronoun confirms, and a potent sense of the tension between inner and outer realities is thus established – a world of strangeness is registered, albeit a strangeness of the familiar, of the haunted presences of the everyday, "the erotica of little things" (124), and of the self that tries to negotiate the prickly challenge of recognizing and ordering everyday existence. *Fighting with Shadows* (or *Sciamachy*, its alternative title) is saturated in the everyday, but in Healy the ordinary is almost always extraordinary.

First published in 1984, *Fighting with Shadows* is ostensibly set in the border county of Fermanagh, in the fictional village of Fanacross in Northern Ireland, and it spans the 1970s and the early years of the 1980s. Thus it is deeply rooted in provincial Ireland just as the Northern 'Troubles' erupted. The Allen family, around whom the narrative circles, coexists in perpetual uneasiness under the dulled glare of violence, poverty, and internal familial strife. In this uncertain world, lives are abruptly ended under the most violent of circumstances, and family members shift between different states of unbelonging, both north and south of the border. At some point the twin brothers Frank and George, and their older brother Tom, all spend time in the South, although the Six Counties continue to exert a magnetic pull for the twins. Frank's son Joseph is also sent south to work in Manager Tom's hotel, in what appears to be a fictional version of Cavan town, and the second half of the novel is largely situated amongst the hustle and bustle of the midlands in the 1970s.

The novel is, in its own particularized way, a fictional record of a specific time and place, since lost to the passage of the years: provincial landscapes frequently fall off historical mappings which usually focus on metropolitan centres to generate their topographies of the past, and *Fighting with Shadows* offers an artistically transposed insight into this lost world. In addition to the Northern Irish Troubles, which hum away in the background for much of the novel, there is also the strange stirring of the "New American Ireland," of the peculiar interpenetration of external influences in still inward-looking towns and villages, of a faded yet exotic era of drugs, rock music, jazz, and localized Irish politics. The lounge of the Cove Hotel, where Joseph works, is haunted by the airs of American and English music, which introduces slivers of pathos, wonder, and longing in the often closed, grim lives of the employees and punters. All of this is a fascinating footnote to the birth of modern Ireland, with its idiosyncratic medley of cultures and a provincial world that still very much exists (and to which Healy's last novel, *Long Time, No See*, bears extraordinary witness). The soulful note of Dinah Washington crooning "What a Difference a Day Makes" to farmers and labourers in Manager Tom's airless lounge strikes a deep chord, and contributes to an incomparable atmosphere – this was a world quite unlike any other, and Healy's powers of observation are stunningly evocative of the time. It is in such moments that the novel fixes the world in its consoling fictions and retains a little of its essence. And yet, for all its potency in the set-piece moments, in the capturing of nuanced phrasing in the home, the pub, and the marketplace, *Fighting with Shadows* is far more innovative and complex than just being an insightful record of minutiae in provincial Ireland. The context is both a function of, and a cause of, the innovative technical heights that Healy reached in the novel, and like all innovative art, the formal demands it initially made on its readers formed a recurring pattern in the reviews it received on its first publication in 1984.

The immediate reception to *Fighting with Shadows*, in the 1980s, offers an insight into historical-contextual obsessions, as well as to the literary-critical expectations of the reviewing industry at the time. The raw immediacy of the Northern conflict in 1984 – especially in the emotive aftermath of the IRA Hunger Strikes – is frequently evident in the recurring critical focus on the novel's significance for the political situation. Similarly, the novel's role in declaring a post-Independence, political statement appears more important to some reviewers than perhaps it would nowadays, with one reviewer suggesting that the novel was symptomatic of "a collapse of Irish Catholic Nationalist self-confidence" and strongly objected to its apparent "self-enclosed introspection" (Brooke, 19). Perhaps of more telling importance is the clear confusion expressed by many reviewers, particularly with respect to the form of the novel, who appear to yearn for a more linear narrative approach (Sommerville-Large, 14; Hazeldine, 88). The benefit of hindsight, of course, offers one greater contextual distance and, in this case, the luxury of thirty years of critical distillation. Furthermore, a consideration of Healy's formal innovation in the novels that followed *Fighting with Shadows* – perhaps unparalleled in post-1980s fiction in terms of its technical range and achievement – allows us to return to the first novel with an informed sense of how complex an aesthetic innovator Healy really was. In *A Goat's Song* (1994), for example, Jack Ferris' invented narrative of his love affair with Catherine, and of her life (and that of her family) before they met, operates within an embedded, framed narrative that runs parallel to Jack's actual existence, ultimately forcing both modes of existence into narrative conflict. Similarly, in *Sudden Times* (1999), the challenge was to locate a form that would serve to imaginatively encompass Ollie Ewing's fractured consciousness rather than simply represent him as a deranged character, and the resultant novel is both a record of the protagonist's consciousness and a powerful reordering of how we experience the world through his eyes. Healy's last novel, *Long Time, No See* (2011) is also a major technical achievement, being largely constructed out of elaborate sequences of dialogue between local characters, immigrants, and various passers-by, in which the imaginatively perceived ordinary world is raised to almost mythic significance.

Several of the first reviewers of *Fighting with Shadows* were also concerned by the fact that the "Troubles remain in the background," and that Healy's "concern for the terrible scenes he describes" are therefore in question because of the narrative distance (Morton, 41; Hazeldine, 87). Such concerns, of course, primarily reveal the reviewers' own critical templates and they appear not to have grasped the aesthetic motivation that lay behind the carefully calibrated, detached voice that refuses any emotional, psychological, or overt political positioning. Several critics and reviewers did, of course, recognize the kind of novel that Healy was writing, and were aware of the potent power of the voice that accompanies (rather than guides) the reader. Marianne Koenig, for example, although troubled somewhat by what she saw as the "difficulty" of the novel, nonetheless recognized the rationale and benefits of the "dispassionate, detached voice [. . .] which effectively allows the author to survey, permeate, and withdraw from its characters at will" (Koenig, 113). And rather than see the narrative distance as a problem, Seán Golden, too, was aware of the potential impact achieved by "representing overt violence obliquely," and that by "ignoring the details and descriptions that we have come to expect," Healy managed instead to imbue in the reader a sense of perpetual dread that would otherwise have been unattainable (18). Golden further vindicates the author's frequently absent narrator by illustrating how it facilitates an integrated, living quality in the represented landscape:

> The narrative voice intermingles with the thoughts and words of the characters to such an extent that it could as well be said that the characters live to contribute to the creation of that narrative voice, which, unspecified, avoiding the embodiment of an "I," shares their lives at the same time that it creates and comments on them. It also creates the living world around them. (Golden, 18)

Critics like Koenig and Golden clearly recognized the novel's technical achievement and saw in its construction a considered mode of responding both to the immediate socio-political upheavals – and, paradoxically, the concurrent deathly stagnation – that gripped the country, as well as the invention of a new formal approach that allowed its author to speak of a mode of experience, above, or beyond, the very material realities that frequently threaten to devour his subjects. The relationships between the characters are marked by a similar narrative distance – oceans of grief and longing and misreading lie in the small spaces between Helen and Frank, and all of the characters do little more than probe each other's outer zones and remain imprisoned in their insulated imaginations.

Golden's observations, in particular, account for some of the structural features of the novel. Most obviously, the authority of the narrative voice is frequently surrendered to the characters' perspective via free indirect discourse – when the primary narrator's voice gives way to the individual characters' point of view, often for lengthy periods. Similarly, the point of view frequently shifts between several of the main characters, sometimes accompanied by shifts in pronouns. In addition, vacillations between first and third person narration, the replacement of the primary narrator with long portions of dialogue, as well as a full chapter of reported speech, as is the case in chapter 25, all contribute to the sense that there is no fixed narrative centre. This elaborately wrought approach ensures that the narrator appears to vanish at times, and lets the world get on with its own business. This is accentuated further by a regular alternating of the inner minds of the characters with a rather panoramic sweep and, at certain intervals, all characters are omitted from the narrative, and images of the landscape, or local historical data, momentarily replace the plot sequence (chapter 26). All such variations are indicative of a desire to reject the single, authoritative narrative voice and, by extension, to decline the implicit notion of the world as a monotone, knowable space – the tapestry of life becomes the primary focus, in which the characters themselves are simply constituent parts of its texture.

In this multi-textured world, many kinds of voices emerge, from the epistolary registers offered in the chapter of letters, to the diverse ways that reported speech is presented, including occasional intrusions such as, "Said the radio" or "Said Maurice Caulfield" or "Said the Islander who rarely spoke" (chapter 22), and with the occasional interspersion of lines from songs by Dinah Washington (chapter 8), The Animals (chapter 37), and the music of the Beatles and Elvis Presley. Everywhere the texture of reality is being woven by multiple voices, ghostly presences, shifts in perspective, and a deeply interconnected world is elevated to become the primary focus of our attention. In fact, as recently as 2011, in an interview that accompanied the publication of *Long Time, No See*, Healy sought to explain his use of vernacular dialogue in the novel in the following terms: "I was trying to stay out of it and let the reader take over and run with it. So I would often put the meaning of a passage in, then take it out again" (O'Hagan Interview). His explanation holds a resonance for all of his fiction, in which there is a recurring fascination with somehow locating a way to allow the world to find utterance and to be witnessed, without recourse to the singular authority of the fixed narrative voice.

In *Long Time, No See* the world is somehow channelled through the orchestra of voices that bear witness to their lives, while in *Fighting with Shadows* the complex narrative design also speaks of Healy's desire to move beyond a linear mode of expression.

This desire is also evident in his evasion of a linear sense of time, so much so that several reviewers appear to be genuinely confused by the precise temporal frame that we fictionally inhabit (Hazeldine, 88; Koenig 112). While this is largely a result of lazy reviewing, a novel like *Fighting with Shadows* is something of a trap for those who read swiftly, searching for the easy sequential temporality that structures many "realist" novels. Healy's focus, however, moves repeatedly back and forth in time, frequently switches tense in mid-flow, and offers up abrupt signals of temporal shifts at the beginning of chapters e.g., "This was a long time ago," or "There was another time" (chapters 34, 37). Such temporal variations are all part of the mosaic-like tapestry of the novel. Healy resists the linear plotting of the realist novel and instead allows coherence to emerge via a series of interconnected patterns that speak of a less-structured understanding of the world, akin to that which Margaret speaks of in one of her letters to Joseph: "life is made up of the half-forgetting" (255). Similarly, the genealogical lines of connection that link Frank, George, Tom, and Pop, help to knit the novel's diverse structuring together, while the recurring images of home that linger in Joseph's maturing mind, long after he leaves, and his familial inheritance of anxiety and diffidence, ensures that the past perpetually haunts the present – again, though, just out of sight.

Aubrey Dillon-Malone astutely recognized in some of these genealogical patterns a connection to the work of William Faulkner, but the echoes of Gabriel García Márquez's *One Hundred Years of Solitude* are also evident in this respect, the structure of which is in part framed around the multigenerational complications of the extended Buendía family. In both cases we have an apocalyptic opening, a drought, the hint of incestuous relationships, while the madness and gaiety of Healy's midlands town reads like a slightly demented version of Márquez's Macondo:

> At two, the bell-ringer sauntered round the sodden streets announcing how the parade would begin at three. His sons swung out of his coat-tails. He was a chimney sweep by trade. Not long after the bell-ringer came the float from the bacon factory, with live pigs chortling through the bars, and then a man on stilts, fearful of the thin snow below and the bunting above. Next a showband playing Country and Western airs on the back of a lorry advertising furniture. The owner of a large supermarket in the town seated, in old-fashioned regalia, on a penny farthing. "Will you look at Fegan," said Cathy, "and a pair of balls on him like the weights of a grandfather clock." Next the brass band marching into step as they played a mixture of patriotic and show business tunes, "Oklahoma" and "Mise Éire," their ranks depleted because of death and lack of instruments. (276-277)

Aidan Higgins declares this mood of gaiety to be akin to "the frantic jig before the drop," and likens the novel to Flann O'Brien's *The Third Policeman* and Beckett's *Mercier and Camier* (Higgins, 193), placing it within a very clear tradition of innovative Irish writing. In *Fighting with Shadows*, the narrative focus shifts, temporal frames vary, and the inner and outer worlds of the characters frequently interchange, all generating a sense of a world that forever lies just out of sharp focus. Far from being a failure of observation, this registers a way of seeing that extends beyond merely linear modes of representation and is suggestive of a world that is not a neat, easily observed set of phenomena. While this awareness is clearly apparent in his later work, already in *Fighting with Shadows* one has a haunting sense of the fragility of human consciousness in perpetual negotiation with material reality. In fact, throughout the novel, several characters experience deeply unsettling slippages in this sense of themselves, as when Frank, one day after a solitary drink, "lost touch with his surroundings and headed towards some house in the town," imagining it, wrongly, to be his own house (9). Similarly, in a particularly disorientating temporal and spatial shift, Healy presents Joseph as he experiences a profound sense of dislocation:

> His bladder began to pain him and out in the yard he stood waiting. And pissing, he went back through all the times he had stood like this, his *bod* in his hands, pissing. Smaller, smaller he went till he shook with fear that his mind might not return to him, but stay in the head of some two-year-old self, and leave him mindless. Only bits of him would travel back. Though he could sense the yard around him, the yard was not there. (75)

From the point of view of the characters there is a general sense of the unsolidity of material reality in the novel; George occasionally believed that his children "Margaret and Jim were only figments of his imagination" (59), while Pop, after having had his cataracts removed, can for a time "see through the ceiling to the sky beyond" (89).

All of this contributes to a sense of the novel being structured not by the tight rules of encyclopaedic reality or linear histories, but with a sense of the world as a product of the imagination. In fact, the novel frequently hints at the idea of the imagination as an alternative ordering system, as when Frank assures us that there is "nothing . . . in your imagination cannot happen in reality" (40). Healy too suggests as much in a book review the year after *Fighting with Shadows* was first published, when he expressed the view that "Irish people prefer to side with the imagination, leaving linear history to those who can chart specifics into generalisations" (Healy, 1985: 13). The general sense of the essential mutability of things, of the powerful ebb and flow of time and space, explains the vast multi-focal range of Healy's narrative, and the subtle manner of its own ordering principles. Indeed, within the novel itself the fiction sometimes self-reflexively hints at this fact – for example, when George's mind threatens to break free of its moorings, while he is imprisoned:

> He heard himself say and think things that seemed rootless, to have no seat in his mind. Yet the outside world could accommodate all this randomness. Anything he thought or said was possible. It was in the yard. It was in the indescribable trees. It was in the things fought over. It was in what remained after the fighting was over. It was the shadow of things long dead that stretched off into the future. That sudden darkening of the fields and the streets that has no explanation. And then the brightening, even a greater darkness. (350)

The "sham fight," or *Sciamachy* of the alternate title, thus points to the struggle with shadows of many kinds: with history, between genders, across generations, and with the self. But above all that, readers are offered an early glimpse of the sheer mastery of Dermot Healy's subtle and harrowing fictional universe. This reissue *of Fighting with Shadows* is an invitation to (re)discover the work of a modern master.

—Neil Murphy & Keith Hopper
Oxford and Singapore, February 2015

WORKS CITED

Brooke, Peter. Review of Dermot Healy's *Fighting with Shadows*. *The Linen Hall Review* 1.4 (Winter 1984/85): 19.

Dillon-Malone, Aubrey. "Vim and Vinegar" [review of Dermot Healy's *Fighting with Shadows*]. *Books Ireland* no. 89 (December 1984): 232–33.

Golden, Seán. "Oriental Sense of the Border" [review of *Fighting with Shadows*]. *Fortnight* no. 210 (3–16 December 1984): 18.

Hazeldine, Peter. "Barricades" [review of Dermot Healy's *Banished Misfortune* and *Fighting with Shadows*]. *PN Review* 13.3 (1986): 87–88.

Healy, Dermot. *A Goat's Song*. London: Harvill, 1995.

———. *Fighting with Shadows*. London: Allison & Busby, 1984.

———. *Long Time, No See*. London: Faber and Faber, 2011.

———. *Sudden Times*. London: Harvill, 1999.

———. "When is an Irish Writer an Anglo-Irish Writer?" [review of A.C. Partridge's *Language and Society in Anglo-Irish Literature*]. *Fortnight* no. 222 (24 June 1985): 13.

Higgins, Aidan. "Cantraps of Fermented Words" [review of *Fighting with Shadows*]. *Windy Arbours: Collected Criticism*. London: Dalkey Archive Press, 2006: 192–93.

Koenig, Marianne. Review of Dermot Healy's *Fighting with Shadows*. *Irish University Review* 15.1 (Spring 1985): 112–15.

Morton, Brian. "In the Border State" [review of Dermot Healy's *Fighting with Shadows*]. *Times Literary Supplement* (11 January 1985): 41.

O'Hagan, Sean. "Dermot Healy: 'I try to stay out of it and let the reader take over'" [interview with Dermot Healy], *The Observer* (3 April 2011): web [accessed 30 January 2015].

Sommerville-Large, Gillian. "Borderland" [review of Dermot Healy's *Fighting with Shadows*]. *The Irish Times* (24 November 1984): 14.

A Note on the Text

Fighting with Shadows was originally co-published by Allison & Busby (London and New York) and Brandon Books (Dingle, Co. Kerry) in 1984; a second edition was published by Allison & Busby (London and New York) in 1986. The novel has since been out of print.

For all of its virtues, the original Allison & Busby / Brandon Press edition contains a considerable number of typographical errors. The 1986 edition corrected several of these but retained some of the original errors. The more obvious misspellings and mistakes in punctuation have been silently sub-edited. In general, the punctuation has been standardised throughout: double quotation marks for dialogue; single quotation marks for quotes within quotes; closing quotation marks after commas and full stops. New paragraphs are indented, and section breaks marking the passing of time get a double line break (with no indentation). Long em-dashes (—) have only been used when a character breaks off or resumes speaking; otherwise, en-dashes with spaces – like so – are the preferred format here.

Throughout the novel, English and Hiberno-English spellings are used instead of the American forms. Healy sometimes uses Irish-language words and phrases; while most of these are understandable in their immediate context, translations are included in a glossary at the end of this note.

Healy's technical innovation is evident throughout, sometimes with respect to seeking ways to permit the voices of his characters to emerge in a direct fashion, without narratorial anchoring. For example, all of Chapter 25 is related via Helen's direct speech, which frequently includes the reporting of other characters' speech. Similarly, in cases of continuous dialogue, in order to maintain the conversational flow, double quotation marks are usually left open.

Several extracts from *Fighting with Shadows* were published as work in progress between 1977 and 1983 in various magazines, journals, newspapers and books. Many of the extracts are direct replicas, or near variants, of scenes in the final published version of *Fighting with Shadows*, with a few notable exceptions that did not eventually appear in the novel. Some extracts, "Legal Times" and "Work in Progress: Dermot Healy" are set in the Basque region, featuring a protagonist named José (see below for further details), later to evolve into Joseph in the published novel. Another piece, indicated as an extract from *Sciamachy* and entitled "The Island and the Calves," was later published as a short story in Healy's debut collection, *Banished Misfortune and Other Stories* (1982); this particular story features characters named Jim and Margaret, as in *Fighting with Shadows*, but the context is significantly different from the published novel.

It is clear that the original novel underwent several transformations, or distillations, in the years immediately prior to its publication. The geographical context shifts, some characters are removed, others are added, and, in some instances – for example, "An Interview in the City" (chapter 40) – there is a switch from the first-person narrator in the work in progress to the third-person narrator in the published novel. Indeed, the first-person perspective is largely avoided in the final version, which is in keeping with the detached mode of narration that is so technically striking.

At one point the overall structure of the planned novel appears to have been fundamentally different from the extant version, at least according to the following comments offered by Healy two years before it was published:

> I would see my book as an attempt to tell stories.
> You know the way Chaucer's *Tales* were about people
> telling different stories to while away the time. That
> was on a huge canvas. My book is about tales told
> to while away the time, because of the absence of

someone. In the book, the young man is dead and
the stories are told about him. The beginning of the
book is a mixture of my own family.*

This description doesn't correspond to the novel as we have
it, although some of that anecdotal quality is retained. What
this demonstrates, as with all of the variations in the published
extracts, is the degree of continual revision and refinement
that was part of Healy's artistic process. It seems quite clear
from the material set in the Basque country, and from his
original statements about the novel, that a dramatic rewriting
of the book took place during the last two years. Even in his
later novels, Healy expended enormous reserves of energy in
the rewriting process, while he was simultaneously producing
a significant body of award-winning poetry, a substantial
number of innovative plays, and a highly-regarded memoir.
The work itself, and the career, were clearly marked by a high
degree of focused industry and diligent attention to his craft.

* Dermot Healy, "Some think I'm wasting my time" [interview with John McEntee],
Irish Press (15 July 1982): 9.

PUBLISHED EXTRACTS FROM *SCIAMACHY*
AND *FIGHTING WITH SHADOWS*:

Dermot Healy, "Legal Times," *Icarus*, no. 75 (1980), ed. Gerry McDonnell: 35–41. [Includes a drawing by Christy McGinn entitled "D. Healy's story."] This story is subtitled "(An Excerpt from 'Sciamachy'– A Novel in Progress)." Reprinted in Dermot Healy: *The Collected Short Stories*, ed. Keith Hopper and Neil Murphy (Illinois: Dalkey Archive Press, 2015).

Dermot Healy, "The Island and the Calves (Sciamachy 2)," *Cyphers*, no. 7 (Winter 1977–78), ed. Leland Bardwell, Eiléan Ní Chuilleanáin, Pearse Hutchinson, and Macdara Woods: 23–27. Reprinted in Dermot Healy: *The Collected Short Stories*, ed. Keith Hopper and Neil Murphy (Illinois: Dalkey Archive Press, 2015).

Dermot Healy, "Work in Progress," *Icarus* 73 (Winter 1977–78), ed. Ed McGuire: 61–66. This is subtitled "(Excerpt from Dermot Healy's 'Sciamachy,' now being forged in the smithy of his soul 3 miles outside Cootehill, Co. Cavan)."

Dermot Healy, "Voting for Dead Men," *Books Ireland* no. 86 (September 1984): 151–52. A Headnote calls this "An extract from *Fighting with Shadows* by Dermot Healy, to be published this month by Brandon / Allison & Busby." [Variant section of chapter 38, *Fighting with Shadows*.]

Dermot Healy, "An Interview in the City," *Cyphers* no. 16 (Winter 1981), ed. Leland Bardwell, Eiléan Ní Chuilleanáin, Pearse Hutchinson, and Macdara Woods: 26–32. [Variant of chapter 40, *Fighting with Shadows*.]

Dermot Healy, "An Interview in the City," The Anthology, ed. Leland Bardwell and Joseph Ambrose (Dublin: Co-Op Books, 1982): 131–40. [Variant of chapter 40, *Fighting with Shadows*.]

Dermot Healy, "From *Fighting with Shadows*," *A Christmas Feast: Incorporating Winter's Tales*, ed. James Hale (London and Basingstoke: Macmillan, 1983): 283–85. [Variant of chapter 24, *Fighting with Shadows*.]

Dermot Healy, "The Midgets on the Pass" ["Work in Progress: Dermot Healey [sic],"] *The Fiction Magazine* 1.3 (Autumn 1982): 64–66. [Variant of chapter 25, *Fighting with Shadows*.]

Dermot Healey [sic], "Helen Allen," *Aquarius* [London] no. 15/16 (1983), ed. Eddie S. Linden: 65–68. An endnote calls it "Extract from *Fighting with Shadows*, a novel by Dermot Healey [sic] to be published in 1984 by Allison & Busby." [Variant of chapter 2, *Fighting with Shadows*.]

GLOSSARY OF IRISH TERMS:

Pages 53, 64: "sheugh"– a furrow, ditch, or trench.

Page 136: "*is m'athair* ruin" – "and my darling father."

Page 139: "tigín"– little house or cottage.

Page 168: "*Is binn, bog ach bréagach a sheinneas tú*" – "Sweet and soft, but guileful / falsely do you sing."

Page 168: "*Is minic do bhíonn an fhírinne féin searbh*" – "Truth itself is often bitter."

The etymology of the name of the fictional village, Fanacross, is explained differently on two occasions in the novel: first by Frank Allen: "Fanacross. *Fan ocras*, the end of hunger, surely" (chapter 1); and then, towards the end of the book, a police interrogator says to George, Frank's twin brother: "'Fanacross,' he says, '*Fánaí na coise*, the slopes of the bank'" (chapter 41). Both etymologies are imprecise and this may be deliberate on Healy's part, implying a kind of ignorance of place that is a result of not knowing the language properly. It is possible to discern a deliberate mischievousness in these misrepresentations, of a very specific kind: "fan" (wait), instead of "fán" (slope), and "fánaí" (wanderer) instead of "fán" (slope), plus "coise" instead of "croise" (of the cross[roads]). Implicit in this Joycean wordplay is a subtle statement about cultural disconnectedness, one which speaks of wandering, wondering, and a terrible sense of loss in the lives of the Irish people.

Acknowledgements

This reissue of *Fighting with Shadows* was conceived and initiated with Dermot Healy's blessing and assistance in July 2013. Dermot had kindly agreed to comment on the final draft typescript and galley proofs; sadly, following his untimely death in June 2014, this was not to be. We do hope that this edition would have met with Dermot's approval, and that its publication will, in some small way, serve as a tribute to his memory. We are very grateful to his family and friends for their encouragement and support in bringing this volume to fruition; any errors in the text are entirely our own.

Immense gratitude and admiration are also offered to Dermot's wife, Helen Gillard Healy, who was deeply involved in this venture from the outset, during early discussions in Singapore and Sligo, and thereafter by phone, email and in person – none of this would have been possible without her help and commitment.

Seán Golden's friendship with Dermot spanned more than four decades, as did his familiarity with the intensely nuanced topography of the work – we have been extremely fortunate to find in Professor Golden a most helpful and gracious guide through the labyrinths of print and myth, at times almost on a daily basis. Brian Leyden has also been an invaluable presence for which we are, and continue to be, extremely grateful. Without the assistance of those who were familiar with Dermot's work and life down through the years, our work would have been, at the very least, far more challenging.

Thanks too are offered to John O'Brien for his visionary Dalkey Archive Press, with sincere gratitude for his continued, steadfast support of this venture, and for his ongoing contribution to literature that matters.

We are very grateful to Dr Michelle Chiang, who offered

much-needed support and dedication in preparing the text for publication. Cheryl Julia Lee was a most helpful envoy sending valuable missives from the libraries of Dublin, for which sincere thanks. Pan Huiting assisted with an early draft of the novel, which was most helpful.

In addition, thanks to Tim O'Grady, Pat McCabe, Bill Swainson, Molly McCloskey, Alannah Hopkin, Aidan Higgins, and Annie Proulx, all of whom significantly intersected with Dermot's life and work, and who were all important sounding boards over the past few years. Dr Guinevere Barlow offered expert advice on, and translations of, some instances of Irish in the novel, as did Dr Seosamh Mac Muirí, who also provided important insights on the etymology of Fanacross, which are reflected in the Irish Glossary in the 'Note on the Text.'

Dermot's friend and neighbour, the artist Seán McSweeney, kindly provided the landscape painting which adorns the cover of this book ("Shoreline Sligo"). We are extremely grateful to Seán for this beautiful image, and to Sheila McSweeney for supplying us with a digital photograph of the painting. Thanks also to Su Salim Murphy for her advice on cover design.

Emma Wilcox, the English subject librarian at the School of Humanities and Social Sciences library, NTU, has, as always, been extremely supportive. Thanks also to Prof Lance Pettitt, Dr Anne Goudsmit, Donal McCay, and everyone in the Centre for Irish Studies at St Mary's University, Twickenham, for their encouragement and advice.

Fighting with Shadows was first jointly published by Allison & Busby (London and New York) and Brandon (now O'Brien) Press (Dingle, Co. Kerry). Due acknowledgement of both presses is hereby registered.

This work was completed with the assistance of a Singapore MOE, ACRF Tier 1 grant, awarded to the editors in 2014, for which thanks and acknowledgement are registered.

Deepest gratitude, as always, is offered to Su Salim Murphy and Niamh Moriarty, for their constant support and encouragement.

FIGHTING WITH SHADOWS

For Dallan and Inor

And to all there who gave me the rooms and the stories – Una, Joe, Eric, Chris, Martin, James Coyle, Dan, Frank, Steve, Dee, Lynnus, Anna, Mick, Barbara, Clive, Val, Bill, Pippa, the folk of Annaghmakerrig, Noreen, Susan, the Breifne, Caldwell Street
– thanks.

Author's Note

Sciamachy: I chose the word as the cog around which the book turns for various reasons. My dictionary gives its meaning as: A sham fight, a visionary fight, a fight with shadows. Each of which will satisfy what I intend. But there are extended meanings. *Skia* means shadow, *Machi* means fight, the latter leading to such words as *machismo*. *Skia* can lend itself to the feminine. The two sexes opposed can then be read into it. Also, there is a further reading in a word allied to it, *Sciomancy*, meaning Divination through the Shades of the Dead. This has always been an Irish way with history. So the collage of events from recent times portrayed in the novel is selected according to that meaning of the word, and the meaning extended into the plural to capture the nuances, hence: Shadows.

(Dermot Healy, March 1986)

I

1

"Anything strange?" asked Pop.

The youth was fair-haired, not of that end of the country. He did not answer Pop, just threw him a casual eye and toiled nimbly up through Fanacross.

"What is this they tell us of the drought below?" Pop called after him.

"It's not that bad," he shouted back.

A small bag hung jauntily by his side. His accent was Southern and his face intelligent. "You're not wise," Pop whispered. But there was no delaying the fellow. He continued his journey up Slianein till he had beneath him the upper lake and the lower lake, and further back the Leitrim mountains, and the Cavan mountains, and driftwood on the shores, and the skeleton of the new pier, awkward and ungainly. I would have you know the times we are in, Mister. The long unending middays. The lorry-loads of watchful pigs descending the mountain by night to a slaughterhouse in the South. How the cattle get dizzy crossing the border for the grants in the North and back again for the grants in the South. The heavy-coated smugglers searching the narrow roads ahead. Another bridge down yesterday. Time, consider time. And worse. Pop would have followed after the young fellow if he could, to explain the unexplainable. But that was the way things were with the people in the border village, that complete strangers passed through, were viewed from every garden and window, and then, never seen again.

As the drought down South dragged on over the long months of the summer, the midlands people no longer knew what nature or man held in store for them.

All disasters became confused in their minds and seemed to come from the one source.

They lost the will to govern themselves.

The colour of the birds seemed parched and lifeless.

The hatred of the midlands people for those fighting in the North grew greater, for was it not those deaths that woke them with feverish temples and screaming children? One day the papers would say that no one had died. The next, they gave the names of those that had perished. Down South, the weather reports gave no hint of rain. Herons glided along the rank garbage that filled the riverbeds. Whole areas of woods fell dead and here was the endless traffic of beetles drilling the bark dry. The inhabitants held their noses and never looked back where the drowned dogs, trapped on the muttering riverbeds, had turned rancid yet still kept their teeth bared. The people kept themselves in a state of constant preparation for a life that was going to begin again at any moment, but each morning when they heard the tap of the bricky's trowel on the wall of an unfinished house and the sifting of dry cement, the bored talk of the builders, the moans of animals in the scorched fields as they thundered along a ditch after the quick step of a passer-by, the heavy breathing of the cows as they dragged their raw tongues along the grass after night had lifted, there was no denying it, no miracle had taken place, the people knew that the same nightmare awaited them.

Yet, because of the new liberalism, the economic boom of the sixties, the midlands people could now afford to question, however naively, their fates and express, however sentimentally, their psychological loss.

Faint voices from the earlier religious days echoed through their sleeplessness. *There will be a ceasing of consciousness. There is a Hell.* The old heroic tradition was gone and in its stead came the terrifying knowledge of another's existence. How, in the lull afforded them by other nations clashing, elsewhere in their own country rebellion had begun. The drought and the war were closing in fast on all sides. And Mr Allen, Frank Allen, had lost his status in that society. A carefree man, he had explored even that fragile tilt of a single love upon which a reputation for respectability is built.

His wife, Helen, slept away from him in a pure way now.

The midlands people had time for each other like never before.

And the border village was constantly filled with rumours of terrible disasters happening North and South, so that the fishermen as they paid out their illegal nets on the lakes never, even on the good days, let the village out of sight.

The Allens, after some years wandering the South, had settled in a caravan where the Erne rose and in the spring of the year the drought came. A tractor had hauled the caravan across the small fields to a muddy spot under a shimmering tree, and the nights there before the drought, a small stream would trickle past, and further down, fill a hole with cool noiseless water. Through the tunnel it formed under the ash trees the stream continued down a gentle fall through bright-coloured stones, turned left across still, boggy earth, making on its descent a playful sound against the deeper flow that came after, so that when the Allens sat out on the steps of the caravan in the early evenings they could hear the stream in all its various moods. It was a good time too at the beginning. Frank Allen found work at a flour mill convenient to the field, and though the work appeared permanent, still he continued to believe that no work would ever be again. Each home made way for a more temporary one. And when asked where he came from, he would reply: "Why, Fanacross. *Fan ocras*, the end of hunger, surely." A man's skin is thinner than a woman's, and when a man panics he exaggerates his love and his loss. His imagination fills with things that have never been.

So one day, on his way home from the mill, after a solitary drink in the pub, Frank Allen lost touch with his surroundings and headed towards some house in the town, knocked correctly on the door, then waited there on the steps, white as a sheet. "No, mister, you don't live here," a lad told him, and shouldering the lad aside a woman in the hall shouted to someone else within, "I know him to see, he lives out the road in Freedmont's field!" Dismissed, Frank Allen returned again, indignantly thinking he was in the right. He stood seeking entry from the street into this house in the South, glancing around unknowingly as bewildered faces mouthed disbelief, and when it dawned on him, as the house grew strange and the faces distant and unfamiliar, a hot flush undid him. He heard their voices disparaging him – the gruff murdering Northerner – like someone who flags down a bus too late. His spirit winced at the exposure of this sordid melee.

He fled out the road cursing his misfortune, as if fate had severed him forever from any security, and his worst fear was that wordlessly the same scene would be re-enacted in the shapeless reality that lay ahead, the same mean refusal occur, outside of his or their control.

The mill closed.

The labourers occupied it for a fortnight till a tired gang from the city drove them from it, but first they knifed the bursting sacks and scattered the flour onto the attackers below, they fucked the seeds across the yard where they burst from the earth the following spring.

Each was fined a statutory sum at the Circuit Court.

The stream in June dried up.

Frank Allen placed an advertisement in the local paper, offering himself, a strong-bodied man with average intelligence, for employment. It was enough to drive Helen insane. He expected, with some forlorn hope, to hear from all and sundry, and each morning he was at the gate watching for the first post van, to see whether the wild dreams he had thought up the night before would be realized.

The reality he kept to himself.

Frank Allen received three replies.

Two down and one to go.

He crossed the field in his wellingtons while Helen followed after with his shoes. He changed at the gate and they parted without a word. He stepped in. There were three men at a desk in the corner of a shed in a builder's yard. Overhead, old stone plumbobs hung from the rafters, moving on their ropes now and then like silent bells.

"What wage would you require?" the head fellow asked.

Frank stalled. "I'll leave that up to you," he answered.

They looked at him. After a long silence the figure on the left said with a smile: "Would ten thousand a year be enough?"

Frank Allen was staggered. That had to be at least twice what they were getting. His slack mouth opened and he looked along the three faces. Again he had come to the wrong door and realized it. Now he saw what was happening. He headed away from there, stood decisionless on the main street, his lungs sending out quick breaths to vie with others coming in. He sought to find an image that would contain his distress. With jaunty stoicism he strode out the road, a naggin of Paddy in his fist. What were brilliant colours now but a furious hallucination of a deeper need.

Refracted life from an exhausted pupil.

His asthmatic speech began.

His lips, ashen and thin, withdrew as he spoke. The tip of his tongue appeared. He gave a cough. Helen, a little tipsy after a single glass, brought her hands to her face as she laughed ... "All down through the piece I loved her, JoeJoe," he said to his son. "Take it from someone who watched politics from the cradle. I served priests and saw them brought down in time." He drank a little. "Good luck, now." She looked away from him. "It was big rebel country, Fanacross, that's why I married out of there. Maybe I wasn't as fond of the work as I should have been. Do you know how I used to get on with the farming?" He turned to his son. "Because the animal, every animal, thinks you are twice the size you are."

"When I was with them, I didn't listen," he told Helen that night as she lay out of his reach crouched tight against the caravan wall, "and when they are not here I hear their every word.

2

Helen Allen one day saw a distorted image of herself in her husband's eye. Next morning, the shape had not righted itself. For days she thought that the caravan was filled with the smell of milk boiled over, and though she scoured the walls and the floor and the cooking vessels, the smell would not go away.

"Do you know," she said, "that you're a cunt to live with?"

"Well," said he, "you're no great shakes yourself."

Helen's earlier life had been full of fantasy. She had thrown herself onto Frank, desiring him greatly. In her excitement it was she made the demands. She did not see his body, but all other men's bodies rolled into one. That he existed as a representative of all other men fulfilled her fantasy and while he would have liked more time, she drove them forward in quick short bursts of bliss. His body was the instrument of her imagination, and his mind a place that she could move easily in. Her early dissatisfaction she saw merely as the ache of not having him completely to herself. So they went wandering, till in time his desire matched hers. And went beyond. But already they had formed certain habits that were not of his making. Too late he learned that he should have controlled her needs and not given way to them. Now as her need for that kind of quick fantastic love dwindled and her desire for affection grew, he found he had become a victim of her earlier fantasy and knew no other way of winning her.

She drew back from the very thing she had once craved and like someone pitiless he pursued the same path, thinking she must remember.

On the good days she returned to her fantasy, going back to the early times in his arms, but it could not be sustained. Coupled with her need of the freedom of the earlier days was a growing suspicion of the new. He knew this distant manner, but it was like reading a fortune. He could not tell the difference between what had happened and what was to come true. She was slipping away from him while he played out the role she had created for him. She saw through him. Her rebukes became painful and wounding.

And all the time he knew that she could only truly live with him when he had become inaccessible again.

It was the way of her fantasy that when it went all his human needs demeaned her, demeaned them both. Her need for security grew with the same recklessness that she had once sought freedom. They had lost themselves and wandered unhindered between each other, not hearing a voice distinct, belonging to the other, that could admit to the flaws. The flaws of one became the justification for the complaint of the other. On the good days they spoke each other's names with raw, tender, unfamiliarity. But the fantasy, like a form of consumption, had made their lives wretched, for he was too distraught to see his way toward her. Her great curiosity about the world of men, her excitement about their excitement, could only be continued in another, but that too would be unsatisfactory. This is a stage in love, she told herself, there is another stage, I must hold on.

And soon she started to wear him down to another need of hers, that he know death in the face of nothingness. Her sympathy was gone. Her caring sense had become a burden. She panicked over the shape of herself. The skin she was in.

Her meanness and temper.

Through work, relief to her senses came.

She worked the walls and floor of the caravan till they were raw, and having got permission from Freedmont she started a garden along the edge of the stream. All other pleasures – those that merely assuage the loss – became false. The sensual loss continued but there was no need to hurry into another's arms. When the enormity of the reality struck her, that her body did not care a whit for the man beside her, that her mind could not respond to his, all fantasy was gone.

For how could she sustain a further fantasy when her flawed sense of herself would break through?

And work alone, in a small caravan, could not cheer up her body like the loved one could.

Her contempt grew.

Could he not tell, as she heard him in the dark compensating with the body's dream, pulling her hand down to his groin, that it was this cold release of the body that built up the barricades while their spirits flew restless about them? Unfulfilling and unfulfilling. "I'll swing for you," she said, pulling her hand back. And as he sought her night after night the more untouchable she became, full of righteous indignation, making promises she would never fulfil, saying: Tomorrow night, tomorrow. Once she could get through this night, that was all.

"It will make us happy," he said.

"You're wrong," she answered. "People only make love when they are happy."

Then an impossible day would arrive. The world righted itself. She felt relaxed. In her isolation, in his isolation, the two met momentarily. But she knew all the time the aftermath. It was like a worm working its way through her brain, yet she thought that in release she might find honest union again. That day she admitted to a lot yet retained the will to carry on. Did he think she was weakening? Anyway, his personality became a protective coat. She saw the shape of herself in his eye and it was a warm image he had of her. She could rest there a while. He was remaking her, she could see it, but she was too tired to care. It was all right, she felt safe for a while.

Patience. To not keep at bay the existence of the other.

All day they built up to it. They went back to themselves, as they had first appeared to each other. She knew it. A time would come when she would have to share herself again. Her cries for sympathy, that had replaced his, had not brought good fortune. The bright blue thread in the patchwork quilt glowed. The sun through the small window. Onto the gas heater. The can of paraffin. He did her back. She did his.

He fondled her back, prised the muscles with the tips of his fingers. He touched the shadowy centres of her shoulder blades with his lips. He worked down the firm steps of her spine. "Don't," she said, "be so soft with me." She arched her neck forward. "Have you found something there?" she asked, as he tweaked a dried-up pimple. "Jesus," she said, "not that hard." Her shoulder-blades arched. She descended to some shady spot, all movement was slowly arrested, she fell still.

Soon Joseph was asleep.

The nightbirds threw a canopy over the caravan.

She was tickling his buttocks and he could not believe it. After all the time he had waited. Everything seemed so far out of reach. He came so quickly that she called out too late for him to wait. Helen gave way with an aching thrust that he would remember over and over in his mind, along with what came after. For recovering herself, she knew no peace. Their love-making had been like a quick dash down a deserted street. Unsatisfied ghosts were at the window. She told him of her frustration, knowing in a deeper way, that his haste had been of her own making. He grew bitter and full of remorse. He does not know me outside of fantasy, she thought. It's not me he sees, but all the others in me. The circle was complete.

And the whirlwind began again. The recriminations took seed in their brains. The distortions started all over.

There, in the middle of the night, unable to take his insults any longer, she leathered his face with her fists. The caravan rocked on the hard mud as another morning of screaming began. A fox, head-down, darted through the field and looked out at the road. A rabbit sat up. Joseph locked himself tight between the sheets in the other double bed, then first one side of him his mother climbed in, and soon after, on the other side, his father. "Christ, I'm stifled," he said, but no one answered. It was as if they had only imagined him.

3

In the morning the smell of corpses of cattle drifted along the eaves and sashes of the tumble-down houses on the road into town, but by midday the wind drove the smell of death before it and the people would forget the terrors of the night before. A form of gentle camaraderie grew up among the survivors as they hauled the piglets away from the dry teats of the fallen sow, and bottle-fed them any liquid available. Frank Allen had expected that the townfolk would accept him down here, but the sight of the stranger from the North only exaggerated their fears. In his eyes they saw the frayed nerves of their future. He drew them, without a word spoken, back into a continuous war. So, with that vigilant humour and desperation of their kind, as Joseph dropped the bucket into the dry well or beat the crank of the pump till the green paint splintered in his search for water, the townspeople offered him nothing from the fresh stock delivered that morning, but sat instead outside the pubs and shops smoking, unconcerned in the hum of the afternoon.

The rope was coarse as the fetlock of a plough house.

Why did his parents not know that in this place the well was dry?

Who came and went from the countryside into the town had to fend for himself.

He queued again by the steps of the hotel whose owner had a private spring well that was still functioning normally. Small bachelor farmers stood ahead of him, and gypsy women and children from the poorer areas of the town, all complaining as they waited. "It's frightful, frightful," whispered an old man in a black suit, a beret perched on his white head, his body neat as a thimble on the married finger.

"What's to become of us?" said a couple going round in circles.

"You can't win," a querulous voice repeated again and again.

Though the merchants kept the Allens' food from week to week till Frank paid up the dole, it was handed over with the fatalism of the subjected. The need for trade just about kept the hatred of the shopkeepers under control.

Well, anyway, their wealth had made Joseph angry.

He carried the half-filled bucket up the hill past the church, knocking it from one knee to the other, tried to stop himself when he got home from telling of the attitude of the people in town because this only made things worse. He made it through his first cup of tea before he told how things stood this day within. He started with one complaint, what someone said to him, and getting an audience he started to exaggerate till his father threatened to go into town and break someone's face, then Joseph said he had been lying, he said, "You know what I mean anyway."

"We must get out of this," Frank Allen said to Joseph and to Helen, "and hightail it back to Fanacross."

And his exasperation became all the greater, for Helen his wife, because of her loneliness, was lengthening her stride away from him. Her sense of objectivity had become obscene, and his subjectivity, unbearable. And each night Fanacross, the home place, spun by them like a comet leaving a trail of happiness in its wake.

"Curse it anyway," Frank would repeat over and over as this deadness came over his soul.

"I would not like to be stuck like this for good," Helen said as she straightened up by the basin.

"First," Frank told Joseph, "you can taste it in the air, in the wind, in the trees, then in all the senses. The lake air." He looked over at Helen. "The lake air."

For Joseph, there was no place to hide from the world his parents had known which re-existed every time the stories were told. "If I was drunk all the time, man dear," said Helen to her husband as she gave him a candid glance, "I'd think like you do," and satisfied that she had hurt him well enough, she gloated in the silence that followed. There followed guilt because she saw herself as a woman who could no longer think of another's needs. Knowing someone else's needs is in itself an act of love. That they trust in you. But I want to be free of all that, thought Helen. You've spoiled it all on me. She lifted a cup of water from the bucket and drank as she looked at him, saying over and over to herself, You've spoiled it all on me.

In September, Joseph's Aunt Geraldine visited from the home place in Fanacross.

Geraldine was a heavy, though sprightly, woman who had been blessed with a hard soul, and allied to that, a sense of humour. She needed all these qualities in good stead when she arrived, for she could not believe her eyes at the demons that had the run of the caravan. Joseph bawling his head off for Fanacross and the pair in the little kitchen arguing over the least thing. So his Aunt Geraldine said: "Stay quiet in front of the lad." The pair would try to pretend they had not been arguing. "Is it money?" Geraldine asked. "Is it work?" she asked again. "If it was only the one thing," answered Helen, "it would be easy." "Well," said Geraldine, "I find the place, if you don't mind me saying so, very unhealthy." A recriminatory silence followed, but the minute Geraldine lighted into the field they were at it again in long hoarse whispers, blaming each other for the bad reception they had given George's wife. Helen shrieking as she cooked the dinner and Frank giving the imbecile's headbutt to a drawer overhead. Geraldine stepped in and marched by them. She put Joseph's clothes on over his pyjamas and took him for a walk. Soon, leaving the strange sleeping landscape behind, they headed out the road where no one saluted them.

"What age were you when ye left Fanacross?" she asked.

"I was seven, I think," he said.

The night air was ripe with the smell of the local tannery.

Calves with their hooves stiffened into the air had been hauled over the ditches. "It looks," whispered Geraldine, "like we are only imagining all this." She walked the faster to forget so the lad had to run alongside her. The sickening smell of rotten cabbage-water would suddenly attack their nostrils, then just as suddenly disappear, and return again, intensified by having been forgotten, like an argument starting up with worse venom than before. Joseph grew weary and wanted to return, but his Aunt Geraldine propelled him forward with lies. "Wait," she said laughing, "it's early yet."

She went ahead of him like an ungainly steer, a shape moving against the trees till there was the backward turn of her face, then the dropping of her hand into his. It told him something of what was happening in her, a sort of spiritual recklessness he could not name. He took short quick dashes up the road ahead and waited in the shadows with his heart pounding. Her step grew faint. He ran back, demented with fear, straight to where she stood listening.

Later still she said: "Look, do you see ahead of you, that's the light in the kitchen of your father's old house where myself and Uncle George used to live."

"Can we walk there?" enquired Joseph wondering, as the light signalled in the distance.

"Of course we can," she leaned down, breathed into his face the full fire of someone living.

So they walked and walked till Joseph thought the feet would fall off him. And sometimes the light was here and sometimes there, higher and lower, and sometimes in the hand-held torch of a drunken farmer crossing a field or in the lights of a Garda car gaining on them down the wandering road, going from sight and returning weaker than before, and nowhere the sound of the lakes because where Fanacross was, there was water.

"Maybe we should go back," eventually Geraldine said, as she trotted behind him.

"No," he said stubbornly.

Blindly he walked through the dark, and sometimes felt it behind him, her dress cold as stone. She stopped to catch her breath. They started again. In error they entered an open field by a bend in the roadway. They found the dry grass beneath their feet. She led him around till she found a break in the silhouette of the trees. They edged forward like children through the darkness that breathed around them like a distressed animal. Their feet found the warm running road. It was here she tricked him into returning. Still Geraldine lied because she could not go back on what she had said.

She followed him back through the silent countryside.

And the one thought that kept going through her head was that this was not her child, he is a complete stranger to me.

"Is that it?" shouted Joseph, pointing towards a light ahead.

And in total silence Joseph found he was back at the caravan where he should never have been at all. The voices of his father and mother carried out from the small rusted windows but this time not in argument. This time it was the gossiping sound you hear from trapped birds. He walked by them without a word, flung his clothes away and climbed into bed. Helen stood up. "What's wrong?" she asked. Geraldine heaved herself into one of the folding chairs. "Now," said Geraldine, her voice embittered by a sense of human frailty and her body tired out after all the aimless walking, "now," she repeated, "he knows all he need ever know about Fanacross."

4

It was 1970. Joseph was seven and they were living in Fanacross. Frank Allen, a tall woollen hat perched like a tea-cosy on his head was crouched on his hunkers in a gap of a field watching the soldiers laying dynamite charges under the bridge to the South. It was one of those meandering days when the birds twitch like midges and everyone appears very sure of themselves. All morning people had been collecting on both sides of the border and, along with the others, with hardly time to collect her things, Helen was shepherded out of the house to a safe position behind a barricade.

The wiring of the bridge was a long intricate affair.

The voices of the British soldiers carried up like the voices of lads in a playground.

There is no telling it – you think you are human because you are looking at humans.

The soldiers withdrew from the bridge, then returned again.

A boat came up the river. The engineers harnessed a charge to the belly of the bridge. Moss floated downstream. Cement flaked into the water. The people grew restless. It was as though they had been given extra time to see all that was happening in a different light. Clouds raced up the river over the green swirling weeds. The odd trout sucked at passing flies. Now it was the Southerners started yelling their abuse from the far side over the heads of the unarmed Gardaí. The village people kept their quiet. They looked at the soldiers who looked back at them like drinking cattle.

The countryside was quiet with expectancy.

Frank Allen stole along the ditch and waited.

Nothing happened for a long time.

The soldiers left the bridge and knelt in the various alleyways in the village or else stood up against the gables. They held their rifles tight against them as if somehow this would deaden the roar of the explosion. There was the sound of hobnailed boots running up the quiet village. "Did anyone see my fellow?" asked Helen Allen. "Ah, he's about somewhere," said a man. "That's no answer," she said. The men stood about with their boyish cheeks. Even in middle-age their faces had not yet been lived in.

The abuse on the far bank got worse.

Suddenly, the Southerners broke the Garda cordon.

They ran onto the bridge. When they got there they didn't know what to do, there were so few of them. The soldiers began screaming to each other from wherever they were standing a series of unrecognizable names. Yet, no one moved. Then at last an officer spoke through a loudspeaker. He said there were only minutes, minutes, he shouted, to spare. His words threw up frightened birds along the river. But the people on the bridge did not move. The officer sounded genuinely afraid. A hail of stones crossed the river over the heads of the struggling Gardaí. It took some time before the British officer realized that it would be his responsibility to clear the bridge.

The guards were making no attempt.

The roll-call between the British soldiers started all over again.

Ten soldiers without guns pulled the protesting men by the heels into the North. But one man outwitted them, he jumped off the bridge into the river below, and resurfacing seconds later, clung to one of the massive granite piers. Frank Allen wondered could the Free Stater swim for he was making a poor job of staying afloat. As the crowd realized what had happened and began to cheer, the fellow brightened up a little, and releasing one of his hands he waved. His coat was being dragged up river.

He should throw that coat away, thought Frank, and make himself comfortable. "What depth is it out there?" someone asked.

The hail of stones continued without reaching the far side.

The officer, ducking behind a makeshift shield, implored the man below to climb up. He was having none of that though, he just hung on grimly and shook his head. Will they try the boat, wondered Frank, or will they let a soldier down to him? Frank edged along the ditch till he was a few yards away from the river. The soldiers scattered this way and that. The cheers in the South rose to fever pitch. It looked like soon more of the crowd would break through. The army motorboat came up the river with four soldiers on it. They cut the motor as they passed under the bridge and knifed up silently to where the man clung. They teased his grip off the wet stones and flung him bodily into the boat where he kicked and struggled like a landed fish.

Now it was Frank Allen's turn.

He kicked off his shoes and jumped in. He swam steadily towards the bridge hearing each time his ears cleared the water the sound of the loudspeaker. "He's nifty," someone said, "whoever he is." Being nimbler than the man before him he climbed up and stood on a margin of rock just under the water level of the pier. He held his stomach and beating heart against the wet pier thinking, Jesus, I hope they have seen me. He wrapped his arms about the pier. He could hear nothing. He saw the neat clamp of the explosives under the arch.

Time was running short and there was so much to do.

Then heads appeared over the bridge and began to shout down.

He heard the cheers elsewhere.

This is all right, he thought, I've done better than I thought I would.

He listened for the motorboat. That's when it started. Suddenly other men followed him. They jumped in downriver from the South and started the long swim to the bridge, bad swimmers every one, trying to get there before the boat could return. Through the corner of his eye Frank Allen saw them coming. "They'll tear him to ribbons, the soldiers will," said Helen. I'm too old for all this, he was saying to himself. It's all happening to some other. Again he heard the soldiers cut the engine and they hammered his hands off the stones where he clung like a leech. They drove the boat at the oncoming swimmers but already some had reached the bridge. The soldiers circled the water not knowing what to do, while overhead on the bridge itself, the crowd from the South broke through the guards. After them came the cattle and the cars.

The boat roared upriver, the two protestors pinned to the boards. The soldiers knelt on their chests, a grip on each of their necks. It was the first time that Frank Allen had ever really looked into the eyes of a British soldier.

A helicopter swung up the sky. The protestors clung like barnacles to the bridge. All night they stayed there. They urged each other on. A boat from the South crossed over with whiskey. That night the soldiers withdrew, and the following morning, the engineers returned, and under the cover of the soldiers they took the dynamite away. That was how the bridge was won. A few days later Frank Allen returned to his home. He entered unsteadily. The swelling in his eyes was just dying down. He did not say much to anyone, except to tell Helen that they threw something into his eyes. It felt, he said, like a handful of burning lime. For nights after she bathed his eyes with cold tea. A month of nightmares followed. There are two parts to me, he told his wife, the one part of me runs the prison where the other part is kept in chains. He knocked deliberately against Helen as if to hurt her.

"Does it make you bitter?" she asked him.

"It's early days yet," he answered.

It struck him that somehow she thought all that had happened to him had been self-inflicted. A few hours later he said, "Well, the water was bitter anyway." Soon all the bad things began. He saw his eye plucked from the socket by a scalpel. Then his wounds healed. After a while one minute did not run into the next. His heroism passed. He was like an animal that had been imprisoned, then released into the night to be later refused by his own kind. He went about the village in red socks. An Innocent. But as the deaths multiplied throughout the province the people knew that innocence would be no forgiveness.

He wanted to talk, but talk ran away with them.

Helen was kneading the uppermost knuckle of his spine.

"He had a sort of frightened look about him, that soldier," said Frank, "and do you know what he kept saying to me?

"'Take that fucking look off your face! Take that fucking look off your face.'" That was the voice that remained longest in Frank Allen's head, and in those days when Helen loved him, he could easily cry in front of her. But the voices can start up anywhere, anytime and have to be controlled. The saga of Frank Allen was only one of the many. It was not his pride ceasing that troubled the people, but that their consciousness continued beyond the times they were living through. The voices they heard told of other duties than caring for an individual who spent his days crouched by the river going over in his mind what had already receded from theirs. As he went up the village his nerves jingled like keys, then, after the long climb up the mountain he'd catch a glimpse of it miles away – the ocean. The Atlantic Ocean. From one day to the next his moods were like that. And last of all, he expected her to forge ahead of him. But Helen was repelled by his dependence. Soon he started announcing that their whole life together had been a waste of time. He could not be spoken to. Angrily he shoved unwanted food into Joseph's mouth. The next day Joseph and himself camped out for a week. Joseph never looked so happy. He ran up and down a pool in the river then turned and hugged his father's knee. And laughed and ran off again. When they returned a week later Helen greeted her husband with sheer hatred, especially when her son for the first few hours avoided her.

5

Sleet, and snow and cold rain. Out in the yard of the house Frank heard Helen talking sympathetically to a man about his failed affair with another woman. This is something to be watched, he thought, sympathy is the worst thing to look for from a woman, for when it runs out on her it's replaced by bitterness. These days Frank hardly got out of bed. Nothing had changed. Thinking always of what might make her happy, and affected always by an insecurity that plagued him. Yesterday Helen said: "I'm leaving you and taking the lad with me." He waited every moment for her step across the yard, the leaving down of the case, the swing of the gate.

I must, thought Frank, admit to a lot yet retain the will to carry on.

There is some justification then, he reasoned, in thinking of myself as alone, and then to earn the material things to make other people happy. It is the way of a family to expect this. If there is any falsehood it comes from my terror of loss. I must never project a false image again. I must build up some strength, so that there be solace for the loved one who travels in fear and can see no image but betrayal of what she holds dearest – privacy, that she be known outside of fantasy. Yet, I cannot be two people. She must be freed of the burden I make for her. If she feels burdenless, then so will I. Thinking such thoughts he came to his decision. He left the house each morning and stayed down the fields, stopping up to talk to whoever would listen to him. An old girlfriend listened so cold-bloodedly to talk of his affair, and saw Helen's position so objectively, that it was reassuring, yet left him lightheaded, that a woman could look so clearly into her own heart and see another woman's there. What was driving Helen to act in a particular manner, said Mary Callaher, was the need to get away. And he thought, how can she see all this? Why do women know so much of women and men so much of men and yet so little of each other? It seemed a tribal war. She loves you, said Mary Callaher, and all that Frank could wonder was whether Mary had ever known true love herself that she could see it so well in the heart of another.

The same night the soldiers came to search the house again. They kept Frank against the gable end of the house for four hours. Here, he thought to pass the time, thinking how temporarily he had treated this home where he and Helen lived with Pop, and George and Geraldine. He thought how much more he should have thought about the need for nice things there – now it was too late. Pop came round to him with a cup of tea which he placed at his feet. "Bend down for that, mate," said the soldier, "and you're dead." You just have to forget other people if you want to remember them, the more so if you live with them. Then you'll have no fear of losing them. Yet, I am not unworthy of you, Helen. You know I love you. What can I do? If all your desire is gone, I can't expect mine to be answered. You expect something of me? Can I deliver it? And will our future lives be free of these terrible humiliating arguments? Dawn dropped over the village, and seeing as they had tormented Frank Allen enough and thought they had broken his spirit since the affair at the bridge, the soldiers left.

Can I describe a world again that you do not inhabit – I mean you have been so much a part of mine that anything I say you will see as a type of subterfuge. I think people like us sink down together. None of us kept our independence. Falling in love happened at different times for each other.

So, one day Frank Allen took his wife and son into the South, they left Fanacross by way of a private bus which had special rates for the traveller. Geraldine was sad to see them go. George hurled their cases on board. The bus turned round. The sweat streamed down the faces of the passengers from the heat of the interior. The father carried Joseph on his knee. It was the first of their many journeys. The family could not take the strain any more. For them the South meant peace. And despite the arguments between himself and Helen, despite the constant

harassment from the soldiers, it was a prophecy Frank Allen
feared that drove him away. It was in his dream. It was in a
conversation half overheard. The bastards will get us. Worst of
all possibilities was the thought of the death of his son. He had
never once feared for Helen's life because that was not written
in the signs that were unhinging his mind. There is a peculiar
way the village people have of leaving home. You'd think it was
the conditions drove them to it, but it's somehow haphazard,
unplanned and has no real, basic necessity. It is a need to have
a life realized elsewhere. A life with a core of truth. It means
that you must never return if your greatest hopes are to be
realized. If you come back it will be downhill all the way from
there. It's a sort of moral cowardice to leave or return to what
you cannot change. The beginning and the end of the journey
are one and the same vision. Yet, there is this nagging need
to have done with the dream by turning it into a nightmare.
Perhaps Frank Allen was too selfish a man to know another's
needs. And maybe Helen should have stood more by the
partner she had chosen out of life. The bus passed the far
side of the river. They'd be back, like the salmon that throw
themselves against unassailable rocks and dams arisen during
their absence. Perhaps that's how fish turned into birds.

The radio was on high in the bus. Stopping a second at the
extreme end of the village, they saw through a gap in the
houses a valley of orange whins ahead. Past the white goalposts
in the football field. A man stopping, looking behind him, in
old dungarees. There is nowhere here that the cows can plant
their hooves firmly on the earth, they are always on an incline,
their legs on different levels, feeding, with necks strained, off
the grass above them. The bus passed through a black spot
where the horizon lies and men drive, in a direction not
cast by the roadmakers, towards their death. The road they
thought they saw ahead was a furrow cast by the quality of the
light and lie of the land. The conductor is collecting money.

The women in scarves open their purses. The long rattle of the handbrake as the bus halted on a hill looking down on the endless quilt of fields thrown carelessly over the earth.

My son, Joseph, thought Helen, my man, Frank. There are times when I would just love to up and disappear.

The green barrel-shaped sheds, like a row of shoes. For a brief instant, a clump of hay pinned overhead to a fork disappearing out of sight behind a low hill. The warm sun coming through the deep ploughed land of Meath, the low bungalows and the arched roofs of densely slated houses. The wrecks of lorries and the spires of churches seen inland through the trees. The driver jumping in his mirror and nobody talking, just a bell ringing somewhere in the undercarriage. The trees, wrapped in ivy, like pumps in winter, sending up sprays of little branches. All the things, thought Helen, I see for the first time again and again. The hot sun returning as we wheel round a bicycle. Through Navan. The granite town hall. White loaves in a window. A guard, after writing down the number of a car with great care, steps back, looks right and left, then carries on down the town with his mission over and the offending notebook safely buttoned away for again. The Boyne, high as the land around because of recent dams, goes against its nature round the new factories in a foam-flecked flood. The road to Dublin. We climb in third gear towards Tara. The tree-lined walks for priests. What about us, I ask you? In one field all the cows are lying down. Drums of hay yellowing at the core and wrapped in tough straw against the elements. A shop window full of little girl's dresses. Dresses and scarves drawn out by pins to their full extent. It's nearly over. I wish it would last forever. Crows fly awkwardly up from the road ahead after picking at the leavings of the flour lorries. Instead of a weathercock atop the house there is a silver horse with front hooves raised one above the other. Growths nesting in the high leafless trees. The driver raising his finger in recognition to a lorry driver who flashes his lights in response.

A pylon, its lattice-work designed by a man who thinks in lines that forever meet. The hangover entry to Dublin where I feel absolutely nothing. The new day should arrive. The nerves grow sluggish. The inhabitants seem to have entered into a cheerful intrigue to admit nothing. There it is in the face of a woman who stands at the edge of the racecourse by a van staring straight ahead over the trays of fruit. She is wearing a blue raincoat. Prescotts, cleaners and dyers. I am in Ireland after travelling down. I love my son Joseph. Have I shouted at you? Forgive me. Forgive me. I love you more than any other person in the world. We have only the one time on this earth.

They stepped down among the crowds of O'Connell Street. And two days wandering the pubs with Joseph tired and ill-tempered till they found a place – This will all happen again, Helen knew, from the ashtray in the back of the seat of the bus crammed with soiled tissues, to the handle that came away in her hand when she stepped into the two-roomed flat and heard two doors down a train roaring over a bridge and two doors up the continuous sound of coins spilling out of the fruit machines in an amusement arcade. This was to be their home for two years. In the deepest recess of the amusement arcade there stood an aged parrot dressed in the dishevelled colours of a music hall singer, the green cape and the extended fan, the horned face always in the spotlight, who roared out in a hysterical Dublin accent a continuous refrain of welcome to the gamblers. "Shut up, you fucker you," roared back the old ladies, "You fucker out of Hell," "Three bells," screeched the bird as she went up the road in the small hours on the shoulder of her owner, a low man with pinched ears. The veins stood out on the lobes. They crossed under the Allens' window, and towards Fairview.

In that whole period Helen did little of anything. She rarely ventured outside the door. On Fridays and Mondays she crossed the streets to a publican from their homeplace who allowed her the use of his bath. Her wash was a quick nervous affair because she could not trust the gas heater chugging like a kettle on the corner. She kept her thin back to the stains like excrement under the brass taps and stiffened as a barman walked down the corridor. She forgot the use of a mirror for ages till one day she caught sight of herself, slightly stooped, without ambition, her nipples coarsened by the lips of the father and then by the lips of the son, and yet what was the sense of blaming someone. Soon she came over nearly every day to wash. It became her obsession. Sometimes she'd stay too long and have to rush back across the street, up the three flights, into the room to find Joseph just as she had left him, watching TV. The woman from next door would look in. "Ay, you're back now, dear," the woman would say. "You'll be the better for that."

"How much did you say?" she asked the shopkeeper again.

"I might as well not exist at all," she told Frank, "everything is always the same."

A man furtively stepped out of the shadows. She was dreaming him. She found him moving over and back, his prick between her hollowed-out thighs, not in her, no. "Don't move," he pleaded, "please don't move." She shook her washed hair before the coal fire. That was that. Meanwhile Frank Allen was plucking potatoes out of the earth at Swords on a day's labour afforded him by a friend from Fermanagh. The next week he was painting a boutique off Abbey Street dressed in a cream-and-blue set of overalls and a little peaked hat. Helen came by with Joseph. She found Frank on his belly in one of the windows between two undressed mannequins drawing a careful brush along the thin edge of the sill. He was so engrossed in what he was at that he never noticed them. He pushed his head through all kinds of women's undergarments to make room for himself as he moved forward on his knees. Joseph dropping on his hunkers squeezed his face against the glass. Frank backed off in fright in finding a head at the same level as his own. "Come in," he gestured. "C'mon and try on some clothes." He had an easy way with the girls there, so Helen spent the morning dipping into all the knee-length dresses of the time, and finding one that suited her, Frank arranged to have the price of it deducted from his wages. He was loath to let her go, she looked so wonderful. His family disappeared into the afternoon crowds. That was that. Another evening, after one of their arguments, he was standing in a bar with a couple of men from the North and every man had his own version of the story that gave them a claim to fame. He found himself exaggerating every like the others. Yet no one would admit it. It was a break of trust. The other might see through you. A Dubliner spoke to them. They turned boastful and proud. They saw through his inexperience. They flaunted themselves like peacocks at the bar. All sexual conversation was rooted in the perverse. They egged each other further on till they even demoralized each other. They would part that night defeated by their insecurities again. Was this what we came down for? Frank Allen went up the loose stairs dreaming of a home. There was concern but no quiet at his centre. He could not be depended on. That was that. She tried to kill him one day in a rage brought on by drink she'd taken early that morning in the pub where she went to wash. There had been a crowd in the bar singing. Some of them had just arrived from Europe. They would not let her pass through till she had a drink. A gin, then, and lime. And pints of Smithwicks after. Through the other door came the sound of the ukulele and spoons. In an old Guinness mirror filled with gilt lettering she saw her high head in the towel looking back, and seated below, the gang singing a short Germanic song with a robust chorus. When had this happened before? The more familiar it became. The women, young girls, sang in harmony. She turned. Everyone had good manners. Everyone stayed still. "Where did you get the beautiful cardigans?" she asked.

"What's great about your crowd is," she told them, "that no one tries to chat you up. It's all so sickening. Sometimes I'd like just to drink a bottle of whiskey down and forget about it all. It's as bad as that." The young Swede was clowning behind his glasses. Max drove his wooden leg off the floor with a vengeance as he smacked the guitar in a blues air. A girl stood up. She had a striped tie around her soldier's trousers and little red wellingtons. She sang "She Moved through the Fair." The luminous dicky-bow bobbed at her neck. As she crossed the street where a little drizzle was falling, Helen heard the whole pub join in. As she ran up the stairs she heard the sound of Joseph crying. Frank was there going through her clothes and complaining, complaining, where have you been. She pulled Joseph away from him. "You don't give a fuck for us," he said. "Leave my son alone!" she screamed. His voice was going on. He stopped her at the door. He raved for hours it seemed. It frightened her to think she was capable of so much violence. First she warned him. "It's a big lemonade bottle," she said. Then she struck him. He shielded his face from a blow of a crucifix that she tore off the wall. For some time he lay on the bed pretending to be paralysed, and Helen cried a little.

A couple of weeks later his bed made out on the kitchen floor was empty. A note telling her where he was gone was pinned to the back of the door. She didn't see it for two days. He crossed over to England without ever once stepping out onto the deck to see the sea. She waited till she heard from him in London, then for days she and Joseph just walked through the crowded city of Dublin. Up and down, over and back. School was forgotten. His first cheque arrived. She walked through St Stephen's Green. Down Grafton Street. Back up Grafton Street. Without Frank she was completely alone. She stood at the back of the bank queue and when they asked her for her identity, she said, "All I have is my son." With the money, she bought Joseph new shoes. Then that weekend,

leaving whatever they had collected over their few years in
Dublin behind in the room, she returned to Fanacross, and
could not believe it as she saw the country gaining on her.
Never again. Never again, she promised herself.

Now Frank Allen saw her each night stretched among
the bodies of strange men. Each face the face of someone he
had known. He worked late into the night unable to sleep.
The worst thing was to realize that he and she might be
incapable of change. That he possessed her against her will.
The jealousies in the end were like jokes. Beyond them was
the woman he loved, he must fight through this nightmare.
Thrown onto himself he knew a state of continual panic the
like he had never known. As if throughout all those years the
man he had been was a pure facade, and the violence a parody
of real life. Nothing inside him was informing the language
he used. If you cross Pimlico towards Vauxhall, the south side
of the bridge there is a barber's shop. Two floors above the
shop Frank Allen caught a vision of Helen that frightened his
very soul. In the silence a voice was muttering heavily into his
ear. Just one more night then I'll go back. The traffic started.
Another day had begun. Someone touched him on the knee.
He darted forward in the bed. But there was no one there. His
nose and face felt extremely dry. He got out and threw open
the window of the room. The sound of the traffic mounted to
a higher key. Just one more night. Soon his steps followed the
others down to the Underground.

He saw a boy running under the railings of a playground.
He was floored. Another night of ceaseless terror followed. He
was disembodied. Just like that his body could change into
hers. Her mind came racing in rebuking him. The room filled
with the jerky noises of past occupants. He could not seek
refuge in sleep for there on the edge of consciousness he was
at his most vulnerable. Sleep contained the most irreversible
evil image of them all. A version of himself that could never
be changed. This is madness, he said out loud, and as soon
as his nature tried to correct his fears, he found himself

slipping sideways into the body of a child. She was mocking this too. Himself in some distant time when none of this had happened. But he was too terrified to stay in the world of innocence. Was that why he loved Joseph so? Again the dawn coming up. The ghosts of his own making withdrew. Was that I? Wanting to conquer but not being able to maintain. Two voices in free conversation passed cheerfully by, like people from some place impossible to recall. He made for the street in a loose ecstatic manner. Through one of the open windows came the sound of a harpsichord. A plane low over the city. That night he packed his bags with six months gone, and caught the night train from Euston, ready, as best he could, to sacrifice everything.

6

Frank Allen came in by the late bus to the south of Fanacross in time to catch the last of the drumlins surfacing as islands out the lakes. He stayed there out of sight till night fell, then slipping from house to house he made his way up the village to the North side, passed the soldiers arrogantly and climbed a tree at the back of the house that looked in on Helen's bedroom. There he stopped, his case at the bottom of the tree, half-drunk and crazed with jealousy. Down behind him the cheers of the greylag geese and swift looping of the eels. Geraldine emptied potato skins into the yard. The yard light went out. George appeared airing his pants by the fireplace, then with a tremor Frank saw Joseph pass and, soon after, with that vision that can make nothing of a shape that the eye knows, he saw Helen moving along the sides of her bed cupping the sheets and blankets in at the sides. For one brief second she stood by the mirror, and with a quick movement took off her knickers and pulled another pair on, so that all her husband above in the tree saw was the quick flash of her white thighs.

It had all happened too quickly.

The tremor in his knees passed.

He began spitting out the debris of his journey. She went to and fro a number of times. She corrected Joseph, then there occurred a sort of intimacy between them, a touch, that lightened his heart. "Everything all right?" called Geraldine. "Everything is all right now," answered George as he pulled the outdoor after him and locked it. "That's right," said Frank. Next Geraldine sat by the kitchen window basking in Nivea. The line of trees to Frank's left blew down the crest of the hill to the lake like a horse's mane. At the water's edge the hills drank, great buttresses of dark green.

In her room Helen raised her arms to take her jumper off and he saw her armpit, he saw her extended arms. Then Joseph, with sleep-cuffed eyes, kissed her good night. She stood in her slip combing out her hair.

He remembered her pregnant. A pregnant woman supporting her extra weight with one hand on the strap of her bag.

"It was a great summer, wasn't it," someone called from the road.

As the rain began he pissed from where he was onto the ground below, one arm wrapped round the trunk of the tree. He never took his eyes off her, and it came to him there, that a man with wings is an absurd sight. The long stern muscle in Helen's thigh as she stepped in forward in her knickers, then as the other leg takes the strain, the muscle passed, returns, goes away. She stood. Her bare legs produced in him a kind of sickness. Then with an unbelievable ache, he saw George enter the room and go over to her. The two were laughing. Frank began shaking inconsolably, even though now she was alone there, smiling at her own thoughts, for hidden in all of their relationship was something he had always foreseen. His greatest hurt would be for him to find her in the arms of another. He saw it all happen before his eyes, and craved to get the other side of it.

That he know a life without her.

She disappeared from view, back into some remote part he could not follow. Seconds later the light went out. He slipped down the tree, and lifted the bottle out of his bag and drank. Then walked down to the water's edge. A small jump. The night shifts on a second, a bigger jump. He entered a small gate onto a path that led up to the lough. The path divides and both are overgrown. Through the night a cabin cruiser ploughs forward. The cruiser's ripples reached him. The moon passed over. Another jump, and towards the left a colourless flag marking a stone. All flags then are a sign of dangers lurking in the depths. The leaves overhead in a group of trees scatter-shine like rain. Each leaf the dimension of a drop of rain, caught before it falls.

A new unexplained crash of waves.

He stepped out of sight.

Frank Allen found his mind hauled to and fro, over heat and cold as he moved along the lake. His heart beat faster or was hardly beating at all. He heard someone speaking of his life. At times the voice was his own. Each self claiming rightly or wrongly to be heard. Or remain silent. A footstep sent up wood pigeons.

To see my life in the life of others, something I've never done, is begun.

"Fuck, I did," he said.

— Sit there for starters.

— Where are you off to now?

— Oh we'll be back.

— And don't be making excuses.

— Oh now.

Early bright green light on the drumlins shaped like the rumps of ponies. Up she comes. The nearest island rises, a tower like a pine cone separating the breasts of the hills. The furrowed brow of the mountain browsing on heather. The deep-scored line of the pink ridge hardening. At the core of the hills is water, spreading inland. Hill after hill came out of the mist. Waves fossilized into earth, and bordered by tense trees. The sun weak on the water. Red berries in hard earth marked by the hoofprints of the Charolais. Bent galvanize. The trees swallow the wind. He pulled up his coat. He came to a place where the hills and the water of the lakes were at one with each other, the one continuing where the other leaves off, where what is at rest has captured the image of what is always in motion. The hills reflect and exaggerate the movements of the water. A storm that left the land suspended.

A woman had forgotten to shut the door on a crazy calf. The calf followed Frank Allen. "Go long," he shouted back at the animal. But the calf still followed. "Go back," he shouted, waving his arms. The calf came on. Frank climbed a cartwheel gate out onto the road. He turned for home. In drink it's this, you must never tell your secret, else you will lose your magic and then your fucking life, maybe. "What time is it?" he asked someone on the road.

"I haven't the faintest," she said.

At the bridge, in an unmarked car, an RUC man was reading a book on gardening. Up the road a stranger stopped Frank Allen. "I can tell you are a Catholic," he said, "from the cross there on your forehead."

Plod on, thought Frank, and take little seriously. A cat was hurled out of a window. She busied herself under the bush where she landed as if nothing had happened. It's not good to be known as a sufferer. True. He met a big-thighed schoolgirl with white and blue ankle socks. Then another lassie in a green outfit, slim body, court shoes, striped tie of green and red. A working woman stopped her. The lassie looks away from the question. She pulls at her hair, covers her mouth but never stops answering, till the older working girl, many years her senior and a friendly soul who persists with knowing eyes, releases her.

Here we are.

He hammered the door, and seconds later Pop answered it. "Well, now," said Pop, "you know what's good for you."

"How are you, Dad?"

"Enjoying every minute of it."

"Aye."

Helen came out from the kitchen when she heard the shouts of Joseph in the hall. The jumper had fallen from her shoulder. She was poised behind Joseph with his schoolbag and raised hand. She looked her husband up and down. And Jim and Margaret, Geraldine's children, stood tight against the wall, wondering.

"Well," said Pop, "this is the end of your run of luck, boy."

"Look at the clatty state of you," said Helen. "Where did you spend the night?"

"Up a tree," said Frank.

"Jesus," Helen called back into the kitchen to Geraldine, "he's rotten as well."

Again it's one of those quiet shapeless mornings when the grey sluggish waters move past. Their talking over, she followed him up to the room. Beforehand she could not stop talking, telling him of Joseph and herself, and sometimes halting on the name of a man, as if she could foresee the jealousy in him. He'd said to George: "How was she, what did she do while I was away?"

"That's between you and her," George told Frank.

"What do you mean?" Frank asked, another nightmare settling round him.

"That's your business," said George. "You will have to sort it out between yourselves."

Frank looked at his brother. What was hidden behind his words? He had to keep back the big clammy swill in him, the rage burning. "She was cheerful enough," George went on. Geraldine made a great fuss over Frank. He would have

liked to pour out his heart to her, instead he felt his face beat
to some inward humiliation. It was falling. He felt his spoiled
forehead looking down his healthy, lightly haired arm. "We
were at Farrell's," said Helen, "last week. We had a great time.
I couldn't tell you who was there."

"There was dancing till three. I wanted everyone to stay on
but they were too tired. And we got peas."

—And we got chicken.

—And we got stuffing.

—And we got cream and apple tart. Now!

—And good singers from the floor.

Frank Allen looked down angrily at his glass of gin-and-tonic
as he washed it round in his mouth, mixing the price and the
taste, then his bottom lip came up. The clack of Helen's heels
on the tiles of the kitchen. She flits into the rooms. Not really
in a hurry at all, she does it again, seconds later. Joseph fell
asleep in his father's lap, his arms round his father's neck and
Frank could see it in Helen's eyes, a nervous, white look that
her son could find love in someone outside of herself. And it's
only you, he was thinking, it's only you, can tell for me the
difference between the imagined and the real.

"There is nothing," said Frank, "in your imagination
cannot happen in reality."

Now he waited in her bed while she washed. The big long
endless day over. He heard them whispering. It could have
been Helen and George. It could have been Geraldine and
George. They were talking about him, he knew. He could
do nothing about it. He heard the wind blowing round the
hipped gable of the house, and the sound of a late aeroplane
banking over Cuilcagh. Then delph and glasses being stacked
away.

"George," she called out, her arms tight about his neck.

"It's Frank, do you hear," he shouted, "Frank."

"God," she said, "I must have thought I was Geraldine."

She held him tighter, spreading herself.
Her pleasure beyond his control.
A distant receding thing.

She felt the power returning back into him. After the effusion from her loins he lay gathering strength for her debasement. It was not enough that she gave herself to him, he must later become alert and rational, interrogating her. Instead of this lovemaking liberating Helen, it became the means of her persecution. She could not admit that the alienation she felt was her thwarted desire to continue her control over him. He demeaned her by becoming independent again. Becoming subtle and abusive. She would never encourage him again. Yet the next morning she touched him, out of some compulsive tenderness she could not fathom. She did not want this domination. Better that he force his way into her. That way she retained her sense of power. Denying him she retained her sense of power, for any sign of affection she gave him, any warmth, was diffused so quickly in the aftermath of their lovemaking, that her desire was always troubled and frustrated by what must follow on. She did not want nothingness. She wanted to be carried through whole and satisfied. So their bodies latched and fell apart, latched and fell apart. She told him of the things that passed through her head in those few moments of peace. Her words unsettled him. He could not speak to her. Every word he said came with great awkwardness, with self-consciousness. There was no excess now. No warm words surfaced from his jealous core while all her physical being poured itself out to him. Her freedom wounded him, it should have given him strength. Now that she learned how to wound him, she entered a vacuum, telling all to hurt him. And feeling for them both only arrived through tiredness and fear. For a few seconds Frank Allen became her comforter, he was her friend in flesh, but she could not hold it. For as the other daylight flesh returned to his bones she despised him. After he climbed off her she still felt the weight of him there.

And because everything she said was contradictory, his need of her was overwhelming. He dreamed of someday having a secure and lasting place, knowing too that on that day his love of her would go.

7

Now, on the understanding that he never share her bed again, the Allen family were on a bus travelling into the interior. A blood vessel in Frank Allen's brain had broken. He had reached a point where he could forgive everything so that he might survive. His love for her must contain everything she was or might be. That she had chosen him somewhere in the past was enough. He had got over that conceit of the lover who tries to prolong the ecstasy of the first days of love, who wants everything to remain as it first was. If I lose her, let it be because of what we are now and not because of what we might have been, had we remained blind to the faults of each other.

That you sit there some feet away from me is enough.

His mind filled with hospitable things, and she was cheered by his warmth, this love that did not need the excuse of hurt to claim sympathy. That begged nothing. Other touches were possible than those that led irreconcilably to the one-dimensional, where he entered her and she could not enter him.

Now, separated like this, she could see through his eyes.

This was how she flirted with the world, to drift off into the mind and the body of another who, excited by her, doubled the pleasure of her love, and returning to herself she'd find herself enriched, full. Through the body of another she made love to herself. And he, becoming her, must seek for her satisfaction beside his own. He'd know then the sheer pleasure of his entering her, the loss of self, all authority gone.

The tanned hide of the mountains receded. They passed through fields of heather burning. Sheep dyed red jumping a drain. There was a big floating salmon in the sky. The heather smoke rose across the blue wash. Light traces of cloud frightened back from some source drifted, white ash floating endlessly. The sheer terror of such an unselfish love made certain things possible, and other things, impossible. "I do love you," she said, "myself and Joseph do love you." Going back into himself and without trying to exaggerate anything, he tried to find an answer, an answer not steeped in recrimination or self-regard. He thought of the word "love," the shapelessness of it. Image after image receded. The violent and the calm. "Thank you," he said. He prayed that this calm might stay, this tightrope they walked between the senses.

"Lacken," called the driver.

"Is that us?" said Helen, shaking Frank.

"Lacken, who's for Lacken?" shouted the driver, who had relieved the first driver some towns back.

"It's us here," said Frank Allen.

"Well?" asked the driver. "Are you getting off?"

"We were a bit short," Frank tried explaining, "and we intended going further." The driver marched down the aisle to them. "You see I couldn't get to the post-office in time."

"That makes no difference to me."

"But I said I'd pay the odds when we got there."

"That's no good."

"But the other driver agreed."

"This is my bus. You get off here."

Joseph began tugging at Frank's elbow.

"I said we'd pay," said Frank. All the passengers tried looking away, the same passengers whose faces Frank had said earlier reminded him of real Irish stock.

"This is my bus. Get off."

"You'll not put my family off," said Frank.

"How much does he owe?" a voice called from the front of the bus. This was a lad that played with a well-known pop band of the period.

"To the next town that'll be—"

"To the town after we're going—"

"That'd be one pound fifty."

"God Almighty, we were only fifteen pence short in the first place."

"You'll be charged a new rate from here."

"Jesus Christ."

"Here," called the bass player, shaking out his shoulder-length hair, "here's the extra."

"Damn it," said Frank. "Thank you. We'll get off here. Thank you all the same." He stuck his face in front of the burly red-faced Southern conductor. "You can have your bus. Aye." But the driver hailed from Offaly, and the state of a man's mind or condition was of no concern to him. Frank Allen looked along the heads of the other stale, embarrassed passengers as he followed Joseph down the aisle. He shook hands with the man who had offered him the money. He handed the cases down to Helen. "Lacken," he said to her, "if you don't mind."

And before he had rightly stepped down, the automatic door of the bus swung to, the engine fell into gear and each face on their side of the bus looked safely down at the three of them as it pulled away.

"This does not look like a bad place," said Frank. "We'll put up for a night here in a hotel."

Helen did not answer him.

"Look," he said looking at her, "why not?"

"I'd like a hotel," said Joseph.

"I wouldn't hear of it," she answered.

"I'll hot-foot about the town and see what the chances of work are."

Helen sat on her case on the footpath. She felt every eye on her.

"I can percept here," she said, "nothing but more the same."

The dull grey strokes of a midland town, with one hill, where that evening when it was dark enough they pitched their tent, an acre off the main road below. They boiled up a tin of stew, and before Joseph was safely abed watched a thousand shooting stars. "There's a pub down there on the left," said Frank. They zipped up the tent and holding onto each other, found their way down the field to the lights below.

An old fellow there eyed them for a time.

Helen had a bandana tying back her hair and Frank a wide straw hat. The bar owner sat with his back to a snug where every so often a slight hand appeared with an empty glass. He rested his paper, filled the glass with gin, the hand appeared again and took the drink. Then he went back to his paper. After another rum the man who was watching them brought himself to speak.

"How are things in Chicago?" he asked out of one sour eye.

"Why Chicago?" asked Helen, twitching.

"I have a brother lived over there," he answered seriously. "He was only a humble chippy."

"A good one is hard to get," answered Frank.

"Youse had me fooled." The old fellow's drawn chin was peppered with slight abrasions of the razor. Up comes a slight from the past. He ducked his head to let it by. A blonde child, shop-soiled at birth, came out to the bar for a lemonade. She laughed indifferently as if the birth-mark could have only added to her charms. She helped herself and went back into the kitchen and, as she did so, Frank, passing the snug, saw the figure within and when he returned, he told Helen to take a look for herself.

"Where's the Ladies?" she asked.

"Out there," said the publican, "as far as you can go."

She looked into the snug saw this little white-haired lady with the biggest white moustache she had ever seen. She was the mother of the publican. He with his back to her reading and drinking within, and she with her paper spread across the small table. The yard would turn your stomach. The shifty eyes of the old man went up and down when she returned. He looked at the barman. He looked then out the door.

Eventually he laughs at his own jokes. One heavily coated elbow on the bar and the puce face spiritless. A fly crawls across the ashtray in front of his rum and blackcurrant. He has to repeat his lines for no one can hear them at first. He pinches his fags. His jaw hangs open as he looks at the time. His freckled hands wait. As he speaks the little clump of dark hair on his cheek is suddenly noticeable. His beauty spot rises. "They couldn't do it to save themselves," he said. The publican drinks a cup of tea and eats slices of a jam roll. "And they with two boys at home." The publican's balding curly red skull shines and his fair-quiffed eyebrows highlighted at the nose, crease into nothing when a frown comes. He is assessing some item he has just read. The old fellow has congealed rum in the corners of the mouth. He called into the girl in the kitchen with honest joy. He squeezes a suspicious eye in the publican's direction. When he comes to his feet he is a ferrety man with a newspaper stuck in the pocket of a brown suit with a square pattern. "I'll give you a shout later," he says going. The hand again proffers the glass from the snug. Without rising off his stool or taking his eyes off the paper the publican fills it, the hand appears, the glass passes on from son to mother without a word.

They woke in the warm tent to the crash of drums.
    "What's going on?" asked Helen.
    On his knees he went forward and pulled back the opening. Outside the field was in darkness but the sound of music and cheers was growing louder. He stepped out on his bare feet on to the grass. He looked down. A procession was coming

up the road from the direction of the town. Every light in the pub was on. Helen clambered out beside him. He could feel her bare leg alongside his. She was wearing one of his shirts. Instead of his smell came hers, fresh and sleepy. The band below drew nearer so that they could see at the head of the procession a clown or mummer leaping into the air. Behind him came three rows of silent men about thirty strong. After these a band that was not in formation, and on the footpaths six others holding flames aloft. Last of all came a crowd of schoolchildren shouting through it must easily have been two in the morning. As the procession passed the pub one by one the lights died out. For a long time only the sound of the drum could be heard. They stood there a while wondering at what they had seen, and entering the tent because of the sudden cold, she was inclined, forgetting the other days, to lie closer to Frank. She bore down softly on him so that the pupils of her eyes slipped round the balls into her skull.

The next morning they woke this time to the drone of cows and the loud sneezing of horses. Shadows lumbered past the walls of the tent. Men's voices were everywhere. A hoof pressed down the edge of the tent. Cows snorted and groaned. The mad whinnying of horses was everywhere. Joseph was already out of bed unzipping the door of the tent.

"We're in the middle of the fair green," he yelled, and beyond him Helen and Frank could see long-coated men prodding their animals into pens erected while they slept.

"Will you close the bloody thing," shouted Frank, astonished.

Joseph, pulling on his trousers, disappeared.

"Well," said Helen, "this is very romantic." They dressed in the tent and emerged expecting to find themselves a subject for ridicule, but business then was at its peak, and they unpegged the tent without anyone taking the least heed of them, except one man who said: "You can get a good breakfast below." He pointed at the pub they had been in the night before. They packed their gear and headed down the crowded fair. Past bulls with numbers taped to their rears, soft rolling flesh under their ears, the two balls hanging like something stripped of all desire. The scrotum, when the penis is at rest, like a loose and useless sack of flesh, and yet there is the need to cup it in the hand less it drag across briars.

The bar was packed and plates of chicken legs were handed up by the whiskered woman and her blond grandchild, while the farmers, their faces purple as Aran spuds, ate greedily.

"Are those pound notes?" asked someone of Frank as he produced some English sterling. "I took them for samples."

"Youse were celebrating late last night," Frank Allen said.

"What are you talking of?" the publican asked.

"We heard the band passing."

"There has been no band around here. You must have been dreaming, boss, that's all I can say."

Frank Allen could not believe his ears. He asked a few others who, hoisting their drinks to get back of the crowd at the bar, just looked at him blankly. The procession and thus the lovemaking could not be authenticated. It was something that had happened in another world. No one had heard any of the crowd marching through the town the night before. There were no flames, no bands, nothing like that at all, Mister. Even his belief that Helen had received him seemed like something he had dreamed up. Some distortion of his mind had made him happy this morning. He returned with food to their table. A grim, drenched, raucous air surrounded them. "I feel dirty," said Helen.

"Do you remember last night?" he asked.

"What?" she said, leaning over.

"Do you remember . . . ?"

"Of course I do," she said, as the first question reached her. "They looked half mad."

Now for the first time Frank knew what a companion was;

someone who shared with you what everyone else denied. He
told her what the others had said. "No," he said, "not one of
them would believe me." Tears of laughter came to her eyes at
the thought of Frank at the bar trying to act naturally. It was the
first time he had heard her laugh so freely in years. Some sort of
crisis was over. Outside they sat on a low wall with their bags
at their feet while Joseph ran up and down through the fair.

It struck them that the Southerners had no enemy except
in their own subterranean natures. A united Ireland was a
final fling before they gave up the drink for good. A secret
binge. Warm air blew across the flat land. The sky was empty.
Helen, exhilarated at the absurdity of Frank being treated as
an imbecile at the bar, started laughing outrageously again.
"And some fucker asked me: Is our cat above in your house?"
said Frank, and feigning great innocence, he leaned forward
on an imaginary stick, and spat, and stared narrow-eyed and
pursed mouthed into the eyes of his wife. "Now while you're
at it, tell me this, is our cat above in your house?"

The next three nights they spent in a bed-and-breakfast in
that town. And this was paradise. Their savings were taking a
fair hammering but Frank found a few weeks' work shifting
rubbish from the Woolworth's which was being redecorated at
the time due to the fact that the management had decided to
drop a number of unprofitable lines. The odd toy that worked
backwards found its way into Joseph's hands. The lad held
the shovel while his father took the brush. The manageress
came out every so often to check on them. Her lips a radiant
pink, she wore a lime-green outfit, red high heels and, going
home, a red handbag. A fierce middle-class town, jeans and
high heels, a man suffering from migraine, the sound of a
crass flute. Ladders straight across his shoulders, a window-
cleaner passes. A yellow dustbin swarming with wasps. A tall
burly middle-aged woman with the buckle of her belt undone
on her high stomach crosses the street to the vegetable shops,

the motor of her car still running. In this position Frank Allen struck up a conversation with a house painter. The house painter explained that no one could make a living in that god-forsaken part of the country. But he pointed out that a caravan was up for sale outside a small house on the edge of the town. "It just needs a lick of paint, that's all," he said. I'll have that, thought Frank. They looked at their savings. They looked round the outskirts of the town for a site. At last they hitched the caravan to an old second-hand Ford owned by Harry Dean the painter and hauled her to the gate of Freedmont's field. Freedmont drove the tractor that took the caravan to her position under the tree. But the Ford stayed where it was on the road, its wheels turned questioningly outwards from the grass margin. The engine had stalled, then went altogether. "You can have the car as well," said Harry without lifting the bonnet. And without another word he stepped back the road into town. So nights there Frank worked the engine while Helen scoured the caravan down. The boy climbed trees. It was touch and go at times. Then came the true image of herself in Frank's eyes that blotted out everything. None of Frank Allen's prophecies told him that there was another kind of death than the one he feared. A living death. That's what Helen called it. They drifted again. And Frank slept, hands tucked to his reclining head beside his son, listening to her every sound, waiting for the day he'd be recalled.

She looked at him, his working trousers hanging loosely from his braces. The striped blue shirt. Green handkerchief and pen in the top pocket of the old tweed jacket. The mustard waistcoat. The fawn shoes. "No, you can't look," said Helen as she paddled up the stream, threw her dress aside and started soaking her thighs and stomach. The sight of her boyish arse made his heart falter as she stepped away from him into the shadows of the ash trees. Further down through the shadows the soapsuds flew across the rocky beds.

II

8

You need strong arms to buckle the mad sheets to the line when the wind is coming from the east. And a strong heart to keep yourself from wandering unprotected into the mind of another. That done, considering other things, Geraldine decided on a walk up the Falls. It was a long walk by the edge of the plantation where thousands of trees had been cut down, and the land was neither one thing nor another, stubbled with shorn trunks and briars. On the road a shadow reached her. A vehicle came down the road and tossed Geraldine into the air. A neighbouring woman found her sometime after. Thinking she'd choke on her own blood she turned the face away. Still Geraldine's heart beat feverishly trying to prolong the moment. The rattle came louder. The woman covered her with her coat. The sky darkened. A crowd from the village saw the two of them. They came up and gathered. Like that Geraldine's life ended. "It was a hit-and-run," Bobby Johnson said, "see where the fucker ran toward the sheugh."

They carried Geraldine into her own house to clean her up before George's return.

And it's strange. At that moment the neighbouring woman could find everything she needed in the house. She knew where everything was though she had never once stood inside the house. It was as if everything had been lain out for such an event. And just when she had Geraldine presentable, word reached him. Then came Jim, her son, and Margaret, her adopted daughter. But before George could surrender to his grief, already he was off seeking revenge. For two nights he scoured the outlying farmhouses on his bicycle looking for a dent in a car, a claw hammer in his fist. When night fell, he positioned himself below the mountain road. He'd stop a car, shine a torch across the bonnet, then wave them on without a word and return to the ditch, his rifle trained on the bend of the road above. Up there he went through all the scales of grief. But it was all for nothing. Representatives of both religions met. The priest came to talk to him. It would be no time at all, he was told, before he'd be locked up. It was not someone in the community was to blame. There were worse things happening. So at last George relented, and had Geraldine's body oared across to the Island.

It came as a shock to the Allens in the South, they were so embedded in worries of the flesh, to hear that Geraldine had been killed.

George wrote to say that his children needed minding. The same morning the letter arrived Helen hauled all their belongings out of the caravan, the tractor pulled the car out onto the road, and the old Ford sluggishly climbed from panorama to drumlin to buffeting lakes. The drought was over. Everywhere fine grass fields that sloped towards the mountain had been stoned off, and muddy hay pinned to the ground with stakes for the sheep to eat. Wild flowers grew from unused troughs. Plastic flapped from the roofs. The mountains drifted, drifted. "There she goes," said Frank. "Christ, it looks more miserable than I can tell."

Wind and water drummed on the wooden porch and galvanize roof of Uncle George's house.

Old familiars went about their work across the fields like ghosts.

The moment Joseph lighted from the car he fell into an unnerving swoon at the sight of Margaret, who, since he had been away, had grown into a girl he hardly knew. Then seconds later Jim, his other cousin, knocked him directly to the ground and ran off in the direction of the bridge shouting something unheard over his shoulder. For Uncle George had filled his son with exaggerated stories of all that Joseph could do now – rise before the crows, lift a hundredweight and speak two languages.

Margaret was clambering over walls following the honk of a goose, her luscious hair stinging her eyes, every small detail of her appearance escaping him as if all her parts had been magnetized back to the pattern of the original ore. She was a whole complete element that had once been embedded somewhere in the great peakless mountains and eased out not with gentleness by those miners, generations from the beginning of the world, who wielded their tools on the edges of the marvellous pits in the clearing of Gospel Forest, loving and attacking all things in their entirety.

She had breasts, no ankles, a check shirt open at the neck.

Anyway, desire was there that sees only the wholeness of things. No matter, no matter. They danced. Tins were being drummed in the back yard. The sound carried down to the ears of the soldiers. To the drivers halted by the bridge. The family searched round the home place for all they had dreamed of. But it was just a dark place at the foot of the mountain. So for Joseph, who could tell nothing of time passing, the short distance to the door took years, his parents followed, haunted by things no one will tell.

The sky-filled river flowed under George Allen's window and inside, a brown and red feather tucked in the wing of his cap, he sat brooding his widowed limbs and ruined demesne. Geraldine was everywhere. Her very words had worked their way on to his tongue and now whenever a phrase of hers would start to issue from his lips, his mind darted like a trapped animal. But the phrase was left uncompleted as he sought blindly for a new response. He saw his brother's family alight from the car.

"They are here," he shouted down the stairs to Pop.

"Who gives a fuck?" Pop shouted back up.

He welcomed the family. The house was as much theirs as

his, he said. "Let me take that," he said to Helen. There was a lot of embarrassment. The two brothers pulled up their chairs.

"My thoughts," he said, "it's true, are not my own since she's gone."

"We'll see how we all get on," said Frank.

"No, I'm glad you are here." Silence then as they heard Helen opening drawers overhead. A few warning cries from the birds down at the river. George turned the talk to the war.

"I've had enough of all that," said Frank, "there are always these boys who will continue into the next world complaining about the flaws in the old."

"Never mind the children," said his brother.

"The mountain," said Frank, "looks like it's just been sprayed with copper."

Across the radio came a selection of Slim Whitman's favourites, "Oh the Wayward Wind" and "Ramona," and it suited the two men as they looked out of the window. Somehow the announcer had just happened on it, something to distract them. George puffed out his shoulders and taking all responsibility upon himself, he pushed with his hands lightly off the wall and laughed. "The crowd across the water must have some designs on us after all," he said. He rewound the woollen scarf around his nervous neck and looked down towards the bridge. It was terrible to see some woman who looked like another falter on the bridge as she passed the soldiers. "But after we've all had our day's fighting," he went on, "the bastards will make up, settle for worse, and the man who believes otherwise will be left wanting."

"Margaret," said Frank, "has grown."

"And so has Joseph."

"You have taken it very well."

"Well, I'll not be in your way here, Mister." The twin brothers looked at each other, as if all those years apart they had been living out each other's lives without knowing, but now that they were united again, all that sentiment would go.

Helen lightly entered the room. "I was just saying," said George, "that it's good to have a woman around the house again."

"You don't know me yet," said Helen. "I've had enough of being used. That fellow there has treated me like a fool."

"You're starting early," said Frank, then he turned out the door for a walk down the village and remembered suddenly that sometimes you feel more at home remembering things from afar, but still, he reckoned the Northern way of life was good. Everybody knew what everybody else was doing, yet they didn't make a meal of it. Their minds were couched in the proper style. Looking up he saw a branch that had grown right across the road. It banged off a lorry sweeping by. That's it. Nature that had followed light had discovered violence. New landmarks fell into view.

Later that evening Peter the musician, who had been taken in by Geraldine that previous winter as a charm against misfortune, strolled through the house and greeted all with the gay mannerisms of the west coast man. He took off his hat to the brother come up from the South. Turned immediately to inspect himself in the mirror. For Peter never told a story against himself less it was through the strings of an instrument. And even where the tips of the fingers faltered, the lilt of the voice persevered. "Did you meet Flynn the butcher on your travels?" he asked Frank Allen without turning his grey eyes from their untroubled reflection.

Joseph's father shook his head.

"He's down there somewhere towards Kilkenny," said Peter, "living the life of a gentleman."

Peter, righting his hat, passed on into the next room.

He took his instrument down.

Marched down to the community hall and there, under direction, the children of the village played spontaneously. Argued fleetingly between the tunes over what they had learned the week before. Dogs and cats fled the sound of their céilí. He had the children march in military style around and around the hall while he pounded the floor with his boots, all this according to the old style of a band he had seen as a child that could never be equalled.

He called a break, lit a cigarette and considered his good fortune.

He was a tall thin man, with many strappings. His long boots seemed laced to his neck. His legs reached right from the stage where he was sitting to the floor beneath, so he appeared as both spectator and player in one. That was a long chin too, and the cheek-bones harboured the cheerful signs of excess that had been for him guiltless and sometimes sickening. Even now he fell into a child's imitation of an adult at prayer as he watched the children in one of their games hold their breath till they fainted.

"Well, take your time," said Peter.

Then starting again on their whistles the band at first scored without imagination among the new reels, then, through gradual embellishment, they preserved, without flaunting their skills, the special airs. After they were dismissed by Peter some ran and some walked from the hall through a world where everything was familiar, and Michael Walkers's lad, as he crossed the bridge over into the South, played a fast version of "The Soldier's Song," throwing his head a bit to the left every now and then to where the barrels of two guns were trained through the portholes of the concrete post on those arriving, and those leaving, whether Fenian or Orange, like the antennae of some machine that were being reluctantly drawn away from each other towards contradictory signals – this one will live, this one will not, and other accursed things.

George's mind those days was like a vast open space. Sometimes he'd be sitting in his garden wrestling to clear his head of the pressure within. The presence of his brother and his wife in the house reassured him, for many times since

Geraldine's death he had believed that Margaret and Jim were only figments of his imagination. The loss of his wife had somehow severed him from his children. The night of their arrival he heard Frank making up his bed in Joseph's room and Christ, he thought, the fools, the fools. If I had my life to live again I'd never waste a minute away from her side. Could they not see the gift they had been given? Jesus Christ!

"What's going on between you two?" he demanded of Helen.

"Just give us time," she said.

"It's just plain selfishness," he said, "that's what's wrong."

He looked into his brother's eyes but could see no woman there. There was no woman in Frank's head, there was no man in Helen's head. They were too frightened to cross the great divide. Go down into that almost impossible place. Guarded by great lumbering animals. Inside, a galaxy of fish. A cave wrought out of the mountain by water. You'll be alone descending, he wanted to tell them. You'll always be alone no matter what. It's the aloneness that brings us together. Float into each other, he wanted to say. He spread a piece of lace across the table. He left Pop's tray by his door. He closed all the windows and doors.

That evening Joseph was bedded down on a new planet. He sat listening to the radio in the high cedar room, without shafts of light to strike the laths of teak or even the noise of the lake, nor bird, nor laughter from another room that signifies we are not here alone, nor argument from the most mundane or comical of soldiers who having such long nights would chuck grenades into the ponds, no sound came up to his room, but that unearthly silence of the night like playing cards tossed lightly on to a table.

The mountains, bolting Joseph's room tight to the earth, held everything in. They shoulder above a young girl washing cutlery in a valley stream, interested in the passing traffic of night birds and ponies, she moved through the night, eager and lovely limbed. One minute it's right, the next minute it's wrong. He is in the right place, then he is not. The next time the breach will be all the greater. Into George's head comes the thought of the barracks below where the soldiers and the prisoners that sleep each side of the bars listen for any sign of the other relenting, for from that weakness you can build a nation. The low bitchy voice of a jazz singer on a foreign station harangued the darkness of Fanacross. All the time fulfilled and optimistic, singing, "What a difference a day makes." Socrates the drunk pounding the stone tablets above at his house. The air sweet with the warm end of autumn and the draughts from the lakes. Joseph, lying there in a painful moment, was united with all the pleasurable moments of people past and future, what was anticipated and what was remembered, what was unique and shattered, lifeless, buoyant. That distracted moment when the sky is wide purple – sympathy, adrift. When flesh holds tight that extraordinary freedom and mystery. Here there was an emptiness in time. Joseph gave out a terrible scream and flattened himself against the bedroom wall, screaming for his father.

9

The pounding of his father's clogs came up the stairs.

He threw open the window against which the hail beat like shingle.

It was the winter. All the autumn and the winter of that year the same nightmare had been recurring. The cold air blew across the room. "What is it, son? Who is it?" Frank Allen stammered, his heart furious. "Where is he?" But there was no one. "I was afraid," Joseph said. He could not explain why he had cried out. He had been lying there on the bed listening to the radio when this terror seized him.

Now it seemed the radio was playing on after some dreadful accident had happened.

"Son of God! You nearly gave me heart failure," replied his father. Frank Allen was not built for running fast. He sat on the edge of the bed, a handkerchief held to the temple over his wide unthinking eye, the pupil worried down to blankness, and he wondered what terror had come over his son that could not be named. To hear your son crying out in the dead of night like a sick animal. For me, he thought, all terror has been the fear of hearing the truth about myself out of another, knowledge that I learn too late to make any use of. He studied his son's face, no feature of which matched his own, yet in a fragile terrifying way they were bound to each other, the father and the son. Whatever this echo was, it too could not be named. Through the window came the roar of the lakes whipping along the banks with broad blistering strokes. The hail changed quickly to snow. The battering stopped. They were cocooned there by the swirling snow.

Alerted to things beyond his control, the father saw in the son the mother imploring him.

Soon the woman would be rooted out, the shape of his son lose an old dimension. Perhaps it was her screaming out of the mouth of her son in the middle of the night, now that she was to be ousted. Always fearing that she will disparage me further or I her. We leave our terror on the lips of our son. Abruptly he carried Joseph downstairs on his shoulders past the clouded prints of cacti and floating white-stone cottages. Nowhere in them the building up of details that speak of life. Hardly a stone there but it has to belong to a pattern that does not exist, or does elsewhere, in more harmonious lands.

He found himself out in the yard with his father gingerly loosening his grip of the gate that opened onto the road that led down to the village. Joseph was hauling at the gate with all his strength. Then shivering in his father's coat he crossed the snow-packed yard. In the warm kitchen the stove was chugging away, showering the warm ash with sparks. The firelight years off. "Well now," said his father, "you are a great traveller." His mother blew on his hands and bobbed over and back in her chair, forgetting where she was. This time anyway. Margaret and Jim came down the stairs in their pyjamas. They stole towards him. Jim sat with his fingers in his mouth looking over curiously at Joseph who minutes earlier he had heard screaming like a madman in the yard.

"Do you think does he know we are here?" he whispered into Margaret's ear.

"There's a door open some place," said Joseph, "I can feel it."

"It's only me," said George entering, "thinking of Geraldine."

There were loud guffaws of laughter as Helen directed the two men to move the dresser. The old kitchen linoleum was thrown out into the yard. They peeled the wallpaper off the parlour walls. Work that had lain undone for weeks on end George now completed. The boys swept out the rooms. The hammering began. "A man is liable to strain himself at this crack," said Frank. Just as everyone sat down to tea Pop threw open the door of his room. They heard him crossing the hall sucking his gums. He cursed them each by name. He cursed the village below. He cursed the wombs that bore them. That I'd live to see the day.

"Jesus Christ!" he shouted. "Have they all gone mad?"

It was the first time he had emerged in ages.

"I thought," he shouted out for everyone to hear, "that ye were trying to bring the place down round my ears."

He emptied his pot of piss into a drain in the yard.

"Fuck off, MacCarthy," he yelled to an old crony well asleep in his bed down in the village, "you were never any good."

"That's all right," he continued, entering, "but look what I
have to put up with." He drew the bolt firmly across the door,
deliberately avoided the kitchen where all were sitting. He
doused the lights throughout the house, and pulled his door to,
after one last moment standing on his leg like a hen in the hall
studying all that had happened since yesterday. "Your marbles
are unsettled," he said and went below. Soon the hail stopped.
The darkness beat a furrow across the lakes. And, following
on, the first eddies of light appeared in the wake of a cruiser
that moved by the islands, the seagulls sweeping down each
side of her with flattened wings.

"Listen. Do you hear them, Margaret?" said George at the
sound of the distant seagulls. "All the dead sailors."

The land tossed like a buoy.

"The old fellow," said George, "is the happiest one
amongst us. He says to me yesterday, 'I have my youth and
health I didn't have when I was young.'" Towards dawn all
climbed the stairs. The house had been possessed once more.

Another day his grandfather got a sudden pain in his side. He
fell to the ground by one of the sheds. I must have tripped,
he thought. He felt he was responsible in some way for this
falling down. He could not remember any pain. I'll just lie
here a while, he thought, pretending to be resting. That's how
Joseph found him. He shook him and shook him. "I was only
pretending to be dead," said the old man rising. He sat up and
clasped his knees. "I have no feeling in my legs," he said. Still he
sat on in the shade. He relaxed. His shoulders going back and
forwards as he rocked on his buttocks. "Which one are you?"
he asked the lad. "I'm Joseph," he replied. "Well," said the old
man, "it's your funeral."

"I'd hoist a can of milk to my head till I couldn't hold
my breath, at seven o'clock in the morning," he remembered.
"They had me at it from dawn to dusk. We had no names for
the cows but for the horses, Cockatiel, Len'air, Leven Le Bin

and Poolya. Poolya was blind. I wasn't to know it. I'd been hired that morning. So the first day I sat on her she ran into a ditch. We fell. So I cupped her ear and said 'I'm sorry' to the horse." He extended his arm and Joseph got under it. From under his armpit came the chalky smell of camphor. "I only came up for a shit and look what happened me." He sucked his white moustache and raised a bleary eye.

"You have to look after the little things," he said.

Joseph supported him to the door.

"Christ, Pop, you are silly," said Frank, meeting the pair in the hall.

"Isn't it terrible pity to have a son like that," said Pop to Joseph about his father. He laughed outrageously to himself, then signalled towards the stairs, the house, let the whole fucking lot go up in flames.

10

The men arrived late of a Wednesday and sat around with their bags at their feet. Out of each stuck the claws of dead birds. Their dogs prowling the yard provoked the other dogs throughout the village. The hunters had not brought their rifles down but stashed them on the mountain. Last month, a soldier had ordered one of the hunters to lie on his belly at the west foot of Slianein. He kicked the hunter's rifle into a sheugh and pumped two bullets into the earth each side of the prone man's ears. "Count yourself lucky," the soldier said stirring him with his foot. The hunter lay on in the field for over an hour before he had the courage to raise his head, and finding himself alone, he returned along the ditches, dropping every so often out of sight to dodge the bullets that were echoing through his head.

Now the same man said with a nod in Joseph's direction: "This boy has grown big as a landlord."

"You were the right idiot to be up there alone," one of the others said.

"I thought," said he, "I'd seen some curlew over Ruane."

They sat around with their palms flat under their thighs and when the food arrived they ate it greedily, lifting their heads occasionally to glare at something unseen. Their crooked hands pausing. A cap on a knee, a voice unsure of itself. Last to arrive was a tall man with a sparrowhawk strapped tight to a glove on his fist. "I'm training the auld whore in," he said. The bird picked a point on the ceiling from which its eyes never faltered. The hunters recalled odd, slight things about those killed in the war. They talked as if they were speaking to strangers, with darting glances, with irony and modesty, yet holding firm to certain unspoken principles.

Frank Allen stood by the window, well out of it. The hunters had brought him back to what he had been before his departure, a man inflicted with the scourge of wandering without cause. The way his father stood away from the others Joseph could tell there was something wrong. He saw the swollen gland on his neck that did not occur on the necks of the other men. The drooped eyelid and brown sympathetic eyes. The laughter lines scored below his fragile cheekbones. But something was hardening in there.

"What you'll do now that you're back?" some called across.

"Look for work," Frank Allen replied.

"There's not too much of it about," someone laughed, baiting him.

"I'll have to find something."

He wiped back the oily hair that was brushed from his forehead to a high quiff at the crown. Twice he spoke unnecessarily to Helen, who did not answer him. The company fretted at the history that surrounded the time they were living through. "It's hard for the people to take back the responsibility they have handed on to another," said the hawk man. "You are fierce quiet there, Frank," said George. "I was just thinking," he replied. There was something callous in the way Joseph's mother smiled quietly to herself at the remark, and during his father's despair his son looked at him with a dreadful patient silence, for Joseph, when he had screamed above in his bed, had seen a point in the future past which neither of them could go. Now he waited till calm was restored, with the silence seen in the eyes of lovers bequeathed to a violent partner.

Joseph, they all knew, would feel bad if he let his father down in the world.

For during his weakness when he had believed that the smell of the thirsty cattle was issuing from his own flesh, Frank Allen had grown thinner than ever. This gaunt parent, this emaciated father. Yet his face was stark with accelerated life. "You boys have a purpose," he said back to the men.

"But I'm not so sure of myself," he continued.

"When I want a man as a friend," said one of the hunters, "I ask myself, would he make a good enemy." The rest laughed good-naturedly.

"There must be a better way than this," Frank said.

"Sure they're only gossoons," another replied.

Frank Allen stretched one hand out over the flameless grate. All that could be heard for a moment was Margaret plucking the duck into the pile of feathers at her feet. He gripped the sides of his seat hard. Nearly every heartbeat could be heard through his hairless chest, and the other men priding themselves on their realism and longevity turned away in sympathy, same as they would talk dirty to Margaret because she was an adopted daughter. Wait till you start, they joked with her. They pretended they knew about these things, that her desire would be increased by their needs.

"Blessed God," Frank Allen gasped as he put his son down in the kitchen the autumn night that Joseph had screamed, "I thought someone had attacked you."

"There was no one," the boy answered.

Margaret brought Joseph with her when she went down the field for water. Outside the spring night had darkened the sheen of the reservoir being built above the village. Soon, new water would thunder through the pipes laid by the money of the occupiers. But they only trusted, as yet, to the old springs. Below them, the two bars were still open. Bats flicked through the heavy stone uprights of the granite church. She showed him through the echoing porch. Sprinkled water was scattered under the font. Come daughters of Jerusalem. Inside a nun sat in contemplation two seats from the altar. Soldiers tramped past. The moon-brightened sky flickered through the top resting stones of the sheep enclosures. In the empty community hall a band was rehearsing some country-and-western airs, the singer proffering his arms to an audience that was not there.

Women with unbelievable smiles pushed through the doors.

And as Joseph walked beside her, Margaret saw the exquisite shape of his bones bundled up like a lyre in his white cotton shirt.

He was all hers.

Wild roses in the forts were well sleeping.

The village below moved like a ship through the dark.

In the room off the scullery, the men had set up their bottles and were trying to identify and recall a figure from another village.

"He has aged onto a stick," the first said.

"Tall, thin and refined," one said.

"He's done up with a stick and lame," George offered.

"He steps about wicked with polish, I believe, a tall man with a cap," the first maintained.

"Count him," said George. "Count him."

Now they sought a figure to lead them through the next election.

"The same man is a mistake," they all agreed.

"But who else have we got?" asked the man with the bird.

"That's not easy," one said, after a silence. "But there's Ferguson."

"There is Ferguson and there's McEnteer," said another, correcting him.

"Nothing startling there," they all agreed.

"Well, make your choice, Ferguson or McEnteer."

"Take Ferguson," spoke the eldest man.

"Take Ferguson or McEnteer then," said George looking around.

The men went back in their chairs. They set themselves to thinking again of the reasons for the present war, of the place that might lie ahead, or was already there but unseen, unfree, and still they were honest enough to know that the real enemy lived amongst themselves.

"It'll be no paradise anyway," laughed someone.

"No such thing," the old man said.

"There'll be purpose to it," added George, "and much more besides."

"If we don't weaken," argued a voice.

"Could someone tell me what ails the dogs," asked a young man.

"The bloody soldiers," said Margaret's father, "motoring past like thieves."

As the night dragged on the whispers of the men grew incoherent against the rattle of the bottles in the crates and the spitting, light wind. The two cooked ducks were torn to shreds. The bones thrown to the dogs. The men's shoulders slouched. They thrust their hands into their trouser pockets and heaved their bodies, and closed their eyes as if dreams were but the drama of answers to unrecollected questioning. Some made their way home over the mountain, arguing the same points, then going off elsewhere. "It's his own fault," George said, speaking of his brother, "he seems to be pushing her."

It seemed a great fulfilling time had arrived. There were many who were ready to believe that those who had come would take care of the people's destiny. They were ready to believe anything. But the next election would pass, and the one after, before such a man or woman was installed. And by then everything else would have changed. Too many deaths would have accumulated. The ranks would divide again, which was only natural. Along the river the soldiers pointed their rifles South at jeering faces they could not see, lights flashed through the leaves. There was the horrendous sound of a car's exhaust. Somebody out there was denying the nothingness a while.

Another time, later in the night, Joseph came down for a piss in the yard. He found the tall man sitting at the kitchen table looking into the eyes of the hawk. The eyes of the tall man were red-rimmed and sore and small tears had gathered in the corners. The boy sat watching the man and the bird for a long time.

Sometimes he heard the man whisper to the bird.

"You hound out the hell, I'll best you yet."

And while earlier that night, when the men were talking, the bird would suddenly take fright and toss her wings, or rise up onto her toes at the sight of the plucked flesh of the ducks, now she perched quiet in his glove, her long eyes glued to his. Joseph dared hardly breathe. Each side of the bird man lay two hunters transfixed by sleep as the still, satisfied sea. Slowly one of the bird's eyelids fell then swooped open. She arched herself upwards again. The man said nothing. She watched him to see if he could tell of her weakness. He made no sign. She hovered. It seemed that the house was slowly drifting from its moorings. The tears dripped down the tall man's nose but still he held the staring bird fast. Once again both the eyelids of the bird fell, like night crossing the land below. The man said nothing.

He watched the great emptiness of the shuttered eyes till her neck sagged sideways and she slept.

"I have you now," he said.

11

Joseph awoke with a start near morning and knew that there had been a crisis during the night. Angry voices were coming up from below. Margaret was over sleeping in his father's bed. Sparrow song was abroad and the sound of a farmer's van filled with vegetables turning toward the road to the South. Joseph grew rigid in his bed. Margaret sat up in her brother's pyjamas. Her breasts rolled forward. Joseph was afraid of her. It was a period of fear for all the children. He was afraid of her because her needs were simple. The van sped over the bridge.

The bright mountainy light edged through the little shutters.

"Your father carried me in," she said.

"When he woke me," said Margaret, "I had this awful feeling of calamity."

Joseph made an effort to look out the window without disturbing her absorption in her speech for she had that intent humourless look of the obsessed. Then it came back to him what had happened in the middle of the night before. His father had come and got them out of bed to sing in the kitchen. And of course they wouldn't sing, but had cried. Then Helen had retrieved them while he drank on by the table. "He took me out of your mother's bed," said Margaret, "and put me in here." She reached up above her head. He saw the blue creases in her young stomach. A blackbird was hanging upside down from a thin branch eating red berries. Tightly clustered berries. Workmanlike and dreadful.

His cousin's tongue was cold and watery, her speech sleepy and dramatic.

There was the odd mad laugh from below. The light grew. He watched the patterns from outside assemble on the ceiling and float across the walls like the souls of real things. The sun hardened. The shadows became more substantial. The loose unbuttoned line between her breasts he saw. Margaret's shadow crossed the low ceiling. She sat by him on his bed, talking away. "He looked like a man fierce cross," she said. "But he told me there was nothing to be afraid of."

Joseph pulled off his vest and reached for his shirt.

"Why, look," she said, "you have little breasts."

She tipped the little pink buds with her fingertips. Someone was burning leaves. Someone else was regaling a man on the road. Her touch turned to a tickle. The pleasure spread throughout his body. She was laughing into his eyes. Her pyjamas were made of heavy warm material. Without taking her eyes off him she nudged one of her nipples up against his. The sun had reached her hair. The sun warmed the eiderdown. It was as if someone light and warm and dangerous was spread across every inch of his body.

Then Jim knocked on the door.

Margaret fearlessly stepped into the middle of the low-ceilinged room.

Immediately Joseph pulled on his shirt.

"C'mon," said her brother looking at his boots, "I have to take in the night lines." She ran next door for her clothes after blowing Joseph a kiss behind her brother's back. Jim watched Joseph dress. Without seeing anyone they slipped out of the house.

The lake pounded with dull and grey movements on the shore.

Jim pushed off the canoe, Margaret started the engine. The prow turned into the waves and Joseph dug his heel against the laths of the boat. "There's nothing to be afraid of," said Jim. On the shore children were hammering galvanize. Margaret brought the boat in a wide circle. She dipped through the little swells, chatting happily over her shoulder.

A ribcage of cloud. The ground like warm ash.

The suds among the shingle, the boggy streams, the smell of wild mint, the bald ploughed land and swooping birds and Margaret's feet and big rocks thrown up a millennium ago, war clouds with a pink edge and a bank of opened mussels where they coasts in to an island. The thin inner shells of the freshwater mussels, a morning blue and night blue, and the outer shell, with dark rings in fawn, circling to an almond core. The halves like the spread wings of a headless bird. The winch. The rails to the boathouse. A late October plant, its pods bursting with poisonous red berries.

They took off again.

And coasted from line to line. With his pliers, Jim tore the hooks from the mouths of the eels and pike. The fish collapsed with a gasp on the floor of the boat.

"It's not so bad at all," said Jim.

"Are we finished at that?"

"It must be all hours."

The green bottom floated dangerously close as they cut through the waves on the return journey, the matted green floor of the lake stayed permanently there, a few yards of swimming undergrowth, unchanging and yet ever-changing, for suddenly there are tall flowers, grey underwater orchids, moving with eyes closed. From another world Joseph saw it happening. He was on the edge of theirs. A woman drove the boat, a man took in the fish and another man watched. From the shore the wheezing ponies; across the lake came geese off the bog. Water continuously reaching them from another place. The drumlins levelling out into islands. The morning moon was there. Margaret held them on a steady course to a red shed on the hill, ducking the spray that flew overhead. She turned the engine off and drifted toward a garden of water-lilies. The bed came away in her hand as she tried to pick the blossoms by their rubber stems. The supple roots refused to leave go of the blossoms. But she persisted. As they pushed away the lily pads corrected themselves and drifted back to their former position. Joseph could not take his eyes off Margaret's feet. Her white feet. The wet purple flowers hung over the seat beside her. The eels flew around the keel. Water trickled through her toes. Her wet feet on the boards, all right. The toes curling as she lifted her shoulders and strained to look over their heads. Her foot flattens. She's onto her heels to look behind. Through us and at us. The island bright, swinging astern. The white sheen of the water. The islands went up and down with the buffeting seats of the boat, then a gradual calmness as the boat shot over sand-coloured depths. The boat shovelled up light behind it and approached the green shingle that smelled of spent petrol. Jim cursed without anger about the state of things. He looked toward the other fishermen, they looked at him and each other while further downstream the rich cruisers beat over and back like shackled birds.

Then a long time standing on the slip in the coldish wind, doing nothing.

"It's the arsehole of the world," a fisherman in time observed.

"That's how he shines," whispered Margaret to Joseph, "a complainer."

"He'd try your senses talking of what can't be because it's over," she said. This complaining or turning the mind to abstract things. This boasting about the past. He sat in his boat one eye trained upriver for the warden's boat.

A cloud lifted above Cuilcagh. The mountain drew her great bulk over bedrock and heather. The eel boxes were handed on. Then Jim spread a green net over the lilac shingle. He dropped to his hunkers and drew the weights and floats apart. "A man gave me her," he explained, "I'll make my living out of this." As the sun strengthened and pulled the sky further back from the land the shingle dried to a dull grey. Hunger

brought them through copper beeches and elms home. He
watched her oval calves and lake-spattered shins. How the
catch of pike on a piece of gut swung against her thigh. Her
warm, leavened thighs. The cups of lilies in her other hand
swollen with colour and water. "C'mon," Margaret called.

Joseph found his father asleep in the kitchen, his face white
as chalk, his bloodless hands draped round his head like a
child's. Frank Allen's breathing was hoarse. His holiday suit
was rumpled, his blue beret in his hands. The plastic coat on
the back of the chair. And the battered case again stood in
the corner. On the floor by his feet stood a glass of sour gin.
Chewed lemon was scattered at his feet.

Helen was in a ferocious humour. She tried to listen, but
her intolerance was getting the better of her. Joseph stood
stock still with fear. The others left him for they knew how
to disappear. They became high birds while he cowered round
the hearthstone, hating himself. He stamped the ground. He
knew something terrible had happened, that would sever this
moment from what had gone before. There were no words for
that. He stamped the floor. His grandfather was roaring in the
basement. His mother came in from the kitchen. His father
was asleep. "Stop it, Joseph," she said. "Stop it this minute."
She held him by the shoulders.

She brought herself to him. "Your grandfather and this
fucker here have been at it," she said.

"Can I go down and see him below?" he asked.

"Not if I was you," she replied. "Anyway, the old bastard is
no company for you."

Up from the basement came the names of women long
dead. A radio smashed against a wall, changed channels and
shot up into an ear-splitting volume. A feverish knocking
began as if the man was pounding the bowels of the earth.

Shaking, Helen said: "There he goes, taking out his
frustration."

"What's he at?"

"Fighting, that's what."

"Whoever he's got," said the boy, "he'll kill him dead."

As suddenly as it had begun, the cheering subsided. Pop had ceased to curse the cauterized darkness round him. He lay down, heart throbbing, on his bed. However much he strained to listen, the boy could hear nothing there. His bladder began to pain him and out in the yard he stood waiting. And pissing, he went back through all the times he had stood like this, his *bod* in his hands, pissing. Smaller, smaller he went till he shook with fear that his mind might not return to him, but stay in the head of some two-year-old self, and leave him mindless. Only bits of him would travel back. Though he could sense the yard round him, the yard was not there.

He was afraid, and much later it struck him what he was afraid of. It was dislike for who he had been. Some unspeaking self in the past he could not remember. Not till he saw this series of scenes of himself pissing, *bod* in hand, did he know he raced through the past. Not till now could he see anything of what he had been. Nor could he understand why he disliked those other selves so. And he was afraid too, because the present was so vulnerable a time. For perhaps now, he was in the body of a man he would despair of later on, and forget, and remember only in snatches. It seemed the past selves had been vulnerable too. Afraid to be looked into. Afraid to be seen, a greedy place swallowing all before it and leaving only its mirror image, the present, the moment I stand here in the yard. He knew self-disgust. He looked into a mirror of the past and found himself looking into the face of himself, as people often do, darting glances to the left and right of them, propelling an arrested pupil up close to the arrested pupil of the reflection, as if trying to find the one standing behind. Beyond this self, the others, separated through untruths and violence. As if each pain inflicted on another kills off a thousand possible lives of

our own. Behind these pupils the vanished ones seek the light
denied them.

In the kitchen, Frank Allen, his skin grey and cavernous, was
filling up his glass again, and deliberately followed every move
of his wife with his eye.

"What time is it?" he asked.

"You've missed your dole anyway."

"Why didn't ye call me?"

"I couldn't think. I couldn't remember."

She shouted for the children who came in and ate like wolves
after their long fast. Frank Allen sat on his chair while Helen
passed in and out without a word. He started whispering.
He clasped his tall thin knees, then lurched to his feet.
"Let me in there among you," he said drunkenly. But it was
Margaret that had to go and fill his plate.

"Why," he screamed, "won't you even do that for me?"

"You've got two hands," said Helen, taking her place last of
all, her face bitter and white. A forced laugh. A drained eye.

He was a tall stiff man, frightened at the end of the table.
His eyes blurred over. He fought for his breath. "It's all to
spite me," he said.

"Think what you like. I hate the sight of you."

"You could have called me for the dole."

"Every day the same whine."

"Stop the lying, the lying to yourself."

"God," she screeched, getting up from the table, "I can't
stand the sound of your voice."

He sat on in front of his uneaten dinner. "You should eat,
Uncle Frank," said Margaret. So he ate. The children moved
away from the table carrying their plates. In the scullery stood
Helen shivering with temper. He stood in the doorway waiting,
thinking that each expression of rage somehow made her look
younger. She became a girl fighting over her most basic right
while he stayed in the place of the righteous who exact from
reality the terrors they have dreamed up in their head. And

find that soon their lovers will become accomplices with the
great hurt imagined. Roars of insatiable fatalists. What was
it that dragged them into such degrading acts? Was it only
his bodily need of her? Aye. That his mind might climb down
to listen to another's point of view.

"I'm sorry," he said.

"I hate someone that has to go over the same thing, over
and over," she said. "What's the sense? It makes no difference
in the long run. Why don't you go off and get another woman?
Hah! With all this talk you leave nothing of me here. I'm not
for taking apart and putting together again as you please." She
stepped further away. "Do you hear?" "I hear you. I hear." The
latch came off the door and George entered. He sat a moment
by the table comprehending. Taking no side but his own. The
honeyed voice and swaggering gait. "C'mon now, man dear,"
he said, and took the shaking Frank Allen out of it. Frank
shook his brother's hand free of his shoulder. Through his
mind ran a litany of love words. They walked down the village.
"I can imagine their every word," Helen said to the empty
house. The day wore on. She threw open the windows to get
rid of the smell of drink. What does he expect if he comes
blundering into my room at night? She lit a cigarette. Skillet
arse, she said. Fucking cunt. Her mind for a while could not
get beyond that point. Overhead was a gold-framed picture
of a green somnolent river that flowed by a Roman tomb.
She could not make out the Latin inscription. Jesus, but
Catholics are common. Common out. Then Helen moved
from room to room to keep a check on her wandering mind.
She heard the calls of the children playing late on the road.

The boys pottering in the loft.

Then they walked by the flooded river skimming stones to
the far side. Seagulls chuckled over the calf's roar. Or else flew
by houses tucked into folds in the hills. Houses built on stone
or else perched without protection near peaks, built by bad
map-readers. Our children cannot be consoled, she thought,
not even by us, for we have handed on the self-same aloneness

and dependence that now mourns our children's loss to us. We have handed on time fleeing under our feet. Miseries beyond telling. What comfort we have given shall be returned to us. What badness there was stays, clawing at us in the dark. It's this way. Death happens midterm, not at the end. We must make our peace with existence, to know the truth of those out there. This, long before we can exist in the eyes of others. Midday we die, leaving room for that conscious life that is endless, misty and crude. The afternoons will have a ring to them. The evenings for learning. The nights for forgetting. That we refuse to relive the pain any longer. The nights are for diminishing the pain. Turning to those in the here and now, not out of selflessness as he wants, nor for forgiveness as he wants, not with rebukes, but with the knowledge that night is here, and what that means.

In another room talk of school literature begins.

The woman sitting there had grown considerably older. Whiskey, tequila. In the same glass following each other. "I love Conrad," says Jim, "and I love James Stephens, too." "And I love D. H. Lawrence," said Margaret. "The only book I know is the Bible," said Helen. Joseph began to rub his mother's feet with methylated spirits. Her blue veins spread out in stiff clusters as he drew his fingers hard against the scored flesh between her toes. "I trusted you," she sang, "You can't be true, My heart no longer sings, Its wings are broken, too." Margaret spread the lilies round the rim of an old brown vase, and said: "And what bed am I in tonight?" "With me, of course," answered Helen, too sharply. Now Peter the fiddler entered the house and asked for a bed for the night. Granted a roof overhead in Jim's room, he went upstairs to leave his instruments safe. He is the type of a man that is never in a hurry, George claimed. Useless to society, said Pop. And yet sweet to listen to. Helen cooked him up a meal. It was that she was not obliged to him. Sympathizing with this wretched creature, his countenance like that of a boiling chicken, freed her. She knew as she heard him washing in the kitchen that the basin would be filled with toenails and fingernails, clippings of his beard and hair. But what matter. He was her toy, her sympathy, that she could be hard on if she chose. Afterwards he opened drawers, checked a shirt of Jim's against his chest, earrings were held askew, a clock set right, a ball kicked, a wheel on the dressing-table fixed. Now he lifts up each statue from the mantelpiece to test its weight and texture. She could tell that lately he had enjoyed few intimate things round which his mind could turn. That fixing and fondling these strange materials prepared him for the day ahead.

"And where's the men?" he asked.

"Where else."

"I'm off on the road for a few months," he reported. "Granard is a good town. They're not short down there, no."

Margaret wore her socks to bed, Jim his shirt, and Joseph went up on the shoulders of Peter nearly breaking his back. On the window ledge of his room he found the lilies spread. And he thought of his two breasts growing where none had ever been and how Margaret had touched them with a kind of stupefying excitement. How his nipples had cowered from her touch while her elbow touched him at the root. The wall of his stomach grew taut. He thought of her sleeping there in the very next room.

Helen walked down through the village.

The priest was out walking too, through cars and tractors parked outside the bars. Curious as a bird he glanced through rear windows. He crushed some pipe tobacco into his fist and palmed the remains into his pouch. He looked up. A woman of high degree. And a child, forgotten by someone, was pushing an ancient pram round and round the monument chuckling. Helen entered the lower bar under the Tuborg sign. Two card schools of twenty-five were in progress. The two men were in the back lounge. "There was no use in stopping up there alone," she said. George was on his feet immediately to buy her a drink. Frank was happy she had come down. He had a big black cat on his lap. He called the cat by her name. Helen interrupted unconsciously from some place distant, it was an irritated thought, too fragile to be grasped. She clung stubbornly to her story and found the dark passages through which the mind will go to right itself. "You know what they say about you," she said. "They say you're only a bollax."

She knew the terror that sustained her there was the sum of herself.

It was that he might recognize her that she persevered. But when memory refuses to budge, sanity comes toppling down. She enjoyed telling him all the bad things she heard about him. He was grappling with a false cheerfulness that might explain away his misery. But scored deep in his soul was an insecurity greater than his protested love of her. George was talking politics, and Frank followed on retrieving. They talked politics out of fear, taking their vengeance on names out there in the real world for what happened here in their own. So Helen saw it anyway. George's passion would infuriate her. Could they kill over a slight in love?

Now look, Helen.

Oh yes, the great and futile objectivity.

Head down, she went across the bar with her bag by the tail to buy a drink out of her children's allowance. She could not remember a word they had been talking about. All that was left her was to imagine the whole thing over. She had two double vodkas and a coke. The late news on the TV was turned up to an intolerable pitch.

12

Old Doc Ferguson leaned closer to detect the cause of Pop Allen's declining sight. "Mastoid, I think," the doctor said. "You see," said the doctor, "the fifth nerve and the third nerve cross each other at the petrous bone, and there is the danger."

Outside they could hear the doctor's children yelling in the car. The doctor focused closer on the alarmed pupil, holding the light bulb in his left hand. Joseph, standing by the window, became acutely aware of the inflamed honeycomb of cells behind his grandfather's ear. The doctor lifted Pop's eyelid as if it were a stopper in a trough. He stared an incalculable time towards a point of light which withdrew continually from his gaze. "Tsh! Tsh!" he said.

"And what are you doing in the National?" he asked Pop.

"I'm sure I don't know," Pop replied.

The doctor packed his things and went out onto the road where the sunset was growing long in April, slung his bag in the back of the car and drove off through the resurrected trees, so full of life that people marvelled how memory had provided for forgetfulness.

Pop developed a number of spasms throughout the late spring which appeared like premeditated contortions, and in the same manner, the jump of the nerve under his left eye was seen as a distinguishing feature rather than a sign of inward pain. No theory had ever satisfied his craving for freedom, yet he had not consigned his will to fate. "Flattery is at the root of it," he told George. "Mark my words." Nightly, he and Pop argued politics, meaning George would drive him to despair. "You're giving me a pain in the head, I say," and Pop would lie down. Then George would hurl himself around the room, where his father lay, working towards an apology, and last of all he'd say, "I miss Geraldine, but that's no excuse I know." This show of self-pity drove George further into righteousness for he would not like his weakness to be known. Each Tuesday Joseph linked his grandfather down to the lake where the heavy shingle poured back and forth through the riddle of the waters. They walked to the village and crossed to the South. They met first an old policeman talking earnestly to a curly-haired chap with earrings. He was camped out on the green.

They were enjoying themselves, the old man and the boy, the guard and the renegade.

Opposite the revolutionary memorial, a granite statue with a laugh on its face and an arm raised in the manner one welcomes home a neighbour's child, was the tourist bookshop with photographs of the village taken from the air.

In the field behind the bookshop the sheep were lazing on the harsh ground, contented; in the field next door, the wide awake lambs were jumping in the air. Pop put out his hand to touch the face of a child whose father he had once known. "He's got the chin," he told the mother, "and the cleft-ash cheeks. I suppose he's got the same bad temper as well." At each pub they passed Pop stood up at the door and breathed in deeply. The boy described all that he could see. They found a rhythm of moving forward together. The blind man sensed the cold spot on the bridge where the soldiers stood. The grandfather and the grandson stood in the small queue in the post-office. "I suppose," said Pop to the man behind the counter, "you have something of mine there." He counted the notes from his pension. "Lead on, Macduff," said Pop. They entered the small snug. The barman already had the glass of port poured. Pop pinned the tip of his cigarette to his cheek, his eyes watered and with the tips of the fingers of his other hand he measured the distance between the bottom of the glass and the edge of the table. Then without more ado he started his mimicry of everyone in the house for all to hear, then while the drinkers laughed, he summoned up all he could remember of what he had overheard in the pub the week before, giving each familiar voice its particular whine and the strangers' a wild exaggeration. This was how he kept stock of the world. "I don't," he said, "miss seeing any of you beggars at all." After the initial gaiety he would quiet down. He measured the distance to the glass, listened to the passing trade. He ordered a drink for Mrs Simpson when she came. And Peter Cathcart. They spoke to each other from their separate places at the bar. And every so often he would lean over and squeeze the boy's thigh affectionately, for he could tell that Joseph had no sense of how affairs were going with his family. "They are a thoughtless bunch above," he said. Then the ghosts arrived, and Joseph shouldered him home through insults thrown from all sides.

Come a certain day, George had it all prepared. Lawyer Smith arrived to Pop's bed. "We are going to take a little journey, you and me," he said. Against his will Pop stepped into his Sunday clothes. He had Joseph shine his shoes. Then he and Frank Allen and Joseph got into the car. Lawyer Smith, as usual, commenced a long conversation about exports and imports. Pop replied that a horse will eat twice the amount of a cow. And if you strike back against your aggressor your offence is all the greater unless you take it the full course. For then you will have to act forever according to different laws. "The worst are gypsies, the best are hoteliers," Pop said. "Take the market, now, to Eastern Europe," said Lawyer Smith. "The worst are gypsies, the best are hoteliers," Pop continued, riling him with his nonsense, "but still it's hard lines when you hear a gypsy apologizing to the crown for the trouble he's caused."

The first part of the journey was friendly.

The men leaned towards each other. Talked and gestured and then as morning slipped cloudily over the twisting roads, Joseph fell asleep.

"You'd best be thinking of the future," said Lawyer Smith.

"What future are you talking of?" asked Pop.

"Don't be difficult, Dad," said Frank.

"Jesus Christ, listen to his eminence."

Pop coughed angrily and spat out of the car window.

Joseph awoke. Some argument had taken place. His father was holding the back of the driver's seat.

"What are we stopping for?" asked Pop.

"I thought we might look over your will," said Lawyer Smith.

"Well, you can do all the looking you like," answered Pop, "you'll not get my hand to anything."

"Christ, don't be hard, Dad. It's only to sort out the house."

"What the fuck are you after, huh?"

"Nothing."

"Aye."

A country family swayed alongside them through the murky artificial caverns of the modern hotel. The women all tissue and the men wringing out their frosted collars. And seen through the twelve-foot-by-nine-foot plate-glass window, a black dog among rocks. No trees. A magpie perched on an orange cow's back. Rhubarb bristling from the earth in a garden protected from the crows by a shorn fanned-out swan's wing.

The necessary papers were placed in front of Pop on a low table.

"We might as well get it over with now," said the lawyer.

But Pop was biding his time, thinking to himself if he signed over the house now, he would be dependent.

"Are you behind this?" he asked Frank.

"It looks like George's planning," he continued quietly. "Well, you can tell him that I'm not ready for the grave yet. I'd sell the place first."

"The price will not be right," said Frank.

"The price is never right."

"Don't be self-indulgent, man," said Lawyer Smith, "do you want them fighting after your death?"

"If they'd stop it now," said Pop raising his voice in Frank's direction, "I'd be happy enough. What do I care what they do after I'm gone."

"You could make things easier," Lawyer Smith went on.

"I'll keep them at it," said Pop, "and divide it between the two."

Joseph guided his hand towards his drink.

Joseph's father drew in his breath and looked hazily towards the out-of-season carpets which were rolled up in the breakfast room. The barmaid, who had wide brown pupils like the sheep in those parts, seemed to understand his misery. "These men tackle their lives with cohesive philosophies," the lawyer indicated a western group seated at the next table. "Just by you on the left. There is no confusion there." "From their accents I can tell they're from Donegal," said Pop, "and that's enough for me." The mother of this group, poised in mottled scarf and heavy coat, leaned upright and forward from her two male companions to sip her minute sherry. Her mouth went back like a young bird feeding from the parent's beak. The men discussed the markets, humorously aware of her arched, inquisitive figure. Her liberation had been late in coming. She was interested, anxious, homespun. "We are doing the place up," the barmaid explained tentatively to Frank Allen as she reached down for the dirty glasses. The lawyer nodded with the sympathy of a man of the world. "It's a frightful job, I know," he said. "Jesus," whispered Pop to himself. One of the sheep farmers arched his fingers and tickled his scalp. The other hand cupped loosely under his chin. The friend had his burly arms tucked to his chest the better to concentrate on criticism.

They bit into their ham sandwiches.

The woman counted some coins out of her purse.

"Between the two of them, I say," said Pop.

Joseph guided his hand as he signed.

"Now, get more drinks," Lawyer Smith commanded with a quick dart of his eyes.

Joseph spoke out his order at the bar. The barmaid did not hear. Her bored face was chinned by a swaying arm. She was caught between two talkative, grinning youths. She took over the conversation in a puzzling, though confident fashion. She watched for their every response. She moved towards them and away repeating numerous phrases. She was talking of the hanging law then up again before the Dáil. "If anybody touched one of mine," she said, "I'd have them put down. Oh yes." Joseph again slowly told his order. One of the youths touched her cheek with his finger. She flicked off the touch with annoyance and turned to the lad.

"Here, this will keep you on the road, son," one of the sheep farmers said as Joseph again gave his order. He pressed into his hand a bunch of purple seaweed. "It's better," he said, "than any of your wild garlic."

"Tell us your story, then," agreed Frank.

"So, since I was a child I had a malformed kidney and had been in hospital most every year," said Lawyer Smith. "Then I met a priest that I was defending at the time. He told me of a nun. I travelled all the way up here to see her, and she was so beautiful when I saw her, like a spring day."

"I'm sure," said Pop.

Lawyer Smith paused. "She told me her story."

The lawyer's eyes, the white brimming with thought, sought out Frank Allen's attention. But Frank was always inclined to wander when people spoke of their own misfortunes. He looked into the fire that heaved and sparked, dusted turf mould off the grate, only too aware of this beseeching intimacy. Frank Allen was subduing his own panic. He was arranging his fate to confound the forthcoming miracle. Yet he tried to put his irreligious thought by him, that he might hear the story through the sense of another man and know him for again.

"She was teaching in a place in America," the lawyer continued, "then during the night a voice says to her: 'You have the gift, go out and use it.'"

In the background "The Can of Spring Water" was being sung by Michael Joseph on the barmaid's tape . . .

"Go on," said Frank.

"I'll be brief. Going up the northern coast I could feel this great calm. Coming away from her I knew I was cured. And

I could tell something spiritual had happened as well. At the consecration of the Mass I could feel people drawn to me. People would turn round and look into my eyes. I had been given the gift, but didn't use it myself." He gathered his groin and shook it generously in his hand. "I had been cured only." He placed his hands once more on the table. "The nun was the one started the movement." His pupils lifted to a point left of Frank Allen's head there they stayed, reflecting in a grave manner.

"I sit here turning these thoughts over in my mind," he said.

"Am I dreaming?" asked Pop.

"I'm glad for you," said Frank. He turned to a drunk whose friends had brushed by their table. Hand up, the drunk man apologized. "Have you a horse for the St Leger?" he asked, leaning down to Pop, his red lips delving sideways into his cheek and the eye above squeezing down. "Ask the man beside me," answered Pop, as if the world he had known was best never seen again. "No offence, then," said the man and he moved after the others to the bar. The tape stopped playing and the radio turned over to the race. Pop shook his head as if he had had enough for one day. The crowd at the bar became terribly loud. When muttering to himself proved inadequate Pop struck his stick off the table. It was all to no avail. Blindly he strode to the counter. The barmaid said with a shrug, "They will keep talking." The drunks shouted out the names of horses they had backed or should have backed. They did not hear the race begin, but kept shuffling and talking and sawing the ground with their feet. Pop was led away towards the door. Suddenly the last furlong was upon the drunks before they knew it. The excitement of the announcer quietened them down. It was all over. What the men at the bar wanted to hear passed by them as in a dream.

"That was a right howdoyedo," said Pop as they entered the car. Frank Allen asked questions concerning the law that the layman craves to ask and with it, too, he was sometimes arrogant, then, given an evasive answer, he broke into a speech. It was a holding speech where the words sought to finish well a heroic talk of the mundane. He ended up on the far side of himself. "The food in that place," said Pop, "would sicken a dog." Outside the world was in torment. "So," said Pop, "the bitch behind the bar would have us all put down." The lawyer accepted that policemen had only the law to protect them therefore they must abuse it more than most. "For once, man dear," pronounced Pop, "you are speaking the truth. The force, I'm led to believe now, is no fit place for a sane man." They spoke of the dangers of the sea. Storms that come out of nowhere on a clear day. Nor would their voices allow Joseph sleep in the freezing back seat among all the files and briefcases, briefs of murders and thefts and assaults, plans of houses, and accidents. Joseph was afflicted by drowned faces, his perpetual fear. He was dreaming himself up close. Nobody was stirring on those steep climbs. Wrens were blown across the road like twigs. And seagulls fell into the freezing valley below, except for one brief moment when maybe twenty of them were stationary above the high bushes, level with the toiling car, before they fell away.

"You'll find yourself a different man," said Lawyer Smith cheerfully as they pulled into a driveway that led around the back of the convent.

The lawns were filled with fallen chestnut leaves. Old dried-up primroses still nestled against the roots of trees. "You are on your own now," said Lawyer Smith. "Me and Frank will take a walk." Joseph and his grandfather entered the convent. The small old man tottered forward like a beaten child. The windows looked out on the hockey fields and the solitary walks that ran down to the railway tracks. Pop had this terrible feeling of committing some crime by walking down the high-ceilinged corridor. He leaned out to touch the saints in the recesses. He felt underfoot the winding carpeted stairs.

"Where are we now?" he asked. They walked for ages before meeting anyone. They whispered to each other. "What's that?" he asked. It felt like a great spacelessness. A place where souls scurried to and fro. A nun led them past the cells and wooden crucifixes to a white bare room stacked with magazines. Pop had barely time to get his bearings when the one they sought entered. She closes Joseph's eyes. Her fingers were coarse but playful. He felt her move towards the old man. "Sit down," he heard her say. Then there was a long silence. "Are you there, son?" asked Pop. Joseph opened his eyes. The healer was gone, so they went back the same way in the wake of another nun. He kept looking at his grandfather's eyes but the old man, as always, had his head back. His listless eyes told nothing. They went along the cheerless corridors and through the doors, above them a conglomeration of mountains and birds. Lawyer Smith was furtively picking flowers for his wife. Frank was sitting with a gardener in a field of hacked cabbage plants, the tide below sliding in over the level of the other tides, running over sands and shingle polished like cut glass, right to the gleam of sunlight striking Pop as he sat in the outdoor toilet at home, straight and upright, tracking his life through the unfamiliar present.

Some months later Pop woke in the dark after the operation for the removal of the cataracts. There was a lot of scuffling going on. They began to unroll the bandages. Light started travelling into his brain. A distant ceiling hovered. For a while he could see through the ceiling to the sky beyond. Then the grey ceiling fell into place again. Gradually he turned his head sideways and saw in the next bed a grinning hag. "Who the fuck is that?" he said aloud. The hag exposed a row of blackened otter's teeth. Pop raised himself onto his elbows. Further down the ward he saw the thin frame of a man's back and the shaking hands tentatively putting the top of his pyjamas on. Pop saw the other old men, their faces stripped down to the singular passion that had driven them all their life. "Merciful Christ," he said, "will you look at the state of the whores." He closed his eyes and was pursued by wild animals. A horse was cuffing his ear with his cold nose. He woke to find his two sons standing embarrassed at the bottom of the bed. "Christ, boys, but you've aged a terror," he said. Behind them a man shrunken to a dwarf passed by carrying a razor and a phial of pills.

13

Summer was peeling the whitewash off the walls. The long drainpipes were empty. Steaming pots were melting down tar to seal the studded boats. The boat people were rolling tins of diesel across the shingle. Jim was sandpapering his upturned boat. Joseph and his mother walked by. It looked like the people had been here a thousand years. Mother and son passed the bowed houses and the two bars at the end of the village. The door into the publican's house with beaten Tee Garnet hinges was swinging wildly.

The pair slipped into the country.

Helen Allen was glad to be free of the house. She and Frank no longer spoke to each other. It was as if their minds had seized up. She was wearing a bright summer dress with polka dots that had belonged to Geraldine. Better that George had not seen her leaving in that dress for his sorrow afterwards was unbearable as he tried to tell the one woman from the other, seeking further signs and finding none. The pair started the climb. Bright streams shot down the mountainside. Under their feet the boggy soil wheezed.

Helen undid her scarf and carried her sandals.

"Wait, will you," she shouted after Joseph.

At length they came into a valley, two fields of which were filled with ruins. Mud walls that contained goat droppings, and grassy furrows where the potato gardens had once been. Crouching rabbits disappeared at their approach into burrows beneath the deserted village. Here the people had struggled on with the land through the famine till starvation began to arrest the children. Then one day a family who had suffered more than most put their belongings on their backs and headed down ridges covered in cuckoo-spit on the long walk to the sea below. The men of that family returned the long trek back to attend the unfertile soil, then back again before night fell to their huts by the sea. The others watched their comings and goings for six days. A meeting was called to which all the starved members of the village came. And they asked the men who had moved to the sea: "Do the fish throw themselves into your nets?"

"They do," the men replied.

"Are there not British soldiers to ferret away your food?" the villagers asked.

"The soldiers," the two men said, "have returned to their barracks to quell the riots in town."

"Do the fishermen allow you the same rights as themselves?" they went on, for hunger had given them great common sense.

"The sea is big enough to contain us all," the men replied.

"And how can you fish since you have no boats?" the villagers asked.

"We steal the fishermen's boats by night to lay our nets we found discarded on the shore," said the wily men.

"That can't go on forever," the others thought and said.

"We shell the shingle for mussels," the two replied, "and killed the two pigs we had. Their skin is drying out upon the shore. Tomorrow the women will lace the willow in. We'll yoke them the day after."

"And what if she goes down?" some jeered after them.

"We'll build another then," they said.

The men set off down the cliffs. The villagers sat around a

fire in one of the houses arguing till dawn. Some still argued that the potato would return. By next morning they all trooped down out of the valley leading the few animals left. They collected debris on the shore to shield them from the elements. And along with the others they returned each evening to their potato plots. But all that summer and the next the blight remained. Each spring they held their breath. The plants shot up whole and hearty. But the roots, when they drew them up with hopeful fingers, were soft as watery peat. No matter if they mixed seaweed with soil, or increased the peat to the earth, added fishbone or ashes to the hard ridges, the core of the plant would not survive. They watched the wet thatch of the houses crumble through two winters because it was unattended by fires from within. The reeds dragged with their burden of mountainy water. Heather and ragwort crossed the stone walls and entered the plots. One or two doors fell from their hinges. It was then that the villagers plundered the old houses to supply the new. Thrushes nested in the recesses where the villagers had kept the small things that mattered most. And sometimes the villagers would search unsuccessfully for anything they might have left behind. They dreamed that their previous lives had contained more than they really had. Finding nothing, they started searching all over again. But when the first roof fell there was no one to see it. They did not return, not even when the blight was over. They adapted themselves to the sea which had more layers to it than the land, and they were thankful for the weapon of hunger which they hid quietly for the years ahead.

Away to the left, on the other side of the valley, men were footing turf by the side of a clean, spare trout lake. The old moon disappeared as it hit the water, resurfacing minutes later when the dark clouds had moved on. Snipe got up and frightened waterhens scooted towards the reeds. The sun shone down.

The lightly fingered sound of the cuckoo came from the meadows beyond.

Helen lay back with her hand across her eyes.

"Look, Mammy," Joseph said.

She turned her head and saw him with his shirt raised. She looked at his baby's breasts, then back to his face grown pink with shame.

"What?" she asked.

"Margaret says they are bigger than hers," he said, pretending indifference.

"Oh, she would," said his mother. "Take no heed of Margaret. They'll be gone in no time."

"How long will I have them?" he asked.

"I don't know," she answered briskly, "but as long as you have the three-piece suite down below, you've nothing to worry about."

Helen lay back. She saw herself from a short distance away. The white stockingless legs ending in a blur. There was no body beyond her thighs. Her skin was thick as that drawn tight about the shell of a boat. Inside her, the stiffening ribs. The wide flare of her stomach. A woman who could not talk to her son. She had lost stability. A beast was being killed by her father. The grass from the calf's stomach burst out and filled the kitchen. Then her father entered Helen's room. She was lying on the bed. He said: "I love you best of all, you are my favourite." He went on talking of the beasts and the weather, cursed with the dark in the things that he said. He waited outside the room spending time while the fluff from the calf's stomach settled. He dragged his feet to the window where there was nothing. To the scullery where there was nothing. He draped his arms about her. He hugged her. She hung on, waiting till it was over. And everywhere she went, the day the sour grass had been loosened from the belly of the calf, her father was after her. In the meadow. In the hay. By the eel-pool. The bog. Her bedroom. Hay somewhere being mown. Milk collected. He felt her hair saying, "I love you best of all, you are my favourite." She lay there thinking, Can my mind be aware of itself forever. She could see beyond this day to the next. The burden of thought too heavy to carry. The weight of thought. Each minute thrown together as one.

A tremor ran through Helen's body. Something was frightening her. She was frightening Joseph. Her eyes opened. Joseph returned her look unashamedly. For a second his senses wavered. His mother knowing this look, lay back and did not trouble herself over him anymore. There was a man there all right. A creature trembling in fear of being alone in the world, who, when he plummeted down would take another with him. These cruel thoughts shamed her, and each day the deception grew greater. Sometimes she feared that she might never be able to return to the person she was and would always remain. She entered the head of a man to tell his story. Her belief strained. What dangerous thing must I leave out that makes me a woman? How can I see out through the eyes of a man? What is the difference? Were I the man entering the mind of a woman I know what he must leave behind. The excess of his need. The emptiness he expects another to fill. Then she saw it. If I enter the head of a man I must leave creation behind. For I, as the man, will create myself again. I will make a new man because I, the woman, cannot live with the old. But it was no joy for her to know she was the vehicle for creation. The man inside her is dead. Am I lonesome after him? That tough body brutalized against its own loss?

"Say Mammy," said Joseph, "can we go down?"

The waterhens. A cow bellowing against the bare shit-stained walls of an outhouse on the hills. In a wheatfield, the flattened place where someone had lain.

III

14

A flotilla of small racing yachts crossed the lake bending and weaving like butterflies. Nearer home the motorboats chugged along, bringing provisions up from the town. All the Allen family were sitting on the steps of the house waiting on George to return with his wages – and with food.

There was not a thing in the house.

"My stomach," said Pop, "thinks my throat is cut."

"Was I in my right mind to return here at all?" muttered Frank.

"Well there is nothing we can do about it now," said Helen against his fretting. Seconds later in her impatience she said: "Why can we never have a place of our own?" Then she added: "You'll just have to stand up for what you are."

The road shimmered like water. They sat on the steps of the house dreaming of different dinners. Margaret claimed she was starting to hallucinate. "I can see," she told them, "potatoes big as turnips cooked in oil. There's lashings of everything." But all that drifted to their noses was the stench of old fish from Jim's boat. The sieving of the big stones by the lake never stopped. Their bellies rumbled. Pop started to fart. "The curse of God on it," he said. Frank Allen walked down the road to meet his brother. The others tightened their belts and waited on the steps.

"Tie me to the blessed earth," complained Pop, "else a good surge of wind will take me with it."

"Look," said Helen, "there's Molly Farrelly who just lost her mother. She was in hospital ages and ages after. Who is that with her, I wonder? How can she have the nerve to go out dressed like that? All the colours are clashing. Maybe it's her nerves." She started laughing.

"God, she said, "how can I talk like that?"

Soon the two men came up together.

The boys ran down to meet them.

"I've a plan for later," George told the boys. He was working now at an electricity plant on the mountains. A villager had to be able to turn his hand to anything. The labourers from the village stole all they could from the site. They came down from the mountains by night with yards of cable, building materials, newly hewn planks. All talk stopped in the kitchen. The steaming plates arrived to the table and Frank was torn with envy thinking miracles only happened in the stranger's house. He stood outside looking in. It was too much for him.

"Now," said George when the table was cleared, "I want you boys tonight."

"Jim," he said, "bring the boat around to the river."

Jim oared off under the mountain. "Here," said George, "youse are old enough." They lit up three cigarettes and ghosted along on full stomachs through the rich shadows, speaking now and then of what they thought they'd seen. They drove screeching ducks ahead of them out of the lisping reeds that were flattened by the dull prow. They passed a crowd of men playing cards under a light by the caravans. Rugs and sheets and clothing were hung on all the ditches.

The sky cleared. The river grew bright as day.

"Here," said George. "Jim, you stop by the boat."

Himself and Joseph climbed up the steep bank, then onto a further ledge. The boat stirred over and back in the water. Jim strained his eyes after them. Soon there was only the deep-throated sound of the night. Then branches breaking. They returned with timber across their shoulders. They piled the timber on the bank without a word. Piece by piece Jim carried them to the boat. The others returned with mesh-wire and wall brackets and new plastic piping. Boxes of gold-plated reed switches. Like minnows. Red and blue volt relays. "That'll do us now," said George.

They waded in. Jim guided the boat around.

Terror seized their hearts when they heard the voices of men
a field away. The boat drifted quietly downstream. "Good men,
good men," whispered George, "you are worth your weight in
gold." At the mouth Frank was sitting in the ditch waiting.
He gave them a fright when he stepped out, a fag in his hand.
They unloaded the goods and carried them up the back garden
and into the house. Then, after replacing the nets Jim turned
the boat and beached her alongside the others at the slip.

"We have never known such good times," said George.

The next night they encountered something flying in the
air that they could not identify. "Keep on lads," said George. It
flew all round them, sometimes swooping inches above their
heads. George sat stock still while behind him the lads waited
the return of what it was. Their two faces looked this way
and that. Their hearts were beating madly. The next night it
seemed that someone was following them up the bank of the
river. Through the silhouette of the trees they saw the shape of
a man intent on where he was going. Again in another break
he was there. They coasted in. George went out to search.
"There's no one," he said.

Three nights they came and went.

All was stored down in Pop's room.

"Where's my fucking tea?" he'd shout out. "I'm dying of
the drought."

"Take your time, you old goat," Helen would scream back,
then strike the floor with her heels.

"Don't you put on airs with me, woman," Pop would
sneer. At last she'd relent and leave the tray by the basement
door. The boat turned up the river. Frank waited in the ditch.
She'd sit by the fire listening to every sound. She heard the
latch undone and the tinkle of Pop's tray going down the
rickety stairs. Not long after, the back door opened. Frank
looked into the room to see was she there. God, she thought,
I'd rather be traveling with them in danger than sitting
here tormented by unwarranted jealousies. She heated up

their food again, then climbed the stairs and got into bed by Margaret. The last night she knew they were out there making very little sound. She stepped quietly to the kitchen door. It was a cargo of men's clothes they were taking down. The next day at noon Pop appeared in an immaculate suit. Deliberately he strolled through the kitchen. He stopped by the window to survey the village below.

"Going walking?" asked Helen.

"I never," replied Pop, "like taking to the streets till they are well aired." He cocked an eye in the direction of the two lads in stitches of laughter in the corner. Each had in their pocket a sum of money given to them by George. At last, the boys had entered the world of their fathers.

15

Haytime came. All normal work was suspended. George emerged in the bright mornings, his coat filled with seed, the turn-ups of his trousers filled with seed.

The weather, loneliness and abstinence from drink had strengthened the colour of his cheeks.

Those times Helen used to cook boiled turnips with scallions through them, and the children loved to sit close to her. Though no one admitted it. For Helen would run her fingers through their hair, again and again, till their scalps grew rigid with excitement. The house warmed up. The boys went the long walk through the mountains after George.

Later in the day along the lower road, Margaret followed.

A gypsy van pulled up with the passenger window broken. The handle held with rope. The children of the gypsy had to climb into the back. Then everyone squeezed over for Margaret including the woman with the burnt shawl and the child who had never lost his milk teeth. The driver began to sing. Went up and down the scale searching for a note to suit his clipped accent. His van was filled with the smell of burnt timber, tar and children. There was a monkey trapped in his wicked eye. He had a good monotonous voice and thought boisterous singing might please. His daughter leaned forward smiling into Margaret's face. The van emerged suddenly out of the mountains to cliffs left behind by an earlier ocean.

Down through the U-shaped valley she could see the lower lakes.

The gypsy cocked one blackened fingernail.

There's good drying out, Mrs," he said.

The van with its buckled doors charged off.

Her wet footprints followed her father up the warm road where he, taking the shortcut, had struck out for the heights, pulling himself upward with heather and moss, able to attack physically what tormented him, till he reached the meadows above.

She did not look back.

Then all through the day she worked the rake with her elders.

Evening came and she was left alone with George there. The sun was going down. They continued to rake in against the cocks the leavings of the workers on the side of the mountain. They dragged upward and rested. He went round and round after the hay. He clamped the cocks with turf. Tin cups rattled in her osier basket. Pails rocked on a cart on the road below.

She loved these times alone with him.

Everyone stood around in the village waiting on the festivities to begin.

The both of them stood after their day's labouring and through the silence came the sound of the politicians talking in the valley below.

That morning a lorry filled with chairs had pulled up on the village green. The usual bunting was hung. The local councillor, while waiting on the men to finish in the fields, played marching airs across the speakers. The crowd roared their approval like cows lonesome for their calves as each politician called out for the damnation of some other. Then they disguised their greed by appealing to the people's humanity. This made the people more attentive. The politicians screamed out the profanity of their days so that their voices carried into the South. Margaret and George stood on the outskirts of the crowd. "Where will they bring us next, I wonder?" asked George. "What fucking madness can they think up now?" A shot rang out. It echoed up the hills. A silence long as any history followed. The organizers drew the banners open across the lorry. The Lambeg drums started up. Not until tomorrow morning would the planet cool.

Margaret came to the door of the barn in the dying sunshine on an errand. Something wanted in the house. Something like that. Opened it. Closed it. Inside was the dark cool of the barn and light sliding through an open knot of wood. It struck Joseph's face. "What are you doing?" she asked. "What are you at there?" She looked down at his hand. She touched the tip of his flared penis with the material of her dress. She sucked his painful breasts. "Please, please," he begged.

She stretched out beneath him on the hay. He inserted a small piece of straw into her blown lips with the curiosity of a child. He moved over and back. She said into his ear, "I'm mad for you." She rested her cheek on his stomach. Somewhere bread was being baked. "Your hair and mine are the same colour," she said. "I've seen all the mickeys in the house but yours is the nicest yet." "Margaret, Margaret," he whispered. She brought up her face and kissed him. He felt the soft rounded cheek in his hand. They dreamed each other. Someone was crossing the yard. She had her knickers back on in the wink of an eye. Her dress fell to her knees. She turned back as if nothing had happened. Fumbling with his trousers

Joseph stood sorting out the harness.

Helen stood in the doorway.

"What's been going on here?" she shouted.

Somehow she knew. "Get out here," she screamed.

She brought the sweeping brush down on the base of Margaret's spine as she shuffled in her bare feet on to the porch. All of her frustration and hatred was in that blow. All the family heard Margaret scream. Joseph ran between the two women. "Leave her alone, alone, alone, you witch," he screamed. Frank caught Helen and dragged the brush from her. Pop stumbled through the door. Screeching, Helen fled to the river. And Frank after her. She ran away from them. Nothing moved. George coaxed Margaret up from where she lay. "Don't hit me," she said. She would not move. There was no sound from insect or bird on the great yellow mountains. And the earth lulled by inactivity grew desperate for growth and space and life from another world.

16

That night George dreamed that he had found the dent on the wing of the car that had killed Geraldine. He approached the small man who was sitting in the driver's seat. "Yes?" the man asked. The engine started. "It's a personal matter," said George. He leaned in and held him by the throat. Immediately, showing no pain whatsoever, except in the pitch of his voice, the man started to confess. "I was only a child," he said. "Forgive, forgive me. I see demons. I am going about my ordinary life then something goes wrong. Don't condemn me. We must forget. It's that you can forget things, no matter how terrible, makes the world go on." The dream was not going the way George intended. For the voice of the man in the car was becoming slowly familiar. The voice was too real and smothering his revenge. George would have done anything to make that voice back into the voice of the man he wanted to kill.

But it was not to be. "He made me feel, at first, the strength of the illusion," the man went on. There were tears coming down his cheeks. "He built me up. The world was made. He'd be a mad rake for me. And gentle too. You'd go to the altar unashamed. But it's the you before the you he knew needs comforting. How can he get back and change all that happened before?" The man in the car was not aware of George throttling him. Only weakness seemed to travel through George's hands. "My imagination is a gaping wound through which my soul has passed," the man said. Soaked in sweat George awoke. He ran towards the source of the voice in the dream and found that it was Helen kneeling by Margaret's bed. Joseph was in the other bed. Frank was sitting in a chair in the corner, his arms on the rests, hands dangling, the head slightly forward, looking blankly at his wife.

"I think," said George, "that I'll move out of here for a while."

He took down the bottle of Powers and filled two glasses.

"There's work at present on the boats," he went on. He drank his glass down and filled it again. "You'll have to be kind to her," he said, "she's not herself." The two men sat a while in silence. Frank went down the tortured path of longing. All the years he had lain impotently by her side. His mood changed again. He turned speechless with rage. Hate streamed through him. He ran up and pulled her away from the bed where she had curled up and fallen asleep by Joseph. He hauled her like a madman across the floor. "Keep away from him," he shouted, "keep away from Joseph."

"I don't blame you," she cried. "Kill me if you want to."

He thought the force choking his heart would make his body suddenly explode.

In this terrible savagery, demeaning them both, they made love. It frightened them. They breathed like dogs. "Please,

Frank," she whispered, "take this guilt away." But all he was building towards was his own release. In a sudden wrench they move that great distance between the body and soul. She called him Daddy. She called him by the names of other men. She felt the small stiff neck of a hen between her legs. A headless bird pursuing her. Its wings flapping with one last surge of nervous life. They were driving towards emptiness. With a terrible cry he fell over the cliff and found her body under him stilled. His frustration gone and all that aching nothingness again. "Oh Christ, love me," he called to her. It was too late. "Love me!" He shook her. He saw her bright tearful eyes in the dark. He'd known them filled with many things. Disdain. Arrogance. Temper. Fear. Happiness. A happiness so real that it had made him cry out. This was the first time that he had seen innocence. Cowering there behind the defences she would soon erect against him. He held her tight knowing an awful truth. That the divide between sex and despair is the same as that between sex and celebration.

He prayed that his mind would not return to the murky depths where it had been for so long hungering after someone else's humiliation.

He had stifled her every cry for freedom.

The insane selfishness that bled him of spirit. He held her. She was going away. Stay! Stay! "I could have killed her," she said out to the darkness. "We are both to blame," he said. "God, what have I done to him?" "Joseph will be all right." He was again outside listening in. Separated from her. But he must persist. "I'm to blame for so much," she said in an even voice. She was taking her own journey again. I must reach the outside of all this before it's too late, he said to himself, over and over. She turned away from him. He journeyed outward alone. In the silence he wiped his groin. He touched her. She did not move. Soon she slept.

The next morning, he walked George down to the bus, then

on instinct, travelled with him to the next town to look for
work. Said George: "I'll have to be careful after this. It'll
not be easy for you. It's the way we are." So, when Helen
descended the stairs she found the two men gone. Margaret
was watching the TV and would not speak to her. Under
the window Joseph and Jim sat playing draughts. Was this
normality? Where had she been? She saw Pop trudging with
his socks to the line. She cupped the teacup to her breast and
bobbed over and back in her chair. God, she said, I must live.
Please let me live.

17

Jim was restless now that his father was gone. He was estranged
from the rest of the family and spoke little. Many days he
spent in his room just reading. He read all the newspapers he
could find. That period passed. He would disappear for whole
days. The others would try to be sympathetic. Only Helen
said nothing. She watched him out of the corner of her eye.

"That fucker, Frank, is having an affair," she told Jim.

Sometimes she would sit by her husband at dinner time,
and before she was half way through the meal she'd empty the
contents of her plate with a sweep of her knife into the bin,
sit down again hungry, and wonder why she had done it. She
covered all the mirrors in the house, had Joseph constantly
searching for things she thought she had lost in the yard or
in the outhouses. There was talk around the village of Jim
drinking. She prepared herself. Oiled her skin and soaked her
hands in Pond's cream. Stepped into another of Geraldine's
dresses and went down the village. She went into the first
pub. The barman leaned forward, blew out his cheeks, his
eyes took a swallowdive through the thick lines on his temple.
"No, he's not here," he said. He expelled the wind from his
mouth and trundled down the bar, rolling the sleeves of his

shirt up to the elbow. He went back to conversation with the others. She crossed the street into the other pub. Jim was sitting up there at the bar. "What are you having?" she asked, sitting up beside him. The eyes of the drinkers followed her. "I'll have," says he, "a bottle of Guinness." "Two bottles of Guinness then," she said. The sharp puncturing sound of the bottletops being drawn. "There youse are." Later they went up the village together. That stopped the gossip.

So ended the journey of the senses they had all taken that summer. Within two months Joseph's breasts disappeared and his fear of turning into a woman disappeared. He had been cut off from real tragedy, those moments when he tried to imagine what shape his womanhood would take and what if any power he would have over men. The abuse and degradation that would follow. All gone. The pain that was pleasurable. Not there anymore. The real woman was his mother out early in the morning searching in the dung heap for a lost wedding ring, for whom all gestures were transitory, and suited her fine. For her language was filled with stoic myths of falsehood. She sought solace in long spiritless silences, and as she went about her daily chores, she was tormented by the image of all the other women throughout the world, safe and snug in their roles, doing what she was doing. And for what? Her past life came back to haunt her. She jumped to her feet and threw her food away. With her body half-washed she stepped into her clothes. Half-dressed she entered the kitchen. Half-way to the shop she turned back. She observed her gestures: a mid-circle with the index finger, a pleat of her dress picked up. And some days later she noticed that Frank Allen had a few gestures of his own. She warmed to that. Several times she saw it, the big friendly hand of himself nearly covering half his face, as for no reason he touched his cheek with his palm. That went beyond reassuring himself that he was alive. That was the big awkward hand of a tender lover. Yes, and then the

air sucked in over his bottom lip, the lip pulled tight against a
row of teeth tipped with charcoal, and out comes the sound,
awe. *Tsh, tsh*, he expresses mock disgust. The tip of his tongue
hopping up and down off the roof of his mouth in a lower key.
Then into a higher key. *Awe!* The conversation goes on. *Aye!*

He crossed his arms and arse-out stood in the yard as if
he was leaning forward on something. He whistled inward to
express mock horror at a thought traveling through his mind.
This was followed by *Oh God!*, then *Ah!* The understanding
falling like a shadow behind the mysteries. The shadow
crossed the yard. *Awe! Aye!*

The fucker is human after all. The loose trousers pinched
above the cheeks of his arse. She noticed that he was wearing
a green gansey of George's. Jim was wearing a pair of her son's
socks. Margaret was in a shirt of Jim's. We are all going around
wearing each other's clothes, she thought.

On an impulse she ran into the house and up the stairs. She
picked out a scarf she kept ready for a trip to the city. It had a
quaint green and gold design like the kind her mother used to
wear. "Please," she asked, "try it on." Obediently, Margaret got
up from the kitchen table. Helen tied the scarf tight about the
girl's hair. "Now look," she said approvingly. Out of compassion
and egotism Margaret peeped into the shaving mirror.

She loosened the scarf a little so that her hair could fall
down.

"Now do you see," continued Helen, "you have nothing to
be afraid of. You are beautiful."

But Margaret closed her eyes. She closed her eyes tighter
and it began again. An embryo tottered past in the darkness.
It grew. A jellyfish passed. A shape arrived. Flesh steadily grew
on the bones. She was remaining in life. The child cannot
stop growing. The world around continued unabated. The
shape grew and grew. Suddenly the hair of this creature fell
down. One day she can see it, the child is herself.

Startled, she opened her eyes and her reflection swam into

view, and behind her, Helen, with wide anticipating eyes.

"See, what did I tell you," said Helen tentatively.

Margaret's stomach turned. For one brief instant she saw the world through the other woman's eyes.

The utter loneliness. The long sharp veer of the senses into eternal night. The thin shape of Helen's shoulders and how she drew the smoke from her cigarette into a ball and sucked it down. Then blew it out on a tight rein. The nervous way she sat. Always on the verge of saying something that might explain away the endless repetitions. How fearing to hurt another you tell them endless lies. Margaret halted before the revelation that anything honest she might say would be misinterpreted by the woman opposite her.

"You should dicky yourself up, Helen," said Margaret, "you should."

So, dispassionately, they trod water. Helen thought of her head like a lighthouse directing strangers through the night, and underneath, this colossal empty place of light, the stiff shape of her body that could never be lit up again. She was emotionless. That morning she had seen a famished greyhound trotting down a country lane. That was her in the here and now. Then there was the ceiling lath down in the shed. A white cat that suddenly jumped in the air to play with a twig overhead. And not forgetting a sprig of hawthorn in a stranger's hat, the exact knavish movement of the hand that had put it there. Through a world of sympathy her senses moved. "I'll have to put on my face," said Helen. It was Saturday night. The cars trundled across the ramps at the bridge towards the darker lights in the South and the longer opening hours.

18

In a period of five weeks three Protestant families were left fatherless in the area. As one of the funeral corteges passed on the TV the Protestant men in the lower bar took off their caps. In the Catholic pub there was that dreadful silence too. Old values had become flagships. What power the people had conceded to the politicians had become corrupted. The politicians had drawn back from the common herd. Their revulsion spilled over into rationalism. Their laws became a means of protecting themselves from the people. The next night the soldiers took Frank Allen away again. He was white with fear. All night they grilled him as to George's whereabouts. "He's fishing South, I say. He's in the South on one of the boats, I'm telling you." They did not search the house, but there was talk that the police were trying to track down the stuff stolen from the plant on the mountain, so next morning Helen dispatched Jim to tell his father what had taken place. He took letters with him from them all. He walked up the leafy roads hearing from the isolated houses the morning programmes on the radio. Later in the day the announcer's voice sharpened with an appetite for dinner. No car would stop for Jim. Murder was in the air. Sheep clambered down the gorse hills each side of the road to watch him pass. They lifted their heads to see if he meant danger, then went back to tugging the coarse grass. The road was endless and straight. He strode out the thirteen miles to the sea. He passed parked cars where people were picnicking. The sea was alive with the sound of engines and pools of oil floated up against the pier. He sat near the ice boxes till the trawlers might come in. One man said they would be in by six, another said seven. He walked the beach over and over, hating for the first time in his life the very sight of the choppy sea saying the same thing over and over. The sea had no knowledge for him that day. The port was humourless and uncertain. Night fell and the floodlights came on, so that where he was sitting on the pier appeared distant from the land behind, like he was anchored forever waiting on his father. The first trawlers came through the mist. Last of all The Silver Spear tied up, the sixth of all out of the stormy bay. Jim jumped across the boats.

"Blessed God," said George.

When he embraced his son it was everywhere, the reek of fish and the scrubbed deck. And oil. "So that's the story," said George. He read the letters and then had a few words with the skipper of the boat. That night they all travelled by van to the South side of the lakes, then the trek across the river on Jim's boat to the village in the North. Through the drifting islands, marvelling at all they saw. Turkeys screeching. The hooting pigeons. The skipper, George and Jim entered the house in silence. They brought up the stolen material from the basement where Pop in his book ticked off each item. Helen kept watch at the front of the house with Margaret. Frank Allen took the planks down the garden. Joseph stacked them by the boat. Jim lifted them in. Laughing, the men carried down the suits of clothes. "C'mon and eat," said Helen.

When George sat down at his own table he could scarcely contain himself in front of the men.

"I'm working now with Davidson's," said Frank proudly. "There's a bus comes through to pick us up."

"We've had a good season with the herring," the soft-cheeked skipper said. "There's no use in complaining."

"Davidson's is all right," said George, "but the hours are long."

"There's no use in complaining," repeated the skipper, "when you have a job to do. But I won't go back to slaving for the stranger."

"You take what you get now."

"Still I'd find it hard to leave this house behind me," the skipper went on.

"When we get the co-operatives going," said George, "we'll get the houses."

"Well," said the skipper to Helen, "I'm sorry that you are spoken for. You are a wonderful lady." They made hot whiskey with lemon and cloves and honey. Soon they were released from their protective things. They wore the coats of people happier than they. More drink. Guilty people are the most disloyal when drink is taken. And fearful people are the quickest to betray. Now that she was leaving Frank her love for him returned with one last spirited cry. The men were a little drunk and admitted many things, withdrew sufficient to allow the other personality in. The skipper was talking of his wife. He was rambling on.

The others grew restless.

"Well," said the skipper, scanning the table, "are you right, George? Have you got everything you want?"

"Yes," said George. "That's it, now."

And after tidying up the affairs of the world they were all beset by a terrible depression. A sense of lying or not trying hard enough. Jim delivered the fishermen to the South. They drove back in the van to the bay. The other fishermen on the trawler came up on deck. They let go the ropes and went off into the dark, calling back their destinations and their actions to each other. There was no need. They knew their job by heart. But they kept up this sense of shared responsibility till they were out of sight, so that they might journey well together, that each man answer to himself for the safety of them all.

IV

19

He licks the back of his hand. Edges the cap forward like an ear over his forehead, then leans downward with his big laughing claw on the head, then the shoulder of the boy. The soft rustle of material down the bar as a woman sits. His hands, like root plants, wringing the earth out of each other.

"Do you know what it is?" he whispers. "Aye. I'd sell a cow, one or two, oh yes. You are in a hurry there."

"And a big cow I might, you know. Ah, this twenty years. Aye."

A woman's clear ethereal air. Like gossamer spun around an elusive human being. High heels and jeans and a slipped button in her blouse, and the snug nipples at ease, swaying gently. Her hands each side of her head. She claps them in front of her face. The thought of it! Aye. She gave a clear watchful gaze, unconsciously she touched her neck. "He was the luckiest man that ever was," someone said.

A farmer surveyed the town, fist on hip, fag in the other hand, head looking down. He saluted a woman with a large brooch on the lapel of her coat. Another woman stepped out of a shop. A sloppy white suit. Artificially curled hair gone lustreless. Full of cheerful talk. Trousers tight round the shins. Little red heels peeping over white shoes of medium height. Up went the finger of the farmer in the air. His hat fell so far forward that he had to swing his head back to look out.

"Good luck, now," he said.

A trailer with a sick calf pulled up. The farmer held her mouth open. The vet entered the trailer carefully. He looked through the fretting full lips into that huge pink and white-toothed throat. "That's right." The bloated sound of the border speech. "It's got cauld again." In spite of this the farmer rose an ice-cream cone to his mouth. Then passed a green lorry of Canada Dry. "I could only see it the other night by the light of a match," said the farmer. The injection only took a second, and the calf tried lunging for the street. With his tongue out the calf was thrown back into the trailer, the spring door hoisted and the bolts shot. In seconds the farmer was away. The vet squirted the remains of the syringe into a manhole. The blue and red tractors passed. Leyland and Ferguson. The echo of the auctioneers' voices. The farmers from the mart returned to the hotel. A woman was at the bar ordering. Toe turned round the heel of the other shoe. Little black socks. A green canvas bag. She paid up and left, despising all those who had mated with the lesser part of themselves. In drink they could shout "Up the IRA," sober they were terrified at this weakness in themselves.

These were Frank's prejudices. He remembered with a start all the lies he used to tell down South, to further himself in their eyes. And the status they gave him that he did not want. At moments of despair our paths cross. He is the better for it. He would carry me off if he could. He is life itself. Here before me. Here after me. He is my love who would join me. He plants trees. I burn them. I argue. He's silent. He had been there before. For one sweet moment I have not. We meet. He hands the burden on. It is you bearing down. The other. The other person I recognize weakly. The other person passing through. Then myself arriving. Helen. Helen. We exchange signals and go on. The other bears me out into the world. I try to say or give my appreciation but know, meanwhile, that I have missed somebody. Somebody has gone ahead into the night. He has travelled in me before. Death and its tributaries. Well, then, Aye.

"Christ, but you women have big appetites," said Pop to Helen. He had taken a brisk trot into his second childhood that winter. Today he had come upon himself as a child huddled up in the corner of a vast place of Evilness. "The old bastard is at it again," he said, hearing Peter singing as he went up the road:

Do you remember the other night
It was in the ale-house drinking
You drank the health of each fair lass
And slighted Barbara Allen

Oh well I remember the other night
It was in the ale-house drinking
I drank the health of each fair lass
And good luck to Barbara Allen.

"Every evening that man is starting anew," nodded Pop. He stood by the door of the basement. Helen thought he looked like a stuffed doll. "I was thinking," he said, "that all the women in the village are set to outlive me." He went down to his room. The night was getting on. Frank and Joseph were off at the mart. Helen was alone in the house except for the old man. She sucked in her walnut cheeks, gathered her hands, dropped her chin a little and let go of what was around her. A while later she thought she heard someone in the hall. But that couldn't be. She started scrubbing down the table. Then a loud knocking began so sharp it startled her. She turned into the hallway. She was wondering was it Peter looking for a night's lodgings. She tripped, and could not stop herself falling.

The pain in her ankle was so bad that it sickened her. She prayed for the knocking to stop. The knocking was making the pain an extended thing that worked its way in waves along her leg.

Whoever they were, they went away.

There was only herself in the airless house. Before her eyes the ankle ballooned. She worked her way along the floor to the basement door and called out. There was no answer. The curse of God on the auld bastard. She lifted one of the wellingtons parked there and hammered. Then sat cursing her fate. These voices came into her head that she could not identify. Then there was silence. All of a sudden the door came crashing in and three soldiers threw themselves into the hall with their guns raised.

"Where is he?" they shouted.

"I've injured myself," Helen said.

They looked down at her.

"We've come to search the house, Ma'am," one said.

The others stepped by her into the kitchen.

"Are you deaf?" she shouted. "I've hurt myself."

"You had better get up from there," he advised.

"I've lost the power of my leg."

"Stay there, then, if you must."

"Come out of the kitchen. Come down these stairs."

"It's best not to worry yourself."

"We'll just be a minute now," came a voice from above, "don't fret yourself."

They were carefully pulling everything apart. The beds were hauled across the floors. The cutlery slapped onto the tiles. They pulled the wardrobes away from the walls.

"Please, please help me."

"The less you say, Ma'am, the sooner this will be over."

Helen could hear the folded sheets tossed aside. She heard them lift the pictures off the wall. Then they met again in the hall.

"There is nothing above," said the first.

"Nothing down here either," said the second.

They both looked over at the basement door against which Helen lay.

"Now, Ma'am," says the first, "we'll have to move you."

"I think," she told them, "that I've broke my leg."

"C'mon now, Mrs."

"We'll have to lift you," the young one snapped.

Without warning they lifted her clear off the floor. Behind her the door opened and Pop emerged in his pyjamas. "By

Christ," he shouted. "It's all right," Helen screamed, "it's all right, Pop." They took him easily by the arms. "Leave down that woman," he shouted. "It's me you have to deal with here." They laughed at each other. Exasperated, Pop kicked out and the last thing Helen could remember as the pain took her away was the little old man pinned to the wall, a rag doll, while she floated over his head, protesting.

For a long time she lay not knowing where she was and trying still to calm Pop. But gradually she realized that Pop was nowhere about. She found that she was in a bed, but not at home. Then looking over the side of the bed she saw Frank asleep on the floor, his head cupped in his hand, and a blanket fallen to his waist. "Bless us," she thought. "What's this?"

"Frank," she whispered, "get up immediately and get in here."

But Frank did not move. He had all his clothes on him. She tried to get up and found a great weight tugging at her body. Looking down she saw her leg, like a thing belonging to someone else, was set in plaster and hanging in the air. And beyond her other beds, some occupied and each in semi-darkness, and a sleeping man in every bed.

"Frank," she hissed, "Frank!"

The years came flying back.

"Oh God, Frank!"

The petals, the roses. Yards of clean sheets. The maniacs in the garden. The white soap. The womb soaped. The groin plucked like a turkey. The aluminium pots, I know them all from before, she thought, but not the men that she saw through the slit of the curtain moving by in their striped pyjamas. Who were they all, she wondered. "What's your name," she was asked. The face was gentle and close. But Helen was impatient. "I don't know, I'm sure," she said. "Now don't be cross," said the voice.

"Who is that on the floor?"

"Oh, him. That's poor Frank. Frank Allen."

"So, now," said the nurse, "you are back in the land of the living."

Then slowly it all came back to Helen.

Like a stranger, who coming closer becomes someone you once knew.

The next time she awoke Frank was sitting by the bed holding her hand.

"How are you, Helen?" he asked.

"Could you explain," she said, "what am I doing in here in the men's ward?"

"The women's ward was full," he explained ginning. "It seems there are more sick women than men."

"I'm not a bit surprised."

"I feel a terror that you should have been there alone."

Helen squeezed his hand. "Don't mind me," she said, "I just like complaining."

He lit a cigarette and cupped it in his shaking hands. "My father is down the village creating hell!" he said as they wheeled her towards the lift. "Poor Pop," she said, "he forgets what age he is." The gates rolled back, and Helen was taken to a ward that contained her own kind, the women and the children, and Lord if she wasn't sorry not to be back among the men and their arse-fallen misery because everything in the women's ward was at high D.

"Good healthy place, the hospital," said Frank.

"God bless us," said Helen.

Oh you, she thought, Christ but you are innocent, even in your tyranny. And the more innocent you are, the more tyrannical you become. Frank threw one leg over the other and wondered what Helen was thinking about. A child went by holding the hand of its mother.

Day two. Helen saw a flood of sunlight cross the ward. Bright decked clothes came into view. American orange crimplene that a body would not be seen in. It gave Helen the shivers. Worst of all were the faded nightdresses of brushed nylon. And then the bright blue polyester slips. If Frank could have stopped his search for lost souls our life would have been different, she reckoned, but no matter. She heard the women in the urinals piss like mares. They argued constantly over the toilets and the baths, while the young mothers, stitched and war-weary, struggled, leaning on the bed rests, as they made their way up the ward. They looked for the lie in the eyes of the older women. Visitors came, crazed demons from the outside. Most of them afraid to keep their eyes on the one they had come to see. Then a few minutes before the bell, the reconciliation. It was the sick relieving them of their miserable consciousness of what lay beyond the doors. And Helen could only relax when Frank stretched out like an islander on his blanket on the floor beside her and talked quietly up in whispers of this and that. The nurse had allowed him one more night in the ward. Someone by the door opened an orange and down the dark ward the smell drifted through the medical odour of arrested life. She listened to the sound of cars coming down the main road at intervals through the spaces of the houses, then flying past the junction at the bottom of the hospital where the engines raced and rasped, they climaxed, then fell away quickly, their coming more momentous than their going. And from her leg, trapped and bloodless in the cold plaster, there came no feeling and she prayed that Frank would not stop talking, even though there were gaps between his words that her mind could not fill. Taking the broad energetic steps of a sportsman, the house doctor, in his white coat and leather sandals, strolled down the ward.

Day three. A small woman in a long fluffy nightgown pulled up a chair by Helen's bed.

"I might not look it," she explained with warm clear eyes, "but I'm dying."

"I'm terribly sorry to hear that," Helen said.

"You look like a woman of good spirits," she announced, "so," she opened her legs and cuffed her knees, "I chose you."

"I'm glad," Helen answered.

"Kathy will be along in a minute," she intimated secretively with a finger to her eyelid, and sat back.

So they waited. She would have no small talk. Soon, one of the young mothers, a seabird, with her nightdress pinned across her breasts, flopped down on Helen's bed. "Give me a minute till I gather my wits," said the woman who was going to die. Helen searched her face and body but could find no sign. The woman shook some pills out of an envelope onto the bedspread, then began sorting them out, meanwhile keeping an eye out for the nurses.

"Two for you, and two for you," she chuckled.

Helen looked at the pills and didn't know what to say.

"They are the strongest you can get," she winked.

Kathy produced three glasses of Lucozade and on the spot they drank the three lots down.

"I get more than I need," said the woman. "My name is Maggie Flood."

"Sometimes," Kathy leaned towards Helen, "they stick in your throat." She shook her head up and down.

They waited for someone to pass over. The curtains grew rather large. The other women looked into mirrors propped up on their sideboards. They squeezed out blackheads. Else they seemed to be continually putting something away. A minute sitting with their hands joined. Then out came everything again. They were all quite happy and big-boned. A window was open. They looked down through their fingers onto the city. Older women felt their way along the beds. Freckles and white flesh. So much red hair. So many pink gowns. The feeling came and went. Came and went and stayed.

Would Maggie Flood have anything to say about this?

"It's weakening," said Helen.

"What," asked Kathy, "goes up the chimney down and down the chimney up?"

"A stud," Helen recalled, "in a man's boot."

The two roared laughing at the childishness of it all.

"What," Helen went on, "goes over the water, under the water, and still, mark you, never touches the water?"

"A negg. A negg." Kathy turned crimson with laughter. "Christ help me, an egg in a duck's arse."

The tears flew from their eyes.

"Oh Jesus," stuttered Kathy, "don't say another word."

"I was sitting in the chair by the fire dozing off," said Maggie, "with the auld bowsy relaxing opposite in his stockinged feet. Didn't my gammy leg take off its own accord and hit the cat. Up she got and took a couple of turns around the room. And next, lo and behold, you took a bite out of your man's big toe. 'What are you laughing at?' he shouts. 'You woke that cat out of a bad dream.'"

The eyes of the rest of the ward were upon the three hysterical women.

"He recovered," said Maggie undeterred, "soon after through the aid of his own beliefs."

Day seven. Out of a sense of forever falling in love with the passing trade, to be irritated by them later, Helen, while the other women talked of their lovers and husbands, kept her thoughts of men to herself. Not because of failed relationships, no. But she thought her own needs came uppermost now. Put there in the hospital through violence, she was enjoying herself. Sometimes there were long moments of pure ecstasy when she did not care if she never saw the house in Fanacross again. Someday she wanted to move over the bridge, go South for good. Yes, and if it catches up with me there, well then, move on again. She was floating a little. The housedoctor spoke to her. He lowered his loud voice somewhat as he heard the hesitant reply. Seconds later he had forgotten and the boom in his voice returned. He dipped. And so the rhythm of his speech took on this artificial pattern, redeemed now and then by unexpected allusions to his own personal and domestic life.

Helen knew a secret of his.

A woman who came from the same part of the country as him, explained as she lolled in her bed that the doctor, though son of a schoolmaster and schoolmistress, went always the road in his bare feet. "He had a terrible appetite," she said, sucking her teeth fretfully, "for snails." "There must have been something lacking," nodded an older woman. "God," said someone else. "In fact," came the joyful reply, "he loved snails."

Now as the housedoctor leaned to address Helen again she felt she was looking into the face of someone who knew one of the secrets of life, and pretending to a slight cold, she tried to sniff him in entirely. Out came the familiar smell of well-read books. Something austere. Yet he knew, she felt, the erotica of little things. She lost what he was saying. Just nodded away. His hand was on the small of her back. "Excuse me," she asked, "what did you say? My mind was wandering." Then in the silence she summoned up her courage.

"Did you ever, excuse me for asking, eat snails?"

An age passed. He lowered her back into the bed. "That's enough of that," he said, in his quieter voice. He shook his head forlornly as if his childhood had even been a mystery to himself. He turned on his heel and walked authoritatively out of the ward. "Yes," said the woman, "he'd lift them out of the ditch or off the road and suck them straight into his mouth. Mad alive, I tell you." "I ask you," said her confidante.

Why, Helen wondered, did he not admit to it?

What held him back?

She returned by train alone, nor did she tell anyone she would be coming that day for she wanted this sense of happiness to last right up till the last minute. The river was warm and covered by

May blossom, the chestnut trees were filled with long candles. Deeper still, red blossom among the unnamed shadows. Everything was so strange. She was thinking that sentiment and truth would always be at odds in the house above. Bless us, she thought, the smell of the countryside. It was nearly impossible to breathe. The rancour of returning to the known was lessened. Everything she had forgotten was filling out before her very eyes. No bitterness now, she said to herself.

She did not lift her eyes to look at the house in case somehow it might not be there.

Getting up her courage she knocked.

Through the glass door she saw this dwarfed image of herself fumbling to undo the lock. It was unnerving. When the door swung open there was Pop, his legs in plaster, crutches like hers under his armpits, and a great deal of merriment on his face. "God, Pop," said Helen. "I slipped myself," he explained, "crossing the fucking yard."

20

The visitor and Helen walked down the village to meet Frank's bus. The countryside around had found another reason for war, and when that war of nationhood was finished, the real war about things more dear than territory would begin. A group from the Workers' Party were drunk outside the *café*, their mouths and minds too full of sour indigestible things for the villagers to understand. All week they had been trying to prompt the people towards their candidate. They worked their way from door to door, getting nowhere. All the people's history was dead, and what was this but an attempt to bring it to life again through a people afraid of starting over?

The bus went over the mountains, disappeared and came into view again, its creamy roof battered by the constant elements.

The men climbed out with their cloth bags, stood around to get their bearings, then trudged off.

Frank Allen, glassy-eyed from lack of sleep, stepped down.

The bus, flooding the divided village with black exhaust fumes, turned again for the mountains.

"I'm glad that's over," said Frank.

Cheerfully they went up the lone road that was cleaned out again and again by the lake winds. Past shuddering doors strung between gate posts. The cold air tapped on their lungs, and suddenly the first lightning struck the mountain at the same time as the echoing thunder, and finding no entry there, it flew across the surface of the lake like a ball.

They were talking within of the Cove Hotel and Mama and Manager Tom, Frank's brother. Frank and Helen exaggerated the stories for the visitor. As each ideal was accomplished, another began before his very eyes. "They're made up for life," said Helen. She stripped the pike of its bones, beat the pan off the stove then turned to taste the soup.

"The rooms up there," said Frank, "are big as houses."

"Trottin' but they are," said Helen, "and the sheets changed every day as if a body never slept between them."

"Sleep," said Frank, shaking his head, "blessed sleep."

"Up there you'd swear," Helen stopped what she was doing, "you'd swear the beds had wings."

The visitor, one hand cupping his knee, whistled. He hung on, not wanting to breach the cold night, yet never spoke. The pair were in their element. When someone came through the front door, the back flew open. The visitor rose to close the back door with a nod, a look across the howling earth, a sigh, then back again. The children piled up by the fire. A hen sailed past the window. Dinner came.

The visitor held up his hand.

"No, thanks," he said.

"Just a spud, then," he acquiesced.

From the minute the plate was placed on his lap, his hands and mouth worked greedily. Each time he lifted the fork to his face, he glanced across with the mad look of someone who knew some secret. Accepting more food onto his plate, he shook his head like a simpleton. The knife came up with a piece of spud, while the fork gathered up the turnip. His eyes clouded over with satisfaction. A chunk of butter and a sliver of fish he spooned in. A piece of potato next and following it, a knob of butter straight into his mouth. A dazed look came over him. He halted. Worry lines gathered across his temple. On. He fought to get the food down before it was taken away. All the time these sudden darting glances across at Margaret. Then Jim. His eyes became mere slits from the strain of eating. The last morsel he chewed. It disappeared. The visitor relaxed. His punishment was over. "Good luck now," he mumbled, gathered his coat about him, and left. It was the height of the storm. As he pulled the door after him, the back door flew open. "You can smell that man throughout the house," Helen said.

Frank rose at seven in the cold house and told Helen to lie on. He stood on the step to see the cast of the sky. The last anger of the storm was pummelling the lake beyond. The smell of ashes drifted out. He shaved over a basin on the window sill. His buttered bread and dry boiled bacon waited on the mantelpiece. He pulled on his warm solid boots, then stood at the bottom of the stairs listening. When they heard the drop of the backdoor latch, each of them upstairs turned in bed, hearing the lake breathe more slowly and furiously than themselves.

A south-east wind blew sharply across the toppled trees.

The cruisers in the marina slewed against each other.

Debris from the storm had reached the village street.

He stood along with the other men waiting out of the wind by the high blue wall of the lower pub. Everyone stood

in tight against the wall. The wind had made their throats
hoarse. Overhead the Guinness sign swung round its bar.
The men shifted from foot to foot waiting. They watched the
mountain road for the bus. Latecomers bent forward with
their hands on their thighs trying to get their breath. Soon the
men settled down on their hunkers, though some still stood,
smoking and looking idly toward the hurrying mists.

"The big spruce is down, I see," said a tall village man.

"And brought the paling with it, too, as well," said another.

The clock swung to eight. A pregnant woman passed.
Peter the musician, back from his journeying, stepped down
out of the creamery lorry. A peacock's feather pinned to
his woollen cap. Woollen socks drawn up over his trousers
to the knee. But their bus did not come. The men became
uneasy, as if what they had wished for had happened much
too soon. Other sounds began which told them that the day
was passing. Hill carts, with the blinkered asses blinded by the
wind, came down, the farmers shielded by sacks on the low
boards. "What, are you here still?" one of them shouted over.
They answered with a scolding look. The reply was carried
off by the wind. Next came the schoolchildren to find their
fathers slinging coins against the blue wall, or eating the
sandwiches that were supposed to do them at noon. "Go on,
go on, g'on, up the road with you," the men shouted. The
wind never slackened. The wires strummed. And some said
maybe there had been some damage done. That's it, others
thought, the road is down somewhere. The roof's come in.

"They'll send us word," they nodded.

At ten the first pub opened. The rattle of sieves and bread
graters crossed the road. The first man entered just for one.
The river thundered through the back window. The others
followed for the warmth. The first drink meant different
things to different men. Their big boots made no sound on
the rolling floor. Most drank Cidona. "You could turn on
yon fire," the drinkers told the girl. "Hauld your whist," said

McEvoy. "The fire will be lit soon enough."

He came in with dripping timber.

"Let's break from here!" someone said.

They trooped across the road.

"Did any of you phone ahead?" McTaggart asked as he mopped up. "We did," the men replied. "It must be that the lines are down."

"The whole fucking world can't have stopped turning."

"You are right there."

"But give it time."

The trade union representative arrived by car. The tale was told to him through the driver's window. He headed off directly to Davidson's. The workers strayed across to McEvoy's and stayed. They stole through the shadows with their drink, going back on rumours they'd heard before that morning. With each car that stopped on the street they left down their glasses. The car passed on. They drank. The wind against the blue wall died down. They opened up a game of twenty-five. "Money," said McEvoy, "has always been in short supply." "You are not suffering anyway," they answered him. "Spades trumps," someone called. "Where were you yesterday morning and the morning before?" the publican asked. "Don't tell me, I know."

"Never mind the mornings, what about the nights?" the dealer chuckled.

"The nights?" McEvoy pulled up his loose trousers and blew through his lips. "The nights? It doesn't pay me to open the door."

Joseph's father took him a stool by the blackened pipe of the stove. He pitched Power's whiskey into his mouth.

The only man of the other faith stood by the bar.

Three of the younger workers started to rile him. "Davidson will have you back," they said. The man said nothing. Said Micko, "McEvoy should intervene." The snivelling abuse continued from these lads who never turned their face to look at the Protestant man they were addressing but spoke their blunt taunts across their empty glasses. The others became quiet. Again old Micko said to Frank, "McEvoy should intervene." Said one of the three lads to the man on his own, "You should have your arse horse-whipped, you black bastard."

The man jumped to his feet.

"C'mon outside the three of you," he said hoarsely.

They didn't move.

"Do you want us to kill you?" one of the lads said. The other two laughed.

The man went out with one long lonesome look around the bar.

"Water off a duck's back," said Micko tipping the Guinness into the red lane of his mouth. "But still, McEvoy should have intervened."

"I had got the measure of that job," Frank told his companion. "I said to myself, this is grand. I'll stop here."

"You'd stop there surely."

"It gave me order. I could order my life about it."

"I don't know about that," Micko McGovern shook his head.

"Now," asked Frank, "What's going to happen, heh?"

"I'm not too sure about that sort of thing," again Micko said.

Around them, three schools of cards were in full swing. Matches counted the tricks. The fire took with the roar of a sea lion.

It was true. The car came back. There was no case to fight for every man had signed on temporarily. For the workers it was like they were returning to things they knew better. They were accustomed to having to fill in their days. Prosperity was a strange and dangerous land from which they had again been rescued. Some left the pub as their money ran out or the women came down for them. Frank stopped a while with Helen in the snug, the weak wintry sun on their faces. He lost track of time after she left. He wondered why his mind would go no further than Davidson's had ordained. Your contract was always temporary. The builders' poppies. And the closed factories. Whatever possible had been tried, they said. American factories swooped down like B40s in the open country. They trekked in, they trekked out. The engines roared. After a few years the planes quit the land, leaving their skeletons behind. Then came the German planes. The Dutch. The huge bombers of the British that needed massive runways to take off with all the grants on board. Aye! The security men kick football down the empty factory floor. The perished goods sold off on a bleak day in January. Fair carpets for the front room. The spin dryer that nearly rocked through the floor of the scullery. Shaking in its corner to a life of its own, and spinning within, a woman's blouse and a kitchen towel.

Frank remembered the faulty light in the hall.

"Are you all right, Boss?"

"I'm all right, McEvoy."

Now on the floorboards that ran to a hollow in the centre of the pub Frank Allen got up a flow of mucus and tears. This was no way to carry on, he knew. Soon as it started it stopped. But nobody around him seemed to have noticed. Who was I a minute ago? Had he cried at all? Too stubborn even for that. Had it happened inside him? He felt his eyes, but they were dry and small. His nose was stiff. He blew his nose into a freshly washed handkerchief but nothing came.

If blood had come I would have been satisfied, aye.

Drink doesn't suit me, he thought.

I make a mockery of other men who feel deeper than me. I imitate their repeating woes. Blood from the nose is the smallest of sacrifices. Aye. Shape up, Frank Allen. Against poverty there are great bulwarks. He made for the toilet. A massive concrete bowl sunk into the floor and around it copper urinals from which water sprinkled. Through the window he saw the army moving across the fields guided from above by a helicopter. "I should not have let the job get to me," he said. Never place your trust so deeply, Frank Allen. Men are too selfish in their need for security. The boat people were checking the cruisers for harm from the storm. The fishermen lifted the planks from behind to the fore as they drew their boats up over the rough shingle. Rain spat through the unglassed lead window onto his collarless shirt. The stiff veins of his neck stood out. He leaned forward.

"Anything strange?" the auld fellow asked. Frank shook his head. The auld fellow pulled back his elasticated cap.

"Brave day," he said.

"Aye."

21

The people were back at the lake's edge after the land failed. But the mist spread round them with the great gift of forgetfulness.

What the politicians said was fantasy, till another day came with good news.

The Council would be laying a new road from the mountain.

When they left the barracks after signing on, the men trooped down to the newly constructed Council yard. They watched the building up of materials and machines. This was an EEC job, no

less. The village woke to lorries drenching the edges of the roads with piles of gravel. Road engineers took sightings across isolated places known only to the Maguires and the McGaurans. The larks in the crannies looked back at them. The contractor at last arrived, a bear of a man who appeared in a different place each day, running the gravel through his fingers.

"I want men that can stomach work," he told Frank Allen.

"I'm with you," Frank replied.

"Is that so?"

"I can handle mud."

"Youse are fierce fond of the dole round here."

"We have no choice."

"Come down, then, of a Monday morning."

With criminal forbearance they broke the rock. After the tar had been spread, the men shovelled out the gravel and then along came the steamroller. The macadam men drank tea with their wives in the caravans. Their children urinated behind the bushes. The tar hissed and buckled, then went smooth as damp sand. Every day was filled with the sound of gravel and shingle being panned by the men and the lakes. Then the great weight of the roller bearing down the steep fall into the valley.

At the end of each day the new road met the old that was forever diminishing. You stepped from one world into another when you crossed the line of moist tar and found picks and shovels on the roadway. The black carcass of the grid where the tar was fired. The two pubs made up for life. More ordinary things were afoot then crying out for tragedy. Sheds of galvanize erected for no purpose at all. The small of Frank Allen's back drilled tight with pain. His head putting untold sums away. Counting in pounds the stretch to the village. No one complained. The tarmacadam men moved ahead on knees protected by rubber pads across the boiling tar, flattening each side of them with a trowel. And as the road came nearer the village men worked slower, arguments arose and the contractor, having gained good time at the beginning, let them prolong the moment before the work would be concluded.

They had plenty of time to think about whatever could

distract them.

What did it matter if they celebrated on Friday nights?

To be guilty of what had not yet happened? To never know the days you were living through?

So when the women went up with cans of tea to the mountains getting closer every day they saw this work lasting forever and when the blasting of rock began the village arrived to applaud each blow of the powder against the limestone, as if a monument were being erected in their likeness, forts fell, the foundations of the new road were heaved down from the old goat road above. Sky goats circled them. The workers threw the heavily gravelled cement over their backs without looking behind so that they might well have been filling a fathomless hole. Stakes were driven into the cliff to hold the tar that came after. There was scorched flesh and bitterness. The new world was within their reach.

The tired men cursed the boulders ahead.

Thus through this mindless satisfying work their fortunes were restored.

The road reached the outskirts of the village in October. In fact it missed out the village altogether. The men had built a road to divert the traffic away from it. Come the wind from the Curlews, the men idle again.

22

It came Jim's turn to go. He walked the same long road from the village to the sea he had gone before. The trawlers were tied tight for the early morning burst to sea. A woman accosted him on the pier. She was arguing with a fisherman who was walking ahead of her.

"See, no matter what you say," she pointed after her man.

"See, that's where he was leaning just last night."

The fisherman stopped. "That there woman is just fading

away," he spoke back. The sea shifted like old village ivy
against the prows of the boats. The two went off down the
pier. Jim could see no sign of The Silver Spear. He sat on
an old barrel there. The fishermen were coming up from the
pubs, he enquired of each for a job, till a man from Swords
in Dublin told him there was a half-share on The Swallow.
He climbed down the oily ladder. The men were frying up
flat fish and beans and then dropping asleep against a wall
of waves for a few hours till speechless with tiredness in the
cold dawn the ropes were loosened, the ship headed off, the
radio opened up. A man there ruddy with whiskey opened
the door into the new engine. They were astonished how
she shone in the torchlight, hardly touched, gleaming gold
and bronze, costing twelve shares, full of sudden stops and
frights, jarring sounds that the fishermen had learned in
time to accommodate in their sleep. Jim chose a bunk above
Maurice Caulfield. The sea went over and back, hollow and
full, water into wood. He smoked in the darkness, thinking
back. When he awoke the men had already started to loosen
the ropes to the pier. The sultry waters were churning deep
under the trawlers. Oil was burning across the morning. A
forest of yellow and blue cranes. Boats wheeling out each side
of The Swallow, their lights flashing. As Jim began doing what
he was told the roar of the engine began with a new resolve,
the boat was filled with the crash of bars and the drumming
of discs. Roaring between his hands to someone on the pier,
Maurice Caulfield stood up to hear the yell in answer. Seconds
later it arrived through the swerving winds. "You fucker you."

First the sky darkened, she lit up, darkened again and the
town fell into their wake like a dangerous sleeping planet.
The trawler pulled over the sluggish water. They let the gear
go. The men worked without speaking. The boat shuddered
underfoot, drawing away from all those unknown ventures
on land. Galvanize sheds, railway buildings. Wrecked busted

trawlers whose names were once chosen with care. Against the nervous rattle of timber and steel the boat turned about, pivoting in the depths.

The town swung astern.

"Take her east," the skipper called.

"There won't be a fucking thing there," the wheelman called.

"You'll not see a sardine where you are going."

"Go down the fucking stairs. You are always on."

"Let the fucking thing go then."

The net went in a straight line ahead. The shot grasped the waves and ploughed behind them as she dropped, the chains jarring against the iron knots. The boat stopped in her flight. The winch let the tickler to the ocean floor. The deep strain of the drag began.

Said the radio: "We shot the net at four, wheeled to the east, took her in early, went up to the hotel for a dance, stopped all night with Dealer and the girls and went to bed no more." Said Maurice Caulfield: "The knife and the knuckle. I use my knuckles. I'd cry if I saw a fellow coming at me with a knife. I broke down like a baby in Lawlor's a few Saturdays ago to a man with a knife." He shook his head. "That's not the way to enjoy yourself." Said Old Caulfield, his hands resting on his paunch on one of the forms in the cabin, a beret pulled over his eyes: "Your man the skipper is using good money for ballast." Said the islander who rarely spoke: "It takes me a long time to get home. It takes three to four hours to the city, then four hours more down South, then two hours by bus, two and a half hours out in the canoe if the sea is right, and I will have one day with my mother *is m'athair rúin*, and then leave at seven in the evening to make the same journey back to the mainland, and that all means getting my brother out for the right turn of the tide, and he mightn't like that one bit, for you can never tell by him." Hours later after a

strange sleep they hauled in. This one was different than all
the rest. This one was heavy. As the net mounted the whole
boat keeled to the right, they hung sideways as the winch
screamed, and at last the first bag swung in, delivered up from
the ground of the sea. The knot was untied by the islander
and the belly burst with thousands of prawns. Whiting
spilled. The blue flash of a mackerel. Crabs. Layers of dark
mud and seaweed. They hauled again. The skipper's eyes went
back in his head. The boat circled the drop but would not
deliver. The men went up with ropes. They drew laboriously
but still the winch would not take the second load. "Pull for
fuck's sake," shouted Maurice. "Take the wheel," shouted the
skipper to Old Caulfield. They fell towards the unsteadying
sea. And this time the second bag came out of the depths and
her belly opened. "Would you fight a man at all?" Maurice
roared at Jim. The last load was golden with prawns. Their
tails uncoiling, their yellow tails floundering helplessly. The
net, heavy with mud was again cast overboard and the skipper
steered away from the drop. They coasted, turned and tied.
A steady run. Then fell where they were till the islander
called them down for breakfast. After that the tailing of the
prawns began. They sat on plastic crates snapping the prawns
in half as they lunged at the fishermen's gloves. They flicked
the lopped heads and claws aside. Under them the boat filled
with draughts of the sea. The refrain "A casual encounter, a
casual encounter" began. What Jim wanted, what they all
wanted, was to lie back, let their arms hang and then to listen
to the seagulls tucked into the rain overhead, and feel below
the endless traffic of shells, stones and fish.

And the next day, and the next day they were on the deck at
dawn, grudging for want of sleep, letting the nets go without
a word. They heard an explosion along the coast. They knew
something terrible was happening within. They saw smoke
billowing. The nets flew across the sea. They slept. And

wakening swung the first bag in and as the chords gave under the quick twist of the islander's wrist a body fell free, still white in parts and muddy after being dragged along the floor of the ocean. They gazed with tenderness on this ravished body as if no hurt this stranger had gone through might escape them or ever be forgot. Their senses were numbed by a delight akin to the greatest jealousy. But the body lay there so long that its presence could no longer be preserved by fantasy. It grew weighty and cumbersome. The genitals had been shorn off. The temple beaten. They thought of what was happening inland, the island adrift in an orgy of death, and where everyone they'd ever known was standing at that moment. The killing was no longer a distant phenomenon. They wanted to be free of the body, knowing that each death meant revenge. "Throw it overboard," said the skipper. "Who gives a fuck?" But no one moved as fish slid over the body with easy familiarity. The weight of the body grew again till the islander, spitting away from himself, drew an old sail over the corpse, and soon after, the town hove into sight.

The islander rested his elbows on the crook of the ice shovel. Jim sprayed the deck while the crans were hauled up onto the pier. When Jim stepped out onto the pier, he never looked back. He went under the mountains where udders of salt and sea-growth hung from the rocks. Smoke from a fire clouded out the pier. "Are you not going with him?" asked Maurice Caulfield. "No," said the islander as he sprayed his wellingtons. "Look," Maurice whispered, "you can see him going round the bend of the pier." He climbed on top of the cabin. "He never even looked back." "He's gone, just like that. I always thought you were with him somehow." Jim counted the money in his pocket over and over and imagined the expression on his father's face. He thought of the newness of the day he was living through. He made enquiries in the town after his father. Rain was spitting out of the sky. "George," one man said, "maybe he is above at Gaynor's or out at Nappy

Quinn's place." But his father was not there either. He was directed across the edge of a new plantation, down the cliff and along a grass verge to the door of a felt-roofed hut with a single chimney. But there was no answer. He climbed down to where a man was drawing lines into the mouth of a cave. The cave was dark and shiny as barrel water. Salt and lime fell through the echoing silence. It seemed like the carcass of the sea had floated in and had been buried there. "Daddy," he called in. George leaped out from somewhere, hammering his boots off the veins of granite. "Christ, you frightened me," he shouted striding out into the daylight. He beat his cheeks with his knuckles, quietly, as if reprimanding a small baby to open its eyes, little touches to the eyes, a last look of self-loathing, then nothing at all.

His father was fresh as a child new out of the womb.

A slaughtered pike under the seat of a rowing boat.

They walked back together. All Jim told him of was how the army had been to the house and how they wanted him. He did not mention that they had called Margaret a whore, or George a fucking murderer. In their conversation they went back the same route they had always taken because you only went by unfamiliar ways if you had a fear of being seen. And whatever your distress, when you returned to the path of the familiar, you forgot the unknown cause of your terror. They went into his little tigín. And stood around steaming by the timber fire. "We were after the herring all week," said George. Two rabbits hung above the window. There was a cat asleep on a magazine on the chair. "It'll be dangerous for me to go above again," was what George said. "I'll stay here too then," said Jim. "That's right," said George. "Say nothing to anybody round here," said George. "It's all talk with them. They don't give a shit about what's happening above." They spoke of the village with sentiment and the town below with venom. Before night fell they took a walk along the strand, and placated by such recognitions they returned, forgetting what they had seen, like all travellers.

V

23

In the house in Fanacross the days passed sombrely. And life, the life of the Allen family, was like those places that stand still when a train roars past. At times Frank and Helen could sit pleasantly still, even reach out in some languages towards each other, but their relationship now seemed like some form of indulgence of the senses.

Frank was spending most of his time now with Joseph.

First thing in the morning they were down the stairs together. They ate before anyone else was up. Some mornings the ridge of the mountain hardened and landed at their very door. Other times the mountain wandered off into the mist, and the lakes beat away unseen. The countryside was a lush unbelievable green. They went down the village for the paper and Frank touched Joseph's shoulder in an abandoned moment as the soldiers moved from door to door. He found it strange to find such strength in his son. They went together for the dole and took ages coming home, chatting, stopping up at the shops and the butcher's, then leaving their bags down they'd sit at the edge of the road up from the village. They'd step into a field to kick ball, Frank would get winded. He was sorry that he was not young again so that he could have the pleasure of growing up alongside his son. Each night was spent watching TV. The TV came on, the family gathered, and the rest of the world withdrew.

Frank let his beard grow, like George. He felt bad about his brother. He looked into the eye of his son and saw seated there in the furthest remove of the pupil the small afterglow of disenchantment brought on by that old, sordid life. The war seemed like something trapped in the present. Each hurt only lasted a day. Each life had its own peculiar warp. It hardly seemed possible that worse could happen. The swallows took over the eaves. Helen went for a week to stay with her mother. She returned with a new spring in her step. Margaret would iron. Frank would cook. Pop would complain. And Joseph would wash up. Then he and Frank would go for a walk by the river. Bright stars of flame, the fuchsia bells marked the way. The great tree was making its appearance. The laburnum tree. There were four laburnum trees within a few hundred yards of the house. For the rest of the year they were untidy affairs, but now they came into their own. The yellow lace hung under the green, the branches dripped. The flowers were like those pads on a piper's shoulders. The fringe of lace. The green. A Northern tree somehow; exotic, colonial, beautiful; poisonous in root, bark and leaf; shedding, after a brief flowering, its yellow petals into a warm level grave before returning to its ragged self on the edge of old estates, in the grounds of churches, beyond the side doors of Methodist halls.

Beyond the red-tiled roofs, bright and shining, a man is walking under trees. In a shady, warm place. You'd think his mind was at ease, but instead he's arguing an old tale and losing again what has long been taken from him. But the cover of the trees makes a warm place to explain loss to yourself again. There is no higher court than the present day. There's the dog rose. When you can tell one bird from another you've listened well. Then the mind is no man's land. The man in his humiliation has become a boaster in pubs. In his exaggerations he has committed political heresies. He remembers with an ache of pain, striking out at his wife, then his child. He remembers no pain they might have done to him. He is courting death. Having stopped communications he becomes fodder for fate. Come the words *honest and explicit separation*. A lonesome succinct place, the path he's on. He is a self-dramatist. The loosely aggressive smile, and a hand trailing a fag. No time now for foraging in another's soul for security. He is happiest alone. He has known only prejudice and sentiment, and these are cold sores on the face of imagination. He has said he was sorry. A swoop of fledgling starlings. There's a man walking a sunny path under trees.

It was evening. The mountains moved over the village like great war clouds. The lakes were covered in mist. Frank was drinking whiskey by the window. He read out a story to Pop from the local paper and began a short letter to George. There was little to tell. Things in the country had been bad for a while. Then he answered the door to a man with a gun who shot him three times through the head.

Helen was first down the stairs to find her husband, his chin on the mat inside the hall door. She lifted the shattered hand, with which he must have tried to ward off the shots, and drew his three bloody fingers into her mouth and sucked them. "Now look, now look," she cried when Joseph and Margaret came down. She was rocking on her knees. "He's shot in the head," screamed Margaret. Helen slammed the front door from where she knelt so that they could not get out. Margaret ran through the back garden to a neighbour's house. Joseph, unable to speak, sat shaking on the bottom step of the stairs. His head was blocked. Helen looked at her son in a crazy way. She was crying terrifying tears, he didn't deserve this, he didn't deserve this, and then she said it, "He didn't deserve this."

The day after Frank Allen died the nurse toned the skin of the dead man with witch hazel and tonic till the yarrow uselessly soothed the pores where all secretion was ended. Lastly they applied the moisturizers with the tips of the fingers, smoothing out the lanolin with the softness of wools till his cold face shone with perfumed fats. The undamaged side of the face still held one arrested gaze. With skilled gestures they powdered the loins, bound the foreskin with cheesecloth and plugged his weakened anus.

Outside the hospital the men walked in circles while the body was prepared. Now, shielded from their naked selves, they grew lax and sentimental. Death was a great barrier against change. It was because they had forgone the very terror they craved. They suffered cramps and indigestion and believed the people of the town were looking at them. They told stories of Frank with that air of authenticity that hides so much by correcting the truth as it goes.

The men were down on their hunkers looking out at the lakes that could barely be seen through the trees, their heads like empty rooms containing all they saw, but which they refused to enter. There followed the wet drizzling drive to the church after the corpse had been kissed like a totem, a flag, to remind you of what you were fighting for. Red brake-lights blinked on the wet surface of the road. People stood on the corners of the village waiting on the hearse to arrive. Cars waited up lanes off the main road with their parking lights on, the same in the lay-bys, the lights ticking away in the dark, sinister and sad, till at last the lights of the funeral cars like dragonflies came down the hill to the village after the hearse.

Eventually then, the shingle beach of the lake filled with cow's teeth and jawbones washed up from an abattoir on a further shore. Away to the left, blue-frocked men were building the new pier. The digger's rollers held fast beneath the water, bracing its tracks on the lakebed as the scoop lifted, trailing lily pads, and threw great mounds of muddy earth further out into the water.

A practical sense of searching for the most important events of the dead man's life ensued. They looked into the reaches of the former living man but somehow he evaded them. Instead, emerged all those that lived about him. More and more the elders were afflicted by the sense of leaving home. Of leaving the path of the familiar. Of the soul leaving the body and leaving no trace of that quiet intoxication.

"In your time, too," said Helen to her son, "you will be guarding over your partner's death, worrying and attending." Margaret scoured herself for the funeral. Combed out Helen's hair and stood back from her. Villagers moved by with wooden upturned lips of surprise. By a wind-whitened cottage this neighbour's child, with fat brooding lips and scurrying hands, played with shadows as her parents and brothers divided a catch of eel on the path for the four houses before joining the other mourners who moved through the death house with stifled coughs. And the heads of the strangers among them, with tender raised crowns, intelligent and human. The old discoloured freckles of the faces of our own kind turned liquid in the candlelight. The family stood against the uneven, rolling walls as the mourners moved through with a penitent shuffle. They patted the heads of the children and stopped to surmise their size, their family names, their likenesses. Frogs leaped off the porch. The children grew speechless and crazy. A carnival marquee was being set up in a playing pitch down from the church. And the village drunks hurled abuse at the acrobats, requesting silence for the dead. Last of all, Manager Tom, hatless and fumbling, stepped out of a taxi and, steadied against the wind, entered the house.

So, all gathered. And a man's voice resurrected itself from the side of the corpse. He sat completely at ease and began to speak while the children and elders continued to beat flies off their brows, and he spoke for all there, his voice remained on an even keel. Then his voice was replaced by a woman's. The people shifted their positions in the death house as she spoke. The story-telling passed on to Peter, and his face was so white it was unbearable, and like the rest of the lilters there was one tune in his head and another on his lips. The rhythm of his voice was the greatest deceit, and still the most beautiful, telling as it did of other concerns.

In the far reaches of their mind the people began abusing him, Frank Allen. They now had no image of him, except a few transparent lines that would not meet. Still the women grouped around, tugging at their blouses and coats, carrying sandwiches, friendly to each other and patient – *since that's the law*. The mourners' hands glowed with rings and ointment. Cans of Fanta popped. The soles of Margaret's feet twitched with anticipation and she could not understand it, this cruel joy. And Joseph was ashamed of the solidarity and sympathy he had accrued from the death of his father. For not to believe was heresy. He saw the pink flesh sprouting out of the tight sandals of the women, then disappearing beneath their black embroidered slips. He saw the quaint, lecherous look in the eyes of the men, their beards sprinkled with grey. It was not just that they were here out of custom. They were collaborating with some higher law, some selfish need of their own. He was drinking gin. When he stood up he was taller than any man there and only longing to hear good things said about his father. Yet, he could not be satisfied. For to begin with, the future was not known till a few laws popular with people were broken. *The future was a broken law*. Else time would have stood still.

Now this day there was only the human voice telling all it knows but sounding unsure because only part of the story is known.

His mother held his wrist in the pew.

The bell sounded in a slow otherworld existence that makes people pray to an image hoisted up out of their lonesome selves. Strangers arrived and threw a flag over the coffin. Leaping madly on the shoulders of the men, Frank Allen is borne out.

Joseph waited on Margaret.

The village opened up like a grave.

It was twelve midday.

An hour later, eight boats crossed to the Island.

The one in which the coffin rested was oared by Jim. And it sometimes stalled or went adrift as Jim fought with time present and time past. He lost one of the rowing pins, inserted a fork of ash, then the funeral found direction again. Midway across they waited. Another boat slewed through the water from the South. In it, George. They started again. The gulls flew off after the mourners arrived. "The young fellow can stop with us for a while below," Manager Tom told

Helen quietly, "whenever it suits you." Seabirds' droppings, white as shingle, covered the other Allen graves. Geraldine, and around her the recent deaths buttressed with stone, and beyond that, the unmarked grave from the Famine. For when the lazy beds failed and the first boatloads of skeletons took to the sea looking for grain, the villagers were too tired to bring any new corpses up to the old burial ground at the deserted village in the mountains. Neither could they use the ground of the neighbouring fishermen who saw them threatening their livelihood. If a corpse was left on the beach, next morning they woke to find it returned to the door of their hut. Shellfish were becoming scarce. All the seakale was gone. So they turned their funeral boats up the river, across the freshwater lake to the Island.

This was a long hard slog to worry over the burying of the dead.

And to worry about those who would be coming after.

Maybe, too, they feared now that the pestilence that was destroying the potato crop came from the dead, that the blight was travelling from their empty craws across the black earth.

Or that the bodies might be torn up by marauding dogs.

Each death meant the continuance of violence.

The soil on the Island was blessed.

Out here they came.

Slipped the gaunt frames into the cool ground, and returned dragging fishing lines behind them.

They lifted their boats at the two dams and shouldered them the two-mile walk to the sea to wait on the cutters of the coastguards to pass. The food depots had now been closed by the government. The coastguards threw handfuls of meal into their boats. The coastguards gave them salt for the herring. The villagers had happened on the cutter one day as they oared awkwardly around the fretful sea dragging their feathers behind them. But these were lifeless plumes. For, feeling a pull on their lines, the fishermen would drag them in only to find it was the tug of the sea going off in another direction.

"Give us food," the fishermen begged.

"It is against our orders," said the coastguards lowering a sack. Then they palmed the remains of a busted bag into the boat. The women pounded the Indian meal for two hours and baked it in culverts off the stony beach. The last poteen had been distilled in the sweat houses four summers before. No matter. They got drunk that day on bread. And no longer did the meal shoot into the intestines of their children like pellets. For the women pounded it down into fine powder, and at the same hour of each afternoon the men sat in their boats waiting on the cutter to pass again, their knees doubled up against the prow. And when another of their clan fell dead from starvation they oared to the Island just as the Allens did, over the same water, knowing nothing of who came after. Helen in the stern, afraid of the water. Overhead, young birds squeaking like field mice in their nests while their disturbed parents showered them with feathers as they smoothed the earth over a generous life.

Water-lilies lifted up like a mat before the cut of the boat. The black depths followed them.

Two weeks later the cutter passed again. This time they had biscuits, Indian meal and salt. Again they had been saved. They cursed the dead for not having hung on just one day longer. So Pop took leave of his son. "You down there," he said. "What sort of man were you? If you took it from me, well, then I shall be cursed too. What is the world of appearances you were tagging along behind? You could have done anything. Anything. Why always expect the worse, hah? That woman you drove mad. Could you not see it? You could take no pleasure out of life without condemning another. Well, you're under the earth now." He spat. "They got you Proinsias." The abuse became like some form of compensation, even praise. "It's not inside the fertile earth we go. You just become the death of ourselves imagined. No more nor less than that."

"Keep quiet back there," Pop shouted angrily at someone behind him. George led him away.

The famine fishermen saw the blight pass over. The people knew never to put their faith in a single species again. They built outwards towards the future. The dead opened up for them a new path of responsibility toward those who came after, and they could tell the one man from the other by the way he applied this new truth. They knew their enemy, and would not relinquish him.

The Island, fertilized by birds, swayed gently in the water. And with Frank Allen's grave tidied, the mourners sat in the shadows watching the trout feed on the still water like a fall of rain.

The mourners returned to the village. The villagers stopped to shake hands with the family. They hung on to Joseph's hand as if he were a ghost. To Joseph they appeared flustered and bullying. It was not that he despised them, but over the years he and his father had idealized them so much that they had ceased to exist as real people. They had become doting and genial and celibate in his eyes. Now he had to learn their old faults all over again.

24

Joseph knew he was being sent out into the world. Conversations ended abruptly were he to enter the kitchen unannounced. He was treated with new and heartbreaking tenderness. Margaret cut and washed his hair that last Saturday night in the kitchen. She rubbed her knuckles so hard against his scalp that he cried out.

"What are you trying to do?" He jerked away.

Pop was the first, though, to tell Joseph what was happening.

The old man would emerge from the basement, pull himself out of the house each evening, his face wracked with indigestion pains. "The devil is mad alive in me belly," he complained. He blamed the women's cooking. "George or Frank were the men for that sort of thing," he indicated the cooker with a jerk of arthritic fingers. "Look at yon hussy," that was Margaret pretending she was doing something.

"Not ours, no man's," he whispered to himself. "Encouraging the young fellow. By Christ, I'd watch my job."

Now that Helen had control over everything he complained bitterly.

The day had come when they would not let him cut the Sunday roast!

Dinner was now pure drudgery. His temper bade him eat with disjointed movements. He farted loud and often, lean wisps of wind, custard-sounding, then looked around to see would anyone dare complain, glared at any sign of embarrassment or annoyance, glared even more furiously at the indifference that now so regularly occurred due to shortage of money and humour.

"A body could be fucked for all you lot care."

"Jesus." He drove his boot at the wall.

Then he enquired daily about the state of the boats, started hopeless tasks, brushed and cleaned the heavy metal soda-fountain, that George, years ago, had collected for scrap, till the taps shone.

The electricity!

Electricity! By night, Joseph could hear him moving about the house flicking off switches. The old man had a horror of plugs left attached overnight. Through the darkness he followed each cable to its socket, and often fetched a chair to the centre of the kitchen and reaching up he tried to steal the bulbs out of the darkness overhead, pawing the air like a man demented. Else he resumed his old blind man's gait, leaning out to touch before he might see. Thus one evening, in the latter manner, he entered Joseph's room to complain.

"That father of yours," he said referring to Frank Allen. "It's a pity about him. No sense. Could never hold down a job. Born, of course, in Clare when I was stationed down there. Bad, bad out. Clare, how are you, nothing good ever came out of there. No sense of humour either."

He tucked a fag against his cheek.

Contemplated a moment a framed photograph on the wall.

"That's a right bitch he married. Hardly two words to say to a body. You'd swear a body had leprosy."

He shook his head.

"From this out I'll have nothing to do with her. What did you do today?"

"Nothing."

"Aye. Well, listen to me."

"What?"

"They have you as bad as themselves. Take whatever you're given. Never say no."

He bent low over the window that looked down into the yard.

"They lined us up ya-boy-ya in the square in the blinding sun, guns trained on us like dogs, we were afraid to move a muscle. India is right. Did they tell you yet?"

"Tell me what?"

"No. They wouldn't have the decency. Mutineers we were called. Idiots would have been a sight better. Eager for a master with the wages. Out there for hours and hours. Dying for a drink. A bad business. I wouldn't have been out there only I was forced into it. The army was worse than the Force from what I saw of it. Are you asleep?"

"No."

"So, you are off to the town. That'll make a right job of you. Airs and graces of that fucker Tom. He'll make a slave of you. Donegal, do you see. But George, despite all, is a right lad. No better man, not in Mills of Dublin, at a racecourse or the building of a Cathedral. Whist now, stop the crying."

"I can't."

"I know, I know. C'mon, till I show you something."

Joseph in his pyjamas padded down the stairs after the old man, whose thin shins, small as a tomcat's, peeped out of his long johns. Unwashed and bony. "Your father," he whispered, "he got the bad spirit from his mother's side, you know." They passed the dark kitchen. "By Christ, the bastard did for her in Clare." He trailed his hands along the wall. Felt lightly for everything he had known while the boy stumbled in his wake. Reached the door that Helen had defended. Climbed down the rickety stairs into the basement that smelt of unwashed groin and tannin. He lit the oil lamp. "A good article." He opened an old desk and took out a leather punchball. He tied it to one of the ceiling beams. "Try on these for size," he said. Joseph put on the huge boxing gloves. "Go on, boy, pull on it." Joseph threw a punch, the ball thumped off the wall and swung by him as he tried to meet it with another blow. "Give him the shoulder," shouted Pop. Joseph aimed, hit the bag again as it sagged. It rebounded into his face before he had time to defend himself. Tears rushed to his eyes.

"Hold on, hold on," Pop shouted, "till I show you." He took off his nightshirt. Underneath he was wearing a faded string vest. He put on the gloves. On him, they looked even more outrageous. His arms were skinny and pale, the armpits like bogholes. Breathing heavily, he took Joseph's place and began punching lightly, his fists arranged in the old style. Sweat streamed down his face. Thump, whump went the bag as the old man weaved without ducking. Their shadows flew across the walls. He sat back on his bed to catch his breath, leaped up again and flailed at the bag.

Thump, thump, thump.

Joseph saw her white feet coming down the stairs.

And still the old man kept beating the bag.

"Look at that, son," he shouted. "I'm the hard man, hah!"

"What in Christ's name is going on?" Helen said in a dry even voice. Pop said nothing. He took down the ball and put the gloves away while she looked from one to the other. She saw the red tearful face of Joseph and the white face of his grandfather. Pop sat back on the bed, fighting for his breath,

"I was preparing the boy for the town," he said.

25

"We were only children, your father and me," said Helen, scanning her son's face, "we were only children – you know nothing of hardship."

She lightly slapped her thighs.

"I had thought I had the confidence to sustain me along with your father, but my hope was always of short duration, for whenever my confidence returned, it sickened me to know that somewhere self-deceit was lurking. 'God is good,' he'd say and, Christ, it used to drive me into a rage, for we were stranded, and always what haunted me was – What life was ahead for you?"

She stared at her son. Lest she wake anyone in the house her voice dropped to a whisper.

"Your father had found work across in England –" she beat the pillow – "and would not return for six months. I was so wound up it wasn't true. I went on fretting for the day of his return, though I kept a stubborn silence when he was leaving. Everything just seemed to pile up. I couldn't see my way toward anything. We had been married long enough to know better. I thought a man should have more balance than going off like that, despite everything, but there I was, listening every night for his step on the stairs.

"Then I began to imagine that I had driven him away because of all the useless arguing that people get up to. Sometimes he could drive you astray in the head. I could barely stand the thought of it, anything is better than guilt. But I couldn't stop another night in that place in the city. You were no help, mister, either.

"Tenderness, there is none.

"Maybe that was only wishing that on his return our joy would be all the greater.

"But what I was imagining somedays was worse than ever the reality could be.

"All the times I had denied him came back to haunt me.

"Sometimes, like a child, you'd be into my arms. His cheque would arrive and not a note in it or else a huge rambling letter that told me nothing. It seemed the words were all made up or false. All dead. Day in, day out, the same routine. And the terrible sense of being one of the many. What was I in the head of the man turning in his sleep by Vauxhall Bridge? Were the same thoughts running through his head?

"So, George and Geraldine said: C'mon, c'mon up to us in Fanacross.

"All right, I'm coming.

"Many a start I made, dolling myself, going over things, knowing he'd be mortified, closing the door behind me. I pushed everything down to the station in a supermarket trolley. That's all I have to say about that. A few hours later, humiliated, we were back in Fanacross passing the eyes of the soldiers. A new lease of life. Call it what you will. I remember logs spluttering, the sap of the ash running down the grate. The house like a new pin. Where was I just yesterday, I wondered. And the first thing I did was break one of your grandmother's plates. The prized piece. The shame of it. That's the way I always was, floppy in myself, losing my balance by wheeling around too suddenly. Leaping to help where no help was needed.

"Always tottering, and daydreaming.

"And daydreaming.

"Not much room for that when Pop started. It was the first night I had ever spent without Frank in the company of that auld get Pop downstairs. Except when he took me out to dance at our wedding. He shook his head like a goat tormented by midges, and I swear it, a meal between every tooth in his head. He was always the same when the drink was in. Yet it was a blessing to hear his cantankerous voice rather than the one in my head.

"Here I was with George and Geraldine, a body could not ask for more.

"Wood burning, hot water always on the boil.

"But before I had time to settle myself George and Geraldine took me to an all-night dance which they promised to keep a secret from your father. Frank was always a jealous man. The band was set up on old kitchen chairs on a small stage and big steaming mugs of tea at their feet. The first stroke of Peter's fiddle set the rest of the instruments going through 'The Field of Wheat,' leaving the dancers to catch up as best they could. When you get by four o'clock in the morning, what you know of the world can only be improved by tiredness. You'd fall into the arms of any man. That's what separation is for. To bring you to your senses. A type of drunkenness it was to stay on to the very end till the hall slowly lit up with rough light streaming through the old fanlights overhead. The couples speaking in handfuls of words. Your heart would go out to them. I went round on my partner's shoulder dreaming of your father. The musicians with puffed faces stood for the 'Soldier's Song.' Everyone came to attention. Schoolchildren came in to collect loose change lost by the men during their night's dancing. Arthur Wynne, he whispered to me, 'I'll be here whenever you want me.' Yes, Arthur. And as we crept in the doorway of the house, Geraldine shaking the shingle out of her sandals, the morning light on us, there was the dirty haverel Pop standing with his back to the unlit grate, half in and half out of his uniform, the beady mackerel eyes on us.

"'By Christ,' he said to me, 'I'll have your good man informed of this when he gets back.' He advanced on the three of us. 'What,' he asked, turning to George, 'are you doing, letting down a man of ours?'

"'We thought a break might do Helen good,' said Geraldine.

"'Is that so?' wheedled he. 'No better woman.'

"'Pop,' complained George.

"'What class of man are you?' Pop raved.

"'Pop,' said George, 'give over now.'

"Screaming more obscenities Pop hauled on the coat of his uniform. He drew the buckle tight as a clamp, then maddened by the prospect of another day at work, he went out begrudgingly through the back garden. I watched him go, his cap on all wrong. He drove a kick at the galvanize gate for no reason, then lo and behold you, a kick backwards with his heel when he had passed through. All this without looking round. Your grandfather. Already Geraldine had begun to clean up after him. 'Don't mind Pop,' she said. His bed aired. His trousers ironed. The path cleared. Well, his best friend was gone when Geraldine was gone."

"And those days from the window you could see the pass up to the mountain flowering with may blossom and mad with midges, and the men striding to work in the valley beyond.

Then your grandfather would say of the workers: 'Those men are an asset to the nation, George.' Then, raising his voice for us women to hear: 'Aye, and later in the day their bloody wives will be at it. Out on the town. As soon as they've made up their clocks, they're off.'

"And Geraldine would shake her head at me, as if to say, no, no, don't say anything.

"Don't say anything. There is no telling.

"And yet each night Pop and the rest of us seemed to have forgotten the day's news and what had been tormenting us the morning before.

"We'd gather round the fire downstairs, the wind so furious it seemed the contents of the house, your grandfather last of all, would be sucked up the chimney and blown across the lakes. I lost track of time. I felt less of a stranger as the nights went on. It was in George's heart that the war was fermenting. Bleeding him of compromise, you understand. 'When it comes to my door,' he said, 'I'll fight like the rest.' Geraldine was playing patience. 'What,' asked Pop, 'was it like across in France?'

"And I told them of two years as a governess there.

"'I'll bet you think you married below you,' he says.

"'Well she might,' said Geraldine, 'considering.'

"'I've always had a fancy to spend a night in Lourdes,' he mused.

"'They drink wine there, Pop,' I answered. 'It would do your complexion no good.'

"'Wine,' he murmured nodding, 'addles the brain.' Up with a finger. 'Now tell me this, how can a man kill a woman over there and get away with it?

"'If,' I answered, 'he is in love with her.'

"'There would be more to it than that.'

"'He has to kill her in a fit of passion.'

"'There is many a man here would like to have been raised in France.'

"'Well, the same goes for the women.'

"'Tell me this, who does the most killing – the women or the men?'

"'I honestly don't know.'

"'It would be a fact worth knowing, my good woman,' Pop reprimanded me.

"'Killing is a terrible thing,' said Geraldine.

"'You'd learn your lesson if you caught sight of the murderer,' answered Pop. 'Before I left the service we arrested a man for the killing of a neighbour. He had never done a thing wrong in his life. I was in on it. I saw him as he was taken through. His head wasn't shaven and he had no shake in his hand. He wasn't ordinary and he wasn't peculiar. He was just like any other man that all his life had been roped to another man higher than him. The higher man fell and took the lower fellow with him. That's how I saw it anyway.' He lifted the wisp of a cigarette to the brown spot on his cheek, burnt there by the tips of countless hot butts. 'We didn't encourage him no whit as he passed through.'

"'Youse were hardy fellows,' said George.

"'Always shot over their heads, son,' replied Pop, 'it wasn't our place.'

"And suddenly we were into the next morning, I was late coming down the stairs to make his tea. Pop was in the scullery in his braces and socks screaming about the customs as he slung the cups along the shelf and slammed the cabinet doors. Geraldine as she stoked the fire was stifling her laughter – 'Listen,' she put a finger to her lips. I tiptoed over. 'The no-good floozy,' he was muttering, 'a French whore, I'll warrant you.' He kicked the empty tins of paint. 'Couldn't make a man a drop of tea.' He stopped by the window and dipped his head completely into the basin, once, twice, three times. 'Out half the night and her good man elsewhere working.' He dried himself. 'Poor Frank, you don't know what lies ahead of you.'

"'No, no,' whispered Geraldine, restraining herself, 'don't go in to him.'

"'And now talking murder, if you don't mind, when she should be blessing her face.' Pop continued within, one fag to his cheek, the other hand running in agitation up and down the breast of his shirt. We got the kettle on. 'Good morning, ladies,' he said coming into the kitchen. 'It's a fierce fucker of a morning out.' And that was how another day began."

"I watched for the post, thinking something would change. Something would bring me to my senses. Monday come, and a week of night duty lay ahead for your grandfather. None of us could open our mouths. He lay up in his bed all day, smoking and drinking cups of tea. Geraldine moved round the house like a ghost. It beat all. The elements drove against the window so that Pop wound himself in the blankets, trying to close out all the draughts and responsibilities from the outside world. Then, come eight, he put on his uniform saying 'Now, do you see, the world is reversed,' and down with him to the customs.

"The lakes pitched and tossed with black rain.

"Through it all went the roads north and south, and each side the banks of primroses, and bluebells.

"'Terrible night,' said Pop to the customs officer. 'Fit for a dog.'

"McKay the customs officer was feeding a bottle of milk to one of his imbecilic daughters, His own wife had given up appearing in public when the first of her five insane children was born. The officer handed the child to Pop, and the little girl took Pop for a walk up and down the makeshift office, holding his hand with a lifeless, disappearing grasp. They went up against the green door. Towards the heavy clouds. Around the desk. They waved the traffic by. The child had complete trust in Pop who warmed to trust in himself through whatever channel it might come.

"'Eileen,' explained Pop, 'wants to know what happened to the blue wreck of the van that was in the yard.'

"'You should have no bother,' said the officer.

"The customs officer and the child walked down the line taking a short cut to their dark house beyond in a circle of elms.

"Pop watched them go, filled up the range and was back up here immediately to hang his coat out on the washing line. Then into the bed again. Anyone could have taken what they liked across the border that night. It worried his nibs not. Morning come, the two alarms went off. On with the wringing coat and down to the customs to meet the first lorries through. 'Terrible night,' he told the officer later. 'Shocking.'

"In the officer's house the two men had breakfast, McKay carried up his wife's tray. 'Who is down there?' Pop heard her say. Then, as was his habit, he changed the young children's nappies, being a practised hand. 'Christ,' he said again, defending himself, 'it was a wretched night.' The children cried in alarm as he left. And now Geraldine had to troop down to the grocer's to get some chloride lozenges because your grandfather thought he had a summer cold.

We heard him say they were not worth a fuck. 'There is a more sophisticated type of thing on the way,' he remarked. Geraldine did not complain, she did not mind his tantrums and I learned to keep my silence. 'Don't encourage him,' she advised me. Well, despite your grandfather I felt at home, though every day I missed Frank. Yet those few months I had away from him seem more important than all the days I spent with him, somehow. The radio always roaring, Geraldine did all the bills, straining her eyes by the window, with a habit of beating away non-existent crumbs as she totted up the figures. The announcer was talking of Edward VII. 'What about Lily Langtry?' Geraldine suddenly interjected.

"Your grandfather came to his feet.

"'God, she was so beautiful, the Jersey Lily,' Geraldine went on. 'She'd bring the house down and he used to be wailing for her. God, didn't she do well. Not even the light of day for other people.'

"Your grandfather eyed Geraldine as if she were an ignoramus, his face and dyed nut aflame. He sat down prepared for further madness.

"'Control yourself woman,' shouted Pop.

"'He stands out there,' laughed Geraldine wickedly, 'confident as you like, a guardian of the border with his cocky eye, like a duck in thunder. He stands out there misdirecting traffic through the country. Directs them as you please. The boys have seen you often enough at it.'

"'You'll wake the childer,' said he, as if he had not heard her. He looked bewildered, as if he were trying to struggle with some matter beyond his understanding.

"'What,' he demanded, 'is happening to your man across the water?'

"'Ah, what would I do without my sister-in-law?' Geraldine said warmly to me.

"'Another fucking dirge,' remarked your grandfather.

"'Wouldn't it be a shame if he deteriorated,' George said.

"'No fucking harm,' Geraldine whispered to me.

"I took away the dinner things and breathed easy when I had left them down without breaking anything. The men, chafed with the wind, started moving across the yard. Geraldine in her blue apron held the bag for Pop while he filled it with turf. 'My brain is overactive,' she turned to him with grave tolerance, speaking in a confessional manner, as if she must be forgiven for what she was, 'I can see things before they happen.' He broke the bigger sods against the step and filled the bag. And seconds later I saw George affectionately kiss her ear as she swept the mold aside.

"Concerning the future, if you were to see us then you would think we had been on earth a thousand years. George and Geraldine took me to the pictures in a nearby town. 'I like those pair,' Geraldine said out loud, 'Laurel and Hardy – will you look at the face of Stan.' She held George's hand to her mouth to stifle her laughter. 'And Chaplin,' said Geraldine, 'not forgetting Charlie, from Limehouse he made his way, some can make it.' The lights were doused, and she bobbed and arched and went into the hysterics at the mistakes made on the screen, grabbing my knee in terror, running her fingers through the bag of sweets, smoking well-packed Players with surprising delicacy, 'But, oh, I like those pair.'"

"Mary McSherry, one of Geraldine's friends, came round. We were drinking from a bottle of port. George, whiskey. Pop went off to work after the dinner we had prepared. We went on talking happily. We drank from Geraldine's marriage glasses, hummed to the radio. Each of us told our story. As you walked across the old pine floor the dresser rocked on the boards, I burned my dress on the hurricane lamp as I leaned over the pot in the yard. Talk of dresses, Geraldine brought all hers down for Mary McSherry to see. That's what we were at when George half awoke and thought to pick off his plate but everything had been cleared away, so instead, with his eyes fast shut, he lifted a butt from the scallop shell. We watched horrified, not daring to speak. He rolled the cigarette butt around in his mouth, rejected it with a grimace and returned it to the ashtray. We relaxed. But without any hesitation he searched round and picked up another, popped it in his mouth, and with a sigh of satisfaction swallowed it down and fell asleep again.

"We laughed so much that George woke, darted a look around, and pretending not to have been asleep, he joined in.

"'Like father,' said Geraldine, 'like son.'

"'God,' said Mary McSherry, 'I have a stitch in my side.'

"Knowing he had been outwitted, George took himself to bed and left alone we talked and talked, scandalizing the life out of each other—

"'One of the princes had a deformed hand right enough,' said Geraldine.

"'Did I tell you of the dwarf I was looking after in Paris?

Loads of lolly, I was more a home help to him than a nurse. He had a chiffon dressing gown and, bless us, a mickey to the floor.'

"'God of God, Helen.'

"'To the floor, woman.'

"'And when I was nursing in Mullingar,' said Mary McSherry, 'each morning Mrs Goldmont, decked out to the nines, up the stairs of the asylum with her and her chamber pot wrapped in Christmas foil. She'd come to knock on Annie Crabb's door. Got no answer. Standing there, I tell you, with a pot swimming with piss and wrapped up like a present, held ladylike before her, if you don't mind. 'It seems,' she says in her best voice, arching an authoritative eye, 'that they are not at home again today.'

"'And Mrs Fair—'

"'And Mrs Nugent—'

"'God, but we were innocent.'"

"And then complete chaos when the outside world came to claim us again. Your grandfather, out of his wits, returned. 'Come down quick,' he shouted. We scooted down the village after him. An ambulance was already ferrying away the customs officer. The customs office was burning. Pop was covered in soot and blood. We ran down to the officer's house where his poor children were screaming and demented. Geraldine sat with their mother as she moaned over and over. The children fastened themselves to Pop, and getting over my shock at their appearances, I mothered each as best I could till we had them all asleep. Mary McSherry installed herself in the house and we returned home. 'What happened at all?' asked Geraldine.

"'I won't have it,' Pop said.

"'What happened?' again she asked.

"'Aren't they all out to destroy each other.'

"'What do you mean?'

"'Will you not be a fucking idiot, woman.'

"'Will you tell us what happened?'

"Geraldine unearthed a bottle of Paddy from her room. Would that she hadn't. For nothing would do him after that but that Geraldine put on boiling water for a bath and soon the two of us women were rushing around the kitchen, stoking up the fire, carrying saucepans and the two gallon kettle till we were blinded by steam. 'They can do great things above in the hospital now,' said Pop, 'you know.' And then he appeared naked as the day he was born, the same shape of our husbands in his neck and thighs, and as he tried to beat us out of the room, Christ, if he didn't go sailing on a bar of soap. He squatted his sooty back and aged bollax there in the bathpan in the warm soothing water for over an hour, soaking the newspapers around him, the single light throwing shadows over us all, and we scrubbed the thin spine of his back, the perch-coloured neck and twisted toes, legs like tadpoles, and never a word of thanks from him, or by your leave. We did it because he was the father of our men."

"And afterwards your Aunt Geraldine said: 'I see myself stretched out cold as death and everyone living on beyond me, even the old man. But I wouldn't have missed it for the world. Yet seeing it makes no difference.' She frightened the life out of me with those words. I see her, wearing a mauve jumper where the wool has matted, and on each breast, a spray of embroidered pansies. That summer the children had boils and worms and Geraldine tossed them away like withered plants because of her faith. She teased Pop's rheumatic bones to life, massaging him by the fire every night. The customs officer's wife came up each night and went over the birth of each of her tortured children with raw tenderness. And the daft children left with a spring in their step.

"And that's what plagues me. That we are trapped in the bodies of someone else, do you see. That's what I mind. Yet, every day there is George and Geraldine denying this. For

where Geraldine failed she persevered, or else turned on the
old man as if he were the cause of her distress. And George
befriended me always. And I was sad when your father came
for me. I can't explain it, there he was, putting his suitcase
down in the hall. All that had happened, all that had not. And
more promises. It was not enough. Myself and your father,
we diminished each other, and the question was, if we stayed
together would others prosper? I had grown strong in his
absence and now suddenly all my ideas of myself were again
under scrutiny. Oh, it was nice – I'm getting it all wrong – to
be in his arms. 'No, no, I'll take no money from you,' smiled
Geraldine to Frank, 'she was the dear friend to me.' And I was
sad to be leaving for I had grown to love this house here."

26

Across the road the lake was idle. And white. Down the fields
came the sound of new milking machines, of water splashing
round the glass churns. Timid-looking landlords in riding
breeches were there in brown suits that had not kept pace
with the thinness of the bodies within. In other fields the
new breed of farmer was abroad, manful technocrat, his eyes
happily married. Below the estates, Peter and Joseph walked
along the shore each evening after his father's death – the
villagers were all getting along there in the mind. This was
a fine time, as the light emptied of its essence, to walk along
the shore.

Said Helen: "He took all my confidence through his constant
barging, and then I had to contend with the promised land."

"I'm mesmerised," said Peter, "with what hands can do.
Let go, and sometimes not quick enough, grasp, tug, tune,
and sometimes not good enough, feel, hold, and draw. I'm
mesmerised by my hands."

"Where are you going with this boy?" the soldiers asked Peter, the peacock feather sprouting from his cap.

"We are giving the horses some air, that's what," answered Peter.

"Leave them," came a voice from within the concrete post. They walked for days, the pair, talking.

"The words are no good," explained Peter. "A man that remains silent is very worthy. Are you still searching? What then? Not to worry. Pass no remarks. We'll stay together. At the moment. We'll definitely. We are doing the best."

"What's wrong with you people," Pop told Peter, "is that you think the world owes you a living."

"It's hard on you, I know," nodded Peter, "kiss my arse."

"God, but that lad is unlucky with his fathers."

There was a life for Joseph that stopped at the death of his father, then another lesser life began, though that earlier life continued out of sight and came to the fore at the happiest times, but still it was painful to be cut off forever from someone you loved. His power of criticism was overwhelmed. He could never grow old enough to criticize his father. Or come to a deeper understanding of another reality, his mother. He was passive. But he was also looking for trouble. Reality just mounted up. Disparate. Clear, distant. Uncontrollable.

A frozen lake met Peter and Joseph, a technicolor of grey, psychedelic greys and whites, white spills at the foot of each bunch of whins. Then, flooded fields where swans had collected in great numbers. A helicopter was perched above the village, roads swung below like bicycle tracks through the snow that fell that day. Joseph closed his eyes and the phosphenes swirled like the falling snow, the weak sun leaped in a flash from one window to another of a red-bricked house on a platinum-green hill. The hazy boggy ground. The sheep were up on the high banks.

"Said Carolan," said Peter, "'*Is binn, bog ach bréagach a sheinneas tú.*' Said MacCourtha: '*Is minic do bhíonn an fhírinne féin searbh.*'"

Your music is soft and sweet but untrue. Even truth itself is often bitter. Peter shared his naggin of Powers with him. They called into a man's house where poteen was to be had. It was a bachelor's house with chickens running around, and a kitchen full of purgatives and laxatives. "Down at the St Catherine's Falls," the poteen man told Joseph, "the eels go through the small chute of the dam in their thousands, and there's a man there that counts five thousand salmon, and then goes home. His job is over for the season. That would be a nice number in these hard times."

The plaster eagles that sit each side of the gate of the front steps of houses in Co. Fermanagh with a fixed gaze of acute mediocrity, without claws, a December chopped ditch running up a field, the stubble of forest covered in light snow at the butt of Binneachlinn, the empty back roads, a woman stirring three chickens round the outside of her house with a length of stick, her head done up in a rag.

"I can't do anything with him," said Helen, "he's running wild." But Pop was not listening.

Her memories were now more real than her present life, so she feared to walk out into the present world for fear the things she would find there would have to be remembered. Her body sought escape through her mind, leaving in its wake a guilty trail. Her mind self-consciously stole away. Trapped in the present, she waited on memory to restore order. And sometimes her stomach took a nervous twist at the thought of a former day, maybe it was her stomach remembered, and her mind followed, some clear day in his arms, where, totally dependent on Frank Allen, there was nothing to be afraid of and she could entertain the new day. And often what she got back from the past were the times when she had been happily alone, independent of everyone. She was aware of the argument against dependency, the worship of independence, but when she had been happy there had been no difference between the two. She felt she was haunted by a sickness, which was in itself a hatred of the same sickness, a self-remembering sickness, a self-hatred which was based out there in some criticism of herself, some happening she could not recall. The seat of the pain, then, is not the source of the pain. Any relief, then, is crushed by the physical, discordant memories. I have failed to understand something, needing at the time a giving hand myself. She indulged in drunken sobriety.

Her drinking hours veered between advice to others against self-pity, and self-pity itself. She opened a book, spread it across her knees, read a few lines and began to dream.

One day he fell off his plinth, the man, the torso stayed agreeably upright while the head fell to the wet tiled floor, it was real, recorded and random, other things would be filled in after. It is the weakness of the joint makes the fingers, the foot, the head, the first to go. Touch and thought surrender to gravity. The headless one remains as a justification for violence. The removal of the head is the taking away of identity and identification. The weak always parts from the whole – that's why the head is first to go. She recognized where she was suddenly – waiting in a car in Enniskillen for a neighbour to return. Helen Allen now made a name for herself for walking the roads in search of Joseph; "Leaving me without a bit in the house," complained Pop, though Margaret was there to look after him. And when she'd return, without him, Pop would say, "That lad of yours is in for a right land." Off again with her later. "You didn't see any sign of that lad of mine?" she asked a man in the village. "How are you, Mrs Allen?" "I don't know what to do with myself," she replied. His plastic raincoat in a ball, shuffling his feet in a carpenter's blue trousers, the man gestured into the shop doorway. "Stand in there out of the cauld," he advised her, "after the shooting you are never the same." His blue and custard cheeks. He picked his nose, righted his Saxo-salt cardboard box of messages, and said, "It's shocking." He gestured at the sky, sucked at his false teeth, he chewed his false teeth loosely against his bottom lip for a split instant of stupidity. The overriding talk is animals. "See, Mrs, I'm sure you'll find the cub," his knees slightly bent, his knees swivelled, she noticed a cluster of grey hair sprouting out of the lobe of one ear. "All is for the best," he said. He would not leave till he had walked her home. He had a streak of sunburn across his upper cheek, and a long step that left his body racing after it. His brows knitted against the cold, he gripped the wings of his jacket with the heels of his palms and lifted his bags again. Snow was being driven across the lakes.

Then there is the countryside that year. Blue mountain grass that would come in summer at Knockmore. The mountain Avon. For burning lime into limestone the fireplace in the bedded limestone. The body of a UDR man in his byre three fields away from the body of a republican in a laneway. Dung slapping on the earth, crinoids, sea lilies, St Cuthbert's beads, the river thrown like a scarf between the hills while the North drifted rudderless. The people phoned ahead before their departure till, reaching their destination, they phoned back to say they had arrived. Cuilcagh, Belmore, The Isle of the Fair Women. Blastoids, their little sucking feet, supplanted by things they have created themselves. An abandoned car in a sandstone quarry, a tremor that gave rise to a fault in the earth, the Little Dog and the Big Dog, the two walking by Melvin Lake, the black bank of turf and the blue-reeded trout lake, black columns of dolomite and crushed calcium, almond rock, molten bubbles of steam, the long dense landscape of mountain over lake, and forest swerving to the left and the right of the horizon. The liberal roads across the bog to the graves of the Beaker people with the unattended vessels within. The horsetail, the common butterwort, sweet-smelling rowan ash in the Correl Glen, Tempo, Lisbellaw,

Boho, and the bottle of the white stuff for the stomach sitting
empty on its side on the delph top of the flush toilet out in
the yard of the pub where inside the instruments tune up like
a herd of animals and birds trapped together. The birds, the
fox, the cows, all looking for a way out, and in their want of
freedom they move between and against each other, they fly
against the bars without recognizing old enemies.

"Curse a' God, son," mumbled Pop, "the fucker from Clare
is dead." He was sorting out bills at his feet. "That's it now,"
he went on, with satisfaction. He lifted up another sheet.
"Now," meaning see. "Now," he's finished, while thinking of
something else. "Now," a backward look.
    "I'll not go, you'll see."
    It was early morning. There were only the two of them in
the kitchen. "Your mother, a'course, sleeps well. Straight out
into a monsoon of sleep. A'course I want to wake. A'course
I do. You know the rest. I'd been better to stop where I was.
Speak out what's in your mind, surely,"
    "I'll not go," said Joseph.
    "Don't, now," said Pop. "Stay easy. No use complaining."
    "I might as well be a dog."
    "Bless your face," Pop answered. "And see that idiot Peter?"
    "What about Peter?"
    "He's not in touch with reality. There is nothing to him.
That fellow would tell you nothing." He drove out his fingers
as if he were gouging the eyes out of someone. "It's a pity
about him, the beggar."
    He got up, "I'm off to the glory-hole," he said.
    "It's no wonder your stomach is at you."
    "Aye, just."
    Margaret was sleeping with Helen now, and the two
women came into the kitchen at midday. Margaret had a salt-
and-pepper hairdo. Joseph cooked a big breakfast for them of
eggs and potato bread. Everyone sat up close to the fire. There
were draughts coming from every door in the house.

"This fellow here says he won't go," said Pop smartly.

"Tomorrow," Helen searched for the right tone, "you'll be leaving."

"I'll not go without Peter."

"Manager Tom," laughed Pop, "will love that, mother of God."

"He will not go with you." Helen was angry.

"Jesus woman," Pop's shoulders were shaking with mirth, "say nothing."

All day she argued with Joseph but he would not relent. That evening he ran out of the house and down a back alley of the village. He saw Margaret going to and fro. She asked the soldiers. She enquired in the shops. But he sat low against the back of the garage wall. He heard them calling for him. He saw a light shining out into a garden. He dropped over the fence to see. And through the window at the rear of a house he saw a man making love to a woman across a chair. The man seemed to be staring straight at him. Joseph withdrew frightened. He must look again. And this time he realized the man was watching the reflection of his face in the dark window, while underneath the woman watched their genitals locking and unlocking with the same cautious joy that a mother watches strange children play with her only child.

Unlike other times, when he returned that night Joseph found he could make no contact with Margaret. He began to imagine that she was in league with his mother against him. Everything had changed. He could not stand her sense of dramatic sadness. He thought up the most dreadful things he could think of.

"Did you ever go to do something," said Margaret, "then think of all the bad things you've done and it would put you off?"

"No," he answered.

She was ironing his clothes by the fire.

"I love you," he said.

"I love you," she says.

"Forever?"

"Yes, Joseph."

From the moment she said "I love you" he lived in terror of her. From the moment he said "I love you" she slowly disbelieved everything he said.

"Were you looking through my clothes the other night?" she asked.

"No."

They looked at each other a few minutes, lying after their own fashion.

"We'll miss you."

More silence. He went out to the yard. Each evening since his father was shot Joseph had laid stones and the remains of a Farmhaul Cob tractor in the shape of a crucifix at the door of the house. When he awoke he'd find them gone. Each night he returned to continue the ritual, haul them back out of the ditches, across the yard and up to the step. Then he'd leap and dance there. Next morning the lot would be scattered by someone, so he had to start all over, each evening, hauling them back again. The exhaust, the plough rod, the water hoses, the radiator, the hubs, the diesel tank, he hacked the axle from the body of the wreck, he levered the block away that had frozen and seized up. They were heavy. He did these things because they had not let him grieve. On the last night, when the clump of materials had been built into the shape he wanted, it was he that scattered them. That'll save them the trouble, he reasoned. Then he went into the house.

Two neighbours shouldered the boat down to the river. The reeds on the banks whipped Joseph's face. Mrs Allen fretted over him, concealing her fears with nervous energy. His stuff was put on board. Old grandfather Allen, white and emaciated as a starved hen, hurled his hat over the gable of the house.

"The auld bollax must be all of eighty-one or two," said one of the fishermen.

Pop climbed on board next to Peter as if this was all second nature to him. They oared down the river to another bridge blown up earlier in the war, and had to steer about the remains of a burnt-out bus that had fallen nose first into the bed of the river. The road from this point on the border led directly to their destination. Women waved from the far shore. Margaret, above at the house, did not wave back. Soon all were out of sight. The soldiers watched them pass under the first bridge. A horse cantered along the banks in time with them. Helen sat in the back of the boat with a rug over her knees. When they got to the bombed-out bridge the men dragged Pop up onto the road, then Joseph, then his bags. Peter made his own way.

"Tell them to look after him for me," Helen called up.

His mother had a black scarf wrapped tight about her head, her arms were crossed, she was smiling up. He shook his hand to her. She moved away, on. Pop sniffed in the Southern air. "Now what?" he said. The high stones in the water leaving after them fleeces of wool. Yellow road signs. The South, a distorting mirror, lying face up towards the North. A young fellow passed down a laneway to their left perched on the curved seat of his tractor like a dwarf, his ears in headphones. The chimney of his tractor and his cigarette hanging to the left. "We'll get our death," complained Pop. Then a long silence. A bit away they could see houses built to withstand short winters. A boarded-up border shop that had seen good times before the bridge went. There was a terrible hint of impatience in the air. At last the Volkswagen arrived. The taxi-driver flung open the doors.

The group climbed in like strangers.

They took the short dash up to the main road. "How are you boys keeping?" the driver asked.

"Good enough," replied Peter.

"It's hard to credit the size of the roads we used drive on, isn't it," the driver called back.

They were relaxing. They were watched curiously by a

man, hip up, a rope across his arm, he watched them approach
from his position half-way across a field, with a field beyond,
and beyond that another that fenced in grazing cattle, the
road goes on, he turns from them, they pass a scarecrow with
a motorcyclist's helmet for a head. "The man that put that
together was enjoying himself," said the driver. A brown goat
with a pale streak on forehead and chest sat chewing at a high
hedge off the road. A rope from his neck led to the fence. He
was kneeling. They drove a long journey through intermittent
showers, through border towns that were announced by
handball alleys standing like monuments on the outskirts.
They stopped high over the town for sandwiches. The car
ran softly over the newly surfaced roads. The air was tuneless.
The bungalows, staid affairs, began. The driver indicated the
cost of various properties. "Youse are made up," announced
Peter. They passed through the drenched light that hangs
over the lakes till they arrived by surprise among the tall
unwelcoming houses and drove past the long army barracks,
nearly recognizable from a past life, with its numerous barred
windows and green gates, down a hill of poor single-storied
cottages, a street of quiet shops, and all of a sudden they were
alighting by the bleak hotel.

VI

27

Number thirty-nine College Street had been a spirit shop, then an inn, known as the Cove Inn, back in the Dark Ages, then a hardware merchants, and much else besides, while number forty continued for some time as a private house in which lived Master Peckham, who reputedly helped Bishop Bedell with his translation of the Bible into Irish. The ground was first purchased fee simple by the Master for the Royal School. In fact he was responsible for the building of both houses. Great things were expected from Protestant education at the time. But no funds were forthcoming for the Master's School of Oratory. Nor for his School of Movement. Number thirty-nine forthwith passed on into the world of commerce. The doors of the twin houses stood side by side, all the windows were out of alignment, while within each the diverse trades were carried on.

But to give the Master his due, the best of stone went into those early walls. No expense was spared. The last of his savings saw the gardens bordered with trim hedges, the oaks and the elms put down for tearing up again in the First World War. His men dug up the gardens repeatedly throughout the winters to let the frost at the weeds. It's still there in the quality of the earth.

The men who built these houses were a roving band of Protestant lads with slanty eyes and blond, spoon-shaped faces who left a string of such houses behind them throughout Ireland.

Under them was a token group of ethnic Irish labourers who heaved the muck, and drained the land and drove the horses that pulled the carts behind them. And both parties were witness to the day the dray horse, loaded down with Fernadolly flagstones, disappeared with a sad look, as if to say, Why does all this happen to me?, into a sudden collapse of earth, dragging after him sufficient debris to cover his own grave.

To the Cove Inn the fly coaches came from the northern side of the town bearing the Dublin mail, the outside passengers, at half-price, hanging on for their lives over the newly repaired roads. The judges lodged in the best rooms of number thirty-nine, the barristers who walked from town to town, in the cheaper ones. Business began to prosper, for in its time number thirty-nine incorporated number forty (General Evaluation of Rateable Property, 1856). That was when the tunnel came to light again. This time it was a shovel went the way of the horse. Rumour after had it that the tunnel led from the courthouse, via the church and prison, to the gallows. From the time a man was condemned he never saw the light of day. The final days of a renegade were made very simple for the forces of law and order. The populace knew nothing of what was really happening. That's the way. At the foot of the wall in the wedding garden that Manager Tom later constructed, there was an old opening into the tunnel. Just under the garden seat where the bride and groom would pose for their photographs. How it came to be there was never explained. Some say the tunnel emerged to provide victuals, a drink for the guards, but it's doubtful.

Anyway, with the building of the hotel it was filled in.

All the fumes of hunger and terror were trapped down there for good.

The last man through was a blind man.

A lifetime previous he stood at the crossroads listening for his victim to pass. He knew the man he intended to kill by his step as another man might recognize a period of history by what was missing from it. He let the blacksmith go. The RIC sergeant. He let the daughters of Riordan pass by. He allowed the English soldiers pass. His ears rose like a pointer. And the captain will never know how close he came to death that day, for it was hard on the blind man to know his victim's step in a world where so many sounded the same, each making room for the other who was set on travelling on.

Then followed on names long forgotten.

Below his feet a river that would later make a border,

Till at last he heard his man coming, and the blind man beat the rent collector to death with an old flag pole left behind after the militia's festival the previous spring. It was a terrible revenge. He killed him so that he might never hear his like passing through his eternal night again. And when the matter had been reported, of the lights beaten out of a living man, the policemen found the blind man still on the spot. He was on his knees by the trounced corpse tracing the cheeks and the jaw, feeling the hair and the ears, the stiff rods of the neck, that he might remember the dead man for good, for all he had previously known of him was his step bearing down the lane to his cabin where everything was laid out to the gentlest touch.

This was real hate, the police knew it.

The blind man had been standing at the cross at the bridge. They'd seen him, arching his ear against the wind, a simpleton they thought him, for nine days counting off the steps in his mind.

Now he sat in the muddy cell in the old prison till the day came, speaking not a word but going over the face in his mind. And true, too, the authorities would have wished not to make a hero of him. He could have claimed that he had been attacked by a wild animal. That ghosts had undone him. Instead he set about accepting his fate, as he had accepted his affliction. And under the earth and over the earth being the same to the blind man, on the day of his execution it was the guards followed him with their lit rushes through the dark tunnel. In fact he led them to his death. But it took a couple of days waiting before they could find a hangman. He had prepared himself and must begin over. He sat nervously in the silence, while the soldiers, knowing that the best way to separate the people was to have one killing the other, offered good money to any local man to loosen the rope, but the first hangman and the second stayed away, something needed on the farm or somebody sick in the family. And as each man cried off the job the sum of money was increased till a hangman was found in Oldcastle, Harry Whelan. It was a child's dream Harry Whelan had of opening a small business. And the soldiers were happy to be finished with the repeated treks under the earth with this bird of a man who balanced himself abreast of every spoken word, and rose a dead eye, and licked his thin lips with spittle.

Whelan came out of the tunnel and loosened the rope.

"They made me come here," he whispered to the blind man as he drew it taut.

These were the last words the blind man said: "He won't be properly dead till you finish me. Don't be afraid, go on."

But Whelan reported his words to the soldiers for he thought there might be some anarchy afoot. The soldiers could make nothing of it. "Do what he says," they reassured him, "we've been up here all the day." And as Whelan tightened the rope to make the drop from the oak a look of great peace came over the blind man's face, followed on by satisfaction. The image of the rent collector had so penetrated his consciousness during his imprisonment that he let his victim's identity encroach on his own. His only sorrow for what he had done was to see himself in the guise of the other. Thus the debt was cancelled. He grew the face, the ears, the looped hair. Yet there was not enough empathy there. He must replace the soul. Out of sight of the world above, in his damp cell, he stepped out of his skin into another, for at heart he was fearful of death, so when Whelan made the drop he found no peace, neither did the authorities, for on the day the blind man died, it was the rent collector they hanged.

Eventually the houses passed into Catholic hands. The name College Street changed after the revolution to Thomas Ashe

Street. It seemed that the day was over when the populace would enact the ancient revenge of starving themselves to death at the door of their enemy. The new Ireland floundered like a broken family. Neighbours closed up their doors. Number forty became a meeting house for one of the new political parties. Here they cursed the Treaty, had utopian dreams and thought to see one day a land of self-sufficiency. On the second floor of the house was the boxing club. After the boxing finished, the dancing began. The new politicians put prisoners of the old regime on a horse to the Free State Dáil. The speeches for their first TD were written by a one-legged barber. Owner of the house succeeded owner, adding latrines and baths and coats of purple distemper. The Second World War scattered the cranes, peacocks and wild geese. Men crossed the border for better wages, though the town with the lakes beyond was still sweet to look down upon after the long ascent. Number forty was derelict a number years as the town suffered from isolation, though some hardy types prospered. Smuggled butter was stored in water urns, changed every day, in number forty's galvanize sheds. A draper, P. Cunningham, conducted a small business there after the war but could never keep a tailor long enough to establish himself. An unpopular man and addicted to sentimental and numerous tales of his family, as all Northerners are, he filled the shop windows with photographs of the goods he intended one day to buy.

Padjo Ferguson and his father installed a Modern Mistress for him, best ranges out, and better still if cherry and holly are burnt for perfuming the house.

And Mr Carr that followed him, was full of class distinction like all Southerners, and he died of a prick of a rosebush in the garden. He had only time to buy in clocks, haberdashery, bicycles and torches. Time to stock up with delph, ladies' hats, tin sieves and leather dog leads. He suffered from a fragmented mind, and sported himself, each Sunday to the front seat of the church, always two minutes late. After the tetanus took him, his mouth worked its way round under his right ear and no hospital could ease the fury that the poison worked over his features those last few days. In his will he left the place to Mama. So one day the townspeople saw her husband, Manager Tom Allen arrive. They wondered what his plans would be. He walked the town first, moved through all the frustration, passed small dribbling facades, finished and half-finished buildings that establish the effort of the works and elsewhere the debris that disperses it, moved below a new roof over grey romantic walls, that was Fegan's, across a street packed with pedestrians and then with cars, through the garish midday lights, the mechanical portrait of a woman outside the hairdressing salon, the signs for Gold Flake popular as memory can make them, then this empty place yet to remake itself according to his needs, his new home, not even the sound of a footfall but garbage righting itself above the tunnel. He paid the driver. Then the racing engine of the taxi that had delivered him returned through the town, going further away, the driver complaining over the long wait, in his mind shifting the fault onto his children. Manager Tom, Joseph's uncle, opened the door to his left and began hauling the rubbish out onto the street.

28

"This is him," said Pop.

"Right so," Manager Tom answered.

"And this is Peter,"

"Aye. Just Peter is it?"

They installed Peter in a dark room off the pantry where by evening shoals of leaves collected in bustling shadows on the bare walls across which he was blessed to find the hot pipes ran. Later the same pipes were to prove a curse. But the room was the right setting for "The Tent Upstairs," for he had never properly bested the air. No mean reel that went against the rhythm of your toe. Better still, Peter felt untroubled by the thought of who made the world as he threw his bag in the corner. One of the maids took Joseph up two flights of stairs without a word. He knew there could be no looking for sympathy from the women here. There was a brisk, busy square beneath his window, a market for everything under the sun, and across the square a convent, whose cheerless bell on the hour scattered the mad daws.

The maid tossed his pillow, gave it two sharp blows and with a backward look at his helplessness disappeared, as if to say, that's that. His room was only one-and-a-half times the size of his bed, but placed so securely above the heights of the town that he felt intoxicated. When he lay on the bed, the springs rallied to his weight.

The boards overhead packed tight as the leaves of a book.

And when he closed the windows and let the curtains fall the room began its orbit round the earth.

It stopped a while over the village, then on.

To the left was the sink that recorded all that went on in the other rooms. A hand spun a tap. The copper piping sent a signal through couplings and screws, a series of loud exchanges began while the compressed water fought to find a gradient. The sinks in the rooms rocked dangerously till the jammed signal got through. The shuddering pipes stopped. Then, in Peter's room last of all, the air-lock crashed down. What in God's name is that? thought Peter. What idiot threw that lot together? After a few nights his dreams, as dreams will, learned to accommodate the sound, turning what was of little importance into a matter of life and death. No matter where he started in his dream he knew what lay ahead, so he tried to change direction. But the dream insists and the winds take him. Revellers climb to their rooms overhead. Wait, wait. It's all in vain. There is no stopping them. Someone spins a tap. The air-lock drops through the hotel like a depth-charge into his room, driving his heart before it, then with a few stutterings as the charge is released into the outdated sewers below, it dies away.

It was Padjo Ferguson was responsible for the installation of those faulty pipes. The day after his arrival in the town Manager Tom hired him. Each room finished meant a couple of days' celebration, then a further argument over the cost of materials. A room finished brightened Manager Tom's life ahead.

Any hold-up meant untold depression and a day spent wandering through the auction rooms.

Mama arrived.

She cooked up in a corner of the courtyard on a weighty gas-ring of the type roadworkers use. She followed the men with the broom and the scouring brush. The first night the pair slept in a proper bed they drank a bottle of Hennessy brandy with coffee made on milk. They sat out on a row of bricks with Padjo, then as night fell they went through the unfinished rooms, the Manager telling where he would have this and that, and Mama saying, "Why, no, I couldn't have that. Not here, but over there." They were talking of a damp empty room in the dark of night. Of things that did not exist, Padjo did not pay much heed to this, remembering the previous occupants. But never that night was a room given such a finish. Imaginary carpets were laid, china placed in the most immaculate positions and the choicest curtains railed. But next morning there it was, damp and empty again, the plaster coming away to the touch and the bottle of brandy with a tincture in it, sitting on a rotten sill.

And all the untouched rooms beyond.

"Good men," said Mama. "Let's begin."

"You can't," joked the Manager, "have two skippers in the one boat."

"The one boat, will that do you?" said Mama, "But two seas."

Joseph after waiting fruitlessly for someone to come and collect him stole out into the silent corridor. He listened for a step on the stair or voices he knew, knowing that soon enough he would have to get over this meeting with strangers. This was no way to carry on, he knew. He wandered the floor of the hotel and at last furtively descended the narrow flight of stairs. That flight ended on the next floor. Remembering his steps from before, he found the stairs led round a sharp corner to the foyer of the hotel.

A stranger bolted out of the shadows and accosted him immediately. "Is there anybody in this God-awful spot?" the stranger asked. "I want to put a phone call through."

Joseph flexed his shoulders. The stranger's eyebrows shot up in wonder. He wore a tartan cap and tassel, a red handkerchief round his neck and a blue anorak. His brown khaki trousers were tucked into long grey socks. Black shoes with high buckles. "Hold that a mo," he asked Joseph. "It's about to come apart at any minute." Joseph took the lightweight bag. The man licked the edge of a brown cigarette paper with one impatient flick of his tongue. He took back his bag. "Thank you, brother," he said, cocking a finger to his temple. "Much obliged."

"A stranger here yourself?" he enquired, chewing on his peppery gums.

Then, losing interest, he put on a pair of rimless glasses to study a map of the area pinned to the wall. "This up to date, old son?" He threw Joseph a sharp eye, tweaked at the edges by little harrowing lines. Joseph looked down at a loss, "Yes," he said. The man snapped his glasses shut with his loose hand and approached him again. "I got a puncture out the road," he said gently, hands on knees, "I need to ring ahead." Then immediately he began his pacing to and fro.

The unwashed hair at the back of his head was brushed down and out straight like the tail of a duck.

"Bah!" he said suddenly, and slipping out the door head down, he trudged off across the square sending mouthfuls of smoke behind him. Joseph waited a few minutes more but no one came. The disgruntled cyclist passed by, pushing his deflated bicycle in front of him. A phone ringing went unanswered. Then, panicking because of the impersonality of the foyer, afraid of more awkward questioning, Joseph fled up to his room, taking two steps at a time.

The first step that Manager Tom took to project himself into the unfamiliar life of the new town was to open the restaurant. This new authority over himself and his fortune left him bewildered. The walls were tiled to midway with small exotic Mediterranean scenes repeating themselves every four squares. Bunches of plastic flowers hung in plastic shells below blue shaded lights.

The very first day, the smell of the chips reached the main street.

And a generation reared on the common potato recoiled.

Business was thriving.

The market people arrived laden over the mountain and braved the scaffolding without. After giving change Mama Allen drew up her wrists and touched her shoulders with her fingertips. She walked between the kitchen and the counter with one hand flung backwards as she surveyed the tables, the other hand swaying gently downwards by her waist. She learnt to abuse the word please. Mountainy men and sheep farmers trundled in. The poor of the town ate out.

A jukebox was installed for the young,

Gargoyles, with puckered beards and smelling of their beasts, spoke of the weather as if she were a real woman. They hurled their steaming coats before the fire and waited, knife and fork upright. Elvis Presley was playing. They let things be themselves for a few moments, forgot their rich paranoia over things strange, saw the Manager and Mama as unspecific dangerous shapes, then sniffing the strange peppers in the air, they escaped their surroundings to wonder how close the electricity poles would come this year.

The men crookedly felt their purses and bald, peeling crowns.

And still the preparations in the kitchen continued beyond their ken.

With chip-drenched hair the girls left down the plates. The men took off their hats and listened with inward glee to the affected conversation of the Manager telling his plans to the young ones at another table. He had the names of the stars off by heart. It was another language and it was weakening to listen in on the softness of his nature. The countrymen attacked their food with returned joviality.

First, turned over their coats to dry the torn linings.

Then, a different record, selected by a chrome-steel arm, began.

They worked their way with plasterboard from floor to floor, heeling barrowloads of rubbish through the windows and down chutes, while below, Manager Tom picked up a gesture of maximum despair. His raised finger said: "Up there! Up there!" A bout of drinking had begun due to shortage of money. And then Lucille was born in June and Padjo Ferguson was godfather for his pains. In drink the Manager's personality diminished to a terrible fabrication, he clung onto his fellow man nor would his feet carry him. Daily he dreamt of his next sobriety, for that was what he was seeking – a cure. The possibility of a cure was what made his drinking so outrageous. The building of the hotel passed slowly for Manager Tom.

But Padjo Ferguson could have told him – years can pass while you are searching for sobriety.

Padjo and his men had to work around the Manager while he persisted with the running of the restaurant. Nothing could overcome his obsession that business should carry on. He could no longer make it from his seat to the till and on the last days of the café, lettuce no long appeared with the fish, the fish batter toughened, chips were burnt. Cathy, his first waitress, fled through the doors saying she would never be back. When at last they got the doors closed for the final refurbishment, his drinking began in earnest.

He lay slouched in the wake of the work, as the old fortress disappeared before his very eyes, dreaming to himself. When I wake, all this will be over. It's an exhilarating day when the diggers come driving the broken-down walls and tumbled-down sheds before them. The tunnel to the gallows was filled, the stream rerouted. Shuttering went up around where the new dining room would be. "What are you at now?" Manager Tom demanded, as he followed the workers around, bewildered that all this was his doing. "The place is a holy show."

"Speak to the men, Padjo!"

"Speak to the men."

"Are you sure he has the dough?" the labourers asked as they cradled their cups of tea.

"That's not your concern," Padjo Ferguson told them. Mama was listening above. Since the work had begun she had kept herself out of the way of the builders in the one untouched room upstairs with her child, emerging eventually to insist on sinks in every room so that everything had to be rerouted, she demanded that they stay with gas in the kitchen, and last of all she refused to part with her hens.

"Mama," said Manager Tom, "must have her hens."

"Throw an eye about you, Lucille," she said, "and see if you can find the hen with the black shawl."

The child passed out under the ladders into the garden after the hens. The men couldn't stand the sound of the clucking hens and sometimes they'd put a bucket over them, or sit them in the stream. Then the knocking in their throats would stop. Lucille would rescue them. And the dun-coloured eggs would appear among the scattered timber and in the bags of cement, and becoming wise to the ways of the builders, the lightened birds waited till the last few seconds before they flew away from the toes of the men as they wheeled their barrows up the gritty planks, or sometimes they scuttled across the newly cemented yard after dropping down from the scaffolding above. The building dragged on over two years. Manager Tom, ghostly from drink, began to attack the earth in the garden. He made furrows for potato sets and rose a number of rockeries with granite dislodged from Peckham's walls. Saying the newly married will like somewhere to go that's photogenic, he crowned the fences with roses and creepers and placed stone figures of maidens, carved in a nightmare by a local mason, at intervals through the garden. The seeds kept pace with the final building of the hotel and as the peashoots shot up along the canes the men were pulling the scaffolding down. The Dublin lad put up the sign for the Cove, and the same day, Lucille, disappeared among the plants, her mouth and hands covered in green, then appeared again, leaving little piles of pods behind her as she worked her way through the forest of peas.

Manager Tom crossed the street.

"The Cove Hotel," he read over and over to himself.

A smell of cooking, foreign to Joseph's senses, drifted down the corridor.

His hunger grew.

Three steps down a passage he found a small toilet. He peed anxiously, pulled the chain like a thief and backed out in fear that all the doors of the hotel would suddenly swing open. Behind one, the midday news came on. Behind another a man and woman were talking with aggressive earnestness. The rest were hopelessly silent. The sound of the traders vying with each other in the street below was the only consolation, so he waited an eternity there, by a window decked with begonias, looking down.

29

"I'm afraid I can't make out what you are getting at," said the labourer, propped on his knees on a ladder in Ashe Street, "not today, anyway."

The Manager moved on, stopping abruptly to study the

catering opposition and count how many people were going through their doors. The orphans led by a nun passed by for a walk out to the lakes, and in their wake, came the Manager, perplexed by the power of coincidence till his will was numb. He loitered a while on the brow of the hill, then crossed over to where a new hotel was being erected. He stopped at various bars, taking a drink in each. "How can you explain it," he asked, "clocks that stop at the same time, and neither of them electric, mind?" "It beats me," said the barman, moving further away with each wipe he gave the counter, "you had better keep your voice down." "Don't tell me," the Manager shouted, "I tell you." Where can I go? "Excuse me," he explained, "I'm not with it." Bloodless, he calculated the climb through the white heather for home. Traffic from Dublin thundered past to the North. Soldiers from the barracks greeted him as they sauntered down to start their afternoon revelries, as strangers will greet an oddity in an unfamiliar place, and then there it was below, the Cove, listing in a sea of troubles.

So, he stopped in an entry off the Market Square.

A baker moved behind him in the twilight, returning from the ovens, his hands protected with rags from the hot trays.

The sweet smell of flour drifted down the entry. Sweeter than any smell on earth, better than bread itself. Tons of flour were flowing down a chute. A man was shovelling flour. The Manager drew the smell into his lungs. The air darkened to his left. Another thin fretting fellow was suddenly standing next to Thomas. He did not wear a coat despite the wind. He had an enemy sleeping with him. The two heard the girls in their gabardine coats singing along with a record through the glass doors of a newly opened Italian café opposite. In the lounge off the alley, soldiers were shooting pool.

In the yard beyond the moon shone on old red galvanize.

"Get inside, I said," a woman was shouting.

On the morning of the proposed opening of the Cove the bank manager refused any further loans. Still, Manager Tom took himself off to the ladies' hairdresser. He returned to find Padjo and his men hard at work. The hotel didn't open that day or the next, but some weeks later the dining room was ready, then later the bar. With each guest room that was finished, the outside world gained entry. The waitresses were on their feet all day. Manager Tom's girls were poorly paid, curt, cheaply dressed, desirable, and always from the countryside.

The day the bar opened most of the townspeople wandered in and out for the free drink, yet after that you'd find only the Manager and Padjo and the labourers.

The rock generation frequented the lounge on Sunday mornings to while away the time during Mass, or else they fell in late at night after the pubs closed and here they drank till dawn, served by Manager Tom who mixed delirious cocktails to gain their admiration. Mama came down at intervals with coffee for the warrior, obliged to accept trade from wherever it was coming. Morning, Tom put on the boiler and ovens for the girls. But none of these acts alleviated Manager Tom's condition, rather they drove a deeper wedge between him and reality. Come the late afternoon he climbed the stairs with a phial of Mandrax and took more drugs than he need have because he had not much sense, wanting to speed off quickly to whatever place would have him. "For sleeping purposes, that's all," he told Padjo, gobbling them down at the bar. The town talked. And still the hotel was not finished, for there was always the final coat of gravel and the three-roomed timber house in the wedding garden that would sport an old fashioned balcony. It was the Manager's dream house, something too sentimental to be talked of. Each evening he paid the men and the girls out of the day's takings. His cheeks puffed out and his thin pupils marvelled at the horror of their own reflection. Mama, for the first time ever, shrilled at him behind closed doors. He hardly ever played with Lucille his daughter. As she grew up over these years he got to know her less and less. He was humiliated that the young who frequented the hotel and were his only clientele might hear of his betrayal, his nerves, the coming of middle age. So he courted the local drama group, and dressed as a duke in tight breeches and flowered shirt, he stepped out to say his humble lines. And stayed there before the packed audience looking around him in bewilderment.

How did I get here?

Then wheeled drunkenly towards the wings.

"I took the liberty," said Sean O'Dowd, "of taking your good man home."

"You'll eat with us," said Mama.

O'Dowd sat at their table. His long white neck shot forward from deep-set shoulders, his feet when he walked slewed forwards and back like a camel's and the head moved gingerly to the left and right interpreting all it saw. The girls heaped out two plates of stew for the men. O'Dowd watched them put the tables to rights.

Manager Tom watched his wife and the other fellow eat.

His nerves settled and at last he went out of himself, allowing another to enter on his blind side.

"It was 1908," O'Dowd told Mama, "my mother remembers it. This girl, she was seven, and her job was not to let the cattle stray down to a certain stream, because the drop was deep and treacherous. She was wearing a Davy Crockett cap, my mother told me. That was the poor man's style then – headgear made out of a hareskin. The sun was at its zenith, so she sat down and began jigging her head among reeds. The city hunters up for the day came out of the Grand Hotel. Guns at the ready. They must have thought she was a rabbit dancing. First one fired. Then the other."

There were bowls of flowers by every window of the dining room. Outside a man dressed as a clown worked his way round the square slapping up circus posters on every pole. Manager Tom studied the shape of O'Dowd, the man he had met in the entry. He was too tall, but neat, despite his circumstances, and possessed of a warm watered sympathy in each eye. A man living outside himself with no resemblance to the Manager and owning up to none of his woes.

"What makes us different keeps us sane," said Manager Tom. "I heard of that."

"You should not," said O'Dowd, "cling to the friendship of men."

"I often tell Thomas that," said Mama. "It does him no good."

"You have a duty," O'Dowd, in a quiet voice, said.

"The horse came across the meadow," said Mama, "but somehow I must have felt something was wrong, so I ran into the house. My brother was climbing down from his horse when his rifle went off. I stayed in my room and wouldn't leave it. That evening, I said to my sister, 'Where is Phil?' She said, 'He's in my bed and won't get out of it.' I went into my sister's room and tried to wake him. I pulled and hauled." Manager Tom saw Mama bend her head and tuck her skirt into her mouth. "I kicked at him bad-temperedly.

"So, they took me from the room.

"It must sound horrid said," spoke Mama, folding a napkin into a diamond, "but there is no such thing as telling the truth. Maybe at first it enthrals others, but eventually it just becomes the sum of yourself. And it's not everybody's story. You can take it or leave it, the same as you do with people." She stopped and looked her husband in the eye. "What I mean, Thomas, is, your isolation is forever, if you want it that way."

A crowd now entered the dining room, and it was about time too, for the loose evening light as it crossed the tables and their decoration, though giving the work done a sense of character and permanence, was also revealing the emptiness. Manager Tom reached out for Mama's hand as she rose – "I know what you mean," he said.

"The first memory I have of my father," O'Dowd said, enunciating each word, "is being carried on his shoulders into a neighbour's house. There was a crab-apple by the door.

My father kicked it away. Only then did we go in. He let me down. My aunt must have said something like, 'He's stinking!' My father put in his hand and felt my bottom. 'He is not,' he answered, all upset."

"Christ," said Manager Tom coming back to himself, "he should get a whiff of you now."

Thomas Allen turned left into the Bank of Ireland. He straightened his spaniel-eared shirt that was patterned with tan-coloured ladies and gentlemen, and with a number of cursory nods, he sat himself down outside the bank manager's door, fists tucked between his knees. It was as if he understood that the world of economy to keep going funds the world of unreality. Priests held green bags of coins to their thighs. Mart dealers sucked in their bottom lips. The money changed hands so quickly that it could stand for nothing else but to satisfy needs created by its own existence.

When the door opened and he entered the bank manager's office, a whole notion of another life had already passed through Thomas's head.

"There you are," he said, and spread five hundred pounds in a fan shape on the desk.

"Things are looking up?" asked the bank manager, appearing uninterested, as if some ethical code had been broken.

"It was a personal crisis."

"Once you have some sort of monetary security," nodded the bank manager, Mr Philips, "normality returns."

"Of sorts."

"On a basis of viability we can always proceed."

"Oh yes, I know. I understand."

So, although there was something left unreconciled or unfinished in his head, as if the new life he thought would begin with his sobriety had not yet started, or was contained somewhere adrift where drunkenness leads, still, with mis- givings, Manager Tom threw off his obsession that with just a little more time he might have been able to see the inner workings of his mind, and be cured for all time, and that afternoon he was back at the sink of the hotel, working himself upwards again, flawed as the rest.

His sobriety was well timed, for besides having Mama as friend, he was able to content himself with a vastly increased clientele when the war broke out in earnest in the North and the old barracks was restored. Nightly, now, the streets were filled with farmers and soldiers, the hotel recovered and was crammed each evening with lonely hard soldiers who favoured Country and Western tunes and a tradition from the old colonial days was revived – local girls married into the army. The town rocked after the Saturday night brawls while the soldiers and their girls danced the night away in the Cove. The old airs that had been meaningless for so long crossed the square. But they had lost Lucille. Fed up with his drunkenness, at fifteen she went to England.

It was the same square on which Joseph was looking down a few years later. And turning once, Joseph beheld a labouring man in a clean blue boilersuit treading air outside the window at the other extreme of the corridor. He was carrying a spot-board by the hawk and splashing gravel against the outer walls. Sometimes he bent down and went out of sight to trowel up more plaster, reappearing moments later, his head thrown back to study something overhead.

Following the plaster, he scattered the pebbledash with pursed lips.

Finding the lad looking at him, Padjo indicated that Joseph should open the window. This the lad managed with great effort. The man swung backwards and forwards on his cement-stained platform, a pulley rope that ran each side of him, in each hand.

"Always work away from yourself," said Padjo, "else you'd get destroyed."

"I'm Manager Tom's nephew," said Joseph.

"And what can I do for you?" asked Padjo wringing a snot from his nose, "Do you want to climb on?"

"I will not," said Joseph leaning out.

"I can guarantee you," said Padjo, "that this item can easily take your weight, and mine."

"You're codding me."

"Look," said Padjo and he smacked the cradle with the heel of his boot. He let the separate hoist with its pile of pebbledash clatter down to earth. Then rode himself out through the air and back. Joseph pulled his knees up onto the ledge the better to study the platform. The ground below seemed a mile away. His hands tightened on the window frame. He let himself further out. And slowly stood up full length on the ledge.

"I made this lift, boyo," said Padjo, catching the boy as he jumped, "and it's as sound as a bell."

The cradle shook. The pulleys jangled. "Are you all right now?" Padjo asked without looking down, as Joseph worked his way nervously along the older man's legs. The platform inched its way towards the stays on the roof. The ground below gently rocked. Voices from round the town seemed to start up any place, any time. They locked still above the level of the trees. The older man mopped his sweating brow. He scored a clean path with his trowel through the caked slime in the new gutters. The undammed water made for the down pipes.

"Now, hold on," shouted Padjo and he released the ropes.

The cradle whistled and swayed sideways, as if it would rather rest between floors than continue with this unceasing courtesy.

They plummeted down to earth outside the bustle of the steaming kitchen.

"Don't believe a word you hear round here," said Padjo, then from an unerring sense of duty, he again hauled himself skywards.

30

The minute he entered the girls fussed over Joseph and tied him up in a blue and white woman's apron. He stepped through the smells of pastry cooling and chickens spitting against the door of the oven. Everything steaming above long hollow flames. On the shelves jellies rocked in their dishes from the pounding of the potato peeler. Steam from the chipper sweated down the walls. Meringues, just piped onto trays, shimmered like cones. The discarded leaves of lettuces were everywhere. He was set to rolling butter balls with two wooden bats, then dropping the patties into a bowl of water where they soaked to twice their size.

Finn the chef was like a hawk on the shoulders of everyone there.

Hurling furious answers to all who questioned him.

But at the height of the dinner all talking ceased – the cursing was now self-inflicted. Blaming someone else was a waste of time. The women cursed loudest of all.

"Oh, Mother Ireland," shouted Finn, "the dumping ground of Europe, all fucking mercenaries, all in off the troop ship." He turned the eggs with a menacing swing of his hand. "Aye, if we only had the communist threat, by Christ we'd all lie up against the sow."

"My name is Cathy," said one of the waitresses. "Will you hold that, child of grace?"

Joseph took the tray. The chef called the lift. It landed. But before they could get the trays on board the dumbwaiter shot away, and leaning heavily on the bell, the chef roared up the chute. "Steak," called Cathy, "for Father O'Brien." "Steak," repeated Finn the chef. "Oh Christ, the religious ayatollahs of the South." The boy advanced with a dangerous sliding of plates. The lift landed. Then took off again at a bounce, returning moments later crammed with the remains of the first course in the meetings room.

"This is serious, Jesus," screamed the chef.

There was little time for butter rolling now.

The play between above and below was unremitting, as was the bustle in and out of the swingdoors that led to the dining room. The girls held one section open with a hip, then butted the other with a toss of the head, the elbow, the knee. They passed through with trays balanced on a single upright palm, the tray going upwards as they went out and downwards as they came in. Then on a shelf they laboured over the menu and the figures for a few moments, Cathy giving a quick flourish to a sum that would suffice, while Liz, intimidated by getting it right, worked it out through nervous lips. And Laura, who they told him was college taught but could not get a job, whose lovely impetuous movements he had never seen before, would tot up the sums out loud as if she was talking to someone. She had only come to the hotel that summer. She was wearing a light dress through which he saw, in the proper light, the gentle kiss of herself upon herself.

"I'm talking to you," shouted the chef. The pencils fell into the folds of their swinging dresses. Laura, patting back her hair, withdrew, calling another order over her shoulder with the daft confidence of those who can pass responsibility on. Finn in turn repeated the orders over and over to himself. He spooned the potatoes, nimbly sliced the joints of meat, then in a meditative moment, when the crisis was at its height, he stepped out into the yard for a big draught of fresh air, making the staff wonder whether service is all.

The Manager eventually stole Joseph away from the kitchen to give him a tour of the premises. His manners and docility were those of a man reserving respect for people of a certain class that secretly he despised. "This is the dining room," he explained as he nodded to those sitting around. "Nothing to do but feed their faces." Manager Tom ushered the boy quickly through the tables. Joseph saw his uncle as a stooped ambitious man who dreamed up outlandish feasts to which thousands of simple spenders might be attracted.

It was a terrible thing to despise those who ate in your hotel. The Manager sped ahead of him at a brisk trot, his left shoulder up like a haycock.

They marched through the foyer into the bar.

"I found this lad at work within," he said.

"Good boy," said Pop.

Lawyer Smith, in disgruntled fashion, was tearing at a ham sandwich. Manager Tom took the lad through every floor of the hotel.

"Away out of that," he shouted to the dumb tramp at the kitchen door. "Are we feeding the entire country?"

The mute tramp growled, bared his teeth and swung his sack to the ground.

"All right, all right," Manager Tom clapped his hands, "come back when dinner is over."

The tramp gave a loud bray and crossed the yard. The Manager looked up and saw Padjo giving a quick lick of paint to one of the sashes above. "You are very quiet Padjo," he shouted up. "Do you think," said Padjo without stirring himself, "that I'm putting it on with a hammer?" The Manager took a different stance. "Would you give the front door another coat," he asked, hardening. "If I was to give the front door another coat," answered Padjo, looking down from his cradle, "it would be causing an obstruction of the street."

The two men looked at each other, then turning back to his job Padjo rained the yard with pebbledash.

"That man," said Manager Tom, "is a law unto himself."

"You can't tell them, of course," he ran a mop across a blocked drain, "Oh no." They entered the room behind the pantry and that was how they found Peter, hunched up among the blankets cursing his luck. In the corner, good God, a Lucozade bottle of piss. Peter had been too afraid to move out. The Manager stepped over to where the musician lay and looked long and steady into his face. "It's Peter," said Joseph, "who came down with me." But the manager seemed not to hear. He followed the musician's every move as if he could not comprehend the half of what he saw.

His thin shanks. His shining trousers.

"By God," at last said Manager Tom, "he has a very glassy eye, our new pot man," and his nostrils quivered.

Finn the chef had it all off. "I can't bear idleness," he said. He set Peter, hungry as he was, to cleaning out the kitchen after the midday lunch. "Who's your man?" Peter asked Cathy, his head low over the broom.

"That's Bax Tartar," says she. "And who are you?"

"My name is Peter, the bigger fool I."

Peter thought the kitchen was a holy show. At one end of the table the tramp was doing his prize-winning crosswords, at the other the driver of the car was asleep in a kitchen chair, an empty plate on his knee, his hat clasped tight against his breast. Distrustful and tired. Padjo Ferguson was on a high stool by the window, his back to the rest, drinking tea from a saucer.

Peter swept round the driver's feet, and took away his plate.

He mopped away the wet stain beneath him.

Waking, the driver threw him a blow of his fist.

The mute tramp roared out his glee.

"Always keep your distance," said Padjo turning, "from sleeping men."

Following on that they had Peter start on the skirting boards of the ground floor. The ploy he was sure was to drive him from the hotel with work. I'll best you, he thought. He got to his knees and worked backwards. A nudge-chortle of laughter. "You're leaving," smirked Liz from under her tight bun, "a worse trail behind you." Peter did not look up, liking his privacy and the counselling of foolish friends in that order.

His quivering image in the glass door, hawk-free. Them all sleeping out the winter in Fanacross. Finn, a deep-browed individual, with the distinction of pencil-sharp cheeks, that nearly needed scars to loosen the tight grip of the skin on his skull, passed out for his afternoon drink like a different man entirely.

Then in the street outside a white van of fresh laundry and a grey van filled with fish pulled in.

The fish man, a young fellow with long fair hair, gay feminine movements and a nose bursting with pimples, stopped up.

"Where will I leave these crates?" he asked.

The laundryman entered.

He had a bald head and earrings.

"Could you guide us in?" he said.

"Right, men," Peter said getting to his feet, "we can only do our best."

The three of them got the materials placed. Peter came back to where he was, moving along the low smells that could only be detected inches from the floor. A pile of dead ladybirds in a nook. Dried spittle. And meantime, too, he was gathering evidence against that arrogant man, Padjo Ferguson. Between the floors and the skirting sometimes clear draughts blew in. At other places the painters had been very skimpy with their gloss, or over generous, if you could count the runs. The skirting board pitted with open knots. It was a Council job, right enough. Under the mirrors came a fierce pong of old tobacco mixed with discarded face-powder. By the door, gravel trapped in the rugs. Pins embedded in the floor by the desk. And a whiff of dead flesh on the steps that led to the toilet. So this is how the other half live, he reckoned, that saunter here.

"If this place was hoovered every morning as ye insist," Peter asked, "why do these smells persist?"

"Keep your trap shut," said Liz, "we are bad enough."

"The mockers last of all," he answered.

When he reached the bar and found the tang of beer, wholesome as corn, was now well mellowed into the pine floor, he was hard pressed to continue complaining. Here were men who stuck out their cranky arses while they leaned at the bar and women with bare ankles in trousers swivelling uncomfortably on their stools. He worked his way past Manager Tom and Pop and Lawyer Smith who sat smoking cigars in the untidy lounge, under P. Cunningham's antlers. The deer was a great mystery to him. The mirrors hazy with condensation, velvet panellings loosening into folds and mouse droppings like hashish on the carpet. If he was going to have to suffer this floor every morning, Peter was going to make sure of something. "The floor is a mess," he said. "It hasn't seen a broom in ages."

"Everything all right, Peter?" Manager Tom glared at him.

So he took a swab of putty out of Ferguson's box and worked his way around the skirting sealing off the holes, and next he doused the carpets in Mrs Horne's Sweet Shampoo while the distraught women looked on. The tune he was playing in his head at the time was a version of "The Mason's Apron," a common enough air, but proper for the rhythm of the work he was at. At last Peter felt he had earned his keep for that day. And when he stepped out later he found that he was in a town afraid of spires. Everything lay very low to the ground. That town was well known for its meanness.

"You have two summonses here," said Lawyer Smith, going through the papers.

"The second time, they had no right," Manager Tom answered dismally.

"It'll cost you."

"How much?"

"It's getting expensive to keep them quiet."

"How much?"

"Fifty pounds, and I'll get one squashed."

"What?"

"Surely," says Pop, "you can manage that?"

"Look at him," said Manager Tom, indicating his father, "De Valera's first miracle."

"And should any stiff bargaining arise, leave me a margin of a tenner," said the lawyer. "It's your licence is at risk here."

"Can't a man have after hours in his own hotel?"

"Not when you have half the countryside in," said the lawyer rising.

"They had the right effrontery," said the Manager, weakly, "to break in on a woman in the toilet."

"I can't promise anything, of course," said Lawyer Smith, then hastily excusing himself he left to get this business, he said, over with quickly.

"The way to treat that man is with utter contempt," Manager Tom followed the lawyer with a fractious gaze as he crossed the square.

"Why so?" asked Pop patiently.

"He eats here for nothing but charges me just the same. Look at him." The lawyer strolled through the rotten fruit with neat steps, avoiding any harm to his shoes. He looked absent-mindedly at an antique stall and lifted a silver pepperpot. "I dare you," said Manager Tom. The lawyer put it down after enquiring the price. "A professional man is cunning as a fox."

"And they have big appetites from what you say."

"And they are big eaters, yes. And complainers."

"Fifty pounds," said Pop in a mollifying tone, "did seem a bit excessive."

"Now see." Lawyer Smith having reached the edge of the square with a quick look behind him nipped into a modern hostelry. "That doesn't look like the guards barracks to me."

"You should have pulled him up there," Pop was thinking out loud, "that amount is a small fortune."

"He is the type of man that leaves me breathless. You just

think you've got his measure, when by God, he is off again on another tack."

The two men sat surveying the square.

"Here." Manager Tom proffered his father a bag of boiled sweets. Pop tried hard to subdue his surprise. Five hours here and not a drink offered. They sucked away in the lounge, throwing the sweets from cheek to cheek with the patience of priests as they sit out the other speeches, when they have finished their own, at a wedding breakfast. Pop was hard put not to order a drink, but out of sympathy for Manager Tom's addiction, he kept pace with his son's silence as long as his nature would allow. But soon enough he felt a twinge of expectation at the thought of a journey round the town.

"I think," he said, "that I'll give Joseph a tour of the streets."

Manager Tom threw in his direction a sharp unfooled eye. It was his way now to deny his companions unreasonable joy with the demon drink. He returned his gaze to the hostelry at the edge of the square. "There is no come back in these affairs, you know," he said bitterly. "You are an old man now, Pop."

Joseph and Pop went off around the unruly town. The people were suffering from election fever, posters of the leaders of the opposing parties faced each other across the traffic-laden streets. The formal witchcraft of the times was being enacted in public places. It was hard to tell who was serious and who was not. Pop read all the proclamations down to the last letter and disputed with various politicians, or their aides, who were making their way through the crowds shaking hands.

"I think," said Pop, "that they are sick to death of their own inadequacy."

"Bad cess to the bastards," a man said to Pop.

"It all looks too easy," Pop whispered to himself. "God but they are the cute bastards," his voice rising. Some said they had had enough of politics. "Bad luck to you," said Pop.

"How about your brother and sister the Protestant? Oi!"

"Get your wheelchair," a fellow put in.

"Ah, bedad, guilt and lack of social justice, good men all," shouted Pop.

"Pop," said Joseph, "you'll have us hung."

A guard approached Pop who was on his toes on the edge of the crowd. He touched him politely on the shoulder.

"Have you been drinking?" he asked.

"No," said Pop, then turning to go he added, "I must try and get back into it."

They passed on down the town. Joseph stopped every so often to look around him, filled with excitement and loss. Already he was composing a letter to Margaret: "You have never seen the likes." Pop propelled him through the crowds with the flat of his hand, through all kinds of unbelievable commotion and strangeness. The boy took the weight of his spare grandfather easily. The elder headed out of habit to the CYMS billiard hall off the main street. He was greeted there by old cantankerous P. Cunningham who enquired about the passing years. They strolled through old pink doors, over beaten floorboards, past the snooker tables with spills of blue chalk on the mats. Through a choice of smoky rooms with showband music erupting in spasms from a burnt-out transistor.

"Look more your age," said Pop.

Joseph hoisted his shoulders and walked on his toes.

A blast of oil fumes hit them. The four men within were seated around a small bare table. An oil-fire with a red wire grid burned darkly in the corner and facing it a chair on which a tall man,

heavily dressed, with white hair and a face ravished by skin disease, sat reading a newspaper from which he never once lifted his head except to shake it out like a quilt of a bed as he turned a stubborn page.

"OK, Mister," the dealer said, "two shillings a deal, jacks

or better, nothing wild, fours pays ten bob, royal flush is a quid a man, if you are not up to the pot you're out . . . He cut the pack.

Pop nodded wisely.

He assumed a playful silence, his bad eyes straightened, his breathing eased as the cards were tossed over the painted surface of the table. He held the cards tightly and close to his eyes, bet small figures, thumbs raised, joking at his own mistakes. He kept the cards in his hand while the other more seasoned gamblers, after a brief look, bet face down. Pop went for every game, unlike the others. And it was time for Joseph to recognize in his grandfather a person distinct, a character with another life outside of husbandry or fatherhood, though each phase had relaxed and formed that sterile face.

There was something of the playful cheat there.

Joseph itemized the postures, the clothes, the passion of the man.

"Take a dekko," said Pop, "and tell me what to do."

The boy stood for an hour behind Pop's back, going from one foot to the other, listening to the repeated lines of the players. As the snooker alarms went on in the hall without, the new players came in with their fees to the man with the newspaper who pocketed them without a word. Pictures of winning snooker teams decorated the walls. Sleek-haired veterans looked along the length of their cues into the camera. There was a prayer exhorting the members to retain a life of grace and health embroidered on cloth edged with shamrocks.

Then Pop drew in three aces. He winked back at Joseph.

"Less of the speechplay," said the dealer, "let's get on."

Pop bought one card but didn't look at it and tossed the other into the dirt.

As the call went round the table Pop increased the opener to ten shillings, and when the play returned at two pounds, he bet a fiver. The shoe shop owner on his left covered his bet immediately, as was his wont, with a sharp clearing of his sinuses. The porter from the hospital studied his hand, then Pop. "Have you filled, Mister, that's the point," he said. "Could be a bluff too," he continued, going back in his chair. "I have a sick child at home," the porter decided, leaving down his hand.

The next player, a clerk in the bacon factory with nervous fingers, counted out six single pound notes into the pot.

The last man, the dealer, tossed in his cards.

Carefully, for inspiration, Pop rose his hand to his short-sighted eyes. And there to find two aces and two kings. The deuce of diamonds sat like an ill omen against his thumb. In error he had thrown away an ace. The deuce still remained and he had bought in a king. Flustered he looked to the left and right of him. Joseph saw a quick tremor run across his grandfather's face. Pop rubbed the offending eye. When he looked up all there were watching him. And all he could think was that he had come within an ace of a full house. He increased the bet to seven pounds. The shoe shop owner looked at him benignly, as if he understood his misfortune, then threw in his hand. The clerk across from him played with his money then offered the extra pound needed to the pot.

Pop fretfully showed his hand.

"Jesus," said the porter, "I had the beating of that."

The dealer nodded a worldly dismissal in Pop's direction.

The clerk dropped a crooked run.

As they passed through the rooms the snooker players were gathered round the old transistor, its aerial drawn out to full tilt, to listen to the last race from the Curragh. The fierce boredom of the interior disappeared immediately they entered the more responsible world outdoors. The politicians' voices rang out through the loudspeakers,

"Jesus," sneered Pop, "I wish the whores would pipe down."

The door behind them, a sparkling green. The flower plots neatly dug and the late autumn plants in tidy, overflowing handfuls. Across the road, lads were hurling sticks up at a tree of ripe chestnuts. And the early evening sky, damp and down-blue, was streaked with the floury paths of jets heading west. Pop celebrated his loss with three stiff whiskeys in an empty bar where the desultory barman could not be drawn into conversation, and only nodded in a fraught, empty-headed way as Pop told the story of the game. The crooked run. That was the high point of the day Joseph spent with his grandfather. And returning, he barely caught the atmosphere of the streets, he saw nothing but flat tense green and heard in the back of his head the sharp knocking of snooker balls, the hiccup of the pockets, the sound of the snooker alarms. Outside the Cove the driver sat in his car in hostile silence, fingering his rosary. And beside him, Lawyer Smith.

"I hope you got that wee job done for Tom," said Pop.

He sat in, waved, and the Volkswagen spun off. Entering the dining room brought Joseph back to earth. The girls and Mama were in full flight going from table to table. Peter hailed him from the kitchen.

"This place is hell," he told him. "I'm tired as hell. What got into me to come here I'll never know."

"Air the rooms," Manager Tom ordered Joseph.

"Air the rooms," he said, "polish the brass, burn the rubbish, polish the brass.

"That's the order of the day," he shouted up the stairs after Joseph.

As he moved along the corridor, alone in himself, the boy was exhilarated by the smell and feel of the carpets, the pockets of warm air, for nowhere in Fanacross would you find such luxuries. He began on the locks of all the doors, working, when darkness fell, without switching on the lights, with his cloth and his spit and a bottle of Brasso. What had been unfamiliar and frightening that morning, the carpeted stairs and the unknown doors, now became adventures into his life ahead. The hotel braced itself for the night like a repository of lost souls. He skimmed the edges of the mirrors, stood respectfully aside when the commercial travellers passed and greeted him with tired, surprised smiles. When the door of a bedroom was left ajar for a moment he marvelled at the comforts and smells a woman or man can bring from their private lives into an alien world.

A scarf. A bag of nuts. A chair, with a writing pad upturned on its seat, pulled over to a window. Excited voices disappearing down the stairs to another floor. A bath running at the end of the corridor.

The girls, in their wet coats, whispering silently as they scooted across the light drizzle in the yard.

"Jesus, son is this where you are?" Mama said finding him there.

"My mother," he said with colossal conviction, "is fine. She just forgets herself."

"And how was your day?"

"Ah, Pop just went mad again."

"Go down now and get a bite to eat."

He found Finn the chef, his face chalk white, still labouring in the kitchen with a pot of gruel. "It's for a wedding cake," he said. Joseph sat up beside him on a tall stool sipping drinking chocolate. The warm light from the kitchen crossed the yard. From the yard you could see the pair talking within unheard. Finn showed Joseph his wounds. The chef's knee and elbow after a series of bad breaks were now sewn by steel clips and the boy marvelled at the hoops of black corrugated skin.

"It's a shocking sight, I know," Finn said, drawing his sleeve down, "I pay for it when the winter comes."

Peter came in, finished for the day.

"This town is full of happy men," he said, a little drunkenly. "I had always plenty of rosin for my bow whenever I came, I have no complaints. I came by here once in a lovely piper's dress, though the reeds of the chanter and drone were very strong that day. I was leading the funeral of a man I never met. A small boat tossed up a man from the past. Archie Moore is it? The face, can't get the face. No matter. She came out, your aunt, your boss, to me on this very street with a Christmas dinner. The plate was dressed up in silver paper and I had it in an auld van. What more can I say?"

Finn whipped the soup and told them of the town, calling it a witches' brew. He dropped back to his heels. Forwards with words, backwards into silence. Joseph listened through his tiredness. He turned once and saw the gleam of Manager Tom's cigar in the unlit dining room, listening too.

31

Souvenirs broke out into new designs.

Brass work of harps and swans made in the prisons were sold to the tourists.

In the early light the sounds of hammering and the silent pauses of soldering began, a pattern eased itself across the square, with pincers and tongs working at tin. Whey-skinned natives drove their pigs into the town during the darkness. All day the animals screamed in carts down by the river. Stalls were erected under the ivy-covered walls, by the stone war monuments. Sunrise – the market traders arrived laden to their plots opposite the Cove. Then, drinking tea from white plastic cups, some of them chatted, others sat alone behind their makeshift counters waiting. The trays of fish were given a new coat of ice. Cheap watches wound. A family of Dundalk Indians sat at various levels of their clothes stall, the old lassie on her hunkers on the ground with one fig-coloured hand shading her eyes from the non-existent sun. The old fellow, on a stool at the end of a line of cheesecloth dresses, called to someone he knew then stared beyond the horizon. And the daughter, fastened

into place by one tiny bruise of a sloe on her brow, sat, under
curved eyelashes, listening to the pop-request programmes
coming over the pocket-sized transistor of the spare-car-
parts man. Next to him, a rack of polythene bags of Armagh
apples. The kettle, boiled courtesy of Manager Tom, moved
from stall to stall. Gypsies eyed the goings-on through the
plain windows of the early morning bars. Quiet horses drank
from buckets under the purple waterpump that was flaking
back to the original Republican green.

An ass's roar drove the jackdaws from the roofs of the
town. Moss fell onto the street.

The traders' children climbed the stone heroes who peered
into baskets of expensive dull oranges.

Military persecutors of a different era, now daubed with
slogans, commanded with a vacant sculptured gaze the quiet
shuffling of the horse ring. The baker went up the street.

A spiral of voices unsettled the occupants of the hotel long
before Manager Tom, already airborne with his nerves, climbed
the stairs to awaken his crew. The girls leaped out and stood
bare-footed in the middle of the floor, hoping sometimes they
had only imagined his call, but when they heard the knock
repeated, their nightdresses slid down their thin thighs. They
stepped out of their nightdresses, snapped their bras in place.
No one would ever dream of going to bed without their
knickers on. The drag of tractors passing. Laura swung the
mirror round. Market day. Someone tiptoed past the door.
That was Cathy. Now there's Liz. Laura tucked the white
blouse into her heavy-pleated black skirt. A minute standing,
then panicking, she fled down the back stairs.

The orphan girls in the convent trooped across the school
yard to the chapel. Their feet heavy with sleep. The young
priest, white-lipped, was already by the altar which the nuns
had decked out with bowls of heavily petalled flowers pinched

back from briars above the graveyard. He heard the orphans
enter behind him, and with a subdued chatter, a slight curtsey
towards the cross, take their places in the front two pews.
Memory of the year the fire swept through the convent made
the two older nuns, shivering witnesses of the fire, touch the
brakes of their wheelchairs for reassurance. The other nuns
silently came from a sitting position onto their knees. The
"s" sounds stopped and began again in a lower key. A spill of
stained-glass sunlight floated down the tiled floor of the small
chapel, sweeping after it the shadow of a fully leaved copper
beech. And still standing with his back to the congregation
the priest began so quietly as he turned it was hard to tell the
Mass had really started till the serving women began the new
responses. Those few women from the town that attended
the convent's early Mass waited for the nuns to lead them,
and when the orphans stared back, the women, saddled
down by handbags and beads, kept their eyes aloft. The scatty
orphans wore skimpy jumpers hanging at the elbows, long
dresses below the knees and thick woollen socks. Besides
the priest, a male barber was the only other man they saw.
Every morning at Mass the orphans turned round and stuck
their tongues out at the women from the town. As they did
it, their eyes were filled with crude merriment, not because
of the embarrassment of the congregation, who looked down
on them, but because some of the girls would touch tongues,
there, in God's house.

Seconds later, to the tap of the tuning fork, the same
tongues would tackle the hymns that were meaningless to
those who sought security in material things, and the songs
of the fatherless and motherless children would drift out over
the square.

The traders checked their watches.

It was eight o'clock.

Finn arrived with the kettle for the market people, then set off among the stalls buying great quantities of vegetables for the week ahead, arguing over prices, feeling the heads of worn-out cabbages, rejecting soft onions, raising his eyes at crates of broken carrots, speaking of the fifties, appraising the cut of the cauliflowers, and then, having found a suitable companion, he'd steal into the low-slung bars for quick, sweet liqueurs. Sometimes he might appear with his wrist in a bangle of copper piping, for he had heard that copper would eventually enter the bloodstream and cure arthritis. The traders, who were owing to him, obliged with good prices as he always bought in bulk, and because they knew he was highly strung they never returned his insults, for if you did, he would stubbornly avoid your stall. The contract for the Cove was a privileged one. The traders made sure to leave a drink behind for Finn. He in turn forgot their names and faces, which they took to be a form of business acumen. They themselves could ill afford to forget a face. He loved to talk in the bars of the preparation of foreign meals, and always he stopped up with the Indians, who brought him cardamom seeds and cinnamon sticks and heard his talk of curries with loud, knowing sighs. He marvelled at the smell of garlic off their breath so early in the morning. They beat backwards with their hands as they grinned, saying, "It's there since last night." "I'd swear you boys," said Finn, "have it with your porridge."

"I'd hate to see your insides." His eyes widened at the thought.

The Indians fell away laughing.

Then immediately resumed their business-like air.

The farmers owed no allegiance to Finn. "Only for the people," he'd say ironically, "the country is not worth a fuck." They mistrusted his awkward intrusions into their affairs. They sat in hostile groups at tables in the bars, fresh-faced after driving their beasts along the lifted railway tracks into town and wanted nothing but their own reasonable company.

But others liked him because he was a great complainer. "Here comes Finn," they'd say, "the dissident. Good man, Finn."

Sticks in hand, the farmers were at the forefront of modern Ireland, yet, with cunning moralism, they disavowed the excesses of the modern world. The rich among them sampled the best of the competition in Europe. The farmers were internationalists now. Their sons drove fast cars. Still, despite all that, some remained outcasts – they frowned on the petty dealings of those who lived in the town, that's what I think anyway, said Finn – they think that the factories, built by foreigners, are a mere fob to keep the unemployed off the bloody streets.

"The worst type of all, of course," Finn imagined them saying, "is a man who cooks for a living."

Oh, I know the bastards, thought Finn.

He sat there eyeing them.

Laughing loudly, then whispering to the barman.

Shadows under his wicked eyes, hair dusted with flour, skinny arms, the straw hat, mouth sucked up into his cheeks. "You!" shouted a farmer. "Stop talking about us."

He got to his feet and advanced towards Finn.

"Here it comes," said Finn to himself, cradling his drink.

"I told you to stop talking," the farmer said and spun the chef round by the shoulder. "What do you know of us?"

The woman wrung out her mop, and looked around the bar anxiously.

Finn stared callously into the paranoid eyes of the farmer, the runs of tear ducts, the unstable chin, the shock of exposed, prematurely white hair that greased the stiff bolted collar of his shirt. The farmer ran his tongue across teeth gritted against widowhood and disorder. They were alone in a vast useless place. The small strong farmer looking up into the face of the thin, wet-eyed chef. His white unhealthy cheeks gripped by a kind of lawlessness. "You," said the farmer, "I'm talking to you." "Yes, I know," Finn answered, "you should have yourself doctored." The farmer turned sideways as if to depart, he looked down, then suddenly lashed the chef across the cheek with his switch. Finn watched the blood fall on his blue-and-white trousers, onto his white runners, as if this was only a rehearsal for some greater catastrophe.

Then, without warning, he headbutted his assailant in the face and flew through the door. They chased him back to the hotel. The traders watched the rumpus without a word.

Finn fled to the kitchen, the morning's shopping strewn in his wake across the foyer, and there he stood waiting, a brazen stitch of fear twitching his temples and knuckles and lungs.

"Going someplace?" asked Manager Tom of the farmers.

He cocked his left shoulder. "If youse would stop your drinking, it would suit you a sight better."

"Why don't you lock up your lunatics," complained one of the men.

"You know who we want," a coarser voice announced.

And suddenly, behind the Manager, on the stairs, Joseph sat on his haunches and began to yell for Peter. No one knew for why. He just sat and yelled. He knew no one there in this longing for affection. The bolt of lightning that severs the one day from the other. No added consciousness of what he was doing. Nor reaction corrected in the aftermath. Like those always trying to get a correct image of themselves. The thwarted emotion driving them to power over others. And the intelligence succeeding only in explaining itself. Here, for Joseph, emotion, fear, came to clean out the remains after intelligence and self-awareness had departed with their gains. He was crying out for his father who had taken half his life away with him. The men grew embarrassed knowing his history, and would have given him status if they could. But he would have none of their sympathy. To him they were blatant Southerners. Peter came in. "Sing us a song," said one of the men, they all knowing Peter for an Innocent. If it suits them, sing, thought Manager Tom. So Peter whistled "McCloud's" and then on into a song. He had the sort of silence that a man might dream of.

"You are a great singer," one of the farmers said, spurring the others on with his laughter.

"Well," said Peter, "it's better than ridiculing the neighbours."

"Tell him, your man," said the small farmer, a wet handkerchief to his forehead, "that I won't forget him."

"Leave well enough alone," replied the Manager, holding open the door.

They passed by his outstretched arm onto the square, shuffling without conviction towards the screaming pigs by the river, while the scene in the bar, rendered both more normal and outrageous as time went by, was re-enacted again and again. Reasons given for its happening when there were none. Then they settled on a cause that returned some pride to the injured party.

When the front door of the hotel fell to, Finn appeared with a plaster on his cheek. "Never advise those with whom you are not concerned about their cheating," advised Manager Tom.

"I was in the jigs," muttered Finn.

"Our depressions should be borne along," the Manager spoke loftily.

"Yes, boss," replied Finn as he gathered the scattered vegetables to his chest.

And the girls, the girls hated the long hours and the endless cleaning up, no one to speak for them, everyone was just getting along with what they had, and the girls would have gladly exchanged their jobs with the maids who entered service in the big houses, the holiday homes by the lakes. Here the city folk came to recuperate from a society allowed fall into disarray. All of this was not their doing, they said when they met. They did not feel deliberately mean. It was the country was politically unsound. "These people are ignorant of the fact that in social justice there is no goal or peak. It is a continuous and debilitating task," that's what Doc Ferris would say, as he sat at the bar in the Cove, studying form through a cramped and cynical eye. "Everything that happens is disparate. There is no great wholeness. Not even in this small nation, God help us."

He drank.

"Oh, yes, Tom, you can throw them together if you will."

"Their heart is not in it."

"Here! Cathy!" Round dinner time, which carried on from twelve to three, a variety of curses in three languages garnished the meals which swung on scrubbed trays through the inadequate kitchen. Always, on market days, Manager Tom hung out by the dining room door. His gimlet eye sharpened for meals undercharged to neighbouring families of the girls. For broken delph. For oversized portions. For businessmen who might steal by the pay desk. After any misdemeanour he would follow the busy waitress across the dining room so that her cheeks flared, through the swing doors, his tongue working like a weaver's shuttle, yet hardly speaking above an hysterical whisper, enquiring as to whether she thought "This was a half-way house?" And standing by the door, any sharp rattle of delph from the kitchen within made him wince and turn his knees inward and his eyes fill with the terror of failure in business and mockery and bankruptcy.

Laura was stalking the dining room, settling everything before Mama came down. There was a button undone on her v-backed blouse so that when she moved the whole of the arched curve of her spine was promised, then artfully denied.

Today, too, she was wearing no bra.

"If I wore something like that," said Cathy, chin pressed to her breastbone, "my diddies would be down here."

Laura went up the garden, with Joseph carrying the

washing, and as she leaned up to peg the clothes to the line, the wet sheets dampened her breasts. The lad turned giddy. Here, on the edge of desire, he teetered. Because he was in love with Margaret, that did not stop him wanting someone else. So he struggled with his desire. His heart raced. The image of the one girl, then the other, swam before him. That dinner time her toe accidentally touched his calf, she smiled across taunting him, he saw a fierce playfulness in her eyes, as if to say, you have no idea how cruel I can be. He knew this woman must not be fantasized upon. She provoked in him a response to a life other than his own. She would be there, as she was now, after all his fantasies were gone. "He's not himself," said Cathy, throwing her eyes up to heaven. "Some people have the morals of a tomcat." "And that's only the half of it," said Finn, hoping to rile the women.

"I was never better," said Joseph, out of nowhere.

And later that day, as the two of them returned with the fresh bread from the baker's, he found it great to be able to stride alongside Laura without awkwardness.

Come half-past three, everyone relaxed and sat back and ate the remains of the meals cooked earlier. "Call your dogs home," said Cathy, looking down at Peter's loose sandals, "they hum to high heaven." She poured tea for everyone before she would touch her own, milk first so that the soaked tea leaves would not come to the top, then a sort of delicious haze descended on her, she drew out a cigarette and snapped the lighter with her hardened thumb. She held the flame awkwardly away from her face for fear of burning her hair, then threw her legs up onto a chair, so all and sundry could see her blue drawers and warm, rounded thighs.

"The auld cunt," she said, "and his medium rare."

She blew out a stiff stream of smoke, tapped the transistor and crossed her legs. A hush descended on them all. They heard Mama pushing the hoover overhead.

"She's obsessed, that's what," said Cathy, without opening her eyes.

Manager Tom, fresh handkerchief in his top pocket, now strode out the front door of the hotel and wandered through the stalls, depleted now, the earlier mosaic of the morning shattered, the cattle dealers gone indoors and the hurrying traders come to a standstill, ready to replace everything on the sagging roofs of their Volkswagens. But still anxious for a bargain the Manager would stop by the trinket stall, where the beaten tin of the morning had been charmed into shape, or else he picked through the second-hand books and magazines, for lately he had taken to reading a great deal. "Another day," he would confide to Mama, "another day nearly done," and hand her a ghastly patriotic picture to hang along the walls of the hotel, a further bunch of plastic flowers for the corridors, second-hand cutlery, old blue prints of streams and bathers, silver forks too large for the hand to handle, and all this had to be displayed before Mama, and passed, and enthused over. These were great bargains. Once he took home a set of medical encyclopaedias which he read from to guests in the foyer, scaring the living daylights out of vulnerable commercial travellers with details of barbaric surgery and the use of leeches which, he claimed, had never been bettered in treating certain ailments of the eye. He read, with awe in his voice, of the amputators going from town to town to saw limbs and never returning for fear infection or some other shocking malady had set in during their absence. He followed Mama explaining to her instances of leprosy in Ireland and showing pictures of limbs inflated beyond belief. But mostly, in secret, he lingered over the well-thumbed pages of *Diseases of the Liver*, the light on in the hallway over his chair till all hours of the night, unable to sleep because of nightmarish visions of what he had been doing to himself these last few years with salt, liquor and meat, and for days after he went round with throbbing pains in his side, growing worse when he tried to put them out of his mind, then unable to help himself, he returned for more suffering to painful passages on cirrhosis and hepatitis, his frayed liver tight as a ball in his side. He searched long and hard for the telling pinprick of death in the pupil of his eye. He was breathless. Was he dying? There, at four o'clock in the morning, he took off his shirt in the hallway and lightly touched the knot of pain with his fingertips. Stood, his trousers round his knees, the book in one hand, while with the other he tapped the wall of his back and carefully worked his way down his fleshy side. If anyone had seen him then! A week later he cured himself by catching up with *Diseases of the Brain*. His fear, then, of his own madness at least left him fully dressed as he walked the floor, trying hard to catch up with his shadow, while inside his head a boiled crab struck out in slow motion at the heated walls.

And Mama, industrious and cheerfully private, in the break from three to five, wandered the corridors, a tray at shoulder level, her eyes to the state of the carpet, hips gently swaying. She picks a thread from her skirt. "Good afternoon." She looks up as she speaks to a traveller, pretending to some mission, then proceeds softly. Her walk was that of a middle-aged clerk, rather than the proprietress of a hotel. At that time, she wanted to know little of the outside world beyond what the newspapers told. She felt blessed to have fallen on her feet and yet was still unsure of her surroundings. "Let them get on with it," she'd say, "that's what we elected them for."

Mama was equipped with a primal intelligence, a mind that at first glance never heard another's point of view, but once her traditional reluctance had been breached and the other's personality and condition had seeped into her consciousness, she could express herself with halting, yet penetrating sympathy. What the girls had left undone she finished. What they missed, she found.

"This is my province," she'd explain.

Then, sitting at a table in the deserted dining room, she'd slice two oranges and suck them greedily, stopping every so often to listen to the intermittent conversation from the kitchen. Then she'd fall into a trance till Finn arrived with her main meal. Mama loved to be served by a man. No one but the chef was allowed serve her. Finn always savoured the responsibility of looking after Mama. And in this he made nervous wrecks of the girls. Getting her tray ready, setting the table as she liked it. He tossed the liver in wholemeal flour, pinched the chicken with tarragon, cut her lamb away from the bone and sometimes served it wrapped in wild mint taken from the edge of a nearby lake, then with a swift jerk of the pot into the colander he drained her favourite vegetable, the sprouts, before they softened.

"Here you are, Mama," he'd smile, and hesitate a moment.

"What would I do without you?" she'd answer.

Suitably chuffed, the chef retired to eat his meal with the others within. The best moment of his day had passed. It took some time before another conversation could start in the kitchen such was Finn's delight at being Mama's favourite. Secretly she bestowed favours on the others without his knowledge but nothing the girls would say could deflate him. "I was a cook in peacetime," he explained one day as he bit into a bunch of lightly fried scallions, "but that didn't mean I had no trouble. A bloke called Charles, Charles something, complained each Saturday about the stew." Finn looked sternly at the girls. "At last, I took him across the hot sands, into the observation post and put a gun in his mouth. I never had any more complaints." He giggled to himself, and lifted a carrot, buttered in dill weed and lightly peppered. "Word must have got about." Everyone at the table laughed, for although they could see the scene in reality, they could also tell the fiction in his mind. "You are a born liar," said Cathy. Next door Mama heard their laughter, Finn laughing loudest of all, for like all failed gamblers he had lost his nerve and could not continue

a fiction to its ultimate without breaking faith with his
characters, without using violence to restore belief in a narrative
that could not be sustained. Mama listened in hospitable
silence, then turned her newspaper over and scrutinized
what had happened in the Dáil the previous day, giving, as
she did so, the women's page a brief voyeuristic glance. Then,
she thought ahead to her week in England with Lucille.

There were many philosophies expressed in the kitchen,
intimacies of optimism and many instances of distrust, and
Joseph, being immature and craving respect and affection,
acted out his immaturity while pretending to be a man.
Mama and the girls saw through him. Yet, when he was
found out in a lie they didn't humiliate him as the men might
have done. His sin was always greater in his own eyes. Then
the question became, for him, whether they forgave out of
sympathy, or because everyone was, in some way, living a lie.
The retribution that Joseph expected never came. But still he
was prevented from doing what he really wanted or saying
what he really meant, or knowing the use of his will, or just
merely letting go because of a superstition that suppressed real
emotion and turned pain into wonder at the world.

Anyway, everyone in the hotel slept well after market day.

Except for Manager Tom. He slept in fits, felt unsuited
to responsibility, feared he was misinterpreting the modern
world. He missed his daughter. His drunk past pursued his
sober mind across unknowable buildings. Burdened down by
frustration and red meat his dreams were airless, yet he had
acquired a certain humour, even at that remove, which was
practised without intermediaries or characters, breaking the
strain between himself and death. He accepted and gave away
at the same time, and when he heard it rising in his gorge,
the bad temper, the impatience, he tricked himself. He slept
alongside Mama in the trunk room with a crucifix and a mirror,
a seldom-used electric razor, her blouses, a grey sink with
suspect taps, copies of local historical books. Self-interrogations

about ownership and violence scattered across the floor.

Here they slept, arms round each other, in a small room wallpapered with childish designs, overlooking the galvanize sheds that once stored the smuggled butter.

Oh God, Mama, and often there he confused sleeplessness with a desire to write an account of his worry, he plunged heartlessly through bitter unsatisfied attacks on his psyche, they'd turn together the other way in the bed, he prayed for the strength to free the girls of their burden while the practical thing would have been to face the fear of being found out. The day Frank, sixteen years his junior, died his ghost was there at the window, beckoning. It frightened him that nightly now he dreamed the dead alive, while Mama, Mama was just tired. And the girls loved this home from home. But Manager Tom was unwilling to leave an idea alone, fearing that he might not satisfy all men.

They argued, he and her, in whispers out in the corridor.

The two were arguing about simple things, spuds not ordered or the like. They try to keep their voices down so that Joseph will not hear. The Manager going away, returning, she all the time standing still. Now the sides change, that's all. Eternally they are repeating themselves. Neither has the power to go. The coupling of fear and inferiority. Sometimes growing for them into greater, grander things but not now when all is hostility – the self severed from the soul, too quickly for the soul to let go.

The particulars become blurred, become generalities, and all changes into the myths built to contain them. Mama flies down the stairs cursing smartly under her breath. The Manager must take his turn at the bar. He descends slowly listening to the voices below. "It's too crowded," he says to himself, "I can't face it." Then in. The drunken traders call out his name. The car horns of a wedding party race down the street. Mama stamps through the Ladies, dousing the floor with Vim and flushing each of the toilets after her. The girls hang out the windows to see the bride. In bad humour Mama strikes out for the kitchen. Peter and the girls hold their breath as they hear her storm across the hall.

Soon, great crowds of people wandered freely throughout the hotel because it was just then that Manager Tom threw open the doors to the tourists. It was the time when the lonely soldiers had claimed all the wild dogs of the town into the barracks. No person in the Cove could have learned privacy. Tradesmen and lords laboured for places at the table. There was meths burning somewhere. And here the guests relaxed when there was enough for all. The butcher's van came each morning, followed soon after by the laundry van. The butcher's lad cut up the beasts. The Manager ate feebly. His breakfast cough drew out the veins on his temples till the flush relaxed into a quiet, embarrassed smile.

Meat eating had driven everyone's brains astray.

Nobody ate fish.

Children were demented by sweet things.

The tourists entering the hotel created a babble like Chinese bells, and flashed their teeth at Joseph in the fleeting smiles beloved of a competitive public. They stayed no longer than necessary and had a practical manner and energy which Joseph admired. Their cases came on wheels. Their vests on hangers. They seemed like free spirits, wandering through alien cultures without hindrance. Nothing was denied them. They were petty and demanding in their eating habits yet exhausting in their honesty. They travelled parts of the country none of the townfolk had been. And benefited from the experience, moving from festival to festival, satisfied with any condition, now that men were dying in a war a few miles up the road.

With confidence at their tables the tourists argued over the menus and the views.

"The utopia of non-arrival," surmised Manager Tom, "though everyone has set out."

"Oh, if I had the money I would up and go," said one of the girls.

The market people expected their trays of coffee at cheap prices. This was Joseph's job. He carried the trays nervously with both hands to the back door, avoiding the waitresses as they flew through the evening meal. The children of the traders played in the crass gold caravans that were filled with silver teapots and huge brass kettles and a variety of mattresses, then, as the hot days arrived, the children shed their thin jerseys and scarves and played down by the river. They climbed the doors of the derelict stables at the back of the hotel where mice nested in the old saddles. From there onto a slated roof that ran to the wall of the Mill, where the paddles had stopped turning. Onto a courtyard filled with a flurry of quartz where men might box to settle an argument while the gypsies silently urged them on.

And in the wall, a red, unused post box, bearing Her Majesty's coat of arms, that had never been repainted.

Carpets of straw, willow baskets, plaited mats, filled the sidewalks.

And during the afternoon Peter sauntered through the china stalls playing "Granny's Gone and Left You the Auld Armchair," or commenced a series of fast airs as he stood on the steps of the hotel, preening himself in the new glass doors, loving his reflection and the flute tilted. Across the square he daundered. Above, through the barred windows of the convent, the orphan girls stole quick glances down. They were making fun of him. One of them lifted her skirt and showed him her hairless thigh. It was no use telling him that she had no one left in the world. For that made him play all the more fiercely. The crucifix in the door shot back and a nun's young face appeared. "Move on, my good man," she said, "or we'll send for the guards."

"The guards, Sister," he answered her, "have enough to do,

with keeping the shopkeepers of the town from beating the heads of the traders."

Tradition was making way for new misfortune.

The shutter shot back, the crucifix reappeared. The girls were gone from above. He walked the square looking back. Country people loaded their vans with second-hand clothes. Young, well-dressed collectors for charity organizations chased middle-aged women with pleas for mentally retarded children. A well-honed stick for driving cattle, with the shape of a fist on the tip, lay forgotten in the Cove next to pools of urine. And young girls, pretending to buy and watched suspiciously by the Indians, shook out linen dresses, held them above their ankles, hand on breast and groin they looked down, and stood uncertain as wading birds while a distance away a companion measured the effect of the pattern against the multi-coloured canopies and cars.

"Equal money on the red," the roulette man called. Local boys stood around trying to ascertain from his eye where the ball would fall. Then, when the market ended, the loudest voices there – those of the religious speakers – would be so suddenly suspended that silence fell like a gap in the wind on the square, and the speakers wound up their mikes and put their loudhailers away, leaving the space to the fire engines which descended with their great hoses to drive the rubbish against the furthest wall of the Market House, and through this soaking mess of fruit and seed and discarded garments and cabbage leaves, drunks and tramps waded to pick at the leavings, or else they came to the back door of the Cove and asked in dumb language for any remains. Farmers fell out of the pubs carried by their women and sons while the sober daughters, empty-handed, followed behind, looking into the faces of strangers. The town filled with the sound of snapping letter boxes as the politicians slipped their leaflets through the doors, and these were the last sounds heard before Finn and Peter, Mama and the Manager, Joseph and Laura and

Liz and Cathleen, and the other girls who came and went, made pleasantly friendly by unceasing labour, started up their fragmentary conversation in the kitchen, and each individual there appeared to be so self-sufficient, in the market and the hotel, that Joseph was stunned by the sheer purpose and intimacy of the people. And every day, mesmerised by the crowds, he explored the different ways to live among them.

VII

32

The galvanize cabin where the labouring men sat on two benches or else stood supporting themselves against the roof, lurched backwards and forwards across the deck of the lorry. The men were coughing and smoking. The cold wind had channelled up through the cables into their hands, their thighs, their cheeks. I thought you were with Ernie, went the voices. No, I was with Jody. Well, I could have sworn you were with Ernie.

The lorry swung around the square and stopped under the monument.

Danny Reed dropped down and slipped off toward the back of the hotel where he kept his scooter parked in a shed. He checked that his chainsaw was in place, then lighthearted, he entered the hotel.

"I'm foundered," said Danny Reed, "I think I'll have a drink of gin somehow." He sat in front of the coal fire in the lounge of the Cove, his knees locked together, his britches steaming. He took great pleasure in having found his niche in the hotel. "Corruption looms," he muttered to himself. With his hand he beat away an imaginary web from his face. He had a flat chest, a flat back and a weathered head. Mama greeted him, "Youse will be soon finished?" she asked. "It was dear bought, Mrs," he replied. Manager Tom greeted him. "Ah," said Danny, "Charles Laughton. Some actor. Do you remember *The Barretts of Wimpole Street? The Witness for the Prosecution?* God Almighty." Another diner, a doctor, entered. With broad fingers spread on one stool, the thumb outstretched on the soft leather of the other, they leaned forward to talk, their faces ear to ear, their heads looking past each other. Danny licked the back of his hand as he spoke. The two parted. The doctor entered the dining room.

"That was a powerful do the other night," Danny said to Joseph who was behind the bar. He waited to see who else would enter that he might have more chat. Danny Reed loved the company of intelligent men, no matter what their class, the bourgeoisie encouraged him, dismissed him. He would hold forth on any subject till the small hours, then drive home the two miles on his scooter to a two-room cottage on the outskirts of town.

The bar remained quiet, so Danny Reed entered the dining room, taking care as he sat down to tuck a newspaper under him.

He glanced up shyly as Liz took his order.

He commenced eating in silence, his hands still raw from the day's work. As he ate he moved his cap around the table. Of a sudden he flicked away a fallen crumb, then fell into a trance, while his lips moved of their own accord. A man struck by solemnity, he made his way through the cabbage and boiled bacon, mopped the plate clean. "I'll have jelly and cream," he said, shaking his head and, palms down, his mind travelled beyond the patter on the wall into a forest of high ferns. No matter, what matter. The ganger, dressed up for the night, entered.

"Are we putting on airs again?" the ganger said.

Hearing the dreaded voice behind him the labourer jumped up angrily, the dessert spoon in his hand.

"Why do you torment me?" whispered Danny, his arms tight against his side, his eyes riveted on the dessert bowl.

"I don't," the ganger answered solidly. "You ought to get that money you owe me now."

"Why do you torment me?" the labourer's chin shook with shame.

"I don't," the ganger looked round with a mirthless laugh.

"Leave me in peace," the labourer pleaded, his voice pained because of this loss of respect.

"You have no friends here," mocked the ganger. He leaned forward. "They are only laughing at you."

The barb struck at some dislocated point in the labourer's hurrying mind. "I'll not take it," he whispered. The debt he owed the ganger became an infinite sum. The ganger spun him on a loose thread because of his inferiority. "I'll finish my meal first," Danny said. He sat down. The ganger watched the black oily teeth of the labourer chew on the last of his food. He let his hands stray. Laura, sensing danger, went out to tell the Manager. The other guests, as they forked food to their mouths, stopped with the prongs to their lips, and stared wide-eyed across at the labourer's table, then feigning indifference they carried on eating, till seconds later they repeated the same frozen gestures, staring across, the food to their mouths, without any trace of self-consciousness, as if the act of eating had somehow made them invisible.

"Yes, we are so grand," the ganger continued.

"Excuse me," said the labourer unexpectedly, coming to his feet in his old dignified role.

The two trod warily out to the foyer.

"Through the back way, men," said Manager Tom. The group arguing the same points moved down the corridor followed by Finn. "I don't know why," said the ganger, "you let that man in. He's just dirt." An animal darted across the features of the labourer and poised in his right eye. "You might think you are all right here," the ganger called back. The four men trooped out across the yard and before anyone there could stop him Danny Reed threw an unexpected fist at the ganger. The ganger was on him, and Finn trying to separate them.

Manager Tom ran for the guards.

Finn cursed and swore at the two men, imploring them as he was tossed to and fro. In the end he had to defend himself against them. They tore the chef's white coat. Tore his body along the cobbled stones while he shouted the most outrageous things that came into his head. He was losing control of himself, and having started out to do good, he had left himself unprotected, and enraged to find himself the victim once again, he could do nothing but scream.

The civic guards came in. The ganger sprinted across the yard and disappeared through the wedding garden. Finn was yelling at the labourer: "You great fucking idiot, you great big fucking idiot!" Suddenly the guards in one quick move grabbed Finn and held him against the door of one of the sheds. He pleaded his case as the girls cursed the guards. Laura was screaming into one of their faces. The guests were at the window. The labourer stole off through the hotel. "I was only trying to stop it," Finn was catching his hoarse breath. They released him. "Jesus," he said, "sure I'm only a country boy like yourselves."

Coming to attention he saluted. "It reminds me of the time when the colonies meant something," he added, "as you can see I never lost my military bearing." He tapped his skull. "It's the hurt mind, the hurt mind, you see. In the wind up of it, we don't know who we are." Getting no response he dropped his voice back into its more normal tone. "I'm not as soft as you thought," he said, "youse thought it would be fierce handy."

One of the guards spoke into his walkie-talkie, then clipped it back on his collar.

"What are you saying there?" queried Finn.

But the guards said nothing. Say nothing their stance told. They stood by the door, each side of it, thinking their own thoughts. "Bastards," shouted Cathy, "Why don't you go after the other pair?" "Best stop quiet and your friend too, Miss," said one of the young guards. If Finn moved, they moved. He sat down to catch his breath. The TV in the curtained-off lounge crackled through his consciousness. The door, after a scream of cars braking, opened into the yard. Three more guards entered. With a slight inclination of his chin one of the arresting guards indicated their troublemaker. They asked Finn to come with them. He remonstrated. In an instant they had him off through the suddenly frightened crowd, along the carpeted corridor past the desk, while Finn shouted, "Stop it, stop it, I'll walk."

As they dragged him off into the first car a hail of abuse erupted from the girls. Joseph approached the second squad car and leaned in at the passenger door. "Can I go down with you?" asked Joseph, "I'm a friend of his." "You can, surely," said the driver. They hauled Joseph, kicking and spitting, into the rear of the car. The driver lashed out with his baton. "Take that, you fucker you," the driver said out of this nightmare and struck at the back of the young fellow's head. They drew him across the backseat. The other two guards sat on his face and shoulders.

Joseph bellowed into the upholstery.

"Take that, you black Northern cunt," the driver said, hitting him again without turning round. "Bastard," the two that held him hollered, urging each other on into a ritual that needed every man's consent. They held him like an animal being injected to death. Rained blows on the crown of his skull till he bundled up and stopped struggling. "You fucking animals, you fucking animals," he repeated, then went quiet. The least move brought another blow. His nose and chin were pressed into a pool of blood on the seat against which he knelt. In minutes he was reduced to passivity, without cunning, a creature that prays for it all to end as abruptly as it had begun. The final image, that of Manager Tom running breathlessly alongside the car as it wheeled round the square.

The guards stood away from Joseph as if seeing him for the first time as the duty sergeant took his name in the barracks. He caught a glimpse of Finn being quickly taken to a different room so that the two might not see each other. All the formalities were familiar to Joseph; still that did not stop him shaking. It was just that he had nothing to lose. It had happened so often to his family. The sergeant was sympathetic and soft-spoken. From the minute he saw the boy's injuries he never looked up again as he took down the details.

"A riotous crowd had assembled," a guard with bulging cheeks explained contritely.

Joseph put his fingers tenderly to his scalp where numbness was spreading like a warm liquid. Hair came away in his hands.

"They tried to kill me," he said.

"Answer the sergeant," a voice behind told him sharply.

A dutiful hand on his shoulder, he was taken through a warm glass corridor that ran by pebbledashed walls outside. The barracks at the time was being extended. As they unlocked a cell a woman stood with her back to him at the end of the corridor, her stomach pressed up against the radiator.

He felt the soft fall of blood from his eye onto his cheek.

A man was bundled up on the single bunk under the only blanket in Joseph's cell. He never stirred as the door swung to. Not even when seconds later a harsh explosive sound erupted in the corridor. Joseph peered through the slot. Stripped to their blue shirts, their armpits soaking in the heat, two guards were cutting through the chain of a pair of handcuffs with an electric grinder. The handcuffs were chaining the woman to the radiator. It was an impossible sight. One of the guards was laughing at the other, for losing the keys, must be.

They laughed back at Joseph's shouts at them.

And she kept her face away from the din, proffering her bare wrist, her coat rolled up her arm.

He could not see her face. She kept her head sideways, her temple pressed against the wall, her chin buried in her shoulder as the metal filings flew, and when the sawing screeched to a halt and the guards took up a new position, the veins in her wrists drummed and clove together, as follows a disturbance in water or some quiet place. The chain gave at last, and the guards let the woman follow after them down the corridor, like a beast trailing its reins.

Joseph pounded on the doors. "Will you stop that racket. You'll only make it worse for yourself," advised the man in the bunk. Joseph did not heed him but continued to call out, his eye pressed to the slot. Someone passing slapped their knuckles against the slot. Joseph shot back. Eventually, then, the assault on his body withdrew sufficient for him to dispense with temper or remonstration. He knew there was nothing further to gain. He sat down, but considered only survival and after that, revenge.

"Allen, Joseph Allen," said a voice through the aperture, "you there?"

"Yes," answered Joseph. Automatically he brushed down his clothes.

"Do you remember me?"

Joseph righted his pupil and looked through the hole.

"No," he replied.

"Do you not remember me from the South of Fanacross?" the guard said grinning, "I'm Cadogan."

"No," said Joseph, "I can't remember you."

"We were at school together."

"No," repeated Joseph, "but can you help?"

"Ah well, I never liked you anyway," Cadogan replied, and he burst out laughing, and further up the corridor there was more laughter from guards unseen. They were laughing at the mad Allens. Like the laughter you hear from a dancehall when you are outside passing by, bound by a different code than the dancers within.

"I told you," said the other prisoner, lying back, his voice tired of assumed innocence.

After about an hour, which he spent stock-still against the cell wall, the duty sergeant came. "You are lucky," he said through the slot, trying hard to ascertain the injuries to the lad, "that you are not to be charged with assault. You'll soon be out of here." The sergeant went away. Joseph sat by the feet of the other prisoner, waiting, but nothing happened. It grew cold. When he roared out the other prisoner told him to stay quiet. "Can't you just take it like the rest of us?" he said. His head grew water-tight. He was back on his feet again. The hole in front of his eyes became like something he was breathing through. He looked through the slot across the corridor, through a window, across the yard, through a further window that opened to the left of the duty sergeant's desk. Here, uniformed policemen passed now and then, till, with relief he saw Finn, going over and back, and he knew that Finn would not desert him. Silently he watched.

"Hey, Mister," he heard someone calling from behind him.

He worked his way along the wall of the cell till he found a pipe leading along the back wall into the cell next door.

"Hey, Mister," he heard again, "my brother is freezing."

"What age are you?" asked Joseph, crouching by the rough hole the pipe made.

"I'm thirteen," said the voice, "me brother is twelve."

Joseph looked round, wondering what to do.

"Are you there?" asked the boy.

Joseph quietly stole the blanket off the other prisoner. The man turned in his sleep. He drew his knees up to his stomach. The blanket came away from under his buttocks. "Take a hold of that," said Joseph. He bundled a corner of the blanket along the pipe through the hole.

"Have you got it?"

There was no answer. The blanket started disappearing. Then, when he had got it half-way through the boy could get it no further. "I can't, Mister," he mumbled back. Joseph pulled it out, twisted it round like a rope but could not get the end through the hole for the boy to catch it. "What's happening, Mister?" the voice asked pleadingly, so close to Joseph that he could have been whispering into his ear. Joseph stamped the blanket with his heels. This time he pushed the end through. In silence the boy hauled. Joseph could hear him breathing as he stopped pulling, then getting only inches at a time, he started again. For a long time the blanket lay half-in and half-out the hole. "Are you there?" Joseph whispered.

There was no answer.

"Are you there?" Joseph whispered louder.

There was no reply. He kept his ear along the pipe listening. After a while the blanket appeared to start moving again of its own accord. Then, with Joseph pushing wads of it from his side, and the boy pulling it through with little jerks, after a great deal of sweating and breathing, it finally disappeared through the hole.

"Are you all right now?" asked Joseph.

There was no answer. It seemed like the gypsy lads had just collapsed where they were under the blanket. Not long after, Joseph heard the guards coming for him, and just when he didn't care any longer, his cell door opened. A square of light fell on him. He began shaking uncontrollably.

Manager Tom was shocked and bewildered. He lifted Joseph's chin and stared with horror at the side of his face. Lawyer Smith was having a few words in the sergeant's office. A policeman gave Finn his overcoat to put over the shaking lad. "Jesus," he said, "look what youse have done to him." The sergeant without once being unaware of what he had told Joseph earlier ordered the prosecuting guard to read out the charges against him. The guard read out the charges of assault, resisting arrest and obstruction in a schoolboyish manner, as if he were afraid of strangers. It was a crazy task. All that remained of him was this function after everything had ended. In some elusive way, he read the charges so laboriously, the guard might have been accusing himself, but when Joseph signed his name to the charge sheet when asked, the burden of guilt shifted to him, the guard was cleared of all incrimination.

"Have you anything to say?" asked the duty sergeant. "Ask him if he has anything to say."

"Have you anything to say?" asked the guard.

"I didn't hit anyone," said Joseph.

"I didn't hit anyone," repeated the guard, and wrote it down in a large childish hand while the sergeant never once raised his eyes as he told the time for court in the morning. They stepped out into the night. The lawyer drove them to the hospital. "They want to make a deal," said Lawyer Smith. "They'll want to drop the assault and resisting, the two serious ones, if you'll plead to obstruction." He turned into the drive of the hospital. "There's worse things happening to others in this country." For once his voice seemed comforting. "I'll leave it up to you." Joseph's ear was the size of an open hand, the veins stood out like bicycle spokes, his lips were furry with dried blood. The doctor swung a pencil at various angles before his eyes, tapped his forehead and cleaned out his eye. The bruises were quickly growing a darker blue than his pupil. The knot of pain, he explained, was at its worst in the uppermost knuckle of his spine. "I'm afraid," said the doctor, "we can do nothing about that."

He softly touched the boy's raw shoulders.

"That's fear," he said.

The hospital bell to casualty rang.

A young speechless woman walked in that everyone knew round the town. They knew her plight, but did nothing. Holding her gently came the father. Behind came the mother, the sister, the younger sister. They sat in one of the cubicles talking away in a secret manner, stopping immediately when the young doctor passed then starting again. The doctor continued to dab at Joseph's skull. Manager Tom looked out of the hospital window on the lamps in the garden and the town beyond. One of the sisters came up to him for a light. "Is everything all right?" asked Manager Tom.

"Oh," said she, "she is there for all time." She took a long drag from the cigarette. "You are one nice fellow." She walked back to the cubicle.

"Out from that," continued the voice of the doctor, "there is nothing to worry about."

"Oh, I know, Annie," Manager Tom heard the girl say.

"You will?"

"I will."

"She was about it all right."

"He came in ..." the mother's voice, "that's where it all started." Each voice seemed miles distant from the other. The Manager felt stranded. A great desire built up in him for a drink where all these voices might harmonize. "Jesus," said the girl, "I have all the luck." "OK," said the doctor to Joseph, "I'll let you go now. Just watch the ear. Well, Annie, what's the trouble now?" Lawyer Smith led them down the steps like a man certain of his role. He was talking too in a general way. Joseph's case, Joseph knew, was only one of the many he had listened in upon.

No one got any sleep that night at the Cove. Lawyer Smith would not let Joseph be. The girls were over and back from the kitchen to the lounge with tea. Traipsing to the bar for drinks. The guests, the girls and the family discussed the case till dawn.

Lawyer Smith was adamant. "Plead to the lesser charge," he maintained, "or they will make your life hell."

Finn felt guiltiest of all. He had been released without charge. He went about the lounge, a glass in his hand, trying hard to resurrect his old self, but every time he saw Joseph, he was back at stage one, lying under Danny Reed in the yard. Joseph had no grand reason to carry him through the night, all he asked was that his mother should not hear of what happened. He slipped away to bed while the rest were talking, and whoever it was came and sat at the bottom of his bed he couldn't tell, but somewhere between stiff colourless dreams he knew someone was there, hovering lest he fall into too deep a sleep. Manager Tom, Lawyer Smith and himself entered the court the next morning. Joseph was white as a sheet from dry puking on the way there.

"Whatever you decide to do," Lawyer Smith explained, "you will always blame me."

Their advice echoed through his head, calling him back to an earlier time he couldn't identify. To his right was the car thief that had shared his cell the previous night. In front the woman who had been chained to the radiator. Along the wall the guard who had driven the squad car stood chatting with two others who had beaten him. When he saw the lad he took him aside.

"You are under my care now, Joseph," he said, and hearing his Christian name on his aggressor's lips made Joseph wince. He tried to see the cynicism, the hatred behind the statement, but the guard smiled shamelessly back.

Danny Reed and the ganger entered.

They waved to him.

And now Joseph got this terrible feeling of foreboding, of loss, for he knew that not here could he shout out any injustice he thought might have been done to himself. In the eyes of all he had somehow invited it. He felt that all the talk of the night before, of taking the guards through a court of law, was just as if he had struck out with his fist in his sleep, but waking, could never tell the power of the blow. A second bruised skin of pain was drawn tight about his head. The violence of the night before was being humanized before his very eyes. That was what this meant, the guard speaking to him like that, the ganger and Danny speaking together as friends. Soon, all the accused from the cells of the night before were moved together, and there was some form of camaraderie on this bench.

Everyone else was different till the judgement was made. And beyond. For no matter the pronouncement, his innocence was gone, in his own eyes and in the eyes of others. And then Joseph remembered that as they hit him in the depths of his being he had said, I'll hoard this, and as they stopped, I'll remember all this for again. "Plead to technical obstruction, accept their offer," again the solicitor said, "because of where you are from, and what's going on, he could give you time."

The judge entered. The court stood.

Joseph pleaded not guilty. A trial by jury a month on was called for. That month passed like a nightmare. Again, in a different court, before the eyes of the jury he pleaded not guilty to all three charges. The jury found him not guilty of assault, but could not agree on the other charges. Another trial was called for. The guards came to the door of the hotel at closing time every night. Attempts at friendship were made. Again Lawyer Smith pleaded with him. He said: "No matter what you do, they have you anyway. The night before the final trial he never slept at all. He felt his strength going from him. He was on his own. On the following morning he nodded his acceptance of the guilty plea. The jury was discharged. When they heard his pleas, the guards smiled, then their faces became impassive again. When he pleaded guilty in the box he knew that he was signing away a part of his life that could never be retrieved. Now he had connived with them. He understood at last his father's destiny, unless you take a side, your life is worthless. They had broken Joseph, but at least Finn had never any need to tell exaggerated stories of his life again. Secretly, he would go over the events of that night and see it all differently. The fight would never start. He would not have got involved. But Joseph, thinking on these things, saw that his own approach to the police would have been different. It would not have been made by a man who had certain basic rights, but by someone who knew the dangerous defiles of life itself.

For rights only satisfied a claim to revenge.

He was seeing it all differently. That was what reality was then, something that was constantly changing, happening so quickly that it appeared too hard to be ever understood. He saw this often in the faces of those who had suffered more

squalid wrongs than himself. Their humorous fight against
the dark in themselves. Joseph thought of this often as he
turned in after another quarrelsome day in the kitchen. And
then he tried to forgive them, the guards. For, if he did not,
they would still have power over him. They could still strike
fear into his heart. For years after he was afraid. Going over
the night in his mind. And after that, the night his father
died. Then, one day he forgave them.

33

The night that the guards hit Joseph Helen woke with a start
in her bed. She had felt the impact of the blow. Terrified, she
hugged Margaret to her. "Oh Helen," said Margaret, "you
must try getting out of the house, you must get out."

Fanacross.

Dear Joseph,
It was not your mother's sanity went but her memory.
She sees things isolated, as they are, connected to nothing
in the past, irreversibly severed from their fellows and
therefore offered up obscene. She fears the coming day
because of its distance from the day before which she
no longer knows. There are no longer any signals from
the past.

You should write to her.

She fears the present day because it ends irrefutably
what has gone before. When her memory ended, the
future went as well.

A wall has become a structure that keeps nothing in
or out. Just an assembly of hollow listless stones. Her
emotions are fossilized. She knows nothing more. Her
story has ended while in the mouth, in the mouths of
others, it has just begun. The killing has started grave

rumours in the locality. Your grandfather sits at the end of the bed, and he tries with his own death in mind to imagine, as closely as possible, a possible life before, and both explore the joy of telling what has escaped them. That old security had within itself ingredients of its own downfall.

We hear not a word from my father or Jim.

She does not speak of your father. I know that you love to hear stories of your father, but this time you will have to do without.

love,

Margaret.

George's House.
Fanacross.

Joseph,

Has anything happened to you. I thought I saw something happen you. Myself and all are well. All kinds of things come back, you might not remember them. The time your father gave Jim all those cigarettes, and he smoked them down by the lake, and he was so sick and afraid to come back to the house that he climbed in behind Lizzie Dolan who was doting and confined to bed. She'd only get up for an hour in the morning. When Jim came back to himself he came out to the kitchen of the house. "Where are you coming from?" asked the unmarried daughter of the house. She would never look at a man. "I got sick," said Jim, "and I got in behind your mother till I was better."

Thinking of it brings tears to my eyes.

Everything has got so fierce pricey that I can't send anything on with this letter but will with the next. Anyway, this year, T.G., is nearly over for all of us. I hope the next brings better luck. They got me tablets here to sleep and I'm not the better of them. I was about the house all night watching the clock. I feel so odd.

Everything else is the same here. You could come down the village from the house and not come across a light till you reach the pub. They are all gone, left, you see, now. That's the wind up of it. I sent all your father's clothes on to George. Your father was not a man to look into the future. Neither was I, I'm sorry to say, but at least Pop is not as bad as he was. He's mellowed somewhat. He's got over the fact of someone else coming to live in the house. Well, don't be grieving.

    You mother, Helen.

The Cove

    Mother,

I'm the best. Jim turned up the other day in the market selling fish. He would not come up to the hotel. He's odd like that. He said he did not want to be putting in on anybody. He says he'll be back each market day. He told me that Uncle George has two shares on a trawler out of Killybegs, and doesn't look back. Mama, as you well know, is always going on about the "appearance of some people." Finn the chef is great crack. He said the other day that "Sure England is only a permanent launching pad for America." Cathy, one of the girls here, loves to sit up to the range and the other night she got an awful pong. It was her slippers were on fire. Peter is off on his travels again. Manager Tom is down with a cold in the chest. He's a dread to complain. They are all butty men down here. Not like up in that direction. It's all to go in the hotel.

    Your loving son,
    Joseph.

Fanacross.
George's House.

Joseph,

I can remember so many things. Like the time I was in the scullery and heard the front door open. Of course the television took a leap, and your grandfather was glued to it at the time seeing he had the eyesight back. "Here's that f—er Macpherson coming," said Pop, calling your father by maiden name. "How are you Pop?" said Frank entering. "What the f— do you want?" asked Pop, "Have you got no home to go to?" T.G. all that is over. It's funny now but I could have throttled Pop then. Still and all he was never mean. He'd complain, then slip me money when things were short on the side. "Aye," he said of your father, "and feet on him like tailor's cutting boards."

I'll never forget the night he had to sleep between George and Frank because the basement was flooded. "Jesus Christ," he said, the next morning, "it was like sleeping between two elephants. The f—er from Clare had me half killed." Well that's all I can remember today. God bless.

Your mother, Helen.

Fanacross.
George's House.

Joseph,

Nothing has changed. When he lived with me I went through the same day, thinking always what might make him happy and affected always by an insecurity that plagued me. Many's a time I asked him to take this guilt away. Now that he is not here it's still the same. He was not with me then, he is not with me now, only his physical presence is removed, that is the only difference. The rows were over. But I curse those that killed him. And I curse the British below on the bridge that I see every day from my window here at the house. That row is not over. All they are doing is creating false hopes for us all. The other day they spat at one of the women of the village from their lorry. I'm afraid that somehow Frank took you away with him. I hear so little from you. But it would be detrimental for me to indulge myself in thoughts of what things would be like if you came back. I would not blame you if you went out with the others wanting to kill. I often wanted to take a life myself, I admit it, and could. But who is the enemy. That crowd down at the bridge? They hate our existence. Where will it all end? A woman should not care what a man thinks. She should look to her own kind. Only for Margaret I would be driven demented. They are trying to assess the value of your father. Seemingly he was not worth much in the eyes of the authorities. He had no job. No pension. No home, really. Was that his fault? Jesus, now I wish I had made more of myself before, rather than depending on him. It weakened me. I could kill all right. But don't heed me, it's all this fighting with the law has suddenly brought me to my senses, love.

Your loving mother, Helen.

PS They are trying to get me to settle out of court for a measly sum that I won't hear of.
PPS When I have digested the half of it I'll send it on to you, seeing as in the old-fashioned way you are the man of the house now.

Fanacross.

Master Joseph,

I see repeatedly in your letters a slight forgetfulness of me. I might as well never have existed for you, but I suppose you have your worries, still a little concern would have gone a long way. Well I've got a story for you.

In my dream my real mother, so high, takes my arm. She is wearing her tweed coat. And a Persian lamb collar. We saunter round this city. For one whole day I forget my present family as if they have never been. Her eyes I need to air my soul. I walk with my small mother to and fro, through the supermarkets, across a broad traffic-laden bridge. The light is on in my room above. I know you are up there waiting on me.

You, jewelled instrument.

My mother says, Why, you have a young man.

Yes, mother, I say coyly.

You must be terribly in love, she says.

But before I can enter the joy of that, something else is beginning.

Our souls leave us. See. They fly right through the walls of our chests. Emptied so fast our bodies fall. The children pipe up like birds in the village. My mother sits sparrowing away till the last mouth is fed. Satisfied, leaving one, two, three ... eight, nine, ten pounds under the clock. I look down from my room to watch my mother, who has been away so long, cross the street below. She stops under a light and looks back up. With terrible fear I see poor Geraldine's face.

I wake because I say I am dreaming – I must not wake everyone with this noise. I make an effort from my subconscious to break the hold of the dream which is all the life I have lived up till now. I wake sweating but quick to judge my condition rationally. I am still afraid for all those voices in the dream continue unabated in my ears, so I woke your mother and say: "Can you hear voices, radio voices?" She rose onto her elbows, looked round and listened intently. Then went over to the window. Out on the road a jeep was parked with soldiers in it. "Oh Christ," she says, "why do they do this to us?" Each night they are around waiting on George to return. The whole point being that they can prove that your father was associated with the IRA. Then your mother won't get a penny. They have interrogated us and interrogated us till I can take no more. Write please.

Love, Margaret.

Fanacross.

Joseph,
This is the sort of mail I receive now. Please read the enclosed.

Dear Mrs Allen,
With reference to your letter of the – inst.

If your husband was a member of the Provisional IRA and was shot leaving the scene of a crime, or because of internal feuding, no monies would be paid out. The victim is not deemed to be innocent in this instance. Therefore his relatives are not entitled to compensation. The same would hold true for the parents of a child who was fatally wounded by a plastic bullet where it could be definitely established that he/she was involved in rioting etc.

I would again recommend that you accept our out-of-court payment of £3,000 as we do not wish you to have to go through the ordeal of a court case after your recent bereavement, also compensation might be withheld should evidence arise that your late husband was at the time of his death involved in terrorist activities.

Yours respectfully,

P. Heaslip, Sol.

What activities do they think he was at standing at his own door? There was a preliminary hearing about the death of your father last Tuesday. It would appear from all that was said that I was the killer. My dreams now are of courtrooms, with last night a small grey dog, as strong and fierce as a badger, fighting with me while other people persisted in regarding it as a harmless pet. It must have been inspired by the barrister's wig. The place in fact abounds in weasels and ferrets, pigs and rhinoceroses. I was reminded of one of those exaggerated stories of your father where he claimed a pom fell off the slip one day into the lake, and further downstream Sandy Heffernan caught a thirty-pound pike and in the belly found the pom suckling six pups. I have to amuse myself somehow. We all up here in the direction seem living in the belly of a pike.

Your loving mother, Helen.

PS Do not even dream of returning.

The Cove Hotel

Dear Mammy and Margaret,

Mama has asked me to ask you if you could come down here March 17th, St Patrick's Day, as she has a little something arranged for you. I hope everything is working out for you. I miss you all.

Joseph

Fanacross,
Stormy and wet.

Joseph,

Well, I have persuaded Helen to go down to see you all, as for myself I am in a bit of trouble and can't make it. I presume I can rely on you to say nothing if I tell you. I became pregnant, and made up my mind to have an abortion. I had shame all right because of the place I was consigned to. I had shame because I feared it would affect the intimacies of my pregnancies ahead. I was ashamed because I had to lose consciousness and all happened outside my responsibility. Because I was ignorant. Because they said I was using it as a form of contraception. There you go, the unwanted pregnancy and the required lovemaking are at odds with each other. It's not easy. It doesn't matter what you say. The republicans care nothing for their women. The Sinn Fein women are liars. They are just Catholics like the rest. I looked for help everywhere but it was a Protestant agency looked after me. It is my right, that's the way I was thinking. The worst about it is everyone going around looking for love and affection. You trust the man. I was drunk as a skunk, and woke up with him on top of me. "Don't be annoyed, I couldn't stop myself, Jazuz," he says, "you have such a beautiful body." Aye. They make us into a mother. All for a few moments of affection. Christ, I hate the Madonnas. Hate. Hate. Hate. And then at the base, hidden deep in the masculine psyche, rarely viewed except in the laws that be, is a belief that woman is secondary. That she complements the inferior parts of the males. I know it, I've seen it. So when I touched him, the same fellow, he was filled with distaste for himself, and for me, and though he willed himself to forget this cursed anxiety, it was no use. So now, here I am in a bad way, I feel awful, no matter how much I wanted it. But I was invaded by him. What he left in me was something foreign. For such a small operation it took the heart out of me because of all I had to put up with, so I'll not go down. Oh, it's great to be loved by the raw recruit but then you lose them to the others. I keep saying there is a continuity to life and life is made up of the half-forgetting. Forgetfulness in a way can provide continuity, at least for us. For the Protestants will have to forgive too. Those who continue to remember harbour the destruction while the English are laughing. I hope you and your mother can talk, and thanks for the long and lovely letter you wrote me, throughout the trip to England, you were with me in a warm and reassuring way and I hope you treat this woman Laura well when she accepts you.

Margaret, love.

PS How is it that we leave our labour and our foetuses in England?

Fanacross

Dear Joseph,

I know now what Tom's wife wanted me down for, and that it's done out of the good of her heart, but tell her I could not take the fuss and the crowds. I'm sure she'll understand. Your grandfather is back complaining again:

"Will you have a rasher?" I asked him.

"I wouldn't eat the rashers round here," he says, "they're from an auld hog who just gave himself up."

"A sausage?"

"Do you know, my good woman, what goes into them? I had a couple last week and I was up on the throne all night. They went through me like whey."

"An egg?"

"Jesus," he says, "it's a terror what you see when you haven't got a gun." Well, for myself, I was never better. Every day I get a little more back to myself. To think how I wasted my life before. It comes back to me. I mind one evening Jim carried you in. After youse were beaten up, because, I suppose, of religion. Your eyelids blue and filled with pus. Tears coming down your face and terrible shivers going through you, so I brushed your face with morsels of meat, picked the blood from your hair. I dabbed at the cracks in your skulls. That's one of our roles. I suppose. You, son, are a ghost I hear behind me as I sit in the house overlooking the lake. Sometimes it's your father. But now at least I get out of the house and love to get into Enniskillen, especially up the stairs into the draper's apartment where I love to go in the afternoons when things are quiet to watch the carefully dressed men smoothing out the rolls of dark materials and the tailors within the small rooms carrying out neat repairs. From the yard beyond the cheers of the coalmen shovelling behind them without once looking, the glasscutters nipping the panes with skilful taps, the ham turning on the slicers, and all the cheeses, the metal cups of money colliding overhead after shooting along the rails from the various departments, and then, in their spring-loaded clips the bills and the change flying back over the heads of the customers. That's my day, look after yourself.

Your loving mother, Helen.

Fanacross.

Dear Joseph,
Someone has to be always falling in love.
Tell her, this woman, Laura.

It channels all fright away, especially the first time, for we'll surely after this find ourselves in some god-forsaken place. I know it, the love. When the fluids that pass between the body and the soul are trapped for a few excruciating seconds in the pit of the loins. It's weakening.

Yesterday, it was one of those days of stupendous adventure when men working are transferred into songs of joy. Oh, I hear myself. How our country must have prospered under water. For I was tired of the reincarnation of men, wanting the whole thing to begin over, from a world of having no reflection of itself, my ignorance of life and other people to be total. The war has driven us so far back into ourselves. So, I walked and walked. The first footsteps from home transformed me without my knowing.

The reeds of the path where I walked had been trimmed by icy winds. The ground turned sodden.

First I saw a bush mirrored in the mist on the lake. The full moon swung by. What Peter would say: "You'd have the moon on a bright night when you wouldn't want it." And then the white sun, half-etched. The bottom half lost in the mist. A goose cranked her wings in fright away, disappearing, a greyness with shadows, car wheels somewhere in the depths of it breaking thin branches, crunching gravel. The guns opened up. In the mist they echoed across three lakes. The pounding breath of dogs and men a field away. The sun was a white round moon, rounded by greenness. No birds or fish flew in it. The bush floated and grew, guns were somewhere about.

Then came a shot, one went east and one went west.

The end of the season was nigh.

January frost sparkled on the horns of the cattle. They tore at the raw hoary grass. Their beards filled with dew. The sun was gone and rusted transparent clouds steadied in the light blue water above the blackening mist. The clouds went under the water. The water was grey. I was tirelessly alone. I could feel everything. The distance between the clouds and the reflection remained on the surface of the water.

Other bushes appeared.

The far shore blackened off and hovered.

Blue again spread over the grey mist.

I wanted the drug to go on and on.

Then the water's edge sharpened. Something was wrong. The hunters were laughing, getting into their cars, doors slammed, I prayed they would go away, pink became transparent on the lake, pink light spread. It was colder. The burnt cloud moved on. Come the curlews. I was stepping out of myself. Come the hoarse big bellied roars of the hungry cattle. Evening, ice was tightening down again. A last shot erupted off the hill behind me, scattering the senses. The shot careered off the lake to the right, petered away among the treetops with an ache like jealousy. Only the bush was left on the grey still water.

I was never so happy.

The moon itself had been behind me all the time. Nothing at all to be seen except the moon towering overhead, and after a while she went too, next minute she was not there, but streams everywhere tumbling down, cheerful sisters into the lakes below. Who can explain what I felt. Then I heard the cows again. I'd seen the farmers earlier hurling fodder beside the fences for the Friesians to eat, then changing the trough of water in the blinding sleet. There they were gathered with fixed almond eyes in the cold. They were there half the night straining through the fence towards the silage and the fresh hay. What I needed just then was a map of the world to enlighten me for my journey, to sweep over the hilarious valleys where the earth's imagination began. In the eyes of the heifers and the bullocks I had seen the female in myself. It was like a place where the human mind has never been.

My love, Margaret.

Fanacross.

Joseph,

Winter is at the wall, a constant rebuke. Myself and Helen travelled up to Glan to one of the old sweat houses. I thought of the old steaming men beating their backs with cold ivy. The stones heated. And eyes cleansed of inwardness till blood courses with some new pleasures of the flesh. The drunken old men gathering inside the heaviness of the damp stone roof. Flailing at the smouldering stones with damp rushes. The cold of the moors. I shiver like a bittern. Warm alcohol seeps from their pores. Steam softens their gums and crooked toes. Myself and Helen stand against the wall shielding ourselves from the wind that comes from Enniskillen.

Hoarse shouts from the stone house would tell of the delirium within.

The cold wind drives out frocks against our thighs.

Old men with wall-eyes stumble into the evening light to watch us walking through Glan. I imagine their limbs are steaming. The sheep nip at our hard thighs. The men jump into the icy pool where the great river leaped up, salmon-shaped. And in the pub afterwards the men tell laborious stories of Glan and their lives, talking prick-shape and bird-shape. Afraid of being alone the whole of their lives. The youngsters in Belcoo grab at me and I think they are talking of truth because they were drunk with desire. They touch my breasts.

Such small breasts they say pityingly. And as we drive down the mountains to the lakes below it seemed the whole Island went under and cast off all responsibilities for the world by resting on the bed of the lakes. But that's not the way it's to be. The soldiers go through the car from bottom to top, speaking in a dignified manner they try to tell us that Fanacross is miles distant while we know it is only over the brow of the hill.

Yours, with love, Margaret.

PS Their indifference gives us great strength for the days ahead.

Killybegs

Dear Joseph,

I have been intending to write to you for a long time. I know something of what has been happening in Fanacross, and I blame myself for your father's death. I am terribly sorry for all that has happened. If it means me appearing in court, and giving up my freedom to protect your family, then I'll do so when the time comes.

Fondly, your Uncle George.

The night after Joseph received the letter from George he was with a couple of lads out round the town, trying inferior acid. Things kept going wrong and the more they implored him, the worse it became. He could not bear the thought of George apologizing to him. He saw George's skull split wide open. He could not make the two parts join, so he fled the lads he was with. The hotel was rocking on its foundations. Each step on the stairs a precipice till he reached his room. Here things settled a while. He watched the shadows of the leaves cast by the street light below crossing the walls of his room. It was a magical reassuring evening that started. He read the letters from

Margaret over and over that he could understand. He lay on the window by the low bed. Old languages that he had been cut off from for so long sought his brain, that tenderness might come back. The simple, healthy and loving came easy now a while, and would be there again, he hoped, in the next place, when he could give, and giving, recall. He knocked softly on Laura's door but she did not appear. Then he went back to playing with the sulphurous colours till dawn.

34

This was long ago. Another separate place in time.

The low moan came up through the depths of the hotel. Mama lay there trying to tell whether the cry was animal or human. A kitten maybe, hurled into the river, that was screaming against the weight of what was bearing her down. The moans became so distant that Mama had to call upon all her sympathies to sit up and listen. The next moan was indistinct, yet seconds later it reached the same pitch. Mama immediately swung her feet onto the cold wooden floor, drew Tom's overcoat over her shoulders and slipped out into the corridor. She braced herself. She tiptoed to Liz's door and was on the point of going away again, when this time, in earnest, the clear heartfelt moan began inside. She knocked and pushed the door in.

"Oh Mama," said Liz raising herself up, so that her unpinned hair fell down her arms, "I'm awful sorry."

"What's wrong, Liz?" asked Mama, leaning out to touch her on the shoulder.

The girl seemed to have woken from some nightmare. In answer she just moaned again. "Now stop this," said Mama. The room smelled of talcum powder and the body tang of sharp sweat. Nylons hung from a hanger on the window. There were posters of bandleaders on the walls. Her clothes were tossed onto the carpet in a heap. And her high-heeled shoes sat one on top of the other, where she had just toed them off without undoing the straps.

Beads of sweat now flowed down the girl's chest.

"Tell me now," said Mama, gently.

"I have a pain in my stomach," whispered Liz, turning her face away.

"Can I get you anything?" asked Mama, patiently.

The girl fell silent. She mustered her strength. She stole a pathetic look at Mama. "I meant to tell you, I meant to tell, I did," said Liz, nearly rejecting Mama because someone more evil lurked beyond, and could not be told. Behind Mama stood another wretched woman that Mama could not see.

"Don't worry, Liz, everything—"

"I'm going to have a baby, Mama," and Liz held her in her gaze.

"What?"

"Yes, Mama," and giving up on Mama, she buried her head in the pillow. "And I'm going to have it now."

Mama ran out of the room and flew through her own door. "Tom, Thomas," she screamed, pulling at him, "run down and phone the doctor! Quick! Quick!" He came straight to his feet out of a haphazard sleep to do her bidding. Mama raced to and fro demented. "Have you got him?" she shouted down. No answer. Back to Liz's door she went, but did not enter. "Tom," she shouted. Again she heard Liz moaning. What to do? "Mama," called up Manager Tom, "he wants to speak to you." "Go on up," she told him, "go on up you and hold Liz's hand." He entered the girl's room dutifully, not knowing what he would find there, and the first moan he heard made him hesitate lest touching her he should break something. Liz turned a tearful, crazy eye to him. Her splayed fingers took his proffered wrist, her belly rose. He was frightened by the hard-skinned strength of her small grip, how her eyes seemed ready to spring from their sockets. "Oh Jesus, Manager Tom," she cried. "Easy, Liz," he said, and added unsurely, "you'll be all right now." "You had better get her to a hospital," said the doctor over the phone. "If anything happens to her there, it'll be your fault." To the hospital, thought Mama, without comprehension. So she phoned the fire brigade. Five minutes later came the siren and the lights, and the girl was carried down the stairs by the helmeted men in their gaiters and capes and driven away into the night in the rear of the fire engine, and she never once let go of Manager Tom's hand, and he, as he took the increasing violence of the grip, was amazed to see that her hair reached beyond the extent of her straining arm, across the thick blanket, to her thighs, and she held him right up to the moment the child was delivered twenty minutes later, so easy, so silently that he did not know it was over till the nurse dropped the dripping newborn onto the scale.

Liz had white hair. Long beautiful hair that would tumble down her buttocks when she unpinned it after work in the secrecy of her room. All day she kept it tied under a scarf to her scalp so that no one would know. She'd turn on the radio and listen to the showband music. Sometimes, too, she would turn over to Radio Luxemburg. At first, she trusted no one in the hotel and spoke to no one. Then Cathy became her friend. So then she'd pin her hair back up to join Cathy downstairs by the range in the kitchen. There the two would sit for an hour or two each night. Here, isolated from everyone, Cathy would play her two-rowed Paolo Soprani accordion with the rose grille and Liz would sit perched on the edge of her chair, her brow furrowing every so often. She answered questions about her past with a clouding of her dishonest blue eyes. It was winter. The fields beyond the town and the wedding garden were abounding in firewood and the girls had boxes of sticks stacked along the range to see them through the long nights.

Liz had arrived that September during the last of Manager Tom's drinking bouts. As yet, the hotel had few guests, there were unfinished rooms, there was plenty of cleaning to be done. Mama found Liz's silence impenetrable. The girl never complained, and sometimes took ages to understand what you were saying because her mind was elsewhere. Inside her head she hummed the name of the man that had betrayed her. Sometimes she saw his father too, a cluster of carbuncles on his left ear. They had broken her spirit a while, that's all.

Now, stepping into a certain pair of white shoes reminded her of her man. Her stomach raced. She relented. She locked her lover in her arms right up to the night the child was born, the night the waters broke down her thighs as she was scrubbing the grease above the cooker.

By then she had been at the Cove five months.

On her knees on the stairs, hoovering. Sometimes standing alone by the river going over something. Life each day grew more unfamiliar and threatening as if some evilness had reached and darkened everything. All round her the nightmare. The remembered hostilities of those who were incapable of love. Hardened beyond redemption.

She wore peasant dresses. The day she answered the advertisement for the hotel she wore a swinging dress. Accepted, a cold sense of responsibility settled on her. She had chosen a place as far away from her home as possible. The town was of no interest to her. Neither was the hotel. This was only to be a pause before she started her real life. Mama took her in without comment. Each night she released her womb out of slacks tied tight with string under a heavy long jumper. The fly wide open over the swollen flesh. Daily, it seemed, her groin was slipping from sight a little more. The hair between her legs now sprouted over the top of her knickers and seemed to have grown tougher. Though sometimes tufts of it would come away in her hand. Her pubic hair had curled up like something exposed to heat. She was melting. She caught glimpses of things long past that continued. She dared not speak to anyone.

He was never mean to me, she thought, I couldn't tell him. This was a judgement on her. Then each night tormented by desire. Her breasts were filling up. Her arched hands at her groin not quick enough sometimes to catch the pleasure passing through.

Liz's pregnancy turned into one long run of desire for the father of the child. Before she had become pregnant she used to merely accommodate him, but afterwards, her need of him was terrible. She had always thought that a woman with child was pure and had no need of men. But nightly now, in her frustration, she even imagined Manager Tom and Mama copulating. She imagined Cathy with some drunk from the bar sprawled across her. The most mundane of men came into her mind. Middle-aged men she recognized on the street. Men who had nothing to recommend them. Plain men, wrought with desire, she imagined, with their wives. Then her lover, last of all, entering her. Above all else she wanted penetration as if this would shift the child.

She was violent with herself.

Each night she knew she was available for a few excruciating seconds to any man. Then, afterwards, the hurt clitoris beat in her sleep.

Every morning Liz stood by the door of the hotel when the postman arrived to see would there be a letter from him.

It was a hopeless idea. He did not know where she was. There was nothing, nothing. Her day began all over. She put it out of her mind. That he would come to search for her. There is nobody ever there when you need them, she reasoned. It's a fact. But next day she'd be waiting and there was nothing. So, each of her days in the Cove was divided into two. Waking with expectancy that something would come in the mail, she imagined a few words that would unravel all this emptiness, spoken in his voice, she imagined a new beginning, and when nothing arrived, then began the aftermath of her day, a sort of unthinking acceptance that things could never be that way, the way she imagined. She had been fooling herself. There were no words to sustain her. There was never anything. The day stretched ahead. Right up to the horizon—

She had perfected being alone. So the night when the baby was born, and she was unable to bear the pain, it was with shame that she cried out, she found herself suddenly pinned to the ceiling of the delivery room looking down on the girl strapped below, the splayed legs small as a little girl's, she saw the sudden cut to make room for the child to enter the world, and from her perch above Liz looked long and deep into the frightened eyes of the other till the screams subsided, she saw the tent of her stomach collapsing, and some time after she descended back into her body only to find that new fears were establishing themselves now that her one brief moment of independence was over. Try as she could, she could not think of a name for her girl-child like she could not bring herself to think of the future either.

"I'm sorry for waking you with all the rumpus last night," said Mama.

"Oh, I love being woken up," grinned Cathy, "because then I have the pleasure of going back to sleep again."

"The poor thing," said Cathy when Mama was forced to explain the visit of the fire brigade in the small hours, "I have always thought the sex thing was over-rated anyway."

"I couldn't for the life of me remember the word 'ambulance,'" said Mama, her uncombed hair sticking out. She had lain in an armchair all night till Manager Tom's return.

"Why was I so blind?" said Mama, as the two women remade a vacated bed. They tossed the sheets into the air and hoovered out the rooms. They worked on in silence thinking all the time about Liz, and themselves, and other people they knew and did not understand. Mama walked down to the florist's. "What flowers do you get for the arrival of a baby girl?" she asked.

"Well, if you go into hospital," said the woman there, "they give you carnations."

"I'll have some," said Mama.

"We don't have any."

That was why Mama bought roses. And some chocolate. She walked back to the hotel to collect some of Liz's things and to the chemist's then for all the items that Manager Tom had on the list the nurse had given him. All day Mama walked round in a dream. The telephone rang. It was someone from Liz's place asking after her. Mama did not know what to say, so she asked them to ring back, then headed for the hospital, thinking what a fool I am to be trotting round the town with a bunch of flowers drawing everyone's attention.

"Can I let your parents know?" Mama asked Liz.

"No," pleaded Liz, that's why I went away from there. I do not want to be bothering anyone with my trouble."

"Even your mother?" asked Mama, upset by her stubbornness.

"She knew I was pregnant when I was leaving," the girl answered dispassionately. "She wanted me to go," and then she began to coil her hair around her head, the hairpins gripped lightly in her mouth. Not till she was finished did they talk again. The babies were brought into the ward. An eternity passed as Liz under the direction of the nurse drew the colourless mouth of the child to her nipple, and failed to give milk. She grew desperate. "No," said the nurse to Mama, "you must not help her, she must do it herself." "Oh, c'mon child," called Liz, "here, here." The nurse took the baby away.

Liz after a great deal of kneading her breast got two drops of milk into a bottle. Afterwards there was a man-fit of weeping. The women talked. Mama knew that the other women were avoiding Liz, and when the new fathers gathered in the ward, she felt bad for her. The next afternoon whoever it was again rang the hotel. Again Mama wanted to tell the truth so that she might wound Liz's mother. Or her lover. The voice could have been the girl's brother. It could have been her lover. She could not tell, nor bring herself to ask.

"She is away," eventually Mama said, "having a tooth out."

"Did he phone?" asked Liz that evening, "did he phone?"

"I don't know whether it was him."

"It had to be him," said Liz confidently. "You see, I wrote to him."

"I said you were away having a tooth out."

"That was right." All Liz's dreams now were of milk and of him. He was pasty-faced and thin. He crossed the field. The calves bolted across the field to a break in the hedge for a drink from the can. Looking up, they slopped the milk down their white beards.

"I do not hate him, Mama," said Liz.

Then she hugged her dry nipple to the mouth of her child, but something inside her was fastened and would not give.

Mama called in the young priest to the Cove to arrange foster parents. That evening the child and mother were moved to a home for unmarried mothers. Mama did not venture there to see her. She felt outwitted by the girl. Here Liz had a vision. One of the statues in the corridor of the home spoke to her. They were useless words yet somewhere back of her head they made sense. The statue had unblinking eyes. The crotch was painted a wild violet. The feet were milky white. "Take the rushes," said the voice, "bend them into a bunch, over and

over. That's right. Go to the Virgin. She will take you in." Liz
again went out of her body. She flew over the Church. Inches
above the Mass-goers. She went right out of her seat in the
church and landed on a hard-edged beam overhead.

There in the second row, among all the other mothers,
she saw herself, crossing herself, doing what everyone else
was doing, she could see her face whitening. Two wet patches
appeared on her blouse where her nipples were.

The young priest took the child away from the home to a good
family that lived in a house overlooking Streaten Grange. Liz
returned to work at the hotel. She kept everything bottled up
in herself. Her unfeeling, yet anxious eyes worried Mama, but
there was nothing she could do or say. In two days the priest
returned saying how the family could not contend with the
baby. The father was being kept up all night by the crying of
the child. "My housemaid is out in the car with the child,"
said the priest. "Are you mad?" screamed Mama. Dropping
everything for dear that Liz might see the child, Mama ran
out into the square. The priest drove them to his house. He
explained there was somewhere else he could try. They drove
to a house in a workers' area on the outskirts of the town, and
while Mama sat in the car, the baby was delivered in. "Isn't
she a cute little thing," said the housemaid wistfully.

Another fostering had begun.

Nights, Liz wandered the hotel like a sick calf. Days, she
worked away from herself, as if no material thing existed. "Do
you think," she asked Mama, "that men only love beautiful
women? Is it just looks that count?"

"I don't believe it," Mama lied.

A few days later the new foster-father came to see Mama.
He said the young priest would have nothing to do with him.
When he told her who he was she ushered him out to the
foyer. He was a thin man with sleepy eyes and whorls of blue
veins on his cheeks. His wife had been taken to hospital, he

said. He could not contend with the baby and four children.
So Mama hired a car and went out with him to collect the
child. When she entered the small kitchen of the house the
three girls in pink dresses were chattering in to the baby, and
the son of the house aged eight was reading out a story about a
soccer star from a children's book. The cot was damp as a coffin
long buried. The baby's back was covered in sores. The young
boy and the father collected the baby's clothes. Everyone stood
at the gate to wave goodbye to their sister. Mama directed
the driver across the mountains to Fanacross, cursing the
young priest in her mind. She was finding it hard to forgive.

When Mama returned the following morning Liz was on her
day off. Late that afternoon she came in with a handkerchief
to her mouth. She tried to fly up the stairs without anyone
seeing her, but on the corridor she encountered Mama.
"What's wrong?" asked Mama. Liz looked bright-eyed at
Mama. Slowly she dropped her handkerchief and exposed her
bloodied bruised gums.

She had had her four front teeth extracted.

"Ah, no, no, no!" cried Mama.

Now it was Liz's turn to comfort Mama. A few days later
she returned home. She had bought a new outfit, a black velvet
jumper and a green dress to below the knee, she was over and
back from the laundry carrying dresses in a polythene bag over
her arm, stepping through the foyer with an amused swaying
of the hips, throwing a big woman's perspective to every side,
and last of all the white hair cropped short. A week later she
returned to the hotel. Just walked in and took up her job as
if she had never been away. That was why she was still there
in the Cove seventeen years on when Joseph arrived. That was
how Margaret was taken in by Geraldine. And that was how
Joseph, when he heard this story from Mama, understood
all the pain and loneliness that had accompanied Margaret
into the world, and why sometimes Liz would furtively make

her way across the square to the orphan's early Mass in the convent. "Oh, and beautiful teeth they were too," said Mama, "but I was so young, I was no help to her." Each evening, then, after her return, Liz and Cathy would sit by the range if they were not off dancing, and if they were not teasing Finn they were speaking of the hotel, the bitchiness, Mama's tantrums, the Manager's awkwardness, the wages, the customers, the frustrations, the miracle of how after a short time working together their periods had coincided, so that if one of them was missing the other could tell. As other girls came over the years they too fell into this routine. Thus the pain was shared.

35

"They are here," Mama shouted down.

The ladies alighted from their car in the square and ran to the door in the teeming hail under an umbrella held by Manager Tom. Mama was caught on the wrong foot – she was wearing one of those imitation Musquash furs, replete with the cooking smells of the Cove. A strange thing had happened during the night. A hare had run through the town in the early hours – a hare's tracks Joseph had followed that morning. First the wind, then the snow. The wind had scored a clean path through the forest at the lake, leaving in its wake a trail of uprooted firs, a lane running by the lake had cracked across, then the snow fell. Miss O'Neill was the first indoors. She was dressed in the colours of a lake flower, her green smock falling over her shoulders like a lily pad. Mrs Wilson was much heavier on her feet. The girls were watching the style, while Mama anticipated a millennium of mistakes.

Laura was sent to call the other women up the town hall where they were preparing their stands.

Liz brought in the tray of sherry, and hot whiskey and cloves. Cathy took in the Royal Albert bone china, decorated with sweet pea. Men on ladders were still stringing the bunting across the street. The women of the committee slowly arrived, and embarrassed, welcomed the two ladies, then Mama – out of her element for the first few exchanges – under the instruction of Miss Prior, the chiropodist, slipped on a record from "Dance of the Persian Slaves" by Rimsky-Korsakov. The chauffeur was forgotten in a pool of water by the front door till the girls took him into the kitchen. Manager Tom served the drinks to the minister and her fellow TD. After the introductions he took himself in his stiff new suit over to the window where he sat, adroit and careful with his words.

A Chinese lady was placed on Miss O'Neill's mantelpiece.

A dancing Spanish girl on Mrs Wilson's chest of drawers.

The ladies, well versed in dealing with the general public, in listening in on people's obsessions, in hearing women decry their position in society, offered some succinct observations, then went up to inspect their room, while back in the lounge the younger women spoke of the great days of the Women's Peace March. Their terror of jostling and the abuse. How the young Republican women had whistled up their skirts. How they had held their placards away from them like soiled trousers, and could only trust to those Northern women who had lived through it all. Now their cause was the local school for the mentally handicapped, and each held on their lap a collection box ready for when the crowds would gather.

George Allen began his drinking bout in Donegal town. He tried hard to clear a space for another human being. The first days South he too had enjoyed the status given him as a Northerner. Now, no more. It was another false role. Below they gave you a shape you did not want at all. He gritted his teeth as he climbed away from the house leaving Jim. All right Jimmy. All right George.

It was when Jim was only six, and Geraldine sat up with him, and George moved round the house listening to his son

screaming out. Then she said, "Get the doctor." He got the
doctor. And Jim looked up at her and he said, I wish I could
give you this pain ... arm on the ice-bucket the barman
listened with head turned. The first hallucination for George
was the worst. After that you get used to it, your life. The
terrible sense of the tyranny around. You are not civilized,
it's what they are saying. A man in a wide-patterned sports
jacket prods the mahogany counter with his forefinger as the
story unravels, mid-frame, a friend awaits, expectantly, the
outcome, his pupils expanding and widening, they are talking
money for sure, the story will reach a conclusion he already
knows. *There is the laughter!* They regroup, heads drop to the
former position to hear a final line from the barman, more
laughter, the trio break up and the two drinkers lift their
glasses with protuberant eyes. Next to them, the women have
shown no interest in the tale, but cupping her chin with her
fist, the elder is unfolding a different tale, she draws her hand
back to rub the back of her head, then forefinger crouched
by her ear, she presses the more awkward, insistent shape
her words make into the ear of her listener. When the men
suddenly burst into laughter, the women show indulgent
smiles. But when the men speak to them their brows furrow.
The friend and his wife leave. George sees the bus for Dublin
draw in outside the pub. Immediately the older woman dips
into a concocted gossipy stare at her husband, telling him
what she really thinks, without dropping a stitch between
the moment her female companion left and her husband
lost his audience. Her demeanour takes on a more familiar,
authoritative key.

He raises a balanced, collaborative hand.

As she answers he draws his fingers up and down, up and
down, impatiently, along the stem of the glass. She reaches
the end of her third story. There is silence between them. He
looks around. She cups her knuckles to her cheeks. George
made for the Dublin bus.

In the Cove it was all go. An old hippy, big camouflage jacket and thin lime-green socks like a child, was out on the street. At the back of his cap an upturned bunch of hair. The screaming of instruments. The people flocking down from the church, the girls in berets and coats, shamrocks hanging from the white blouses of the waitresses. The minister, Mrs Wilson, found in her room a picture of a room stuffed with pictures and men with elbows leaning on the rests of chairs, heavily oiled wallpaper, and in the background, beyond the fine chairs and tables and stools, a piano, where a young woman is seated. Mrs Wilson cannot see her hands, but can tell she is not playing. She is composed, her fingers holding the silent opening chord of a tune learned in childhood . . .

George was thinking of what he was about to do. These were all fine thoughts, yes, no mention of the mad lurking voyeurism in his heart, sadly there, but rightly there, wringing its own terrible realization out of the future. He stopped the Express twice to urinate before they reached Monaghan where the scheduled stop was. Here he had a double whiskey in the Ulster Arms. "Where are you headed?" he asked the conductor who was sitting reading the *Independent.* "Galway," the man answered, "for my pains." "I think I'll be with you," said George. So he got his case out of the Dublin bus and journeyed to Galway.

A hill of whins.

The broad plains.

Sheets of cellophane thrown over the turf.

Liz from her window watched the newly married couples as they walked through the wedding garden. Nights she'd walked there, not knowing why, till she came across the damp confetti, sometimes, where the red hot pokers glowed.

A woman ahead of him in the bus, the wee bitty bitter lips squeezing down and the eyebrows squinting at new things.

Describing the old when young, the young when old, there is no comfort there for either. Nothing will change, unless you speak of something beyond the observed and the heard. It's in the instrument of the body and beyond that, the commitment of the mind. Cake-faced, fools mingling on a street, bastardly language. Is my story so? He caught a reflection of his brother in the bus window.

Clear daylight in Galway.

"Will there be an end of it?" they asked.

"I can't complain."

"We grew up like ducks, meself and the brother, the one trotting after the other."

"I'm going up in the direction, I'm going North, but not quite yet."

"The electric chair is best, I'd settle for the electric chair."

"Aye, once they wouldn't make you foot the bill."

He stepped onto the train for Dublin in the company of a woman who told him that her mother-in-law was shook, well-shook, and was in Jervis Street hospital. From the windows they saw a lake of swans, their arses in the air, dipping in rhythm, maybe a hundred or so feeding below water, their long white necks in the depths like tubular feeler, after the ducking, they grandly floated by, a sudden spreading of wings like a beautiful afterthought, while others flocked awkwardly across the reseeded field, then turned, and headed back for the safety of the water. "You don't mind," said the woman, "I'm Maggie," as she unearthed a half-naggin of gin. "I've been on the dry myself three years till yesterday," said George, taking his half bottle out of his pocket. "At least," said Maggie, "we got our telephone installed." They passed black-headed yellow-eyed sheep on their hunkers, munching. A blackbird at the top of a leafless tree. A green pool frozen, a swirl of frozen veins, then the pylons. "I came up the hard way," said Maggie, "but even the auld security brings its own horrors. I had a man in London, Bunty he was called. 'C'mon,' he said,

'we'll get married in a posh Church off the Brompton Road.'
He took me up to see the church. Christ, the poor fellow, he
hardly reached my shoulder." She took him in. "Where are
you for?"

"I'm headed North."

"You'll be buying sterling then?"

"I don't think so."

"My man was very easy going. Still is. They called him the
Smoke Doctor. He was a chimney sweep." She rapped the
table with her laughter. "Christ, but I've cried bitter tears."
She bit the gloves off her hands by the tip of the middle
finger. "You know what I mean." She nodded her head
vigorously. "My brain is dangerous, dangerous out." They
saw young schoolgirls running round a playing field in pairs,
the stragglers walking or running singly behind. What was
George thinking? "I can see," said the woman wistfully, "that
you have your own troubles. Don't weaken on me now. Not
now, just when we've got to know each other."

Everyone in the Cove was delighted that the ladies had chosen
their hotel. Mama's new political passions did not now appear
so timewasting. She had lately become treasurer of the local
branch of one of the political parties. She felt proud of her
arrangements for this day, and the day that would follow it.
At two, the bell-ringer sauntered round the sodden streets
announcing how the parade would begin at three. His sons
swung out of his coat-tails. He was a chimney sweep by trade.
Not long after the bell-ringer came the float from the bacon
factory, with live pigs chortling through the bars, and then a
man on stilts, fearful of the thin snow below and the bunting
above. Next a showband playing Country and Western airs
on the back of a lorry advertising furniture. The owner of a
large supermarket in the town seated, in old-fashioned regalia,
on a penny farthing. "Will you look at Fegan," said Cathy,
"and a pair of balls on him like the weights of a grandfather

clock." Next the brass band marching into step as they played a mixture of patriotic and show business tunes, "Oklahoma" and "Mise Éire," their ranks depleted because of death and lack of instruments.

Down the street, they saw him, Peter, fresh back from Dundalk, under the awnings of an impressive draper's, keeping time like a drunken half-moon.

Amid the melee Joseph flew through the crowds searching for anyone from Fanacross. "Bedad," said one man, "are you Frank Allen's lad? He was a brave goalkeeper. He'd stop turnip seed. The goals shut down when he was in them." He shook Joseph's hand warmly. The villagers and farmers had gathered round the horse ring where a special spring sale had been arranged. Inside the horse ring was food and drink. They stood round in the cold March wind drinking beer from plastic cups, happy that the burden of hoarding money for the saint's day was over. Their fast had ended. Lent had given them a great thirst and now they could spend as freely as they cared. Tomorrow, after St Patrick's Day was over, they could take up their old abstinence again, that is, if they could fight off the sickness left over from today's debauchery. Just like the old poets would finish their day's work translating the religious epics, and only then in the chaste evening light that satisfied labour brings, would they take up their pens and write their own cheerful verses in the margins.

Coming up O'Connell Street George and Maggie watched an American majorette hurl her staff into the air. "Beats all," said Maggie, "the poor thing must be frozen." It was explained to them that there was a pub stayed open through the day near Gardiner Street, so here they headed through the crowds that were going up to the Railway Cup Final in Croke Park. "Hit him again," said a Leitrim lad in the pub, "he's no relation." "Sure we'll stop in here out of the cold," said another, "and watch the whole show on the box." Maggie leaned forward and touched

George's knee. "I'm really glad we met," she said. "Let's go to town." "We will, surely," answered George. "There's only three kinds of music takes me fancy," she recalled, "only three kinds, fairground music, ice cream van music and church bells."

"The mummers beat all," said George, "I never saw their likes."

"Tell us," she said, warmly, "tell us, George, all about your life at sea."

Sixty years ago to the day, St Patrick's Day, Countess Markievicz and her astral double, her fellow patriot, Maud Gonne, had come to the town and inspected the ladies of Cumann na mBan in the town hall. Now some of those old ladies of the revolution, feathered and painted, with sprigs of shamrock hanging from their chests on safety pins, were introduced to the new women of the Dáil in the residents' lounge of the Cove. Here they watched the parade with blinds half-drawn, their fox furs drawn tight about their independent thin necks and in each eye a curious appraisal of those political females, the minister and the TD, that had made it. They appraised the cut of their clothes and their sincerity. And when it was called for, they gave dignified support of the knowing kind. Mama had not known what to wear for the occasion. All she could think of was something authentic. Something subtle, not attributable to the world of men's vanity. So she had her black shawl about her, her cheeks sharp and shiny as the heels of her leather boots, and the same precision was repeated in her shiny knuckles, in her temples, in the enquiring joints of her fingers. Along came the pipeband from across the border disregarding all formation. Some walked the footpath and formed a circle to tune their pipes. They fitted their saffron shirts and woollen berets and tugged at their purses. Trembled and halted on the chanters while the bags of the two-drone warpipes filled with the frightening blue purpose of their cheeks. The drummer kept in step though standing still beneath the Cove. He looked up at the women and winked. Then, chins down, the pipers swung their bodies up the street.

"Oh, Mr Lemass was not all he was supposed to be," said Mrs Wilson to some question, "he never took note of national resources. What did he do for the land, I ask you?"

"Time will tell, time will," answered a bright young housewife, who ran a boarding house for fishermen.

Peter passed below. And he was followed by a dark hatless youth playing an accordion come from some town where beggars were still artisans. His box swelled till arms and heart were at full stretch. With a riddle of his fingers he let the air escape. Up like a lake of startled birds. Then stewards wearing badges passed by, looking about them with importance, their coats belted up against the inclement weather. "They are mainlining shamrocks today," said one of Joseph's friends. The old stewards supported each other up the footpath where a way had been cleared through the snow.

Next came the stragglers looking for idiots to laugh at.

"And we," said Miss O'Neill, "the only country in Europe with no language of our own."

These boys had a swaggering step. The sub-language of knowing heads, and laughs, the nodding of heads. Putting up their fists to each other, clapping each other on the back. They lived at home with their mothers. They spoke to each other with arched eyebrows in sly whispers. These were the lonely ones, pretending. The parade gave everyone great entertainment. The parade of the saint going by the door like a river. Upstairs the ladies sipped their sherries and gins and the old ladies cracked their finger-joints at people they knew. Mrs Gough read out the minutes of the last meeting of the Irish Countrywoman's Association. The various stands for the sale of work were allocated. Feet pulled smartly together, Mama came into her own as she spoke of the unemployment, the false hopes, the misery, the economic crisis for those living by the border, the dead border towns. "Aye," said one lady

who ran a newspaper shop, "are they trying to bring us closer
together by having people buy cheaper north of the border?
Hah?" She clicked her heels for emphasis. They spoke of their
sisters in the North, and Helen came to Mama's mind.

The two uncomfortable ladies from the Dáil listened
intently, and nodded and asked questions.

Outside, frozen children dressed as angels went by in slow
motion on a float, each of them wearing a green silk sash.
Over their heads a harp blew angrily. No one was smiling.
Below in the bar Cathy was having the time of her life
overcharging the strangers, and around her reality ceased to
exist as the drunken narrators multiplied. A tall man with
floury eyes came in. She took him to be a man looking for
trouble. She would not serve him. "Look, Mrs," he said, "I'm
one of the Hills of Latt." "I don't give a fuck if you're one of
the mountains of Mourne," Cathy answered, "you'll get no
drink here." "You're hard," he said, "hard out."

"Tell us this," asked Maggie, "were there turncoats in your
family that you got a name like George?"

"Me father is a man that gets strange ideas."

"And what of your mother, had she no say in things?"

"She died at our birth, myself and my twin. He came last
so that the father always blamed him."

"I'm sorry. My auld one could never stop talking. She'd
been vaccinated by a gramophone needle."

"The last time I saw Pop he said to me: I have a mind like
a babbling brook."

"You remember enough to do you."

"You do." Out on O'Connell Street the army band passed
with the music propped up before their instruments. The
music sitting on the top of the saxophone. The cheers rose
from Croke Park. The hawkers entered the pub. Says one: I'm
not the best. Says another: Sure we all know that. None of us
had the heart to tell you. By God, he could field it well, called
one of the football fans. The streets filled up with orange peel.

Maggie was growing fond of George. "Look at me," she said.

He took full advantage of her gaze. "Will you stop this night with me in the Gresham?" he asked.

Maggie cared not. "The Gresham? The Gresham. You must be made up. Well, George, you don't do things by halves." Then seeing as he was sincere, she felt his knee and he awkwardly kissed her ear, and all there could go to hell as far as George and Maggie cared.

The ladies were driven round the northern towns of the Republic so that they could see for themselves the effects that the war had had south of the border. They passed the few caravans parked in the rundown yards of houses belonging to republican sympathizers. Here the families of men on the run, or those evicted from the North by circumstance, were still in bed though the day was darkening. Clones they came on. And Belturbet.

Down at the entrance to Monaghan, they came across the first election posters being raised to telegraph poles. The ladies of the Dáil smiled. They could not help this condescension that slipped momentarily over their faces.

Throughout the day the Cove was full. Down the road at the hospital another tragedy was being fatalistically borne. You'd see big men in little caps crouched round a tall man on a bicycle, some on their hunkers, in their Sunday suits. They were there because of the plight of a single one of their brethren found dead after lying for two weeks inside his house, the maggots had entered him – strewn around him lumps of turf, and rolled up in his pocket a Sunday newspaper. He had died on the way towards lighting a fire for himself. None of the men moved. Each with an eye in the direction of the hospital, they waited the removal of the remains.

"It reminds me of the time," whispered Maggie, as she tiptoed into the bathroom of the room they had taken in Gresham, "of the time we were taking a piss in a bucket at the edge of the carnival tent. 'Slant it, girls,' said Mary Tomelty who was on guard, 'the boys are coming.' So I had to piss to the edge to deaden the sound."

George was lying full length of the bed smoking.

He was looking at the ceiling.

"I cannot imagine," she said returning, "another man the spit of you."

"Aye, be God," remembered George, "and when the auld fucker would hit the one of us, the other would cry. I was, Pop told me, put to sleep in a basket and Frank in a chest of drawers."

"He raised the lot of you on his own?"

"He did. Then he'd get sorry and tickle me who was crying and wait for the laughter from the chest of drawers."

"And what of me?" said Maggie entering, "my father fell back dead as he sat up chatting on a tailor's table. He was thirty-two." The phone rang. Soon after a waiter pushed their trolley through the door.

Of those drinkers that arrived to the Cove one would sing a refrain and another might take it up, then the songs would peter out, and some would shout Mammy, Mammy, Mammy, and the laughter would begin again. A stock of pet names were parried. And arguments ended with the husbands and boyfriend calling up the absent loved one—

"If you don't believe me, ask Lily."

"If Mona was here now, she'd tell you."

"Elizabeth was there and she saw it too."

"She is not here, speak for yourselves"—replied the vain bachelors, and the married men felt uncomfortable, knowing they had addressed their absent wives to support their weaker stories, or else invented lies because they had no companion to remind them of the truth. Their sexual partner could betray them all, she held the key, that's what their faces told. And so, because of this dependence on the women, the men grew lightheaded, they chose the loudest love ballads, or else silence, or grew morbid as if they suspected the women of betrayal. After the funeral, the countrymen with grey sprigs of dried-up shamrocks sagging from their buttonholes arrived. The rhythm of their narratives going backwards and forwards in time. They infected the townsmen with their abandonment. Out leaped one old fellow, he kicked out, keeping his neck stiff and back stiff. He dribbled and danced, beer sneaked down his unshaven chin.

The countrymen stripped down to their shirts and shiny waistcoats fastened with safety-pins. These were men of little property or none at all. And the soberest ones danced longest of all. The melee moved out onto the streets. Then the soldiers who lived without women began abusing the townfolk who had advised their daughters against them. They riled the countrymen because they were ignorant. And there was Joseph, perched on the mill wall to watch the factions.

"It's us that are keeping you," someone wailed.

"It's the army protects you," a soldier retorted.

"What fucking army?" a farmer jeered. "What fucking army are you talking about?"

"Say nothing to the ignorant bastards."

"The filth of the cities."

"Bloody criminals."

"Rednecks, the lot of you."

"Any day, boy."

"Any day, boy."

The military police and civic guards intervened and the main combatants shook hands. "That's always their tune," said Manager Tom. "They have to take out their frustration somewhere." Out on the streets with their fallen banners and slushy surfaces everything appeared rosy till the fight started all over again in a different place, and this time the fight was in earnest, and the guards let them get on with it. Shouting out their pointless victories the men were led away by more peaceful companions. The soldiers, pale from drinking, drank cider out in the square eyeing the people, till wearying of the day, they disappeared.

"Jesus," said Finn, "I hope they have not gone up for their guns."

"That was good crack while it lasted," said Peter. "When the firewater is in, the blood is up."

"And how did the trial go for you?" asked Annie, the woman who had been there in the hospital with him.

"The guards did for me," answered Joseph.

"Aye, well let me tell you this," she said, swaying gently on the stool of the bar, "the worst crime in this country is a drunken woman. I took him before the court, I did. And there they were, the all-male jury, sniggering away. 'Best,' said the judge, 'keep youse together for the family's sake.' What sort of a fucking idiot was he?" She drank and looked at one of her hands. "He's gone anyway. And the last night he beat me and chased me naked through the fields, and that's this fucking country. That's the way it is. See. No matter what you say."

Next morning Maggie took George's arm and walked him to Connolly Street station. He stopped to phone ahead. "It's best," he said, "that you leave me here."

But Maggie came on.

A priest was sitting in the station, waiting. He said he knew in his heart a great desire, so he told Maggie. She was drinking with George and the priest was drinking too. "The day that the women denied us," said the priest, "we made of that rebuke a holy thing."

The Belfast train pulled into the station. George took Maggie into his arms and could not let go of her. He thanked her for everything she had done for him. "Are you married or something," she asked, "that you have so much to hide?" "At least," he said, "on those grounds I'm straight enough." "Good luck then." "I'll see you." He was sharing the table he was at with two Belfast students going North that he could not talk to. He drank, thinking that his needs might appear more attractive than his giving. The snow was still on the mountains. A pair of horns adrift in the fine white dress of a black-headed sheep staring at him. The woman's glove in his pocket that he squeezed. The Northern accents. There was no talk of the North for those who lived in fear, not like those down South, who, like Maggie, could humanize him. His emotions were fossilized in preparation for any catastrophe. He was haunting the shore while everyone was swimming freely out to sea. Swans again. Hierarchies of birds looking out to sea. The bridges flashed overhead with a roar. Armagh. The mountains again. He saw things that did not need to be named, these were the mountains. He squeezed the glove. The train slowed into Portadown and two RUC men got on, they came from carriage to carriage till they found him. "You're George Allen?" they asked. "Aye," he said rising. That night all of the arms dumps in the region of Fanacross were moved for fear George Allen would break down and tell other than what had brought him North again, for it was known by all, that the man who is on the point of confession may suddenly start to inform.

36

The prominent tables at the dinner dance of one of the political parties in the South were occupied by newspapermen from the provinces, elected representatives preparing themselves for the new assault on the electorate, the chairman, elder sportsmen and priests, including Fr John of Fanacross. At the next table sat the committee members, building contractors, the elected Country Council men, younger sportsmen and establishment musicians.

Next came the nurses, salesmen from the major animal

food companies, urban council officials, creamery managers, representatives from tourist organizations, men who delivered oil, and coarse-fishing experts.

The money from all this was going to the forthcoming election.

And beyond, talking in their own country accents of what was familiar and what was forgotten, were seated secretaries reared in the small border villages, their fingernails buttered with plum varnish; then Lawyer Smith, sporting tweeds and a briefcase and the smile of the religiously secure, who saluted Joseph with the spontaneity of a man at a dress rehearsal, as if Joseph were one of his clients he had defended sometime back, God knows when; there were married women who were out and in from the line all day but still laid out their sheets by night on the grass for the dew to bleach them in nature's way and their sons the publicans who bought drinks for the table and slipped tenners to drinkers in need; civic guards just out of the training centre, fresh and courteous civil servants who laughed into their laps at the goings on of certain parties; farmer's sons, early risers and boisterous, telling how the country was way behind them; then merchant's daughters only waiting for the dancing to begin in order to see what the other girls were wearing; garage men talked cars, tyres and petrol and never lifted their heads from the meals till their eyes narrowed with wind; unmarried women who nodded unbelievingly at all that was said, clapped the celebrities as they were announced, but still kept their handbags shyly round their arms; and lastly the young insurance men, who ate up all their desserts, and were dressed in bright pink shirts and quiet suits; and through this crowd Laura and Liz and Cathy carried the steaming trays of turkey and ham and clear soup till the minister came to his feet, then all went silent.

Afterwards, business deals were discussed by men with hands cupped to their knees or else tightly pressed against their chests, photographers slipped through the tables, a young footballer pissed into a potted plant in the foyer, grunted and returned to the hall without remembering where he was; the minister, benign as ever, went aside with a few people to consider aspects of their case in these troubled times; solicitors relaxed by fooling around with international affairs and the secrets of those committed to trial in the city; the priests traced a family line from townland to townland with its success abroad and failures at home, then stood respectfully aside while some of their old students careered across the floor; the ladies in polka-dot dresses from the agricultural ministry complained of the quality of the meal.

There was much derision that a pop band had been hired again this year.

The dancing commenced nonetheless, and soon the floor swayed with assorted, thunderous steps. Most people had brought partners to protect themselves against infamy. Still, certain single women dancers attracted attention to themselves by dancing together, while old couples manoeuvred themselves into quiet corners where they waited for the old popular airs; the secretaries kept their partners at bay, all that could be seen was the white of the man's eye, and the reformed drunks danced sedately with their wives and attacked savagely the break-up of other people's marriages; Isn't it terrible, terrible, about the children; the businessmen watched from their seats and said, The patriots have brought us back a thousand years, we're fucked, there's fuck-all in the kitty; Get up the yard, the older guards shouted at the new recruits as they swung by in the arms of a woman – A good jaunt would do him no harm; husbands and wives wandered lost between the frontiers of childhood and parenthood; the nurses arranged their cuffs in the toilet, the insurance men shook the change in their pockets, undid their ties and took off their coats, so that when they shuffled onto the dance floor, their wide trousers rode down their thighs; and the elder sportsmen knew what was wrong with the country – Shoot the bastards, get rid of them, that's what I say; and the girls of the hotel tripped in and out of this company avoiding all intimacy, sidestepping the arms of the drunks who were caught between extremes of lugubriousness and gaiety; and the lights swung round the American décor, even onto the civil servants who stood well back hoping someone might approach them for a favour so that they could have the pleasure of considering it, then growing perplexed with drink they talked to their superiors in wild and formal language, and at last grew weighty with their infinite responsibility to the nation, and that was Ireland, Republican Ireland.

It was the night that Margaret had come down to see Joseph. They had only time for a few words before Manager Tom lumbered her with a partner for the dance. Her partner, once the meal was over, was happy to leave her to her own devices. She walked through the dance hall of the Cove like a stranger. She drank at the bar behind which Joseph was working with Laura. She went outside to clear her head. The cold air trimmed her eyelashes so that the bare pupil shone religiously. She returned to her partner out of manners, sat down beside him and thought: How much sharper and braver I must have been as a young girl. This place was foreign to her.

She was besieged by sentimental thoughts.

The place about her seemed contaminated by gaiety. The first drinks made her lightheaded, and when she heard her partner monopolizing the conversation, going over and over a route that was painful to her, she could not find words to right him, till she said: "Youse know nothing of the pain, the terror we live through, nothing at all."

"That's an extraordinary way of tormenting yourself," said his woman, across the table. "You are a nice-looking woman and I'm sure people can get on with you."

"Oh, they can," said Margaret.

"Sure, what can we do?" said some other voice. "Isn't it obvious, it's the United Ireland?"

There was that drunken silence you sometimes hear at a melee when every voice becomes separated, strumming out its own cause, then easily forgotten. "That's an extraordinary way of tormenting yourself," said the strange woman again as she looked Margaret in the eye. "You are a nice-looking woman and I'm sure people can get on with you."

Margaret headed back up to see if she could find Joseph alone. Christ, but he's become sure of himself. How is your life now, she thought, who have foresworn me for another. Is she just another language you are leaning while you still think in mine? Every lover I take makes you my lover for life. She got up and went to the cloakroom and put on her light-blue, belted raincoat. She did not hear him calling after her. She skimmed her lips with Vaseline against the cold. She strolled along the foyer, behind her plastic flowers were pinned on an espalier, the square outside shook with traffic.

He has slighted me, she said.

She walked about the town. She felt as if the town had become a living object that had grown eyes and could not stem the flow of its inner self. Here she was abandoned. They are abandoning us. Joseph was a party to this. He did not even bother to take the time to talk. Meanwhile, he was running round the hotel looking for her. For one split second as she stood out on the roadway she looked back and saw the lights of the hotel shining above the town, the light spouting up like a jet of water from the head of a whale. She felt then the quick of that person, Joseph, no matter his aloofness from her soul that can always be felt she knew, in the moment before you lose a person forever. She thumbed a lift from a furniture van heading north. "Have you room? I'm heading to Fanacross." "A' course," the driver replied. This is the way things will be for a while, she thought. She had just come down on an impulse. It's not his fault. This is the way things will be for a while. Things can't go on like this forever. The van pulled out on to the centre of the road along tracks ploughed into the snow.

The crowd from the hotel spilled out onto the pavement, and Joseph could not be consoled. He blamed everyone there. It was just bad temper. Then he found her letter at the desk telling him how George had given himself over to justice above. That the compensation might come through. Joseph's humiliation was complete.

"But why did she not wait?" he asked.

"Maybe she was not herself," said Manager Tom. "Well, anyway, George has redeemed himself." They started with hoovers across the hall, and with the brooms across the dance floor. At that moment the gloved hand of a British soldier with fingers bare from the middle joints was frisking Margaret as she crossed the bridge. Through the river fog she saw the village getting nearer to the church on the hour. "Thank you, are you finished now?" she asked crossly, and saw in the yellow light his blue cheeks antagonized not by the weather but by the English temperament. There is so much to put up with his eyes say, it's scarcely hidden behind his smile, his smile is lowered by cowered lids, not maiden-like, but condescending and treacherous, as if to say, there is agreement all round about this. She passed out of the yellow light into the darkness over the bridge. "Goodnight Miss," he called after her, and his voice was Welsh she realized, Wales where railway destinations sound like the names of magic mushrooms.

She entered Fanacross, once a military outpost for Enniskillen, and now an outpost again. Good luck, Joseph said, thinking of her so intensely that she was there and nowhere.

VIII

37

There was another time. It was back in the early years of the war. Terrible things began to happen. A butcher was found cut up in pieces in his own fridge. There were brothers pitchforked to death. These were atrocities that led to meetings between Protestant and Catholic at which each community said they were not involved in any of these crimes. Later, in both cases, the British army were charged and found guilty.

And in February of that year these atrocities were forgotten by the occupants of the hotel. Meaning they understood how much further there was to go. It seemed a long distance. It was the year that Joseph and Helen and Frank Allen were camped by the lower reaches of the Erne in the caravan. That Cathy had her womb removed. That Laura saw her father force his way past her mother into her own room. It was the year that Manager Tom read of Cromwell, for he was at the time seeking illumination from history, trying to get beyond a certain barrier, for history in the province of Ulster was whittling away at its own image. The people were still set on conquering the past. They were shouldering all those conventions which had been brought to an extreme by some other, till they, in time, would find another extreme, these, the common people. The print went grey. The manager's eyes grew unsteady. He would have liked to lie down.

"How are you keeping?" asked Finn. "Is this what you are up to now?"

He lifted the book. "Aye, that man Cromwell was a man that deserved a good hiding," he observed. The churning of the potato peeler came through the dining room. The clash of delph. The till ringing up. The same benign achievement, dear to the Manager's ear, of money settling into place. "I never wanted to work for a living," said Finn, "I suppose I'm not built that way."

"What's the odds," asked the Manager, "on you having the dinner ready for one?"

"Here comes I," sang Finn, "and as everybody knows I'm Oliver Cromwell with my copper nose."

In the corner of the bar the Manager caught sight of the big horrific face of a man drinking alone during a loud children's programme on TV. Then Cathy crossing the street with a tray of tea things to the solicitor on the second floor of the house across the square.

New lounges were unfurling like the stars and stripes throughout the country. The Saturday night crowd entered the foyer. A highly tanned and well-dressed clientele, fresh from water-skiing. The old elegance of the place drew them in.

"It was a beautiful day," a cheerful chap remarked.

"Youse are twenty years too late," the Manager replied.

Manager Tom was thinking of pollution.

It was the smell of the new American Ireland.

Through the veins of the worker ran the streak that Connolly had cast. Through the employer the new capitalist refrain, each working against the other, and then daily the piggeries unloading their slurry into the lakes.

On hot days the stench was like ether.

And stretched out on the banks, newly painted boats with their oars crossed. Round went the butterfly wings of the sails. The pigs injected with tranquillizers to keep their weight constant. Gas was escaping from a rotten place underground. In a cottage above Fanacross someone was preparing the flame.

Dependent upon the mood of the people, tried out by the seasons, the island of Ireland floated.

The island veered sharply across the sea. Prodded forward by the horns of swimming cows. He thought of where George was now. Where Frank? Why was Frank so proud he would not call? A guest passed with an umbrella hanging from a strap over her shoulder. Then a traveller, a slight pucker or

hollow under the nose and above the thin lips, the whole
mouth appearing to be on the verge of an overpowering
sneeze. "God bless us," thought the Manager.

He looked up and found a new guest standing before him.
Cathy was above Liz's room having her hair cut. Finn nowhere
to be seen. The Manager, over the noise of the band in the
lounge, screamed up the stairs. He was not in benevolent
mood. Over the speakers came the repeated lines:

> Heavens above,
> In a street called Love,

as the guest signed in, and up in the room where the music was
pounding the floor under her feet, Cathy heard the Manager's
summons. Mortified by the state of her cropped hair, she
took up the guest's lightweight bag, while Liz followed after
with a tray of sandwiches and tea.

The guest was of medium height, but ungainly.

Yet, he had a fully travelled face for a young man. He took
the tray without a word of thanks and backed nervously into
the room. The band moved on to a Jim Reeves ballad. At
midnight the new guest came down to put a call through
to Manchester. "There is no reply," said Manager Tom. "All
right then." He backed off uncertain and looked through
the glass doors at the dancers within while Manager Tom
studied his posterior. Is he under the influence of drugs or
drink, the Manager thought coldly. The man excused himself.
Manager Tom mopped out the toilet, and made himself a cup
of coffee. At two, just as the dancers were trooping out into
the square, the young guest again appeared to have his call
put through. And again, there was no reply. Disappointed,
he stood by the desk a moment, as if he were on the point
of telling the manager something, then he dropped his eyes,
and apologized for coming down at such a late hour. "Think
nothing of it," said the Manager interested. The dancers were
stepping out onto the wet streets. The guest followed them

with his eyes.

There followed the slamming of car doors.

The side-streets filled a moment with indifferent and humorous banter. The Manager read on. The guest moved maddeningly over and back in his room, stepping out every so often to urinate in the cramped toilet at the end of the corridor. Manager Tom hung the next day's menu on the dining room door, then picked up the visitor's book to put it away in a drawer. He noticed that the letters in the new guest's signature were not joined. And the address seemed old, forgotten, a place remembered. It was an address from a schoolboy's copybook. It seemed that it would have been difficult for him to dream up a place he had never been. The Manager started putting out the lights. Each of the new tilted lampshades, bought by Mama, had on them a map of the world, with Ireland, a small girl-child illuminated darkly from within, hugging up her breasts and knees, going back up into the womb of the globe, or just recently dropped into the Atlantic to learn to swim for herself. A *Síle-na-gig* displaying her groin while in her head unnatural forces, made natural by their universality, were at work. Her bellybutton, a crater left by a bomb. One by one he extinguished all these illuminated miniatures, and settling in comfortably by Mama, read Cromwell's letters home.

The next morning the young man's face was white from lack of sleep and weathered by a night's anxiety. He took his breakfast without recourse to conversation, as if his accent would somehow betray what was in his head. He felt that the people at the next table knew what he was thinking. He tried to clear his mind of everything for fear his thoughts were travelling into the minds of others. "It'll never happen whatever you're thinking of," said Liz startling him, "We don't get too many from England this late in the year."

"How far," he asked awed by her naturalness, "are we from the border?"

"It depends," Liz answered thoughtfully, "what road you take."

She cleared away the delph, and brushed the crumbs into the palm of her hand. He imagined her long white hair piled each side of her skeleton in a coffin. "Are you staying long?" she asked. He gave her an aimless reply. Mama expected to find some signs of holiday about him, but there was none. He had no fishing rods, he stopped round the hotel in the same clothes in which he had arrived and when the girls came up to make his bed, he stood by the window, not daring to leave his room, and for days his single bag lay unopened at the foot of his bed. Each night he came down to put his phone call through. "The lad," said Mama, "seems sorely tried by love." As always there was no reply from Manchester, and hearing this, he would retreat furtively up the stairs, deeply embarrassed. His appearance at meal times became haphazard, and fearing that his guest might take flight with his bill unpaid, Manager Tom, after a series of one-sided conversations, called the rent in. The young man without demur obliged, adding that he would like three newspapers delivered each morning, the *Mirror*, the *Sun* and the *Guardian*.

"You can get a great view of the islands from Douagh," said Manager Tom, as he cupped the telephone to his ear.

"I am a bit preoccupied at the moment."

"The fresh air will do you a sight of good."

"Yes. Thank you."

They waited. The telephone rang on. "I'm afraid you are out of luck again."

"Goodnight, then – I'll try later."

"Will you hit that switch on your way up?"

"What?" he hesitated. "Oh, yes. Goodnight."

False. False out, thought Manager Tom.

"He has killed her," said Cathy, "and he can't understand why they haven't found the body yet."

"He found her with another man, and left, and is not able
to keep away," said Liz. "He gets through the day, but when
night comes he has to speak to her."

"What's happened is this," said Finn, "he has a fatal disease
of the mind. In the mornings he feels bad. As the day wears
on, he feels better. His disease takes the form of believing
there are two of himself there. He has a double existence, you
see. The first fellow diagnoses the disease the second fellow
has. As the day wears on, he tries to phone through to say he
is feeling better. But in fact he is phoning himself, the bollax.
No wonder each morning he feels bad again."

"Someone," decided Manager Tom, "has given him the
wrong number."

"Nothing?" asked the guest that night.

"Nothing," replied Manager Tom, settling his arms
comfortably under his chin, wondering which direction the
conversation would take now.

"Tomorrow," asked the guest, with more confidence than
before, "could I have the *Irish Press*, the *Irish Independent* and
the *Irish Times*?"

"And the *Irish Times*," repeated the Manager, writing it all
down. "You do, if you don't mind me saying so, a sight of
reading." A school of amateur actors in town for the drama
festival and resident for three days now entered the foyer and
because it was after hours, at first respectfully ordered drinks
into the lounge, though once installed their various humours
became conflicting. "This will be a late session," Manager
Tom explained to his guest who was not inclined to go. "It's
hard to get these poor bastards away from the footlights."
Then deciding he might have been too severe the Manager
added, "I should know." The guest mumbled. "What was
that?" asked Manager Tom. "A gin and tonic, if I might,"
asked the guest, and then he took a seat in the dark corner of
the unquiet lounge, for the façade of order was broken as the
actors' psyches, unburdened of authority, dwelt in other more

frivolous roles than normal life had extracted from them. These were the extreme friendships, founded on illusion and seemed to suit the new guest well. Manager Tom listened, his arms propped on the counter of the bar, to their various stories. Each half-hour he fetched himself a cup of coffee from the kitchen. Finn, attracted by the noise, sat at another table drinking pints of Guinness in the dark and humming away to himself. Water for the hot whiskeys was warmed up in the microwave oven. The guest drank an inordinate amount of gin, sometimes standing a long time before the Manager, holding him in an empty ridiculous gaze. Towards four Finn and the guest met at the bar. With his back to them, Manager Tom heard Finn say: "Did you get through to your mother yet?"

"You what?"

"I'm sure," continued Finn, "she misses you sorely."

The actors broke into a series of Gilbert and Sullivan songs.

At five, Manager Tom shepherded the raucous and glassy-eyed company to their dreams. Doggedly, he collected all the glasses and emptied the ashtrays, then snatched a few quick moments with his book above in bed to find that the two kingdoms were united on 2 March 1653, and finally, that Oliver Cromwell was declared Lord Protector on 30 January 1654. The image of the various hangovers that would be rife throughout the hotel the following morning brought Manager Tom great satisfaction as dawn fell on the topsy-turvy town. And while the stranger wrote into his diary the events of his day and what tomorrow's must be, Manager Tom woke out of a painful dream about teeth. His mouth was trying to reject his false teeth put there by a life of constant sweet-eating. In his dream the teeth were stuffed with meat. The plate broke in two. He had no teeth left at all. Frightened, he touched his jaw to find all was as it had been, then, sweating, he continued through Cromwell's travels, changing the hand that held the book because of the cold, and rereading again and again the lines that delayed interpretation, he willed his mind on to further understanding, while the stranger in his late-night drunken notes was defying understandings of the world, at 6.30 A.M.

"Morning," said the stranger.

He had on plimsolls and a jogging suit.

"Good morning," said Manager Tom who was seated in his favourite chair in the hotel. It was at the end of the second floor corridor by the large windows that looked across the town towards the lakes and the mountains south of Fanacross.

"How is the head?"

"I'm off for a run," the guest grinned sheepishly and continued down. Much to Manager Tom's amazement, seconds later he saw him footing it across the square, and there was something relentless and foreign, disciplined, in his posture. Well, well, he mumbled. "Ah-hah, and how is Finn this bright morning?" asked Manager Tom as the chef appeared with the daily papers. "Oh, but it's true that the Allens have long livers, but no hearts," answered Finn. He drifted lightly away, sneezing at every step. The mountain grew lead-blue, and behind it, another mountain, peacock-blue. They steadied out under the bulkhead from which the last drumlins had fallen. Sharp rays of sunlight stepped across the water. Their source a high, cold, cloudy white. Now rose a flock of birds so dense that they darkened the lake below. As the clouds moved, one shrill beam of light searched the nearest mountain.

It seemed the seams of granite glittered.

"Look," said Manager Tom to Mama.

Racing behind a sudden streak of lightning, the storm crossed the lake, and intoxicated, the two felt as if some revenge was being taken in their name. The wind pounded the scullery doors, the chestnut trees, the boats on the lough. In their raincoats they walked the town up to the Barrack hill, down Main Street and back round to the square where one lone trader was huddled by the gate of the Market House, the polythene over his stall held tight with pegs. Already the actors had started drinking again, and cleaning up their rooms Liz and Cathy had to put their scripts in order. They found the toilet smelt of soot and freshly urinated drink. Thinking of the actors Cathy was struck by a terrible sense of loneliness she could not locate. Somehow it was to do with their little jars of toilet necessities. "We are at your mercy," the actors told Mama as she broke the seal on another bottle of Bushmills. Miniature sailboats floated across a beam on the wall. In the lounge, the guest, brimming with health, again took his place of the night before. The Manager relieved Mama. Mama seated at her dinner table sorted through bills while she waited on Finn.

A crisp otherworld reality settled in.

Later in the afternoon a wind-swept crowd of Irish soldiers in civilian clothes entered the lounge. Their drinking had already begun elsewhere. One of the actors was playing the piano. He was playing a Scott Joplin tune that was popular at the time. The guest moved across and joined the soldiers, and for the first time Manager Tom saw him laughing. Twice he put a phone call through to someone in Dublin, and speaking low, winked across at Manager Tom.

"Don't get carried away now."

"Why should you say that?"

"Those are hardy men."

"Indeed they are," he laughed ironically, then went back to join the company.

Manager Tom moved on to Cromwell's career in England. Cathy took her place behind the bar. The Manager for a few seconds was struck dumb by thoughts of his daughter Lucille. He tried to imagine her face but all that would come to his mind was a look, a glance, that she was returning to him sometime. The look would not surrender her face. The look was destroying him with its tenderness. The guest rushed up the stairs and came down moments later with his bag. Wet-eyed,

Manager Tom saw him. Suddenly the whole lounge went silent. Cathy came out shaking. "He's got a fucking gun in there, I tell you," she cried. Manager Tom plucked up his courage and stepped into the lounge. One of the soldiers was running his eye over the revolver which the guest had handed him. There were murmurs of approval. "Now, didn't I tell you?" the guest was saying. Seeing the Manager advancing fretfully, he came unsteadily to his feet, saluted him, then taking back his gun he advanced and placed it on Manager Tom's desk. Fearing that his final hour had come, the manager stood his ground. Turning round, he saw the stranger drop his various means of identification on the counter, then, tongue curved over the upper lip, kiss curls flying, mountain air on his cheeks, he again fell to attention, eyes up.

"I surrender," then he said.

"I surrender too," said Manager Tom. "God's sake, who are you?"

"Corporal Wilson, Parachute Regiment," the soldier said tipping back his head, "I deserted Saturday night."

The next evening the staff gathered to see the British soldier appear on TV, flanked by the President and Vice-President of Sinn *Féin*, standing like proud missionaries who had lately won over a convert. The soldier decried the military occupation of Northern Ireland. He was a socialist, he said. The horrible things that he had seen in Northern Ireland were beyond belief. His voice returned to its earlier nervousness. He ran his fingers along the pocket of his suit. "I should have realized he was a military man," said Finn, "he was a good riser and carried himself well."

"I'm sad for him," said Liz.

"What will become of him now?" she pondered.

"You can be sure of it, there's Irish blood in there somewhere," surmised Finn.

"Look, will ye," Cathy waved them quiet.

The camera began probing the interior of the Cove. To the soldier's bedroom where the voiceover told the story of Corporal Wilson and how his day was spent in the hotel. Drawing himself up straight as a rush an actor from the troupe told of his surprise at finding the man's real identity. "I could have sworn," he said, "that he had the words of Sean South!" The staff were shown going about their normal business and lastly there was a cut-away to Manager Tom's bowed head as he read in the foyer of Cromwell's proclamation to the doomed towns in Ireland, asking them to hand over the civilian population in order to prevent loss of life. With each refusal the orgy of violence began.

"We get all types here," said Manager Tom to the female interviewer whose condescending eye and television accent he could barely tolerate, "he was nothing out of the ordinary."

"Will you look at Finn," shouted Liz.

"In his farting jacket," Mama laughed.

"Could you find nothing decent?"

The voiceover began to fade.

"What would have happened if he'd got through to Manchester, I wonder?" queried the Manager.

"Well, anyway," said Cathy, "we're famous at last,"

38

From morning on people were shepherded down, from the mountains that looked north and secluded damp cottages on the sides of loughs, to the voting booths in the town. Some of the dead would vote today, and who the living would vote for were long dead. The predecessors of the dead would be chosen. They were voting, the old people, for dead men represented by the living. Some, too, were voting for men on the edge of death whom they had never known in life. The hunger strike then happening was a time when the paintings

on the wall had become real for some. A few Fianna Fáil and
Fine Gael people would return to earlier prejudices than
those their parties advocated. By giving the Sinn Féin party
their vote, these people were thinking how much they might
win from the enemy without conceding through violence all
that had been secured through peace. For the worst violence,
they knew, would occur among those who wanted to be on
the right side. This was not known to the drivers of the cars.
The wives and sisters of the major party candidates drove the
cars down the windy hillsides, their thoughts elsewhere, their
future compromised. They joked with the old couples about
acquaintances, knowing in their heart of hearts that they were
collaborating. The old couples listened and nodded. They
knew of earlier collaborations between wealth and poverty,
piety and violence, men and women. That their benevolence
had been reached through sins long forgotten. "After the
frost, came the fog and a bad doing ... the bombs," said old
Treanor. Yet they racked their brains to believe. The lakes
gained on them from below so that soon the windscreen wipers
seemed to work like oars parting the waters.

A rainbow, then more black clouds. The rays of the steel-
slanted sun pirouetted like the legs of a compass above the
town.

Off the damp breathing streets tea was served up by more
party women including Mama, in the rooms of the town hall.

There was drink, too, in any of the bars, free drink, and
much infuriating rational talk of what could be fulfilled, and
the women were vociferous witnesses to this. Their time had
not yet come. They held to the notions of the men more
strongly than the men themselves. In the politics talked the
women could view their own humiliation, if they cared. But
because of the panic of the times there was little dreamlike
speculation. The thrill of competition and prophecy was
abroad once more. The election, on the heels of another, had
come before the parties were prepared. This was a battle for
power and nothing else. It was not denied.

A village band from the north side of the border marched up the main street of the town bearing to the fore pictures of the hunger striker. The townfolk watched the band pass with puzzlement in their eyes. The band was playing "Roddy McCorley." After them came the other party cars with speakers blazing. The Taoiseach veered left in a helicopter towards a landing site in the military barracks. He flew by with such a roar that the dogs of the town lay on their backs and howled at the skies. Black flags flew from the poles.

The evening before the strangest reunion had taken place in the Cove. Lucille had returned from Manchester town where she was a cancer nurse. "I wouldn't miss this," she said, "for my life." She had her hair cut short in the punk style, wore plenty of green makeup and explained to Joseph that she liked the blond streak in her hair because it was cheeky. If there is a God, she told him, he's upstairs laughing. The two McGaherns took Lucille out that night. The town was rampant with expectation. The girls started with hot whiskeys in the Cove, the elder McGahern girl abstaining because of her nerves. "God," said Lucille, "I'd love a good jive." So on to a modern lounge attracting a young apolitical crowd where showband singers hung out by the door, keeping time with an empty glass and a well-turned heel. Here, more hot whiskeys. It was Lucille's round and she was a long time at the bar. At last she brought the girls their drink and then took a faltering path through the crowded tables, nodding at faces she didn't know, till she arrived at the table of the Minister of Finance. He was sitting with a couple of party devotees paying the necessary respects to a premises where naive votes were to be had.

"It's my birthday," said Lucille, and pressed a hot whiskey, with cloves and lemon, into his hand.

The two girls nearly died. The elder sister came over and in her halting manner apologized.

"Lucille really means well," she said.

"Indeed it's a pleasure," said the minister, eyes twinkling, "and who have we here?"

"She's Lucille Allen," explained the McGahern girl.

"Bedad," says he.

"Ha-ho," said Lucille, curtsying.

The minister sent over round after round of drinks. A man selling *An Phoblacht* moved from table to table. Lucille was the first to buy, much to the girls' embarrassment. The paper announced the death of another hunger striker. The seller was sporting a badge of the hunger striker who was contesting the election here in this Southern constituency. The Sinn Féiner was treated with good-natured and dismissive enthusiasm. The crowd went back to their drinks. The minister and his cronies reckoned that the IRA had brought this hunger crisis upon themselves. They had driven themselves into a corner. Violence had not reached here yet, that was the difference. Cars were parked by every doorstep in the town, and the cottages on the hills were filled with the gay, soft, separate movements of actors trying to be. A small drizzle of rain fell on the mousy-grey lakes. Everyone was in hell. Strangest thing of all for Lucille was to find a tune she couldn't place going round in her head. Though she hummed various parts of the tune no one could tell. Said Maria McGahern: "It's like something you'd hear in Church." The harder Lucille tried to fit the parts of the tune into a whole the more they began to disappear entirely, till she was left with a vague memory of something she had never known, as other people can know mysteries and magic because they follow roads that lead to unsettling places. But this was not for the market people. Today's prices had made the produce of their gardens and farms a total loss, so they sat late under a single bulb in a room back of the Market House, huddled against the stone walls, arguing over their affairs. At their feet, cardboard boxes of day-old chicks. The guards go by in pairs, keeping their torches lit in their blue pockets. Carefully avoiding the cowshit, they slip into the alleys and wait. "Youse are in for a bit of a shock tomorrow," Lucille told the minister in her English accent as they left the pub. He hunched his shoulders. The men with him brushed her aside. The wind from the gallows blew through the tunnel under the town, and most ferociously where it met the obstacles under the Cove. And the girls, Lucille most of all, the elderly McGahern told after, talked dirty among themselves till the small hours.

Mama looked in on Joseph. He was on the sleeping pills. He'd wake up in the late mornings like a beached whale, his consciousness gone out with the tide. Mama was talking him back in over fears never admitted to. He saw Mama go up a black hole into the ceiling and then come back down with whatever she was looking for. So after she was gone he tried to go up there too. But the attic was covered in soot. And black. His arms were weak so he let himself back down to the floor. Then he drifted through the various rooms of the hotel looking at the sleeping bodies to see which of them owned his mind. But no one would admit to it. Each had their own independence.

Nobody there had need of his soul.

He was a man without a spirit.

He was reluctant to let go of his dreams. In his dreams he could eat his fill. He had the constant company of his father. He could know by times the honesty of his mother. He was flooded by memories of his father. He sat up in the bed searching for the tender voice. Nobody cared these days how long you slept. The North was hibernating. There was sleet in Belfast. Force nine on the radioactive Irish Sea. A rock band, backing the Fianna Fáil party, set up their gear on the back of a lorry in the square. From such platforms throughout the country the future would be decided.

The night before the election an RUC man was shot in front of his wife and children. "He had it coming," said Lucille, "he knew what he was in for when he joined." "What have the

RUC ever done to you?" asked Laura. She was distraught to
hear this said in the kitchen. She had never seen anyone die. A
relationship of sorts had grown up between Joseph and Laura
based on their mutual terror. It started by her telling him her
dreams. "I worked last summer in the Isle of Man. The Isle of
Man," she laughed bitterly, "wouldn't you know." They sat in
her room smoking a joint. That evening Laura had retched up
her evening meal at the backdoor of the hotel. He had held
her forehead. He was going to nothing. He wanted to become
lightweight. "Last night," he said, "I dreamed I put my hand
between Margaret's legs and I knew I was using her. She was
being very business-like about what we were at. My mother
was at the door listening but passing no remarks. 'Must get
up now,' I said to Margaret for fear we be found. At that there
was a horrible, scornful, belittling laugh from my mother. If
I had said nothing she would have taken no notice. But I had
called attention to myself."

"And I thought you were there," said Joseph.

"Trust you." Laura turned up a bar of the electric fire.

"Mine was a family dream," Laura reckoned.

"I wanted my mother, I was asking her, to come down
here," she said, "but like all Protestant women she wanted
to hide. You people never hear of Protestant women like my
mother. They are cut off from the world. Lost to the world.
They only appear protected by their men. In the dream I leant
out to touch her dress but she pulled it back sharply. 'That's
no way to carry on,' she said. We are not silent, but there is
nothing happening either. Then one by one the walls of the
room in the house we are sitting in fall down so that we are
exposed to everyone in the street. This does not matter to us.
I keep on asking her to be my friend. 'Of course I am your
friend,' she answers sharply. But she is not really listening,
instead she begins to pick up the bricks to build the walls
again. All this is done as if she were about her normal duties.
To get her attention I kneel beside her, and though it's against
my wishes, I hand her the bricks. The people on the street see

us and yet they don't see us, I am caught up in her labour for I am afraid of my father. Grimly, my mother builds the walls again. And as the walls rise somehow the light is going. When she replaces the last brick I know we will be in darkness. I try to persuade her to stop. It's dark. The walls are up again and I can detect her lips in the darkness. They are the huge crimson lips of a doll.

"This is where you make your appearance – don't raise your hopes. You are in my bed. I get up to get something in the outer room. Here, fully lit up, sitting round, are all my relations. Trying to reach what I want I begin to bump into them. I begin to knock down things.

"I began to knock down things. Now do you see where you've led me?" Laura pursed her lips, "And I so careful always."

Beatles numbers crossed the square. The rock band were singing "Help." Idling in their white shirts, frozen, their flageolets held against their thighs, the village traditional band, once trained by Peter above in Fanacross, stood together watching the platform with awestruck eyes. The South to them was a great mystery. It appeared to them that the parties in the South had the outside world on their side. They explained to Joseph that their man had only days to live. The police stood around this group waiting for any trouble. A man at last came with their coats from the bus, and he brought steaming bags of chips and sausages. Eating, they stood watching the rock band till they quit playing and the speeches began. Then they strolled round the town.

"I have no vote," Peter told the man in the hall.

But the canvasser was a persistent type. He went after Liz and Laura. Mama and Joseph. The sort you disagree with on television but safe here in the hotel saying what he liked, thought Cathy. Then back to Peter. "Here, have a drink," he said. Peter must have felt he was all right. He joined him. Said the canvasser: "And maybe we might be able to get you work back in the village for they tell me you are unhappy here in the town?"

"Everybody else is voting for our man," he advised in the bar, then pulling down the lower lid of his right eye, he continued, "a little bird tells me you are on the register."

"I'll be happy to do whatever you want," Peter told him.

"Good man."

"I know nothing at all about my papers. You might as well be talking of the harvest moon. I let Manager Tom look after all that."

"Quite right. A decent man. I'd say he might be a little hard on you, but decent – don't get me wrong."

He promised to have a car round to the hotel to collect the staff at six. He showed Peter how to mark his card. He was reluctant to leave as if going round talking to the public about the state of the country was an awful burden to him and sometimes he unwittingly carried on the poor man's chat with someone gone far beyond that, then recovering himself, he'd say, "It's been a long day. Don't forget us anyway."

The town that day was full of people feeding off their own hysteria.

Peter set off among them.

A man can be as free as a bird.

And indeed it was lucky he wore his cap.

He played a couple of tunes first by the font, and then by the archway, it was there he first noticed them flying about. Then the whole hive of bees took off from the town clock and landed on his head. But Peter had retreated to another room of consciousness. I know how to beat them, he thought. So he played on regardless till a butcher attracted them away with a porringer of jam. He said Peter was the most sensible man alive.

"There is nothing flying," said Peter, "but respects the resin."

They had a special Mass in the midday and Peter played among the canvassers who were carrying the placards of their representatives to and fro at the gates of the church. They tried to put Peter out of it, but he said, learning fast: "If you want my vote me lads, you'll leave me alone." He said more. He said: "The foreigner stopped the likes of me playing music on the streets during the Famine, when dogs went round thin as hurley sticks, and you'll not pick up where they left off." He was embarrassing the party people. One of the women coming from Mass said, "Good man, that's the way to talk to them." He tightened the strings till they were taut and musical as the force that holds the water to the earth and let go from sadness to "Mocking at the Earl."

"What's the name of that air?" he was asked.

"I couldn't tell you," he replied, "unless it's a children's game that auld men play and is called 'Mocking at the Earl.'"

In a pub in Bridge Street, as he watched himself in a mirror, he was told that he was a great man to study his face for all he might find there. "I see nothing worse there than in another man's," he explained, because he would not begrudge the fellow his friendship. "The road from my father's house to the village is there and everything I saw, not minding what I missed, and when I mind nothing of that there is the road my mother took away from him when there wasn't anything more to hold her there. There was no evil in either of them." Then returning to his face in the mirror Peter cried for each of his parents in turn, and then together, because even then, wherever they were in the world beyond, he felt they might still be fighting for his sympathy and attention. "I have no way of telling any world other than the one I know," he saw, "until I look on another face and I see so far beyond me that my wits run astray, so I turn to my own face for consolation, and there I see weakness and ignorance and exaggeration and everything that a man hates in himself and blames on another, but then a child can sleep on a hard floor as well as a soft if that's all the one he knows, and get up, right as rain, to check everything in the yard and on the kitchen table to see how they work for again." He looked at the face of the man beside him. "But I will not keep from you what I have, or say that you would be better off without me or I without you. You are a good listener, and a man is in control till he starts talking, and now, it's your turn."

"That's all right," the stranger answered immediately, "because you are talking of things that are not real."

A great pressure lifted off Peter's head when the stranger spoke so honestly, and he thanked him. He threw his money on the bar counter and said: "You'll have a drink, have your pleasure. You are a right fellow." "Keep it," his companion said quietly. "You have more need of it than I."

"Go out of that," Peter replied, and his soul thrilled for the man opposite him and he called a glass of whiskey.

"Here," Peter says, "there is more where that came from."

The stranger leaped to his feet, a flush of bad temper on his face, impatient as a dog tied up in lambing time. "No, I told you," he shouted and moved further down the bar. "Don't be annoying the customers," next the barman said. Peter implored his friend but the man pushed him away. He felt the coldness in the bar, it was as if a well had frozen over and every face there was his own face looking back, except for the eyes that were all reflections of an alien torment, he felt trapped forever, what flowed loose and free underneath gone from him.

"Thank you all," he said, and backed out.

They took George out again and again from the Maze, so that suspicion would be thrown on him. "I came up here to admit to having taken up a gun after the death of my wife," he started each day, "I never used it."

"Come now, there is more on your conscience than that."

"I came up here to clear the name of my brother," George persisted.

"We are going easy on him, aren't we?" the voice said.

"Youse killed my wife," said George, "and maybe even my brother."

"And you were fucking the arse of his wife when he was off in England."

"Isn't that why your wife killed herself, you Fenian shit?"

"Fucking the arse of his sister-in-law."

All to be seen of the conversation is the human hand in rhythm to something, clapping lightly the curve of the back of the chair of the man who is talking, fingers alternating as to which finger should bear the weight.

"I'm thinking we should look after you. You see yourself as a good man? The violence? We know."

"It's hard on him, we know."

Again they turn their backs. Again the hand circling the plush velvet back of the chair in which the other sits. They look back at him as if to say he's not important. The sharp head of one nods back to the original movement. As he leaned forward George was saying to himself, I am by nature an informer, I want to know the cause of my own guilt. This makes me a criminal, clear? Up here it's clear.

"Tell us now, and it will go easy on you."

"What are the British doing in Northern Ireland?"

They turn back again so that his question hangs uselessly from his mouth. In his mind this question has become a concrete thing. He is left plagued by something left undone, yet stubborn enough never to find it. I am me, not an assortment of others, I am me. How do you see through other people's eyes the man they see? Don't, now. Don't.

"There would be plenty of pleasure for a man like him in Australia?"

"Your own crowd, George, will have you put down like a dog."

"You stole bomb-making materials with your lads from the factory on the mountain, we know. Your brother was in on it."

"We can forget that."

"You killed my wife, you bastards."

"You had made her life sad, George. You are up to your neck in it now, George Allen."

"It was a British jeep killed my wife."

"And you'll not see daylight again."

"Are we animals, is that it?"

"He came up here of his own accord." The man laughs. His laugh is not true, for he is poised on the wrong leg. He throws open his coattails to show his gun. "Here." The cigarette. "Take your time now. We have all the time in the world."

"Too late for all that now, George."

One heartbeat. Two heartbeats. That terrible thing of the morning breaking with a new frightening consciousness of the day before, he woke knowing he had on the day before committed himself to an irrevocable decision. *A decision made by a drunken mind.*

Peter sings a love song in the lounge. He stands singing to himself unaware of anyone else. Cathy is working behind the bar. Each verse grows the more lonesome. He wets his lips, spits and looks at her grinning. He finishes his pint and takes another as he tosses a handful of loose change onto the counter. A loudspeaker blares on the street. He takes up his position and sings again, rowdy, uncouth looking, rocking gently on his feet, as if he were out on the lakes with the village in sight.

The Sinn Féin band walked down the street followed by a small crowd, among them Lucille, holding high the head of the hunger striker, and afterwards the crowd retired to the bar of the Cove while the members of the other parties gathered in the lounge, and Cathy could hear it – Look at the scum beyond. Manager Tom moved to and fro, his talk always of comedians and politicians interrupted by fast perplexed silences. Again, he found himself at odds with his daughter but did not say a word. Mama was in her element. The crowd moved on into a further interior where things were moving too fast to understand them properly. Till a part of their life was compromised and could only be reclaimed with great difficulty. They were arguing the cause of the common man who would live in a world not yet realized. And elsewhere, how men fear the other side of the story that keeps them from knowing the injustices inherent in their own. Of the power wielded by certain men. How close the vote would be. They toasted each other. A posse of soldiers, needing further humiliation to contain them, jogged down the hill, their great boots pounding on the slippery pavements. Above in the city of Dublin there was a snapping of rails as a train moved further down the track, bearing the Taoiseach back to his own constituency.

The town the next day was full of the roar of domestic animals and cattle being driven in lorries to the mart. The count began at nine. The wet pictures of the leaders of the parties hung askew from their holdings on the sides of the streets as if some all-night party was just over. The nuns in the convent persevered with their prayers at early Mass, trying to get beyond the human condition to the divine, and finding there the same flawed reality that had begun their recourse to God in the first place. Above the town rose the echoing voice of the auctioneer. By midday the tallymen could not give an account of what the likely outcome in the locality was to be. The news of the count continued throughout the day on television. Groups of people gathered round to watch. In the studios some of the party leaders were breaking down the information in reasonable tones. They continued to disbelieve what had happened, that government was changing hands. They disputed their losses till they were drained even of acrimony. Somewhere was a hidden constituency which would right all this. Others were gaining in importance and spoke with conviction. Candidates interviewed, who had won seats, seemed indifferent to everything as their names were echoed by party followers on the steps of the courthouses.

They gave guarded statements. They gave promises where essential. No one mentioned the North.

The party people in the Cove lounge became displaced as if they had taken a drug that would not reach their brain. The radio was turned up so they could hear beyond the recorded voices what they craved, a world where earlier promises were not so readily compromised. Soon enough, though, the two main parties began to trek back into their subconsciouses, like long camel trains coming in from the desert, bringing with them safe commodities for society's survival. The lounge was full. Ham and peanuts were walked into the sodden carpet. "Tunney," some shouted. "Gargan," the others replied.

In the bar the others waited, heads tipped back to watch the television. Here stranger news was coming in. The hunger striker was getting there, and what's more, the rumour was, and afterwards realized, that many had voted the hunger striker first, and the Fine Gael man, a Protestant, second. The Minister of Finance elected on the third count arrived to the hotel. Manager Tom welcomed him by the door. Everyone rose and applauded the minister when he took his seat in the lounge. Tunney was a well-groomed individual and had the mannerisms of a doctor. He listened intently to the views of others, approved with his chin, a little academic condescension, then withdrew to consider. He sat down among the elders of his constituency, those that had started their campaign a lifetime ago and spoke plainly.

They ticked off the winners as the news came in.

And awaited the remainder with stoical comments.

The minister listened with the patience of a man who had served his party well. Still, something was wrong, though that would in time be forgotten. They were on the verge of losing a seat. Business went on. Finn was outside chatting to the chauffeur in the minister's Mercedes. He, too, was listening to his radio and smoking there in the darkness, cigarette after cigarette, Finn cared little as he muttered glibly about the affairs of the world. Within the hotel voices were filled with argument and precaution, nightmare and lucidity. Towards eight the minister's wife arrived in her own car.

She entered the hotel and joined her husband.

"It looks bad," said Manager Tom.

For everyone said she had second sight, a great deal of sense and was the equal of her man in political cunning. "Cathy," she said, "make mine strong." The older party men had their eyes squeezed tight with listening above the noise. The minister's face went red momentarily. It became apparent that his party was out of power. There was jubilation across the street. Then the Cove bar grew rapturous, and broke into a mighty roar, as the news came through on Radio Telefís Éireann that the hunger striker had been elected, though, it was added, as if this would somehow stem the tide of anarchy, he had not reached the quota. All human beings have a failing for power, for celebration, so when the Sinn Féiners were asked, Is it true? Did he get through? That is correct, they answered. That loose-hearted, sentimental republicanism that had not been seen for so long, took hold of the hearts of the crowd. The politicians and the theorists became a sort of infringement on the screen now that the election was over. They only attracted the attention of those who wanted to argue over the same points.

The lounge emptied. The ex-minister made his escape in his wife's car. "There's democracy for you," said Manager Tom. "It makes you proud of this country. He took a second car for fear of losing." The chauffeur after a polite interval followed. The boys' band went home in their bus singing.

The restaurant was going at full speed. The election people were eating with great haste anything that could be prepared. It had been a long day for the girls. Laura had been on her feet since morning. She stood by the kitchen table making sandwiches and did not look up for hours. Sometimes she'd throw the whole lot there and go up to one of the sheds at the back for a smoke and put on her thinking cap for a while. From this out, she was thinking, I'll have to mind what I say. Joseph, she knew, would have preferred to have her talking to him always of things that concerned himself and of those other unidentifiable beings, her family. She had over a time built up another frame of mind she could easily enter.

She went back into the kitchen well-stoned. That's Cathy for certain. "My brother once had been taken away with his nerves," said Cathy. "He came back six months later. 'Pick it up without touching it,' he'd say when he dropped something. For the whole six months we couldn't visit him and then when he came back he went funny. For a whole year he went round crying and whingeing and nearly drove the mother mad. Imagine," said Cathy, "the nerve of him saying 'pick it up without touching it.'"

The kitchen was cheered by Cathy's story. Then one of the party men, braving Finn's stare, came into the kitchen, tucked his arms round Laura's waist and asked for a chicken curry, a great sentimental Irish taste at the time. "I'd love to give you a turn," he said. "You are very forward in your statements," she said, and grew still. "Ha-ha," he laughed.

Her nostrils dilated.

"Let go," she mouthed coolly, "or you'll be sorry."

He held her closer to spite her.

She drove the fork lightly into the back of his hand. He jumped back like a frightened cat. "Look," he yelled outraged. "Look what you've done. You black bitch. Jesus Christ." He would have hit her had there been no one there. And she was prepared for that eventuality too. She went on slicing the bread as Finn wrapped up the distraught man's hand in a bandage. "I suppose I deserved it," he said turning maudlin. She went on slicing the bread. She sliced off the crusts, slapped in the ham, the leaf of lettuce, spread the butter on the next thin slice and smacked the two together. The man was led back to his table. The schoolgirls brought in for the day to help stared at Laura. Then they returned to their labour, wondering at her inflexibility and how Finn had carried on without rebuking her, and when she served at table, Laura took stock of the man she had wounded – a square, fat figure in wide-arsed trousers, his mouth continuing around his cheek in a non-laughing scar, there was evil in his carriage.

You've put on some weight son, someone said to him.

I've put on some weight.

Must be the marriage.

Must be the marriage, aye.

Lines of steel Guinness barrels up the archway of the hotels were rolled in. One wildly agitated man was clapping his knee as he sat below the monument. Across the road the Market House was having its old granite blocks whacked into shape. "Come here," shouts some mother, "or I'll smack you very hard." A moment later she does. She pulls her child's socks out of shoes similar to black dancing pumps, each having a single gold thread. The girls are walking round the town with their hands stuffed into the pockets of their swinging dresses. Laura suddenly heard the motorbikes of the Border Lords revving up outside the chipper. They flew by her as she returned with six fresh loaves across the square.

Towards midnight Peter entered very distraught.

"Come out quickly," he said to Joseph, "till I show you something." He pulled at his arm. They went out into the yard, the two of them. Peter searched the sky, shading his eyes with his cap. Nothing there. He prodded Joseph further on into the wedding garden. They walked to and fro over the cool grass as Peter held his head back and looked up there for something. He let his coat fall. His grip grew tighter across the lad's shoulders. They wheeled about there it seemed for hours, through the stone figures and flowers, searching the sky. At last he sat down. He said: "It was up there a few minutes ago. I saw it with my own two eyes." They waited on his vision to come again. It didn't. Somewhere over the rooftops someone opened up an accordion. The air was sucked in with a great wheeze then the instrument was still.

"By the sound of that," said Peter, "it's a Hohner C sharp."

He pulled up his coat and replaced his long boots and let Joseph go as if he were a stranger who had failed him, someone who had mocked him because of his lack of education, or worse still, failed to match his intelligence. "No one will believe me," he said sadly with a last look at the sky, and they went in.

39

Looking out of his window Joseph thought, this day is a day somewhere before Christmas. The quality of the light told him. Everything in the hotel was unnaturally still. Outside, there was some kind of cheerful expectancy.

Even the kitchen had a warm winter mood. Everything was moving at an easy pace, which created an air of the temporariness of things, their vulnerability. The last of the hunger strikers had died. A dozen soldiers died. It was a bad time.

So, in the Cove, guests those days were treated like royalty. The hotel was preparing itself for its first wedding in ages. Two guests, Mr and Mrs Moss, had arrived a few days early. Joseph carried their tray up to their room and knocked at the door. Mrs Moss was really Cathleen McManus from Glangevlin, up at Cuilcagh. They were both still asleep when he knocked and she opened the door in her dressing gown.

He saw the slight shake in her chin. With a finger to her lips she beckoned him in and crept back beneath the sheets,

"Pull the curtain," she whispered, taking the tray onto her lap, "this man of mine is out for the count."

She poured out the tea in a grave, careful fashion, and, with a modest smile, dismissed the lad.

"Harry?" her eyebrows arched. "Harry." She tipped his ear like someone righting the hands of a clock. Her husband opened one eye, then the other cautiously. He took in the ballooning wallpaper pinned to the walls. The sad frame of the window shedding mould onto the sill. Then the tray of breakfast things on doilies.

"This is the life," he said, coming onto his elbows.

"She came to the door without a stitch," said Joseph. "She did not," said Laura. "No, she didn't," he replied. Sometimes, for Laura, Joseph pretends to know much more than he does, and she takes infinite pains to go over his story in case she might have misunderstood him. The truth always comes out in the end, because he has learned that the truth is an even greater invention than lies. The council, who are drilling the roads from morning to dusk to lay new water mains, now drive the Mosses from their bed. When the workmen stop drilling between one and two the town relaxes. The people after a few seconds adjust the pitch of their voices because all morning they have been screaming to be heard. The schoolchildren just released from the convent pile into the drains after old coins because someone has told them that there is treasure buried under the town. They hunt the earthworks in a fever. The garage workers drive slowly up the town, knowing too that things are bad, people are going North to get their petrol. Then, as the work recommences at two, the town braces itself for the terrible noise. Suddenly the whole footpath caves in. It could have been an opening into the old tunnel. You can hear the drill, hemmed in by fallen concrete, whirring to a stop. Danny hauls it back up. Danny Reed who had caused so much heartbreak over the affair with the police. He starts

it up again, pounding like a beast at the foundations of the
Cove. He says to Joseph: "I can't hear a fucking thing with
that machine. Today at dinner I bit into a chicken bone and
nearly fainted." He lights a fag and he and Joseph consider
the long cracked passage he has made behind him and the
dry untouched pavement stones ahead. And all the pavements
of the town to go. As he holds his cigarette the movement of
the drill continues up through his hands. His drinking has
increased to such an extent that Cathy, hearing him start up
again, says: "There's that auld faggot Danny Reed, and a face
on him like a full moon in a fog." As the drill continues its
short malevolent bursts and Danny has to take the strain of
the weight as the concrete gives, Joseph can tell Danny is sorry
that the easy work on the building of the pier at the shore of
the lake has ended, where at least his tools did not scream the
outrage of the materials and the earth, and his ears had not to
carry the ceaseless traffic of his blood.

Coming down to the foyer Mr Moss righted a picture of a
patriot which hung awkwardly on the wall. He inspected the
photograph of the President of America and shook his head
with an impatient sigh. He offered his hand to Peter who was
cleaning out the lounge. It took Moss aback to hear the robust
way Peter had of talking, of gesturing towards something
unseen, and how, when he offered his limp, workman's hand,
he closed an intimate eye. "Ha-ho," declared Peter.

"Nippy," said Mr Moss.

"I'd put it better than that," answered Peter. He
straightened up and took a mouthful of his cup of Bovril. The
beef tea pervaded the room. "God is good."

Mr Moss excused himself and sat down in the foyer on a
low hall chair, joining his hands on his lap. He crossed his legs
and surveyed the street that was coming apart at the seams.
The moustached smile and straight back of Mr Moss. And
the curved humorous eyes that changed perceptibly as he

watched a crowd of uncaring drunks pass by. Mama arrived and stood by the desk with that habit she had of tucking her elbows against her breasts.

"I am waiting on my wife," said Mr Moss.

"You will be for dinner again tonight?" she asked.

"Yes," he said, "we are eating with the McManuses, I expect. You might hold a table for four."

Mama nodded. The clock swung towards noon. "Coffee?" asked Manager Tom. "Thank you, no," said Mr Moss. Manager Tom viewed himself in the hall mirror, and checked, as was his daily routine, for any flaws in his peeling face.

"Did you ever," he asked, "get a ringing in your ears?"

Moss hesitated and with a smile answered, "No."

"I am cursed with it," replied Manager Tom, "since I took this place over."

Now Mrs Moss put in her appearance. A small dainty woman, white-headed before her time, like one of those pieces of wedding cake, wrapped in tissue, that are preserved in the musty drawers of sentimental guests. She had been a long time away from home. Mr Moss put on his white raincoat, and linking his hands above his buttocks he strode alongside his wife across the square.

They drove up the mountains in a hired car. Their first stop was the graveyard where Mrs Moss laid a bunch of wild flowers on her father's grave. Goats and sheep each side of them were eating grass. The kid goats beat their hooves on the fallen tombs. A white-headed sheep, the bottom of her mouth working independently of the rest of the body, stared at them. Little pools of droppings were everywhere, and sometimes as the pair walked along up a hill of flattened ferns above the graveyard, the goats stopped to look at them, their horns balancing like hands in prayer. They sneeze a farting sound. Then leave, return to look, their beards drop in curiosity. And sometimes too, if Mr and Mrs Moss happened to walk into a flattened area where the animals had been, they found the warm dung smell of the goats. "He was only forty-two," said Cathleen Moss, as she stood back from the grave, "he had a lovely death."

The wind careered off the mountains, came coldly past the north wall of the Church and straight into their faces. Mr Moss had the feeling that someone was watching him. He swung round to find a middle-aged man, with raspberry ducts under his eyes and a cap perched on the back of his head, leaning over the wall. "It's a cool day," the man said, twirling a stick, then he let a roar after his dog. "He was a saint, the man McManus," he rose up a pair of startling blue eyes. "The rest of us couldn't bear investigation."

"How are you?" asked Cathleen.

"I can't complain." He slid away and continued his journey, talking to himself. "That's what comes from living by yourself," she said. Alien for a moment, Mr Moss stood on a wandering sod. There at the end of the wall, like an hallucination, he saw a grinning head shape, stolen he surmised from some earlier pagan site. But as he approached the place the head disappeared. It was just the cratered pattern of the limestone had for a second formed the face.

The dinner things were taken away. Humming, the Manager asked: Had their meal been OK, now? A sour smell of sweat reached Moss's nostrils as the man cleared away the plates, then, returning to his position in the foyer, Manager Tom stood by the curtained windows and looked forlornly out onto the square. Mrs Moss brought her aunt, Mrs McManus, a glass of port. Moss drank a pure orange. Cathleen Moss, who prided herself on her cooking, was dismayed at the overcooked vegetables. Throughout dinner she had displayed other anxieties, and could only be brought into the conversation as the talk returned to the McManus's shop here in the town, where she had worked for two years behind the grocery counter. The talk centred on how things had changed in the town, and above in Glangevlin.

They talked of the forthcoming wedding.

"Youse were great to come over," her aunt spoke from her warm untroubled soul.

"I had some leave due," Moss drew his chair closer to the table.

"This is his first time in Ireland!" said Cathleen with a benign look, as if he should be forgiven for what he was.

"He had more sense," Mrs McManus obliged.

"Will there be anything else?" asked Mama, standing there.

Cathleen Moss declined on behalf of her party, then with the side of her hand smacked her napkin, that bore old coffee stains, lightly, into its old triangular shape. "This place," she said after Mama's departure, "has certainly come down in the world."

"The Allens were never what you might call business people," Mrs McManus declared confidently. "He's an oddball. The drink, you know." Her voice dropped to a shrill whisper. "The young fellow's father was shot." She gathered herself back into her chair, "Oh, now."

Moss nodded sagely.

"Isn't that an army town you're in?" asked McManus.

"Harry," said Cathleen carefully, "is a clerk in Aldershot."

"Youse have had your troubles there as well," coaxed McManus.

"Yes," replied Moss genially, "it goes hard on the Irish population every time."

"It's too bad."

"We have Irish friends," said Cathleen, "and English friends. Of course it's only to be expected. You can't cut yourself off. But we don't do much entertaining. You reach a point where you just need each other's company. It's not like here, where you can come and go in and out of people's houses."

"Well, I'm afraid you can't do that across the border either," said her aunt. "You'd get the snot blown off you. Yes. That's the finish up of it."

Stories of the old days began to spin. Moss, as each story reached its designated humorous finish, laughed heartily. "I have heard a lot of them before," he said, "they get funnier every time." The Manager, recalled from his reverie by the white curtains, brought in brandies. There was a moment's exhilaration, then the party were back where they started, in the present, as if the past had grown inhospitable and sentimental, a place called on to authenticate the violence that had occurred since then.

"You can see," said Mrs McManus, "that we are not as bad here as we are portrayed."

"That's true," Moss smiled, then judging the distance between those gathered there, he ventured – "and neither, perhaps, are we."

"You never said a truer word," said McManus recklessly.

Cathleen asked of John her cousin.

"I couldn't tell you," Mrs McManus replied, scattering crumbs from her lap. "He's a law unto himself. I couldn't care if I never caught sight of him again."

Again Cathleen's gestures grew superfluous. Her aunt suggested that they go to view the wedding presents, some of which had been laid aside in a room upstairs. The men retired to the lounge, where no one was speaking as the news carried on, distracted and poignant, from the mouth of an amiable woman on the TV.

No comment was made. Everything stopped for the news.

The two locals at the bar held tight rein to their feelings because talk only made things worse. His colleagues followed the cortège of an RUC man's funeral. The red nose of a camouflaged helicopter swung up the sky. One of the locals, with a gaunt fit face, in donkey jacket and jeans, looked up. "What the hell," he asked, "are they sending over those soldiers to be killed for?" The music sheets sat on top of the trumpets of the accompanying band. The Rev. Ian, dressed as another Carson, waits under an umbrella in the rain by the grave. The pastor's speech from the pulpit, as a voiceover, follows the coffin through the graveyard. Moral judgement, he says, can become clouded in a time of violence. We have to come to terms with men of violence. The policeman's cap and gloves sat atop the coffin on the Union Jack. He is cut down like a flower, the pastor said.

So, while the women sorted through the toasters, rugs and sets of cutlery, Harry Moss sat curtly before the television, he saw Haughey's face, then Fitzgerald's face, the two leaders of the country, as the picture waned, the reception was barely adequate to say the least, it was the voices remained longest in the mind, then a swarm of dislocated angry dots rose so that the individual components of the picture drifted away from each other, and all became unrecognizable but, even so, Mr McManus sat unperturbed before it, as did Mr Moss, neither of them acknowledging the other's existence till the women, somewhat saddened by all they'd seen, came down.

"Your aunt," announced Moss, "says that we could easily make a home around here."

"She is dreaming," said his wife.

Somebody has tried to teach that woman to be a lady since she left here, Mama thought, as she watched Cathleen Moss move across the square, the white hair newly and tightly permed. Her right hand made a loosely swinging fist, pewter rings shining, while from the raised palm of the other hand, a pair of black gloves dangled. Her head arched down self-consciously. The bag in the crook of her arm swings so-so. She raises her eyes as if to a new and unexplained sight. Then she repeats the same superfluous rhythm which Mama recognized – the rhythm of many women who expect they are being watched, by women or men, it doesn't matter, the farcical posture soon has a charm of its own. Behind it, the twin defences of rigidity and vulnerability. An old- fashioned pursuit of the ladylike, still despite all, a grand, if contrived, failure. Her dull rings go well with the pale nylons as she sports along in a Fraulein's pencil dress from one of those old Hollywood movies, firmly buttocked, in the blue-rose pattern of the old pinafores. She stops to talk a second to old friends without once looking into their mocking eyes, just plays with a pleat in her dress and does not seem to mind the cold.

And Mama had some comfort thinking that a woman tells her most loving stories when she sees herself as all women, but the most distinctive when they are peculiarly her own.

On Thursday afternoon, to the Allens' surprise Jim arrived at the back door of the hotel in a little white Ford van. He threw open the back doors to display the refrigerated whiting, mackerel, pollock, prawns and cod. "By Jingo," said the Manager, "you are the one that is doing well." "I have something else you might be interested in," said Jim and slid back a sheet of polyester to show a quantity of smuggled whiskey, gin and vodka. "Bedad, you've cast your net wide."

"Joseph," commanded the Manager, "take every drop he's got."

"And what," asked Mama as she watched the drink stored out of sight, "will you say if they ask you where this drink came from?"

"I'll say," he replied stoically, "that the fairies left it there."

Jim closed the doors of his van but would not come in. "Do you hear at all from your father, from George?" asked Manager Tom.

"I've just come from there," replied Jim, "he's in good health. They are holding him on remand, over and over." Jim wanted away. One of his hands clasped the other. "I best be off," he said, "I've a fair journey to go." "Will you be back again next week?" asked Joseph.

"I will."

"All the best now," said the Manager, "take care."

"Aye."

He reversed back round the yard, waved and drove off.

"Don't," said Manager Tom to Joseph as the two stood looking after him, "tell a soul about this."

On Thursday night Mr Moss found himself at an all-male gathering in an old-fashioned pub. They were there to give the groom a sending-off. The young men were sprawled on wooden chairs half the size of their bodies so that the legs of the chairs crouched like cats about to spring. The groom's party did not find Moss easy to talk to. His disarming geniality appeared a mere pretence, and struggle as they could, they could not breach the inner reserve of the man. His affability ranged over simple things, domestic trivia, the exact distance from one place to another, but otherwise he could not be drawn into their unserious world. It was the groom's night though. He was carried away by the enthusiasm of his friends, yet made sure that Moss, who this night had acceded to brandy, did not want for anything. He missed the English beer, he said.

"You'll have to see Douagh," someone advised.

"Sure there is no difference between us," said another, "we are all the one."

The songs were of women abandoned by soldiers.

The voices were making Harry Moss disorientated. They sounded like drunk men in a cell claiming sobriety. Each man threw money into the centre of the table and more loaded trays of drink arrived. Sometimes Moss found two or three of the lads talking to him at the one time. He felt he could lead the speakers off on any trail he wished for always there was this repetitive need to be liked. All his ironies were lost on them. All their exaggerations foundered in his consciousness. And occasionally roles changed, so that Moss's thin exterior showed a warm, less simplistic side.

"We have, myself and Cathleen," he explained in an aside to the groom, "a good independent relationship that can leave us wanting each other a lot of the time."

The groom nodded his understanding, then shifted his head to take in a joke about the Irish army that was travelling across the table.

"Yes, there were some right fools in the British army as well," continued Moss, his face and demeanour adopting a comedian's pose. "Here, was I, your Sergeant Moss at one desk, and over there, yes, was your Major Trenchant at the other. The telephone rang. 'It's for you,' I said, 'Major. Major! The CO wants you.' He started out from behind his desk and bolted to attention in front of a plain closed door."

"I can see it," one of the lads laughed.

"A bloody closed door."

"He wasn't right."

"If you haven't got a head dress on. Like. And you meet a commanding officer, you go – Eyes left, eyes right," explained Mr Moss, darting a glance each side of him. "Well, all right, Major Trenchant was just out of the old asylum. Wasn't he. The Royal Victoria Military Hospital in Netley, Southampton. So, I meet him crossing the square. I have nothing on my head. So it's, eyes left, eyes right. The same thing happens later in the day." At the thought Moss started laughing as he threw his listeners the signal. "Don't the same thing happen the following morning. Eyes left. Eyes right. 'Look here,' said Major Trenchant, 'I don't want sergeants in my corps shaking their heads backwards and forwards like a yo-yo.' 'Sir,' I said, 'it's the compliment of dress to officers.' He marched off in a huff, and later that day the Colonel called me in. 'Look,' he said, 'Major Trenchant tells me you've been acting like an idiot.' So I had to explain. Didn't I. All about the regulations. And what had happened. The colonel had an upper-class accent. 'You've got to allow for certain peculiarities,' he said, keeping as straight a face as possible, 'I'll have a few words with him to explain that my acting sergeant was above approach.'"

"Jesus, that's good," the groom laughed.

"And Major Trenchant was, if you will, a strict disciplinarian."

Moss hurled an extra fiver on to the table for good measure, but at that moment everyone decided to head to the Cove for a final fling. "The where?" asked Harry Moss. "Where you are staying," he was told. Here they ran into a school of girls with the bride, all with shining cheeks from the fall of hail that had greeted the men as they stepped down onto the street. The two parties met in a raucous rehearsal for the next day's wedding. Moss stepped into the toilet where Manager Tom, in a bid to muster up trade, had piped music installed, and here Moss swayed gently to and fro to a Christmas carol, then purring softly, he joined his wife at the bar. He explained that he had had an enjoyable evening. She laced her arm round his waist. The groom leaned towards them.

"Eyes left, eyes right," he said.

"Ah yes, the Queen's Regulations," said Moss straightening to attention. He grew bulkier, and at the same time boyish, as he must have appeared to his first wife. "I do love you, I do," said Cathleen into his ear. Laughing, she pulled the hem of her dress down over her knee. The two crept away while the festivities were in full swing and she was pleased to find their room neat and tidy as a doll's house.

As he slept soundlessly beside her Cathleen Moss read into the night from a recipe book she had bought that day. Then closing her book on the flower of the bloody cranesbill, she dreamed of her climb up into Glangevlin, a place abounding in dock. She dreamed of the gub of land in the oak forest. The sharp rock in the little Oakwood of the sleep. She dreamed the hollow in the black precipice.

She dreamed the Middle, East and West rock in the yellow hollow.

And finally, the gorge of the water channel.

The drill started up and rain sifted through the bags of oat seeds.

"I worry about you," said Cathleen.

"Ah, worry of that kind is like jealousy," he answered. He swung round to her in his morning suit, then turning patrolled the room again, as she carefully sketched in her eyes. "I'll wait for you downstairs," he said. He found the solicitor's clerk, a blue vein grovelling beneath his left eye, the only occupant of the lounge. Outside he saw that a broken gutter was spilling down the side wall. Padjo, older now, was up on the rickety ladder doing a holding job.

"It's the children of this country I fear for," Padjo called, "the auld people should be put down."

Through the window Moss saw the wedding cake being raised onto two sets of pillars, that sank, if he could have seen it, into the icing that had not been let set long enough by Finn.

"Do you see this town," said Padjo descending, with laboured breaths, the ladder. "You would be afraid to dig up their back gardens for the quantity of unbaptized children you'd dig up in every square yard."

Moss was surprised to find himself the recipient of all these outrageous confidences. He was more surprised when entering the bar to find the young fellow Joseph pouring whiskey from full bottles of Powers into other empty bottles of Powers. Isn't that a futile exercise," he asked looking into Joseph's eye to catch a glimpse of the severed parent, "what you are at?"

"There's no great concern," answered Joseph in the remote manner of an anarchic servant.

"Aye mister," said Peter, who next appeared from behind the counter, "if it's going to be done, it's going to be done. Still I'm sure you'd find it hard to justify."

Tables were pulled together in the dining room. It was very early. There were shouts from the kitchen. The hauling of beds overhead. "I think," explained Padjo, "that the Manager was thinking of saving a couple of pound." He winked, then grimaced, as the first drink hit his throat. "I'm tired myself of the whole sordid affair." He dabbed at his nose. "Who are these parties anyway that are getting hitched today?" he gestured towards the dining room.

"McManus," answered Moss, "McManus from Glangevlin." He was amazed to hear that he had caught the proper accent of the place. The girls appeared with bowls of flowers, whistling as they moved along the tables. Like scullions in a fairy story. He began unconsciously to hum along with the air of "The Lonesome Boatman." A series of short curses erupted from Finn in the kitchen. This was followed by a quaint relay of idiotic advertisements from Radio Éireann. The taxi-driver righted the wing mirror of the wedding car.

Mr Moss sat on the bandstand as the dancers regrouped. They danced to the left, and then to the right, blocking each path he might take while new lines of dancers formed up behind. Despite his protests he found himself forming up with the others, his left hand raised into the hand of his partner, the other stiff by his side. The music quickened as his turn commenced. He was jerked to and fro. "That's the style," someone called. His partner tucked her head against her shoulder and neatly tapped sideways, then back again, now another blonde lady took his elbow and wrist, and he hers, and she kicked from heel to toe, one foot taking his weight as she swung him round and round so that he had to pull sharply and persistently against her to keep his feet. She swept the floor with him. The room flew by like a merry-go-round, except for the woman's face. His hands grew sweaty and his hold on the woman loosened, but just then Peter signalled with his bow the final two notes of the reel.

"You'll have to forgive me," she said, "for liking the regular beat of a Cavan tune."

Moss hung on to the woman.

The room swung round and would not stop.

"Don't close your eyes," she said and let him go. He found himself in the middle of the wedding party, quite alone.

The bride and groom appeared in their going-away outfits. The entire party, including Mr Moss, followed them out onto the square. Confetti was tossed into the air. Mr Moss allowed himself to be propelled by a group of mountainy men towards the bar. Numerous drinks were pushed his way.

"I see you're with the other side," the blonde woman said.

"Yes, through my wife," he answered.

"We all have our troubles," she laughed, "Harry," she added. That extraordinary friendliness – your first name on the tongue of a near stranger. Her blonde hair was shorn drastically at the forehead. She had tiny brown eyes in a long pony's face.

"Whisper," she says, then into his ear, "so you are one of the married ones that are happy."

"Yes, I am."

"Naturally."

She drank greedily. Her cheeks shone. She was wearing wine trousers, skirt and jacket, white vest, white court shoes and had one of those half-tanned faces where the features are hard to separate from each other and seem branded on. Again he was in her arms, stiffly holding her at bay, her hand between his upright thumb and forefinger, his other hand spread against the small of her back. They turned their heads gaily in unison and swept across the floor past his wife in the arms of an old friend, and wheeling round returned. "So that's her," she said. She stepped on to her toes and whispered into Moss's ear: "I know what you want." He looked into her eyes. Her hand fastened like a claw on to the back of his hand. "I can give you what you want," she said. Her nails brought blood, then without letting go of his eyes, she slipped into another's arms while he was confronted by the father of the bride who told a number of stories damaging to himself. "Your daughter looked great," they told him. "Yes," he replied, "she was very attractive altogether." He pressed fivers into the hands of the staff of the hotel. The drunk dwarf, a cousin of Cathleen's, weaved his way through the tables to talk to the seated couples. His large lonesome eyes going from one to another. His chin fell to his chest. He passed on to the next couple, but losing enthusiasm he sat into a chair, his bottom teeth appeared.

He buried his head in his arms which were crossed tightly across his chest, as if he were hugging himself, steeling himself against every word, then seconds later he rose, drawing on another burst of energy and swaggered up with amused eyes to watch the band.

The blonde woman again embraced Cathleen Moss. "Oh the things that have happened to me," she cried. "Can I get you something?" Moss called over her shoulder to Cathleen. "Why don't you go away," the woman snapped back at him. "No, it's all right," said Cathleen, stroking the woman's back. "We'll be all right," she said and winked at him. The two women got up from where they were and moved to a more remote spot and here the woman cried and cried her heart out to Cathleen, who went on stroking her and listening.

The hired suits and dresses of the guests had lost their Sunday-best appearance by the time the remnants of the wedding party had gathered in the residents' lounge of the hotel. The talk was of the quiet beautiful world of Glangevlin. It seemed to Moss by then that he had only certain confused memories of the wedding – the father of the bride, his hands spread on the table before him, crying a little as he said goodbye to his daughter and roared into the microphone the security of his days, the daughter looking straight ahead, the mother looking down at the table laughing at him, the priest, like a conspirator, rising to his feet for the final prayer, and all the chairs going

back, as the guests rose also. The men in the lounge tucked
the little glasses of whiskey into their heavy calloused hands.
Cathleen beside him was talking to a nun. Passing out of
the toilet he heard Mrs McManus, who was patting her hair
before a mirror in the hall, suddenly fart. It ballooned round
her skirt looking for escape, then deflated with a loud cackle.
She was mortified. One of the men sang "Ramona," "The
Whistling Gypsy," while another prepared himself for "From
a Jack to a King." Moss fell into conversation with a man who
had worked for two years in Camden Town, and didn't care if
he never saw the place again. He was a rotund figure in a blue
suit, his stomach started at his chest, a wide tie hung down to
his thighs, and between sentences he worked his jowls, as if he
were digesting a past that had somehow demeaned him.

"We could build roads there all right," he remonstrated,
"but not here, not for the life of us."

Under the table Cathleen kneed her husband as the other
called on him for a song. He let their pleas die out. Moss
was proud of his wife's appearance. He had chosen her outfit
in Ealing Broadway. Grey dress, grey socks, black shoes.
Tight-fitting green belt and green shoulder bag. A black scarf
wrapped tight about her head. She was looking over at him as
the nun continued to talk to her in a rush. Manager Tom had
Joseph bring the eight guests left a drink on the house, and
while he was taking their order someone entered, someone
came in, no one could be sure later, he looked round the
guests and left. A few minutes later another man entered with
a gun wrapped under his coat. As he pulled out the sawn-off
shotgun Cathleen Moss, as the first blast started, had already
thrown herself over her husband. The shot peppered her back
and thighs. The gunman turned and ran. Into the ear of her
friend the nun began chattering the act of contrition like a
bird, while Moss, blood spilling from his face, held his wife.

And there's guilt coming from the need to tell your story
over and over, and there's panic, coming from the need for

everything to be rational. This waiting in the mists for a soft landing. So the town was filled with rumours that Moss was a spy. They said he had been looking for information about the town. That he had driven with his wife freely across the border in a car hired from Hogan's self-drive. The truth no one knew for certain. Being ignorant was their greatest anxiety, yet their greatest defence. Thus they passed responsibility on. And from this ignorance grew other tensions. They said he should not have been there at the wedding. It was stupid that he should have been there. Could they have found a concrete reason for the shooting then they could have apportioned blame. Word went round that Moss worked for security at Aldershot. They spoke too about the persistent rumour that a local man had pointed Moss out to the gunman who was a stranger. The story was told over and over as each tried to discover in it something that would relieve them of blame. That was their condemnation of the deed. For others, it was easier. It meant one less. He was a spy for certain. The clerk from Aldershot, who was only slightly wounded, returned to England some days later while his wife, in a private room in a Drogheda hospital, wrestled with life and death.

What she took to be the island was the mainland all the time.

And what she took to be the mainland was bounded on all sides by water.

And what she took to be home was already moving away from her, with all those she thought knew her, who could never know, not this time round anyway, that she was alone. Some time later a man was arrested for the shooting and the guilt of the townfolk was appeased. The guilt handed on, the act rationalized. The circumstances forgotten. A month on, her mother arrived to find Cathleen sitting up doing her nails. A month on again, she was sitting up in bed with her false eyelashes in. A few weeks later Moss met her on the tarmac at Heathrow. She crossed to him without the old rhythm, the ladylike gait that Mama had once admired. But in another way the crippled lady was no more. She had lost an audience of observers she had always imagined was there.

40

The town was a pale ghost of itself for a while, and since they believed someone must suffer, the people stayed away from the hotel. Loyal to the last, the solicitor's clerk came each day to his familiar table. But few nightly came to the bar or the lounge. The Cove, the people surmised, invited disaster. Mama and Manager Tom started losing control. Two new girls were let go. The part-time staff were given their cards. Soon the beds were no longer changed daily, Mama's temper got worse as she fought with dust covers and butchers, and Manager Tom withdrew to his room, appearing only when someone of substance came into the bar. There were no more weddings and little music. It became obvious that there was not much sense in keeping the dining room fully staffed, and since Finn was the highest paid, he was the first to go.

"You see how things are," said Mama, "we will be sorry to lose you."

"I was due a break anyway," he said.

He folded his clothes into a small case, and headed away as if he had never been there. It was the same bag with which he had arrived. It bore an old label for France in the summer of 1964. The few words he had learned there had been appended to meals, to people, to raucous interior conversation about the state of the world. He left little envelopes of money behind for everyone, then, with a few glasses of Irish Mist instilled, he went west on an expensive National bus to the Galway Oyster Festival where he reckoned there might be contacts to be made, he bought a new jumper and trousers, he lay in his bed smoking, he drank, he considered America. Thus the outside world threw open its doors to those who had known little life outside of the Cove.

"Peter," says Mama, "what's to become of us?"

"Sell all, Mama," he said.

"No," she answered, "the tide will turn."

Sometimes, on good days, Manager Tom went out and sat in the wedding garden. Then he set Joseph and Peter to clearing out the vegetable beds, he dreamed of going vegetarian. They set a host of new plants, turned up the rhubarb, clipped the fruit bushes. They built new rockeries. Some days that was all they did. They took no wages. Other times they helped Mama put the kitchen to rights. Mama's leg seized up. She got an ulcer. At nights Joseph heard her being sick in the toilet with a young girl's cry. Under the rubber lining of the fridge they found blue mould, under the bread cupboard, silver beetles. Every few days the hotel was threatened by the Health Inspector and Peter followed him around with a broom. And a paint brush. He set them interminable tasks. "You and me are going to have a day out soon," he told Mama one day. "Where?" asked she. "Down to the courthouse," he said. "As long as I had millions," Mama said softly to herself, knocking her fist off her thigh.

"If you hadn't the money you might be off to the Home," she said, wheeling on Manager Tom who was caught on his journey between the room and the garden, clapping along in his brown carpet slippers.

The Manager stopped, looked into the bar where there was no one, into the dining room where an old holidaying couple sat, visited by tremors and silence. He looked out on the square and recounted the number of people that had eaten their midday meal in the Cove. He wept a little because business was failing, not with tears but low whistles and shakes of the head. "I always associate such business with terror," he said without turning around, "the fear of being unable to deal with the public."

"Hm," said Mama.

"All my scholarship was in vain," he said laconically. All that came to the bar now were off-duty policemen. A drunken newspaperman who they found one night curled up in a ball in his own urine in the toilet. Peter had the job of lifting him. Looking down at the state of his clothes the newspaperman said: "Agatha won't be pleased. Agatha won't be pleased." Mama was not pleased either. There was a bucket on the stairs to collect rainwater from a leak caused by a missing slate. The yard was scattered with rubbish. Then one day the For Sale sign went up to the right of the front door of the Cove like a stiff uncompromising flag.

Peter stood behind Joseph who was watching the TV. He said: "'I think I'll be off." Laura got up out of her seat and gave him a kiss.

"Have you a place to go?" asked Joseph.

"I have all with me that needs be," said Peter.

So they parted to see each other again someplace. Peter stood on one road for an hour, then changed direction. He hitched towards a midland town that at least had a railway station. He sat at the granite railway station for half a day watching destinations like a hawk. The other side of the railway station was the handball alley. Come evening he followed some of the railway men over there for a game, and he found they were fairly handy. But he showed them a thing or two even though he hadn't been in an alley for years. The ball fairly flew from his hands, he cupped and drove it like an enemy and for his pains it lodged in the wire netting over the front wall. This was it then. Off with his coat, and on to the sidewall, then edge up along the iron posts till he reached the top. He could see for miles. But his knees began to shake, so on. He got it down somehow, anyway, to a roar of applause from the boys below. That night he spent in the alley, shut off from the winds. The next day he mustn't move because there was nothing in his head but looking at the four walls and sometimes he was above looking down from where he had been the day before, or else he was looking up at where he had been. Things stopped like this for some time. Then come evening the railway men returned.

"Are you back to show us?" they said, and laughed.

They played another few games but Peter was losing his touch because his hands had swollen. But there was nothing better than smoking a Players and drinking their weak tea as he lay with them on the grass behind the back wall. That night he tucked himself into his corner and attempted a few tunes to satisfy the spirits of the alley. The notes flew around the smooth walls, contradicting and harmonizing with what had gone before. Slip jigs he found worked best for the largesse of echoes. The strings powdered his cheek and chest. His thumb painfully flicked the bow, and it seemed to him then that the right instrument for an alley would be the mouth organ, especially on a darkened night when the notes ask, Is there anybody there? "Is there anybody there?" someone was shouting into his ear. He had fallen asleep with the fiddle in his hand. It was one of the railway men, all responsible men.

"Get up," he says, "and come down to the station."

He did. They were all sitting round a slack-heaped fire in an iron stove playing cards. They discussed his condition from all sides as trains galvanized through the night. They put him to hauling bags of oatmeal into the storeroom because he was hungry for any kind of work after being broken into the world of work over the years in the Cove. He told them stories of the hotel. Then at four they escorted him onto the city train under the protection of the guard. He was a tall gangling man that never spoke a word throughout the whole journey, and did not share his sandwiches or his tea. Not that Peter minded, seeing as they passed great stretches of flat land where the farmers were burning the roots of maize and lorries of seed kept pace with the train. They shunted into sidings for deliveries of net bags of cabbages and washed potatoes that would have delighted Manager Tom's heart, then reversed back onto the main track with torches and whistles working in unison. Through tunnels where sound collided with the darkness, and the dawn breaking ahead like an oncoming train and then each side of them monuments and churches built by superior men, and factories the size of a busy village. The first thing he heard in the city was an ice cream van playing the theme from *Doctor Zhivago*, a clock beating out a hymn upon the hour and the stationmaster whistling "Tom Dooley."

"Watch yourself up here, man dear," the guard said to him.

"The hitchhiker," said Peter, "was travelling along the road. He was having no luck. Along comes the sports car. The driver pulls up with a great show of brakes. He takes off with a spin. Looks over at the hitchhiker. The needle tops the sixty. He looks over at the hitchhiker. He crossed the hundred. He looks over at the hitchhiker.

"'How are you now, I'm over the hundred.' 'Fine,' says the hitchhiker, "ain't I doing the same speed myself?'"

The first few days he hung round playing when he liked and living off the wages he had saved. He had bright daffodils in his cap. A man directed him to a doss-house where certain parties used to peg their boots to the floor with the legs of their beds. They tied their belongings to the radiators in the manner of a ship's cabin. Peter was delighted with the city and his lodgings. A fellow called Gennicks there, a broad individual with a taste for drink and a need to refer to all manner of men as egotists, reckoned Peter should throw his hat on the floor outside one of the busy quarters.

Peter took him at his word, but the premises he chose at the time were strike-bound so there was nothing doing. He got himself out of there fast. Next he settled for a spot in the city centre where the people looked at him in his tattered frock coat and scalded trousers and wondered how the likes of him could ever air such sweet songs. The operating theatre of the hospital opposite was always lit. A yellow room above the street inside which green and blue figures hovered. Peter kept a wary eye on it. For a quick movement meant a burst blood vessel, and no movement meant concentration, emptiness, death. Worse was to be found next door. Beside St Brigid's hospital, a butcher's lad was always cleaning out his window, stuffing pink sausages into a bag with skilled scoops of his hand, flicking at mince with meat-stuffed fingernails. He often shouted over at Peter for a certain song so that he could provide a laugh for his customers. Peter did not take to him at all, thinking him a mean, spiritless type. Peter was in this position early and late making a great deal of money but it was not long before the authorities got wind of him.

"Do you know that playing in a public place is illegal?" the civic guard asked him.

"Things foreign are an adventure of which there is no telling," Peter answered him.

They generally left him in peace though, because they were only human after all. After a few weeks in the city Peter made a welcome discovery. He found a music shop with a sight of instruments for sale. Inside it was like a dream where everything had its likeness. Best of all were the brass instruments, a fret to play and keep clean, like a drawer full of spoons. Tom Higgins, the owner, told Peter that he lived for music but hadn't a note in his head. Down into the cellar they went where the wall was lined with guitar cases in the manner of mummies' tombs. Smart as newly hewn coffins. After giving a little speech, to echo a speech he had heard a politician make as a child, Peter played and sang into Higgin's tape recorder. Higgins said: "Come back Thursday," but he had no need to tell Peter. He used to return every day because he could not sleep for thinking of the simple wisp of the bugle, the glittering inverted saxophone, the clarinet, bassoon and piccolo, the bells, valves, keys and turning slides, and he would imagine the instruments playing as they should, under the boxing club back in the town, passing up to the Fair Green, with the men shaking out the spittle from the bells as they passed.

He got a stitch in the heart to think of the Cove that had been the first home he had ever had, after the other homes that he had forgotten, which came to the mind like an air breaking in on an air, and so on.

Thursday comes, he arrives at the shop and the blinds are drawn. He knocks at the glass door very lightly, afraid to set off the alarm. He has a great fear of alarms. He is about to go off wandering when Tom Higgins comes out, "Good man, Peter, come in." The place was lit up like a country-house dance. He was introduced to all the television people, and there was no doubt that if he had minded his manners over the years he might not have become too serious before his time. But having not changed from what he was he had multiplied his many disillusions. But he sought advice from every corner and his terror of the proceedings was overcome by his performance. "Youse are not here to arrest me, I take it," he said. The cameraman took his lights, the soundman his timbre and the introducer his name.

"Well, now, Peter, we would like to hear a number of tunes," he came close, "anything of your choice."

"If I could play the trumpet I'd be a better man," he answered, "there's a sight of money to be had from dance music," then he swung the bow a couple times, eased the grip under his chin and straightened his knees wondering was there a critic here worth his salt for they were a soft-looking lot who pretended to know better, they were in nice ganseys though, there was that. From that moment on Peter never looked up, except to say once in a break between local reels from the village and its environs, "Can I make a request, do you think?" The announcer nodded, so Peter said, "I'd like now to say Hallo to all the folks down at the Cove Hotel and to let youse know that you'll always find me with luck at 23 Maine's Parade past the clock," then he threw a fierce show of decoration into the final piece to settle affairs. Afterwards when they were winding up over a few drinks he refused their offer of money if they would make sure his message went across the air. They promised and gave him the money all the same.

And though he found the television people condescending men, their civility he praised.

Over the next few weeks he made friends with the firemen in the station across from his lodgings. Here the volunteers used to sit reading newspapers and looking at the passing traffic. The talk there was mostly of bad pay, theft, inferior housing, lack of waterpumps and modern ladders. He was very impressed by the men, and the day that he bought the oboe the first tune he played on her was in the station. He set her up like a telescope, clamped the double-reed in his mouth and fought the treble pitch for hours and hours, thinking the oboe might make a fine street instrument if he could master it.

At three fires he played for the entertainment of the crowd as the men fought the flames behind him, and here, outside a flaming meat-refrigeration plant whose entrance was blocked by a sea of tyres, he was photographed by one of the national papers. For nights after the smell of burning rubber was in his head, his old heavy coat was saturated and his straw hat was full of ashes.

That's the way things were with him.

In his lodgings he was set to cleaning out the kitchen each morning. He was a good hand at that after his apprenticeship at the Cove, but conditions here were very testing. For honesty and hard work were not enough to fulfil the lady's wants who ran the house. Her cheeks were hollow and perfectly tuned with the barest of muscles, though compensated by a large chin. Her eyes were full of feverish lights and her lungs weakened by sudden ailments so that she walked about clenching and unclenching her breasts, and he always heard her breathing behind him with an open mind, for her approach meant further work, the stairs today, tomorrow the floors, next week the potatoes, cabbage and delph. He longed for the easier regime of the Cove. But he had to comply for he had started to piss in the bed and each night he rocked himself nervously into a sleep of disarray knowing she would be there fretting in the morning, the auld geranium.

"Some morning," she says, "you'll have gone through to the floor below."

"As long as I don't bring you with me," he answered. "Let us sing of the days that are gone, Maggie."

"Don't give me any of that auld comeallyou," says she.

"There's music," he says.

Strange for a poor man to be at war without a dictionary or a sword. And the worst crime of all to be brought low in middle age by a weak organ. But the looseness of his kidneys were soon succeeded by their refusal to work at all. He tried barley water and Kuyper's gin but nothing happened and the burden at the pit of his stomach grew till eventually he had recourse to a doctor that attended the poor of Maine's Parade each Tuesday afternoon.

He teased his fingers along Peter's bladder till he cried out.

"Are you married?" the doctor asked.

"No," Peter smiled.

"Have you ever been with a woman?"

"No."

"I see. Well, we'd better do something about this."

The doctor shipped him off to St Brigid's hospital that evening in his own car. Peter told him that if he watched the television at eight o'clock he would see something worth his while. He undressed while the nurses prepared a bed, then they escorted him into a shower room where he was scoured and washed and had his hair and fingernails cut. "We can't let the surgeon see you looking like that," Sister Lily said. "Christ," asked Peter, "am I for the front room?" "This will hurt," he was told. The doctor brought the catheter to the tip of his cock which he rubbed quiet as a mouse while the others held his arms. The pain shot up along his spine as he inserted it till the fluid broke with a cathartic swill and one heavy pain went to be replaced by another in a higher key, as if his body were held in place by a tiny paralysing nerve while the waters pursued a pure legato and a cry launched itself from his burnt tongue, but following on he no longer panicked but kept himself rigid while the organs worked of their own accord, draining him, and he cursed his virgin cock, so small and sore, and his wizened sack that had not tempted him into another life. From a room far off he heard himself playing another role on the television as the spools of the hospital sucked him dry. "There, isn't that better," said Sister Lily. They wheeled the television in and he caught one look at his face as if he were a stranger. He went down the same road his face always led him, but this was different, this image did not reflect his every move as he made it, like the mirror did. Never mind that time had passed. This was a continuous performance, something that could not be controlled by the man he now was. Now he was flawed and drained to the core, here he was acting the candyman. And he became distinct from any person he had ever known and they from him so that he was tortured by loneliness, never having been responsible for his own identity before. The people in the ward clapped when it was over.

"An arrogant man can only return to the same place over and over," Peter told them, "the simple man can never return. It was nothing boys."

He was greatly comforted by the respect and goodwill shown to him by his fellow patients and the nurses. He had his first meal in bed and was easily kept in place by two pillows, light and soft as a bed of water lilies. Later still the man in the next bed started to cry. "Will you cut out that racket," called Peter. In a break from his tears the man said: "I've cancer, so I'm going to die." So Peter cried with him. The man started to moan with pain, then an accident patient was taken in to the bed alongside the man with cancer. A big rush of colour came to swallow him up, the accident victim. He felt a great deal of happiness, Peter could tell it by his face. *Yet the man must make a swathe through the ball of colour.* It surrounded him greedily. They took his pulse. They were nearly giving him up for dead. Then a few minutes later he returned to wrestle with the pain. In grunts he told his story to the man with cancer who he could not see. In grunts of pain the other answered. Grunting they kept each other alive and were thankful for the entertainment. And Peter felt he was in a big dancehall where a waltz was playing, no longer arguing that every man should think like himself, that everyone be the same, for this uniformity was counter to his whole being; he celebrated the disparity between people that makes them understand the need of others and he swore that as long as he was on the face of the earth he would no longer compromise his identity by mere self-interest. This was the run of his thoughts when Finn entered. Peter saw him before he saw Peter, which was always the way with him. Finn and Sister Lily looked bewitched as they stood at the foot of the ward under the night lights, they looked at each other as if they'd known each other's likes a long time, and Peter was stricken by a slight ache of jealousy. So that when Finn came up, Peter had an empty look on his face.

"Up the half-acre," said Finn, being a Cavanman.

"Why are you talking to her like that?" questioned Peter.

"But she's a cousin of mine," said Finn. "She's my Aunty Gerty's daughter from Mullahoran."

"I could die of shame," Peter whispered.

"Is that fellow allowed a jorum?" asked Finn, "for I'm travelling far tomorrow."

"Oh, he has ways and means of getting rid of it now," Sister Lily smiled and sat upon the bed.

"Well," said Finn, as he pulled up a chair, took the top off a bottle and poured two drops of whiskey into borrowed glasses, "how is the star?" Then turning to the other beds, he called out quietly, "Is there anybody there wants to join us?"

41

In a room reached only by artificial light, George watched the puce face of the new man that entered. How the lips and nose were propelled forward in some obscene kiss, into a swollen spoiled pout, so that when he spoke, he spoke with the dark heavy corners of his lips.

"And who are you?" he asked, as if he didn't know.

"George Allen," the prisoner replied.

"I see you're from Scotland yourself," he smiled.

But little emotion ascended to the searching eyes in the top of the interrogator's head. It was as if he was using the joke to call to mind the prisoner's past crimes. But his eyes did not weaken. The intelligent leer increased into a cunning nod. White-eyed he watched the cowering, thin-lipped figure of George Allen as he gruffly questioned him. George had his arms wrapped round his chest in the manner of a country-man. Fear had gathered in his Adam's apple. Somewhere on his being a smell of womanly scent that could not be located. Yawning, the interrogator's chin disappeared. He turned sideways out of habit. George yawned too.

Tiredness elongated the features of the interrogator, till his thin blond hair edged back. He leaned onto his hand. "Look," he says, "we are not interested in what you think you have done."

"Tell us," he paused, "about . . . Maguire for instance."

"About James Ellis."

Again, starts the roll-call of names. The familiar names of the villagers assume a crude importance. George hears the words Sinn Féin. The words sound like they come from a voice trapped in a tin can. A voice through a loudhailer heard from some fields away. Sinn Féin. Sinn Féin.

Throughout this new interrogation George Allen was allowed one brief walk outside, of ten minutes duration.

Each day it rose his heart, the stroll at noon. Being walked along the fence he took such deep breaths that he grew faint and lighthearted. A butterfly darted down, glided past, a sign released from a summer happening elsewhere. It flew past the unsweetened shape of the prisoner tottering purposelessly alongside its fellow.

Beyond the fence was a small plot of grass before the inner wall. A crowd of sparrows landed in a flutter there. They fell back before touching earth like a handful of seeds thrown carelessly by a sower into a light gust of wind. George and the guard turn. The seeds regroup, watch the one way, pirouette, flitter, then with one nervous shudder take off again.

A single hooded crow, her skirt pinned up behind, walks the green verge. George winces as his mind recalls what lies ahead. His next thought embraces a recurring dream of him entering a pool where the fish act very peculiarly. They are black fish with ancient eyes and sucking lips. He is reduced by circumstances to bearing their sad looks. Stiffly, their tails sloping up, they suck at his shins.

Terrified, a lone bather, he stands in history watching the waters rise.

He found wounds on his body in the mornings after the sleepless nights that could not be accounted for. He heard himself say and think things that seemed rootless, to have no seat in his mind. Yet the outside world could accommodate all this randomness. Anything he thought or said was possible. It was in the yard. It was in the indescribable trees. It was in things fought over. It was in what remained after the fighting was over. It was the shadow of things long dead that stretched off into the future. That sudden darkening of the fields and the streets that has no explanation. And then the brightening, even a greater darkness.

"To get at my brain," he said, "you will have to shatter my forehead."

And in my brain when you get there all you will find will be a view from the trees. At the best time of the year, hopefully. The brain controlling all it had, the body. A white speck become friendly on the sleeve of a garment. "I am against violence," he said. But then you are leaving alive those who plotted ahead with the death of others in mind. He knew that others would have to take the burden he had handed on.

Sentences were put his way that he might endorse their validity. They were amused and annoyed by his childishness. Once he found one of them speaking to him in Irish. That frightened him. Though he did not know the language still he saw it as the sacred tree of the tribe. He grew flustered. He looked up at the lace-work of the branches of the oak. He knew nothing.

In the absence of real life, he lost his sense of landscape.

He invented another where peace, as precarious as the human personality, reigns.

They invited him to view himself as the sordid one. All this condemnation of violence was outdated. It was a matter of truth. He must review his life. The assault his people had made against the Protestant people settled, as a crow, on his shoulder, signifying the death of the warrior. The death of the spirit of war. Now they could easily move in on him. The living were more dangerous than the dead.

The dead are enshrined in the walk of the living. Dissolution begins. Gone are the living in the argument of the living. The walk, the gesture, the eye preserves the fire of the dead.

His relationship with the men changes. It becomes very simple. We are people like yourself, they say. They inform him that Frank Allen would have been a sight better off crippled because then there would have been more compensation available. They tell him the type of sums available.

"The law has it all sewn up," the interrogator said, "they are the ones that are making the money out of it."

They change. They become practical and correct.

"You keep your Republicanism," they say, "we will keep our Unionism."

"Why," asked the fair-haired one, "does your crowd never read the Bible?"

The man is articulate and curious who questions him. George looks forward to the moment he arrives. "Fanacross," the interrogator says, "*Fánaí na coise*, the slopes of the bank." His interrogator grows informal. Normality leads them down a terrifying road. He is defending something basic as life itself, he says. The Institutions. The Catholics, he says, are petty conspirators. "See, whenever there is a priest about how they grovel?"

"I was up shooting duck," George says, "I have a licence."

"What they say of me is untrue," George says, "I've been the last while at sea."

"I am not religious," explains George.

The interrogators and the prisoner await some understanding, like animals in separate cages watch each other for some movement that may return them to their previous natures. For their nature now is only made up of symbols. The gun, the drum, the pike, the flag, the fiord. The shape of the head. The accent. But they soon know there never was some innocent time. It is the want to return which is innocent. Yet, sometimes this rebuttal of an innocent state may be just another disguise that can explain away what is happening. They were looking for an opening into each other's psyche that was closed up centuries ago. The guards walk past like trees.

His body is like a shadow behind those eyes. He throws on the table photographs of mutilated corpses. He stabs his finger towards a single grey body. *See that*, he says.

The doctor patched up Geraldine's face, and afterwards the wound looked like the fossil of a fish neatly pinned to her cheek, a fish that swam a millennium ago between continents that have since disappeared, with crude fins following adventurous boats in which merry families sat crossing uncharted seas, the elder drawing on his oar, the children frightened and exhilarated by lightning and storms, till reaching a land of genuine promise, and knowing what people can share is limited, they celebrated their safe arrival.

But there were always those searching for the weakness of the enemy. The vulnerability of those who live terrorized by the weakness of themselves. "The Catholics, no wonder I hate them," he says, "when you see what they do to their own. You know what I mean?"

"There was always something bad happening in the world," said the Bible man, "now it's our turn." Later that day George saw a pure flash of hatred in his interrogator's eye. It was as if his intelligence was a mere front that hid this deep fire of hatred. George was terrified. All that he had prepared for that day was forgotten. "The people," he mumbled.

"Who are people?" shouted the interrogator. "Tell me. Who are people?"

The other interrogator's bald head suddenly emerged from his overdressed body. There was a great deal of insanity and loneliness in that look. The bald interrogator leaned back into his seat and stared straight ahead. The silence turned into an appeal to George.

"What are you thinking of?" he was asked.

"I was thinking it would be nice to look out a window on to something," said George.

All of a sudden they dragged him through the door, down the corridor into an office. The bald man drew the window sharply up while the other pushes the prisoner's head out over the square some floors below.

"Now we will see your true colours," the bald one
screamed, "do you get me?"

"Jesus Christ," said George.

"Now, can you see?"

Terror thrown like a flame at the face. Is it sunlight? Something
falling close at hand that the alerted senses turn into a threat.
But even when recognized as peaceful, this terror will not go
away, except that he compromise, and say, disbelievingly, I am
happy, these are friends, this is sunlight. Not flames.

"Would you like Hong Kong, George?"

The need of sleep rocks his mind to and fro.

"You'll meet plenty of B-Specials there."

The miserable sound of water going down a toilet.

"You remember enough to do you," answered George.
"You can be sure of your past."

"Frank Allen told us all about you, George. The day the
Brits took him up here he told us everything."

The room swung to and fro like a hand-held lamp. Through
his tiredness they were only a blur. "I was up on the mountains
shooting duck after the death of my wife," he said. "I came up
here to clear the name of my brother," he said. They tried
breaking him down to terrible nightmares where he suffered all
he had been accused of. Then those terrible sentimental waking
hours where there was no material thing but the long racing
feel of his stomach. The bombed-out houses of Fanacross grew
new delicate blooms that are not or never were. Our children
become us who cannot relinquish the time we were young. Our
institutions will call upon their loyalty. All without a self, craving
and clawing at what's seen, not seen, will never be seen.

Not till the personality find status here.

Everything materializes again. They will have no truck with
anything that has not about it a suspicion of immortality. The
others are clinging to lesser existences. The interrogators come
in with a vengeance, stand off. Now they offer him again

a new life elsewhere. "In here, out of the public eye," the bald one says, "we can afford to compromise." "The hunger strikers forced our hand," he says. "It is disgusting." The light is switched off. The room backs away. It might be blue. It might be green. It might be any colour the place we are in. From time immemorial it has been like this.

Every few seconds George expected them to come again. Woke starting out of his skin. His hair seemed to have spread a rash over his skull. The light outside could not get through the darkness. He tore at the flesh of his neck. Then he'd dart awake again to be prepared. If he fell into a deep sleep he would have no defence. He found himself sinking. He darted awake again. Then down over the bank. In his dreams he waited for them. Each dream took the form of expectancy. But instead of the interrogators, one bald, one fair, came the next dream in which they were expected also. On the point of their arrival, his body would leap in the cot. But they did not come. The next dream started, and when they did not arrive there he dreamed in the dream that followed that they were part of his subconscious. The interrogators lived in his head. Right at the core of his being. This dream brought great terror to him. They had made an enemy of him at last. The dream brought him awake. Sweat was teeming down his unwashed body. It was a delirious relief to know himself outside of what he had dreamed. There was no one in the cell. Where were they? Why did they not come? He began praying loudly to himself, over and over the same words, and then sleep stole up on him, and still they did not come, his interrogators, who know the meaning of such dreams.

42

Enniskillen. A bunch of police cadets in tracksuits jogged across the road to their barracks after an early morning's exercise in a public gym. All were watched over by older RUC men with machine guns. As they crossed the cadets looked nervously at the faces of the drivers in the stopped cars. Even above the sound of the muttering engines you could hear the soft pad of their runners. The gates of the barracks closed behind them. Joseph sat back. The bus hummed under his feet. The traffic was allowed pass. The cars raced between the lights at great speed, as drivers do who fear to be in transit between two points, and impatiently strain against their seatbelts, gear poised, for some new and resolute journey ahead.

The nervous pain was there again in the uppermost knuckle of his spine. He watched the bold and cheerful and unselfconscious way the Northern schoolgirls stood up to chat to a retarded lad. In his raincoat he looked shyly at them. But their eyes were not mocking him. They continued to penetrate beyond his performance, aiding him towards trust in themselves.

Then past the bus swinging a shopping bag went a tiny blonde female mongol, her arm in the crook of her boyfriend's elbow, her face a cheeky satisfied woman's walking in any century.

Then the working girls stepped along meditatively with crossed arms down the street.

Belfast. Two country people sat beside him on a bench down from the courthouse. Oh dear, she said, as she sat. The man hoisted the three net bags to the ground and lifted an ice cream cone to his mouth. Then he rubbed the fleshy unwrinkled shield of his ear with one rigid finger.

There, she said.

They looked about them. Their lips sagged.

In a boilersuit reeking of oil a blonde mechanic went by carrying a transparent bag of pink sausages in his black hands. The old pair squinted as the sun rose. What their posture says is that there is no room for turning now. Joseph looked at the pure granite wall of the court, the clean wandering line of the cement filling, and then elsewhere the dilapidated houses. The old lassie with satisfaction bit into the wafer of her cone. Two off-duty RUC men in their green trousers and blue jackets passed by like Catholic priests who had lost their vocation. Behind the high wire fencing a number of armed policemen exchanged positions. The pair continued to look down the street. The old fellow was gritting his teeth. When you get the weather for it, she was saying. She licked her fingers and handed him a handkerchief. He blew his nose. It seemed as if they had been pushed into another flawed world with the entrails still hanging out of the old.

RUC men gathered, the aerials of their walkie-talkies jigging in their back pockets. Guns neatly perched in black holsters. Their faces unexpectedly unsoiled by alcohol. Joseph stood up.

His mother stepped out of the car.

"You've put on some weight, son," she said and sat beside him for a minute. He looked at his mother. The cheeks of her jaw mussel-shaped, lips set with a hint of blue, the face tapering away. Her hands bruised together on her knee. "You're pale," she said. His loneliness exposed her to hidden hurtful areas of herself. His needs had gone beyond her experience. "We must talk," she said, "after all this is over." A police landrover pulled into the courthouse. The old man on the seat cleaved the air with his hand as he hailed a UDR man he knew. He tottered over to him and stood, dropping his paws onto his knees. His wife followed up confidently behind. A few words. Across the road priests, brimful of liberated gods, stood on the steps of the cathedral chatting, undecided as to which direction to take today. "Right then," their young neighbour impatiently said, dismissing the old couple. He made quickly for the gate. A firmly toothed man of the world dismissing a fellow spirit tottering on the edge of the grave. "It's a terror," he called

back, his square-jawed smile telling all. The old couple made
their way to the entry. The Allens, after an appropriate time
had elapsed, followed them and Helen's purse drew a whine
from the metal detector at the gate and then again at the door
into the courthouse.

The killer of their father and husband sat, out of uniform,
between two prison guards who stood behind him. Armed
policemen were everywhere throughout the court. The only
other civilians besides the journalists in their separate pew,
were the old pair. The judge was listening to the details of the
killing. He spread his fingers about his cheeks and underlined
the odd phrase or statement on a sheet before him. At times
it appeared he was talking to himself, but he may have been
just repeating something from what was being read. The
confession today would be gone through twice. It seemed
strange that the bloody details of the case should have to be
seen through the eyes of the judge rather than through those
of Private McCreedy the murderer, or Helen, the wife, or
Joseph the son, but through some mishap in the past, some
relinquishment of the right of revenge on the victim's behalf, or
else some dulling of the colour of the deed, an interpreter was
called for, that the reality be given status, that the arbitrator,
having consumed much crime in his lifetime would be able to
judge one crime from another, and so it was that through the
judge's eyes one hoped to see the extent of the guilt and what
punishment would be exacted, and the judge knowing this,
never turned to look at the accused, nor turned to look at the
relations of the victim, nor had any picture in his mind of the
dead man, and thus he was excused from all complicity. His
small glasses sat round and stiff on his nose as his silence and
idiosyncrasies brought his audience, with psyches unharmed,
through the whole gory story, as if they were listening in on
what had happened to other people. Then, as that part of the
story ended, the judge took off his glasses and pinched the

bridge of his nose with forefinger and thumb and exposed
a pair of weak, unnaturally dull eyes, dulled it seemed from
listening and retaining, all character faded from his face.
Perhaps, too, this was a pose for now it was the moment that
those involved in the case took stock of each other, and of
him. The stretchmarks of the judge's spectacles to his ears
burned a livid blue along the soft grey skin, with a movement
of his fingers he called the prosecutor to his feet, and despite
the plea of the defence, the statement was called for, and
accepted, it remained only to hear it in his own words, it was
proved that it had been given up without intimidation, there
were questions, yes, a series of conversations took place, yes,
and all these exchanges the judge handled without animation,
with sufficient emphasis to keep his identity intact while he
must forage among others, of his own class or of other classes,
who have acted outside the law through righteousness or fear,
then he allowed them swim into view, those he must keep at
bay, as if the distance he kept would mark the extent of his
judgement, his lips moved, he tried hearing the words of the
confession through his own voice, a battered and forgotten
bible jumped in the glove compartment as the jeep on the
night of the murder shelters in the shadows above Fanacross,
it seemed a giant shield rose over the horizon, it's only the
mountain, they drive under the towering mass as if soon it
will close over them, it was like the top of the world had come
sideways and was wandering in the dark over their heads, like
a shield come free some place.

"I want to say how sorry I am for all that happened."
    "You are Norman McCreedy, a former part-time member
of the UDR?"
    "That's right, sir, surely."
    "I would like you to tell the court what happened on the
night in question in your own words."
    "It's wild hard to start. Your Honour. I was not myself at

the time." His two hands came up onto the rail. "I have two children, one born without eyes." His rounded upper teeth appeared. "Myself and the Mrs have not had it easy. No one else in the family has had that affliction. They tell me now it was drugs she was given here that were barred elsewhere. My Mrs could not be consoled. Not even by anyone. She blamed me. We didn't get on. I was not myself." He looked for a moment down at the old couple at the rear of the court who fell back into an earlier state of taking the hurt upon themselves, yet willing him to get on to where some other superior judgement could be known, that was beyond sympathy, that might strengthen their resolve, that it be known that this act was the result of many others not being named here this day in court.

His voice took on the keen of the righteous.

"I hold no grudge against my fellow man. I am sorry for what has happened."

With a swivel of his pursed lips, the father's finger rises, then he kneads his hat in his hands as if he had hailed someone he did not recognize.

"There's rocks on my land and I was clearing them away when I was called in for special duty. There's bedrock all over the land. That's Fermanagh land too. And I was right glad to get away. They said we must keep an eye to the mountain. There was talk of an individual who had been stopping traffic with a gun up there and threatening people. They said he had gone down South but was back again. We procured our guns and went up there." One of the prosecutors rose, making room for another. They leaned so close to each other that their spectacles nearly touched, and not until they were properly seated would the man go on.

"We were at Hare's Cross for two hours. You can be well exposed up there. We set up a roadblock and asked about him. No one had seen him. But there again, you see, it's a Provisional IRA area, Your Honour."

"There's a wee stretch of wall where we waited, with the miserable sound of the water going down the mountain. The Lord has made everyone different, and a man must respect that. I had no hatred in my soul except to do my job. My job is to protect the people of this province. My life is no more valuable than anyone else's. These are all fine thoughts, you might say. But there it is. And if we did wrong. And if we did wrong in the past, there's wrong being done to us now. I just wanted to get my job done, that was all.

"It's not my job, Your Honour, to think of these things. There's men educated for that. There's educated men, though, who have no liking for us."

His eyebrows rose up and down, so that the whole scalp moved independently of his head.

"I am not blaming any man. Only myself. I did not confess to bring down any other man, no matter what they say. There was only myself involved. True."

He bared his teeth, hunched one shoulder and tilted his head towards the judge. "I am a church-going man." His voice dropped to confide something that could only be understood between the two, then abruptly sought a higher key where the satisfaction in confessing could flood his very soul. Awkwardly he tried to resume but nothing would come, the past halted somewhere back of his mind and would not pass through that moral space to his tongue, that he might be freed of it, so instead he began at the very beginning, more tired now. "I'm sorry for all that happened, you know. All of it."

"We were," said the judge, "on the mountain." The distinctly different accent of the judge seemed brisk and odd, the RUC men shifted their guns to a more comfortable position.

"That is correct, sir," the soldier, roused again, answered. "We were on the mountain." His eyebrows resumed their old rhythm as he refocused.

The woman behind the counter would not change Joseph's punts into sterling. Helen foraged in her bag. They sat together on a forum in the entrance hall of the courthouse drinking their sweet tea out of plastic cups. The place filled up with barristers and their clients from the other courts. Two skinhead lads stood eating Mars bars. They sat, silently looking after each new person that crossed the tiled floor. Sunlight gleamed through the high shuttered windows. One of the lads held his box of matches crookedly in his left hand as he lit a cigarette. It seemed his hand was bound in skin-tight cellophane. Then as the fingers did not unlock but kept the loosely clenched fist, Joseph saw that the hand was false. Helen, too, lit up a cigarette.

"It takes it out of you," she said.

"He seems like a lost man. It's hard to fathom him," Joseph replied.

"He's lying through his teeth."

"Any word of George?"

"They won't say it to my face, but I know they think he has informed. Margaret has got a grant to Queen's. I miss her about the house. She has gone very much into herself."

"And Pop?"

Their barrister, trailing his gown, came over.

"Ye must be glad," he said, "of the way things are going. Now look they've made an offer to us so as to prevent the trial for compensation. They'll give you £10,000. It seems to me to be satisfactory."

"No," said Joseph.

"We are going to see this out," Helen answered.

"You may regret this, Mrs Allen."

"I don't know, I'm sure." Her fingers sought Joseph's elbow. They looked up at him together. "Well, we will have plenty of time to look at this again," he remonstrated quietly. "No," said Helen. "Right, I'll see you inside." The skinheads lit up more cigarettes. A woman in a blue raincoat and red high-heeled shoes clattered across the tiles, sniffing as she went, as if to say she was above all this.

"That night we were pinned down for some time by a single gunman. The shots came from the direction of what we took to be a deserted house up there, Carlton's. Not on the mountain, but half-way up the mountain. When the firing stopped we made our way there. The lights were on in it. We fired a number of warning shots." He looked down at the palms of his hands. "Towards the house. The lights were on. We called out to the occupants of the house to come out. But no one came. So we blew the windows in with shot. My sergeant called on me then. Sergeant Cathcart. With Private McKay we went to break in through the door but it was ajar. Well, you know, it's a two-roomed cottage but there was no one in the house. But on the table a sort of coffin-shape under a tricolor. The flag was thrown across what looked to be a coffin. We didn't know what to do. There was a single bulb lit. Just the one light on. The coffin surely, and the flag over it. So, I can tell you, we got out of there before it blew up in our faces."

The judge turned toward the prosecutor.

"Yes?"

"They thought, I believe, that it might be a ruse, a bomb of some kind."

"I can see that."

"The house was watched for three days. Then the British army blew open the coffin." He paused. "It was a coffin."

"Nothing," said the burly prosecutor, "there was nothing in it."

"We were not, Your Honour, to know that."

"I'm sure the prosecutor realizes that. Don't you, Mr Bailey?"

"Sergeant Cathcart thought he saw some movement down at Fanacross. Lights or something like that. So we drove down towards the village. And stopped short of it at a spot known as Lee's Folly. I was not the better of what I had seen. This was serious, Your Honour. It seemed like some sort of blasphemy. I was right glad to be out of there, I can tell you. Sergeant Cathcart, he took one side of the street and I took the river side. It's a bad place for two men to be in our position. They might as well be sending you to your grave. But the village was quiet. We started to return on the one side. Sergeant Cathcart, he was ahead of me. I heard some noise at the house of the Allen family and stepped into the shadows by the gate."

"Surely you should have contacted your officer first?"

"I was thinking sir, of his safety, and my own." He looked towards the prosecutor, then towards his defence counsel, and went on. "I slipped along the wall. There was someone inside the door. I knew. And I thought it might be George Allen. I knew the man we wanted a little to see. I kicked at the door, and stepped back. I could see him standing behind the glass door. He called out: 'Who is it?' I said: 'The UDR.' He seemed to reach for something. I had my gun at the ready and when he did not step out, I swung out. He was holding the door open to me. I thought this man was going to destroy me. So I shot him. I shot him twice, maybe three times. God forgive me. Only afterwards did I know that I had not shot George Allen. I had shot his brother. The two, Your Honour, were twins. The dead man an innocent, harmless sort of a chap. The other, a wanted man. But I know I should not have shot anyone. I know that."

"You say that you then ran back up to your jeep?"

"That is correct, sir."

"And you say that not one of your colleagues had heard the shots?"

"That is correct."

"Do you expect us to believe that in the dead of night the other men could not have heard the shots?"

"They did not. I returned and nothing was said."

"Private McCreedy, is it not true that locals wrote in of seeing the jeep you were in parked near the village on the night Frank Allen was killed, and that this information was eventually to reach the ears of the RUC and that explains why, after all this time, you came forward to confess?"

"No, sir. That is not true. It was my conscience made me come forward.

"McCreedy, are you a member of the UVF?"

"No, sir. I am a farmer, and was a part-time member of the UDR."

"Mr Bailey, have you evidence to this effect?" the judge asked, "for you are imputing dishonesty to the other members of the force involved and those men are not before the court."

"It has been alleged, Your Honour, by some people that that is the case."

"That evidence is not before the court."

"McCreedy, you say you kicked Frank Allen after he was shot. After you shot him?"

"I kicked him."

"You kicked a dying man?"

"I kicked him. There it is. I wanted to find the gun he was carrying. I turned him over. That's it all."

"You did not beat him up before shooting him?"

"Your Honour, how could I beat a man at the door of his own house? Someone would have heard." He turned towards the prosecutor again. "I shot him. I kicked him over. And ran away. No one put me up to this confession, Your Honour. I was not intimidated in the making of this confession. I just wanted to make my peace with God." He swallowed hard, his brows danced, a small stubborn shoot of a man, he wavered. "I know I have sullied the uniform, Your Honour, by not owning up immediately. I want now to say how sorry I am to all belonging to him." He looked to see if there were any other questions coming his way. But the judge was amending his notes. The defence counsel watched the judge. The prosecutor rubbed the back of his neck. And the parents of the UDR man seemed deflated as if he had not reached the heights of strength expected of him. He should have known the righteousness of his cause. He had tried to appease too many gods for he had been groomed in sorrow for too long now. To them he was a scapegoat. Their eyes burned at the injustice of it all. "I'm sorry," he said down to Helen, seeking her out as the probable partner of the man he had killed, but he could find neither forgiveness nor hatred there. He was reminded of the day he had lifted his sightless child on to a pony and how she had cried out an inhuman cry as the pony started away from underneath her.

Helen and Joseph booked into a bed-and-breakfast off the Lisburn Road. They were driven there in the late afternoon by their barrister who told them of the anticipation they should feel and, of course, sympathized with what they had been through. His friendliness seemed to indicate that he was glad they were there, alive, with all their faults, but should they disappear, die, well then, in time others would take their place. Their rooms had rich heavy carpets, bedside lamps, gold-varnished mirrors and a view of the back yard of a Chinese restaurant where the waiters were gathered for a quick smoke before the early evening's business began.

The waiters drew heavily on their cigarettes and chattered away, like all secret societies, without looking at each other. The smell of the cooking of chestnut and scallion rose.

"Are you hungry?" Helen asked.

"Not yet," he answered. "The Cove destroyed my appetite."

"Well they were kind to you, I shouldn't wonder."

"I was just thinking that I've never been in Belfast before."

"It's a choice place." She opened her bag, and slipped out of the clothes she was wearing down to her old-fashioned slip and bra. While he looked down through the lace curtains at the waiters below laughing Helen put on another dress and threw a scarf like a cape over her shoulder. "Do I look anyway decent?" she asked. "You look grand," he told her. Coming down the stairs they heard the singing kettle of the landlady. The breathless air of sentiment in the Belfast accent. The pulmonary strokes of a helicopter passing overhead. The sudden cold gusts from the side streets. A line of jeeps, the soldiers in the back with their rifles lowered. The two walked over towards the botanic gardens. They entered the domed glasshouse and turned right towards the plants, the humid heat reaching as far as their cheeks, the condensation dribbled down the panes. "I was here once before," said Helen, and as they walked along it seemed the fern, the holly, the great sprouting plant like something overgrown, the bitter mandarin, all the unknown plants, were deep in conversation, in as wild a chatter as the waiters had been.

The defence brought up Frank Allen's action at the bridge all those years before. The time he and Helen had spent in the South was gone over. There were hurtful things said. It was alleged, on scientific evidence, that Frank Allen had handled a gun some time previous to his death. There were traces of powder on his clothes. The prosecution held that such powder could have come from McCreedy's gun. The defence said that Frank Allen and George Allen had always been inseparable and George Allen was wanted for questioning in regard to the death of a UDR man. He was currently in custody. Attempts were made to see Frank Allen as guilty of his own death, by association and by family, for such are the disciplines of law and the disciplines of history, to differentiate between those who died and those who should have died. To spur on redress, already realized in hands more passionate than theirs.

The defence went on to the position of someone like McCreedy who must live in terror of his life day and night.

In the event Private McCreedy got four years, which he spent in prayer in the Maze, nightly tortured by one face becoming another, then back again, so that he, like the others, could never properly identify the enemy. The enemy could be discovered in daylight if he looked towards the republican quarters and his allies could be found here in his compound. Yet, he could never separate the one from the other for he was held by some on his own side in as much contempt as he was on the other. His job of work had severed him from their respect. His crime had severed him from self-respect. He had come down in the world, for like as he might excuse himself and find the righteousness and vigour his people expected, still, the killing took its toll. In time he blamed the politicians. Then the British. He saw himself as a further victim. He cursed the South that refused to understand him. Then aggressive again, he waited to find George Allen suddenly come into his sights and he tried to imagine what it would have been like if he had killed the right man, then he forgave himself for killing the wrong, and there was solace in prayer for this view, same as the protection you get from carrying a gun, he looked out at the daylight, and saw nothing, and went over and over the event again, day after day, he prodded it awake, or it him, till it was erased, and soon for him no one had died, they were sleeping. It was a flicker away in the past. He was forgiven. He thanked God for peace of mind. It was like it had never happened. It had all taken place in his imagination.

43

"What will I come back as in the next life?" asked Cathy of Laura. "There's one for you." Joseph was out in the garden side-dressing the path. The girls were pounding the lounge carpet out on the grass. The sheets on the line blew round them in the hilarious wind. In the dining room Liz swirled the tablecloths like sheets, then she stood a minute, head, tray and cloth hanging. Laura approached to tell her something. Talking, she touched

Liz's waist, she played with her belt as they looked into each other's eyes. "Manager Tom is going spare," she said.

"I thought he was going to make for me," said Liz.

The fans in the dining room stopped turning. Cathy stood with a single plate filled with the leavings of others, as a once-rich elderly lady, having dropped behind as wealth found new owners, though the good days had left their mark in the cosy arrogance of her mien, sought special service. From the kitchen the continuous clash of cutlery, and plates landing or being eased away from each other. Laura caught Joseph looking at her as she leaned over the sink. There, hanging loosely in her blouse, her slack breasts tormenting him.

Her hair lightly spotted like the thrush's breast.

A rip in the sleeve of his jacket sewn up with wide stitches like a crocodile's mouth.

A stranger, a potential buyer of the hotel, stood looking at old photographs of the town on the walls that were lit by unobtrusive lamps. The Cove in its early days flanked by the pump and the old Fords and the laborious cattle being driven up to the Fair Green. A few members of a pipe band, in saffron skirts, hooded shoulders, capes and green tunics, stood under a plant in the bar. They were on their way with their hanging groins and fur tresses to a festival in Granard.

That night the door of Cathy's bedroom opened and in came Joseph. "Get out," she said immediately. "The cheek of some people. Who do you think I am?" "Shh," he murmured, "everything will be all right now." "Will you get out. I'll send for the guards." He bundled in beside her like a man without a soul. Where does he think he is going? He did not answer her and then Cathy realized that he was lying there, perfectly asleep, his dreams swirling by him. His pupils clad in the light skin of sleep. His lids twitched, sheltering in the fear of something thrown at the eyes. What drove him in his sleep towards me? Who does he think I am? Had he tried all the

other doors? He lay there as if there could be no wakening of
his capsized limbs.

"C'mon," she cried, "c'mon, wake up."

She gave him a dig with her elbow. His speechless lips
fluttered and filled out.

"I was going someplace," he said, "but I got caught up on
the stairs."

"That's enough out of you."

She put her arms around him and jerked him up into a
sitting position. She hauled his legs on to the floor. "C'mon,"
she whispered, "do you want me to lose my job? Not that it's
worth a curse now, anyway." Shivering in her nightdress she took
him across the landing. He reached towards her. She slapped
away his hand from her bosom. Then he walked straight ahead
without touching anything in the darkness, and coming to
his room he pulled the door after him. "I ask you," said Cathy.

The next morning there was no mention of the night before.
Though Cathy often caught him following her with his eyes
as if she reminded him of something that could not be told.
There was nothing for it but to keep going. For Laura, to fight
off the nausea that came from the smell of the churning grease
in the chip pan. Something burning. Mama's stricken chin as
she cooked, now that Finn was gone. Wild bursts of Mozart
came down from Manager Tom's room. Cathy, tall and heavy-
breasted, in a black cardigan and skirt, stood in a corner of the
dining room. She felt the white-crinkled collar of her blouse.
The grey passivity of the meals filled her with thoughts she
did not like. She moved quickly between doors, two golden-
ringed fingers playing with the top button of her blouse. "All
right, dear?" she asked the only diner there.

Laura went early to bed that evening to read the book she
was at at the time, *Jane Eyre*, and she heard the occupants
of the hotel all mount the stairs with their habitual pauses
and sudden starts. It was a quiet night so that you could hear

the river, far side of the square, splashing against the wall of the butcher's. That only happened on the quietest night. The soldiers called out to each other in Cork accents about some horse that was running tomorrow, then they stopped to urinate by the wall of the Mill. Their voices dropped lower. A woman was speaking to them. The two soldiers and the woman walked over and sat under the monument on the low wall. The woman shook a pebble out of her shoe. First the one soldier cupped her shoe to his mouth, the high heel sticking out from his forehead, the toe jutting out over his chin, then the other soldier took the high-heeled, white, misshapen shoe to his mouth and breathed the woman in. The woman talked on unconcerned. Laura could hear them for over an hour as they passed a bottle of cider to and fro. When it was empty they headed towards the hill. The woman flicked a finger inside the heel of her shoe, and as she reached into her pocket for a cigarette she found there a child's dummy. With a laugh she stuck the dummy in the mouth of her favourite soldier.

Laura heard footsteps start across the landing. The sound of bare feet on the carpet. They stopped by the door of her room, then went on. She waited a while then slipped out into the corridor of the darkened hotel. She stole into Joseph's room and found his bed was empty. Then she heard the handle of the front door being tried in the foyer. Coming down the stairs she found Joseph silhouetted there among the pots of plants and flowers Mama had placed against the glass to catch the morning sun.

Laura slowly released his hand which like the hand of a robot was working the handle up and down.

He followed her without the least hesitation.

Then in the light from the street she saw it, his cock standing out, blatant as you like, through the slit in his pyjamas.

"Wait till you're asked, Joseph Allen," she said.

But he did not respond, so, terrified out of her wits that Mama would come and find them like that, with the tips of her fingers she pushed the warm shadow back into the folds of his pyjamas. His body shook like a tuning fork. The impression of his member remained like an arched rib in her hand behind. They took off again but he broke free and headed towards another door. "Curse a' God," said Laura, "you'll have the whole place up." She led him by the hand to his room and this time he left his door open as he went through all the habits that he must have gone through every night that he came up. He pulled out a drawer and touched a jumper making sure of what lay under it. He sat on the bed and touched the bedside table. Then, in that intimate way people have of talking to themselves he said "That's everything now," and rose and closed the door against her in the corridor.

The next day the dummy, as he was called, came and threw his bag onto the kitchen table and started on his crosswords, scoffing every so often. His teeth worked off each other with a loud gnawing sound. His liquid eyes followed the girls around till his meal came. They said he had won thousands of pounds on the crosswords. He grinned, teeth upwards at Liz and a low animal whine came out of his loose throat. "The horn is at him today," said Cathy. Nothing would do him but that he teach Joseph and Laura the basic alphabet for the dumb. He caught a hold of Laura's hand, and scattered the vowels across the tips of the fingers. "S," the little fingers joined.

The crack of a finger across the palm signalled the end of a word. Laura spelt out Joseph with great care. The dummy roared out his appreciation.

The voice trapped in his maw sending out long, low-pitched roars.

Laura's hair seemed to Joseph to be illuminated from within through a warmth that was painfully private. Each was surrendering without a word. The dummy thought all their happiness was due to him and when he had to go, he turned petty and bad-tempered like a spoiled child. He crossed the yard hurling shrill abuse into the face of Mama who was steering him forward with the head of a broom. "He picks on lonely women, I've heard," said Mama.

"The nerve of him," said Cathy.

Laura's palm sweated.

"Men," said Liz.

"I always found my brother George a bitter man," said Manager Tom.

"And why," he asked, "do you think Frank never came to see us all those years when he was down South?"

He looked out on the square.

"If Frank had only come to me."

Tears kept falling down his face.

"If Frank had come to us," said Mama.

"Those pair of boys," he mumbled, "they were so close, I did not know them, I went with you and I don't know you. Oh, Jesus. Oh, Jesus Christ Almighty."

Away in the distance the doorbell rang. Laura woke out of an artificial sleep and rushed down the stairs to find Manager Tom unlocking the door. Outside was a soldier in uniform, his heavy coat thrown over Joseph who was dressed only in a white shirt. He stood shivering on the step in his bare feet, totally unaware of where he was. "I found him," explained the soldier, "walking along the river."

"Come in, come in," said Manager Tom, throwing back the door.

The soldier drew Joseph into the hall. Water ran down his long thin thighs.

For the first time Laura saw Manager Tom touch another human being. He threw his arms round his nephew.

"God, son," he said, "what's been happening to you?"

But Joseph's eyes retained that unseeing air. He heard only accents foreign to him. Bodies emptied of the identity he craved. "I'm sorry," he replied, "I'd like to sit down."

"Get him to the fire," said Manager Tom, his hands trembling. Laura brought out warm towels and began towelling him down in the lounge. He shook like a leaf. Mama arriving down was terrified that he had lost his wits. "Speak to us, don't go away again," said Laura. He was looking for his breath. His eyes glistened like river stones.

"Laura," he said, seeing her there.

"Boy, but you're soft," she whispered, overcome with relief. They were drawing a robe of Manager Tom's over him. "You look a sight."

"Laura," he repeated.

Mama, with a tray of rattling cups, crossed the lounge. The soldier and Manager Tom rose. "He's back to himself," said Manager Tom.

"The whiskey," said the soldier, "is very good in the tea."

For a moment the pleasure of his old carousing crossed Manager Tom's face. He looked at his nephew and at Laura, her bare feet drawn in under her nightdress. "Here," he proffered the bottle, "come on the pair of you."

He doused their tea with more whiskey.

"Well," Laura rose her cup, "this beats skivvying."

"I didn't know where I was," Joseph said.

"You were a right handful," nodded the soldier. "I took you to be a man out of his mind."

Laura drank her full cup down, thinking to get the whiskey quickly into her blood, fearing that the next day, all this intimacy would be over, and she would be back, wherever that place is, that she was always. She felt Joseph's eyes on her, but she could not return his look.

"I'm sorry for frightening you," said Joseph.

"Go away out of that," she said.

"Listen to her," said the soldier.

"Well, now, anyway," he said to Joseph, "you don't have to think any more. A fellow like me tries to keep the best side out. I know rightly what goes on. When they bombed the roads to this town they put an end to it. First the railway, then the roads. It's a married man's army, I pay £50 tax. There's insurance for flying, then the cabbabo, in case you get blown off the face of the earth." He reached up for his cup. "Sooner than go to the bank I tried to put a few bob together myself for a house. Ah! Do you see this?" He stretched out his arm to its full extent. "Anyone that comes within that distance is dead. The Special Branch crowd are glory hunters. We had to dive on the rifle of a young fellow to stop him shooting one of them. He took them to be Provos. I've nearly nineteen years done, next year I'll be on the pig's back. Curraghwile, the bend for home. I'll be retiring. I had an experience, you might not believe this. But the barracks is haunted. I didn't see anything mind. It was roughly 5.30 in the evening. There was the gate and I couldn't open it." He shook the air vigorously. "I could not budge that gate. Brother Martin of the Sacred Hearts, who is our chaplain, said he could well believe it, what with the monstrosities that go on round here. Yes, well, I'll love you and leave you." He stood respectfully aside for Manager Tom to open the door. Head down, a small man, he faced into the night. "The whiskey," he said again, "was very good in the tea."

That Saturday night, three weeks on, Laura went up the stairs and went through it all again, the making up. Then descended the stairs and on through the darkened hotel. Cathy had gone to work in a hamburger joint. Liz had moved into a single-roomed flat in the town. The manager and Mama sat up in another dark room of the hotel watching the TV. All was closed down. Joseph was waiting on Laura in the hall of the hotel. They passed through the dining room, out the backdoor.

They took a walk through the town. The stones at her feet falling away from a building, a mountain, a house.

In the dancehall the girls were dancing in groups together. Their forearms coated in light. The boys breathing in the washed flesh under their shirts and walking about with great comfort in their narrow shoes. She was laughing at the thought of Mama ironing Heart's Delight sheets in the kitchen. Laura was wearing little green elf slippers. Sure of the shape of herself. Liz with her head held back sharply went by in the arms of a man. Joseph was sitting with some other. Laura sat down beside him. She put her arm around him. A friendly arm over his shoulder. He was so conscious of her every movement. Her hand touched his back light as a quill. Her hands drifted under his shirt. "Don't ever think anything bad of me," he said. They walked down the steps of the dancehall on a frosty night. That feeling of a life, like a sharply etched landscape, before them.

He tucked his arm in hers.

"The kiss is sweet," she said.

Word came that Helen had received £40,000 compensation. So, Joseph travelled north to Fanacross to help move her furniture to a small house she had put the money into, over the bridge. He went up with Jim in his van past the green lakes under a dark sky. They stopped to take in the air. A mother sheep, wobbling her belly over the heads of her lambs, fixed her eye on a distant place, and went still. They sucked. Clouds darted down the mountains like smoke. Seagulls were blown up like bits of waste paper. The waterfall, a strip of lace, fell over dark boulders. A pyramid of coal by a green shed. A red Volkswagen van in a wet field. Boggy still river. A stream cutting its way down a further mountain throwing up a thicket of trees, like pubic hair, on the bald slopes. A labyrinth of drainage schemes in the valley below. As they drove on, two lines of trees moved against each other in different dimensions, the nearest going by like sentinels guarding the others not

moving within. Moss-covered rocks. Great bog-swish, and
the incessant comfortable roar. A bank of fallen firs. They are
approaching home. In one of the sister streams the molten clear
water before the fall at the rocks forms a silver chalice. Dun,
cinderish swirls of mountain grass descending to another shelf
of cinnamon trees, trees with scorched sightless eyes on their
trunks where branches have been lopped off and the wound
painted black against rot. Redcurrant bushes. The tricolor
painted on the bridge. His mother appeared at the gate, her
crop of shredded grey hair falling uncombed into her eyes.

It was a dangerous sentimental business clearing away all the
Allen belongings for the move to the South. A day came when
they ended up on three chairs in the bare kitchen. "That looks
like everything," Joseph said uncertainly. Very little came back
to them. The crudeness of the building stripped of its warm
familiars began to show through. There was nothing to remind
them of the day when Frank Allen was taken so quickly that his
after-image stayed, as if in a reckless moment they had looked
up at the sun, and blinded, could not see what it shone upon.
They at last remembered Pop's room. Everyone had forgotten
about him. They went down the stairs into the basement. He
was lying in bed, half-dressed, his eyes glued on the ceiling.
    "I see youse have come back for your few quid," he said.
    They started carrying his stuff out into the garden. He sat
on the edge of the bed, hands on his knees, his unlaced boots
on his feet. With each object moved his smell waned. Last
of all was the wardrobe. "Do you think," said Joseph, "does
it come in two parts?" Pop kept a wary eye on them as they
tilted it forward. The top flew off and crashed inches away
from Pop's head on to the bed.
    "That's right," he said, "finish me off."
    When they came for the bed he was seated, breathing
furiously, on the bottom step of the stairs. They broke the
irons apart. The headboard was wrenched free from the base.

They rolled up the mattress. They shovelled his papers into a cardboard box. They put his shoes into a bag. He followed them out to the furniture van, and did not look back as they crossed South to the bungalow, a quarter of a mile away. His was the first room got ready. All the old furniture looked out of place in its new modern surroundings. The stuffing was breaking through. He lay in his bed listening, then when night fell he got up to make himself a cup of tea but he could not find the kitchen. He walked around the house watching the hands of the clock. It said two, and then five minutes past two and then it was two-thirty. But still he could not find the kitchen. He went round and round searching for the dimensions of the old house that he had known so well. He heard water flowing but he could not find it. The clock says three. Then to bed we go again, up all night looking for a way back into the old house. The clock says five. Helen found him by the back door listening for the river.

"What are you doing Pop?" she asked.

"Mind your own business," he said. "What sort of a joint is this?"

When she showed him how things worked he said it was all beyond him. She found he had lit a fire and boiled up the teapot in the grate of the dining room. He watched through the window the lads cutting the grass. It seemed incredible to Pop that those young about him would grow old. That he himself had struggled through all those humiliations and tempers into this antiquated self, though cheered by less recurrent intoxications from the soul. His soul had gone ahead of him.

He fell sick. He stayed in his new room with its radiators and blinds. And in his mind first George appeared, a hand arched hurtling against gravity and just as he reached the top of the arc and relaxed to descend with ankles tucked, next Frank appeared. Passing each other the twins cheered. And the oil drum, buckled as her womb, rolled beneath the plank and screeched hoarsely. It was as if George had drawn Frank from memory, etching him from his own likeness, and then Frank had drawn George from his own scared image, till they beat at her stomach in unison. George took the lead into that first silence, then Frank after, and ears cupped Pop listens for his wife's voice. Tom holds his fists. The village pitied him because he was alone. The motherless twins loved all the old women in the village. *Why is the light in the yard creating with familiarity the day of my birth or death?* A flame flaring up as a farmer cracked a match over the diseased tongue of a calf.

Helen and Joseph came in to see him. "The boys have done a good job, Pop," she said.

His breath came hard and heavy.

"Joseph has been telling me all about his travels. He has some funny stories to tell. He says that Tom is destroyed by wind."

She laughed. Pop kept his eyes aloft for he was following a certain path and any deviance now would only drop him back into pain. This was a path he must keep. His breath halted a second.

"I have no time for frivolity now," he said.

For he had to spend a lot of time trying to keep from falling. Words only succeeded in disorientating him. The sound of his own breathing became something he could balance with. His breathing kept him upright. Then one day he dropped the baton. His arms went out each side of him to keep him steady. He held up the left hand, palm outward before his half-turned face and averted eye, to block the light, to infer that he would return to the argument again, to stop anyone following him.

About the Editors

Neil Murphy teaches contemporary literature at NTU, Singapore. He is the author of *Irish Fiction and Postmodern Doubt* (2004) and editor of *Aidan Higgins: The Fragility of Form* (2010) and of the revised edition of Higgins's *Balcony of Europe* (2010). He co-edited (with Keith Hopper) a special Flann O'Brien centenary issue of the *Review of Contemporary Fiction* (2011) and *The Short Fiction of Flann O'Brien* (2013). He has published numerous articles and book chapters on contemporary fiction, Irish writing, and theories of reading, and is currently completing a book on John Banville.

Keith Hopper teaches Literature and Film Studies at Oxford University's Department for Continuing Education, and is a Research Fellow in the Centre for Irish Studies at St Mary's University, Twickenham. He is the author of *Flann O'Brien: A Portrait of the Artist as a Young Post-modernist* (revised edition 2009), general editor of the twelve-volume *Ireland into Film* series (2001–7), and co-editor (with Neil Murphy and Ondřej Pilný) of a special "Neglected Irish Fiction" issue of *Litteraria Pragensia* (2013). He is a regular contributor to the *Times Literary Supplement* and is currently completing a book on the writer and filmmaker Neil Jordan.

About the Author

Dermot Healy (1947-2014) was born in Finea, Co. Westmeath, but grew up in Cavan near the border with Northern Ireland. He edited the regional magazine *The Drumlin* (1978-80), and co-founded the Hacklers Theatre Group in Cavan in 1980. Following stints in London and Belfast, Healy settled in Ballyconnell, Co. Sligo, where he founded and edited the journal *Force 10: A Journal of the Northwest*. Healy was an accomplished poet, novelist, playwright, screenwriter, and all-round literary enabler (he taught creative writing classes for prisoners as well as for local community groups). His debut collection, *Banished Misfortune and Other Stories*, first appeared in 1982, and this was followed by four novels – *Fighting with Shadows* (1984), *A Goat's Song* (1994), *Sudden Times* (1999), and *Long Time, No See* (2011) – and a memoir, *The Bend for Home* (1996). Healy wrote the screenplay for Cathal Black's *Our Boys* (1981), and played the lead role in Nichola Bruce's 1999 film, *I Could Read the Sky*. He also wrote five collections of poetry and thirteen stage plays (his *Collected Plays* will be published by Dalkey Archive Press in 2016). Elected to Aosdána in 1986, he was the recipient of two Hennessy Literary Awards, the Tom-Gallon Award, the Encore Award, and the AWB Vincent American Ireland Fund Literary Award. Dermot Healy died at his home in Sligo in June 2014.

This new edition of *Fighting with Shadows* (2015) is part of a multi-volume sequence published by Dalkey Archive Press and edited by Neil Murphy and Keith Hopper. It also includes Healy's *The Collected Short Stories* (2015), Healy's *The Collected Plays* (2016), and a volume of essays about his work entitled *Dermot Healy: Writing the Sky – Critical Essays and Observations* (2016).

IRISH LITERATURE SERIES

DERMOT HEALY
THE COLLECTED SHORT STORIES
Edited, with an Introduction,
by Keith Hopper & Neil Murphy

Dermot Healy wrote intricate and innovative short stories that, along with works by Neil Jordan and Desmond Hogan, relaunched the Irish short story tradition. Set in small-town Ireland and the equally suffocating confines of the Irish expat communities of 1970s London, Healy's stories show compassion toward the marginalized and the dispossessed. Gathering all of Healy's stories together for the first time, this collection includes the long prose-drama "After the Off" and Healy's final short works, "Along the Lines" and "Images.".

Available at **www.dalkeyarchive.com**

IRISH LITERATURE SERIES — DUAL-LANGUAGE EDITION

MÁIRTÍN Ó CADHAIN
THE KEY / AN EOCHAIR
Translated by Louis de Paor
& Lochlainn Ó Tuairisg

"One of the most important writers of the twentieth century."

—*BBC*

In *The Key/An Eochair*, one of Máirtín Ó Cadhain's most Kafkaesque novellas, J., a "paper keeper," accidentally traps himself in his office when his key breaks in the lock. *The Key*— a mixture of satire, farce, black comedy, and, ultimately, trage-dy—describes the attempts of J. and various other characters, including his wife, civil service colleagues, and superiors to ex-tricate J. from his confinement. Yet all efforts to free J. must be in accordance with civil service protocols, and no such proto-col exists for J.'s unique dilemma.

Available at **www.dalkeyarchive.com**

MICHEÁL Ó CONGHAILE
RAMBLING JACK / SEACHRÁN JEAIC SHEÁIN JOHNNY
Translated by Katherine Duffy

"A powerful piece which blurs the distinction between reality and imagination to such a degree that the reader must give all his attention to the text to realise its potential."
—*Irish Times*

Rambling Jack / Seachrán Jeaic Sheáin Johnny portrays the imagination of a lonely old man who becomes obsessed with a beautiful young girl in his village. Every moment is filled with thoughts and fantasies about her. Eventually lines cross as this fantasy becomes a reality, paternal feelings and sexual urges mix and they become lovers. *Rambling Jack* is a brilliant, poetic account of an old man's wandering mind.

Available at **www.dalkeyarchive.com**